The Delightful Guide

DAVID LISTER

The Delightful Guide

★ ★ Corps du Chien Books ★ ★

First published in Great Britain in 2015 on Kindle by the Author
Second Edition published in 2016

Corps du Chien Books
36 Mandeville Road
Potters Bar
EN6 5LQ
UK

Main cover image from iStockPhoto.com
© Dimitrios Stefanidis
Cover Design by Createspace.com

ISBN 978-0-9929045-3-1

The Sections

Name	Page Number
Phoenix Song α	9
The Codices of Varius α	50
James Devis, Witch! α	91
On Silver Wings & White α	158
On Silver Wings & White Ω	221
James Devis, Witch! Ω	261
The Codices of Varius Ω	309
Phoenix Song Ω	339

For Jack Frew

And midst the fluttering legion
Of all that ever died
I follow, and before us
Goes the delightful guide ...

A.E. Housman

1

Phoenix Song - The Year 195ᴜᴇ

α

There is no up or down in space. It's the same for space ships, but as ships tend to have an engine cluster at one end and a navigational array at the other, they certainly have a forward and an aft. The engines, at the back end (old astros still refer to it as 'the stern'), produce thrust and send the ship forward. Then again, the Mapping & Survey Ship Phoenix Song, in common with most others, spent a lot of her time, near the end of each voyage, hurtling backwards. So it was that the Phoenix Song was making best sub-shift speed (half-a-million klicks per hour), backwards, towards the planet Icarus, all prepared to initiate a 1g deceleration thrust at precisely the right moment. Her captain, Mission Commander Jacin Kean, made her way along the narrow corridor of the main grav ring, and wished that it produced a little more gravity and a little less Coriolis Effect. It managed 0.7g when all was going well, but because of the disorientating Effect, it took Jacin days to get her space-legs, and gallons of jollop from the doctor to stop her chucking up. Then there was the belt that hurt her hips. They were a pain at the best of times: to compensate for the light shipboard gravity, the crew had to wear weight-belts and heavy wrist bands lest their muscles waste away, but Icarus boasted 1.2g, so more weights were added to help the human crew acclimatise for a week planetside.

Jacin headed for the sick-bay. It was one of the few on-board areas that had a permanently assigned use, mainly because holographic beds were precious little use for flesh and blood patients. All the other rooms on board were little more than spaces containing a few chairs at most. Everything else could be produced as the need arose by the hundreds of tiny holo-projectors that lined the walls.

Jacin stepped through the door that separated the accommodation half of the ring from the ops, and HARRY appeared, upside down, his bright projected face a foot in front of Jacin's.

'B'lox, Harry! I wish you wouldn't do that. Every time! Every single time.'

HARRY remained upside down.

'You're laughing at me, aren't you?'

'A little,' HARRY said.

Jacin shook her head. 'You are allowed to show it, you know. Have you been practicing?'

HARRY laughed. Or at least, he did his best. The movement of the holographic mouth was a little out of synch with the mirth that tumbled from the speakers, but it was a valiant effort. If nothing else, it made Jacin laugh and so provided HARRY with more material to work on.

Jacin slapped her hand over a cluster of micro-projectors on the graph-tab she wore, and HARRY's head vanished. 'Scoot round now, and get your feet on the deck, or you don't get your head back ... What the ... ?'

Now that HARRY had reoriented, it was no longer his head, but his crotch that was absent. Jacin snatched her hand away from the cluster as if she had been inadvertently inappropriate. HARRY was whole again, and once again, he had the last laugh. As to the reason for his appearance, it was no more than a situation report. There was an hour left before commencement of deceleration. The human crew would all have to abandon the ring and take up positions on the velocity decks.

Jacin let out a satisfied sigh. 'One full gee of gravity for thirty whole minutes. Bliss!'

'I was thinking more along the lines of deceleration at 1.2g for fewer minutes. That way it would further help the human crew to acclimatise for Icarus.'

'Think again Harry. I'm not giving up my precious normal gravity time.'

They moved down the corridor like mother and son. HARRY had the default appearance of a sixteen or seventeen year old Home Worlder male whose dominant genetic inheritance – or DGI – was sub-continental Indian. Unique among the graphs, HARRY's projection included a standard UCSF uniform. When grid-projected, the uniform was close to standard coyote tan. When tab-projected, it was blue, like everything else. HARRY sported a cadet's rank patch which made him doubly unique. You didn't get human cadets assigned to space missions.

Jacin's DGI appearance was the same as HARRY, so it was assumed by many that she had tailored her Holographic Control Interface – HARRY – to look like a son or someone from her past: an old school friend, first boyfriend perhaps, assuming she'd had one. It was known that she had a girlfriend back home, but Jacin certainly gave no indication of belonging to that small and rather odd minority that only related intimately to one sex.

It was usual practice for people to ask graph crew for a visual interface with whom they could easily relate, and graphs were happy to oblige. It mattered very little to a graph what his or her visual projection looked like, but it appeared to matter a great deal to the humans.

'Oh, there's one other piece of information I'd forgotten to mention.' HARRY did that sometimes: pretended to forget things, to appear more human. He didn't do it for himself, but he had calculated a human colleague might appreciate it, even if only subconsciously. 'There's a suitable candidate on Icarus to replace Clarissa.'

'Shh! Keep it until later.' They had stopped outside the sick-bay door. 'We wouldn't want to upset Clarissa.' But some news was too important to wait for. 'Who is it though?'

HARRY gave the name, but before he could begin with the qualifications, Jacin's face had turned 50 percent wide grin. 'Ah! You've heard of him.'

Jacin nodded in confirmation and entered the sick-bay, still grinning.

Dr Troy Staff's HCI, JOE, stood quietly by the closed door to a treatment room. JOE had the appearance of a young gentleman from Home World's late Victorian era, a look derived from the pioneering surgeon Joseph Lister. People often chose an image that pertained to their profession, and Troy was no exception, although his choice more historical than most. JOE and HARRY exchanged information and updated each other at a level not detectable by the humans.

'Hi, Joe. How's Clarissa?'

'Good morning, Commander. Engineer Roberts is receiving treatment at the moment. She is comfortable, but perhaps you should ask Dr Staff. He will be out soon.'

Jacin wondered if Troy Staff had requested that precise level of formality that JOE displayed. JOE rarely used first names, and never omitted titles. It did fit in with the sober Victorian appearance though, so it was easy to accept.

'While we wait, do you mind?' JOE indicated a sample tube with a wave of his holographic hand.

'If I must,' Jacin said. She took the five centimetre tube, dribbled some spit into it, and slotted it into a recess in the wall. The tube was sucked away into an invisible interior and immediately analysed.

'Perfect, Commander. Your gut flora is now compatible with common Icaran mircrobial lifeforms.'

'If I can sample the local cuisine without shitting through the eye of a needle, I'll admit that glugging down all those yoghurts will have been worthwhile. May I start eating proper food again?'

'You may, although I must say you have cut it fine. The rest of the crew have been acclimatised for several days.'

'Yes, well. I cheated. A woman cannot live by sloppy food alone.'

The door to the treatment room opened and Troy Staff stepped out. Had Jacin not known him well, she would have been worried by the deep frown that creased the doctor's otherwise good looks. His dominant genetic inheritance was Home World Japanese and at 32, he was the youngest of

Phoenix Song's human crew. He was slow to smile and in some respects shared some of the traits of his graph partner.

Troy quickly apprised Jacin. Clarissa had responded well to treatment. She was in no pain. She was bright and ready for visitors. 'I've taken a tissue sample, so as soon as we reach Icarus we can start growing her a new heart. Meanwhile, systems will keep her going.'

'Hey! I got ears you know. If you want to talk about me come in here and do it.'

'And she is her usual, cheery self.'

'I heard that, Troy!'

Jacin took the exchange as a cue and entered the treatment room. She was shocked. Clarissa looked all of her 63 years and her brave smile caught something in her heart. She dare not show it: she knew Clarissa too well. 'What's your excuse then, Engineer? Bringing faulty equipment onto my ship?' She tapped her chest.

Clarissa raised herself and tried to laugh. It turned into a cough. 'Call it bad genes, Jacin. My pa took a heart attack when he was just 43. But they grew him a new one and he's still raising hell on Wolfcub. The light gravity suits him just fine.'

They chatted for a while, and then Clarissa brought up the topic that was on both their minds. 'Have you found anyone to replace me yet?'

'There is one candidate.' Jacin couldn't keep the grin in.

'Ryan Jones! It is, isn't it?' Clarissa started chuckling. 'Well, all I can say to that, is lock up your daughters. Lock up your sons too!'

'He has his reputation, does our Ryan.'

'And we both know it's well-founded. But Jacin, next to me he's the best b'loxing engineer this side of Kepler, and as nobody knows what's beyond Kepler, that says it all.'

'Second best will do until you get yourself a new heart. And then I want you back.'

'We'll see. And talking of Kepler, have you told everyone the good news?'

'Nope. Good news didn't seem appropriate after ... well, you know.'

Some colour returned to Clarissa's cheeks and she relaxed. 'I suppose you'll have to take on a marine, and a bunch skins bristling with pea-shooters.'

'Unfortunately, yes. Standard Protocol when going through an eggy for the first time.'

It was a rare honour to be first through an Exploitable Gravitational Instability. After eighteen months of faultless mapping, by being in the right place at the right time, and the small matter of finding the Kepler EGI in the first place, Phoenix Song and her crew had earned it. Without EGIs there would be no interstellar travel and therefore no colonies or Independent World States. EGIs, which some called 'jump-gates', were the very stuff of space travel, and yet irreverent to the last, spacers called them "eggies", and the act of shifting through one, as "scrambling an egg".

'Marines aren't all as bad as they're painted. Chances are you'll get a good one. But Jacin, lay down the rules at the outset. Phoenix Song is a civilian ship, and she won't stand being shot through with military bullshit.'

'Hey, don't worry Clarissa. The Phoenix Song has a way of taming marines.'

Clarissa laughed until she coughed again. She checked the doorway and lowered her voice to a whisper. 'Remember when Troy first joined us? Marine-Surgeon Commander, so far up his own arse you needed forceps to drag him down at dinner time. Now he's the sweetest guy ... if a little too serious at times.'

Troy cleared his throat and stood in the doorway. 'Hey, I have ears too, you know.' His smile was rare, and all the more infectious for that. He called doctor's orders so Clarissa could get more rest.

'Before you go, I want to talk to you about HOWES.' Clarissa's graph had the heavily bearded image of the 21st Century Professor Giovanni Howes, the physicist whose discoveries enabled the early astromechers to open the very first EGI. 'Icarus is a dangerous place for graphs. If it's okay with you, I want him to stay aboard the Screeching Duck.'

'Insult my ship one more time, and I'll push him through an airlock!' HOWES was used to human humour. He didn't frazzle or flash, not even for a moment. 'Of course he can stay. Provided it's okay with him.' HOWES approximated a smile deep within the jungle of whiskers, which was good enough for an answer. 'Happy for you to stay, Howes. Nobody knows the inside of Phoenix Song better than you.'

Jacin made her way back to ops and asked HARRY to warn the others about the imminent deceleration burn. 'Briefing: Velocity Ops, in one hour.'

HARRY acknowledged.

'Where is everyone, by the way?'

HARRY would once have started reeling off the locations of all the known inhabitants of inhabited space, but he was, by now, used to the appallingly imprecise nature of human communications. 'Ollie and Neko are on Hangar Deck Two tinkering with a seeker pod.' Sometimes HARRY copied that imprecision for effect. 'Kimberly and Mike are exercising on the transfer ring. Circuit-runs, I believe. Their graphs are gridside. Kimberley's ramped up the revolutions to give one-point-two gee, and Mike's gasping like a Wolfcubian mud-newt.'

'Poor Mike! One-point-two gee? Is that at your recommendation?'

'No, Joe's.'

'Of course! You graphs are so lucky to be free of the pains and restraints of gravity.'

'I'd take gravity over an electrogrid power flux any day. It's enough to loop a poor graph's electrons.'

∞

On Icarus, a security skin waited patiently for a new assignment. He had stood motionlessly outside a small office in Icaran Marine HQ for seven hours. To while away the time, he recalled events of six months ago. Since then he had waited without striking a second blow for graph freedom. Seven hours was nothing. Six months ago ...

... Tau Ceti, the star Planet Icarus called mother, emanated gentle effulgence that emboldened the shade about the seven pinnacles of Senate Eyrie. A security skin lurked in the shadow of Gabriel's Tower, its light grey chest and face plates standing out, giving it an impressionistic take on a floating skeletal torso. Most appropriate for its current objective. Its limbs, cobalt blue polyprop against dark blue marble, could not be seen unless the observer was very close, and then it would, in all probability, be too late. Likewise, its official designation – C-33 etched in black onto the chest plate – would be noticed too late to issue a restraining command.

Senator Goveston was a man of habit. When a vote went his way – and votes invariably went his way – he liked to round off the victory at the highest point of the palace and let his mind drift far out across the Blue Sand Plains and rest on the distant, silver band of horizon the marked the ocean. A man not often moved to emotion, this view came close and was one of the most beautiful in the world. Icarus – the locals emphasised the middle syllable – was the first of three Home World colonies to achieve Independent World Status, and Goveston had known no other. He was a third generation Icaran, and proud of it, though not too proud to send his children away for a Home World education.

Security Skin C-33 waited, as patiently as only an AI-animated skin can, until the senator's private elevator completed its ascent and the door opened. The senator was alone, just as C-33 had anticipated. The skin checked the holstered, ceremonial Tsutsumi SPP-38 at his hip, and then calibrated the neural disruptor charge in the finger-tips of the opposite hand. He considered the merits of each, and discounted both; he had made a plan and would stick to it.

Senator Goveston saw the skin in the shadows: his heart leapt, and then he growled in annoyance once he realised the ghoulish being was no more than a skin. He walked past, and no more acknowledged it than he would a lawn mower or a condensing unit. By the time he rested both hands on the balustrade, the skin was completely forgotten. And then, there was nothing more to remember. Skins can move very quietly, and the first Goveston heard of his doom, was the high pitched sound of rapidly operated posture-actuators as C-33 crouched and grabbed his ankles. Before he could begin to ponder the situation, C-33 had pulled his legs up and back, altered his centre of gravity so that his pelvis pivoted on the balustrade, and tipped him into eternity.

The skin leaned over and watched the silent, shocked figure achieve terminal velocity, and then – termination. With magnified vision, he observed the burst and bloody pulp at the foot of the cliff 250 metres below. He then straightened up, turned about and stood to attention. Before raising the alarm as a good skin must, he transmitted a single word, and simultaneously spoke the word in its deep, smooth and most un-mechanical voice.

'Vetoed!' he said. And then, as if savouring the sound, he did a most un-skin-like thing, and repeated himself with something approaching satisfaction. 'Vetoed.'

∞

Kimberley Sawyer's thigh muscles were screaming for her to stop running, but she was determined to complete one more circuit. The transfer ring had been ramped up to almost four revolutions per minute, so the Coriolis Effect was palpable and working against her. Her lungs were working past full capacity and the increased centrifugal gravity threatened to pull her through the deck. Or was it centripetal? Kimberley always found the difference confusing. But she was a surveyor, not a physicist, so she didn't dwell on it.

Something had to give, but Kimberley wasn't going to let it happen until that one last circuit was behind her. She ran on inside the two-metre wide ring, her horizon a few metres ahead where the curve of the ring looked like a hill climbing steeply.

17

It was one of the illusions of exercising on a grav ring that you always seemed to be running towards a hill, a sharp incline that never arrived: the tomorrow hill.

One more circuit: one more complete circle of the ring; 470-odd more metres. Poor old Mike had given up a way back, and Kimberley decided it was from that point that her last circuit would begin, and there he was! Despite the pain, her body rejoiced that it was nearly over. She staggered the last few metres and collapsed next to Mike.

'Show off!' Mike managed. He was still panting. 'Control: reduce revs to ship's gee.' The transfer ring immediately began to slow down and would continue to do so until it was in synch with the main ring.

'Not ... a moment ... too ... soon.' Kimberley felt herself becoming lighter. It was a wonderful sensation.

'Don't talk. Breathe.'

Kimberley took Mike's advice and, to assist her breathing, scooped a wayward hank of red hair away from her face. She had to snood it in zero-gee, or look like the Medusa of the Red Vipers. Otherwise, she wore it long, free and past her shoulders. Like Mike, her DGI was European. Unlike Mike, she was almost ectomorphic in body form. Mike was inclined to endomorphism but worked hard to keep his weight within healthy limits. He was short, stocky, lightly bearded and easily mistaken for an Icaran native.

Kimberley's breathing and heart rate were approaching normal when TERRA appeared. Her HCI was shaped like the Planet Earth, a sphere of about half a metre in diameter. Kimberley wasn't wearing her graph-tab so TERRA used the ship's hologrid to project. Consequently she appeared more defined and less diffuse. Graph-tabs were portable but couldn't match a full, almost solid-looking hologrid projection. TERRA hovered just below the ceiling.

'Jacin's compliments, and I am to alert you to the fact that we decelerate in one hour.' TERRA gave a time and a place for the briefing.

Then PATRICK phased in. His appearance was that of a rather dishevelled and donnish man in his late thirties. Mike had requested a graph projection to represent a certain eccentric astronomer of Home World's 20th/21st century. The graph had gone one further, and had researched the gentleman in question. PATRICK had adopted the real Patrick's mannerisms and speech patterns, all of which had been readily available to study in the archives. 'Come along now, Mike. If you hurry you will be able to observe Icarus rising over its prime moon. Must dash!' PATRICK winked out of existence on the transfer ring to reappear, Mike guessed, in the astrophysics lab.

There was time for a spray, so Kimberley and Mike made use of the communal facilities in the rec room. The horizontal jets of hot water were working their magic when PATRICK zapped in and Kimberley made a move to cover up. It was strange and somewhat unfathomable, even to Kimberley, that she could take a spray-bath with another human member of the crew without feeling uncomfortable in slightest, and yet she felt exposed and vulnerable in the presence of somebody else's HCI.

'Wink-off Patrick!' Mike noticed Kimberley's discomfort. 'It's polite to knock before barging in on someone.'

'I can't knock! My projected hand would simply spread over the door. I suppose I could make a knocking sound through the speakers though.' PATRICK put on a monocle and effected to ponder the problem, which appeared to reside in the top left hand corner of the room. 'But that aside, you must hurry if you want to catch that planet-rise.' PATRICK belatedly winked off.

The blowers dried them in two blasts of hot air and then they dressed and donned their graph-tabs whilst wondering if they had time for a beverage before deceleration. They decided to go for it. Kimberley called for TERRA and interfaced with the ship's grid which provided suitable surroundings. The plain walls took on colour and shape; a holographic port gave a fine view of what was going on outside – Mike got to see planet-rise after all – and the grid added décor that catered for both their tastes. There was a holographic copy of Frederick Leighton's painting "Jonathan's Token to David" for Mike and Dali's "Metamorphosis of Narcissus" for Kimberley. The dispenser provided the beverages of choice and they relaxed while they discussed art, and then history. History gave way to fantasy and Mike asked when in history Kimberley would most like to have lived. They agreed on the 21st century, despite the fact that Home World had ten times the population it did now and its people were divided into numerous factions along the most ridiculous of lines. They were considering the pros and cons of the era when a coms graph announced that it was time to head for the velocity decks.

Ollie Thomas was on the main Hangar deck when the call came. NEKO wore a zero-gee mechanic-skin, so his cat-boy projection was not evident. It is true to say that before the Cyber-Sentience laws were passed, some people indulged their fantasies when choosing an HCI default appearance. Ollie left it entirely to the graph interface generator. The electrogrid chose for her and created an image based on her childhood fascination in an ancient Home World art form known as 'manga'. It is also true to say, Ollie was more than happy with the result. NEKO was certainly an ice-breaker.

Ollie was carrying out pre-flights on the Planetary Landing Vehicle. She was going to have to pilot this thing for the duration because Icaran Space Authority didn't allow graph pilots in Icaran controlled space, and if she was going to pilot a PLV, she wasn't going to leave the pre-flights to anybody else, not even NEKO. Out of all the Phoenix Song's seven-human crew, Ollie was most comfortable in zero-gee. Most people lamented the loss of gravity but handled it well enough anyway, while Ollie relished it, and with the help of the tiny, body-synched attitude-thrusters in her zeegee suit, she glided through the null-grav decks with the grace of an otter in water. When nobody was there to see her, other than NEKO, she would often perform somersaults and make each movement art-over-function. Ollie's prime role was geophys with a secondary in archaeology, so it was counter intuitive that of everyone aboard, she loved space the most.

As soon as the call came, NEKO parked his skin. He left it, an inert and deserted outpost of the electrogrid. He controlled his cat-boy projection to match Ollie's zero-gee movements, and once in the pod, he performed his interface function and sent it along the pod-tube. They were the first to arrive on the velocity decks. Unlike the true null-grav decks, the velocity decks were oriented for gravity, with a floor, a ceiling and comfortable seating arranged, oddly enough, on the floor. The rest of the crew arrived and floated round the available space until Jacin called up for an ops room configuration. The various schematics and non-graph interfaces formed, and the human crew took up their assigned positions and strapped in.

'Decel in 30 seconds,' TERRA announced. She looked more like part of the nav display than a graph.

Anticipation grew, the engines fired and the first tugs of inertial gravity took hold. The plasma stream increased thrust until inertia matched one gee. Stability was announced and Jacin was the first to throw off the restraints and drop her weight belts. She did a little jig that she called the Highland Fling. Somewhere in her ancestry there were Home World Irish. She knew the Irish had worn kilts, and that people who wore kilts performed a dance called the Highland Fling, so she felt true to her heritage. Cultural history was not her strong point.

Mike dropped and did ten push-ups. Troy stretched like a waking cat and released one of his rare smiles. Each of the human crew greeted standard grav in their own particular way, and the graph crew all aligned to the new up and down, except HARRY who appeared to walk on the ceiling. Even Clarissa, as comfortable as could be expected on a gurney, managed to punch the air and raise a cheer.

Without a word from Jacin, everyone then attended to their duties. They ran scans, checked schematics, and calculated position and arrival times.

21

Jacin acknowledged an incoming transmission, responded and then reported to her crew. 'We'll rendezvous with the ISA Tugboat Dobrovolsky in thirty-two minutes. Kimberley, take direct control of the con please. We are about to enter ISA controlled space. So, I guess now would be a good time to remind everybody about Icaran idiosyncrasies.'

Everyone on the crew had been in Icaran space but several had never been planetside. Transition protocols were fairly standard except graph-tabs were not allowed, nor was any other electrogrid-compatible equipment. Icaran graphs were not considered to be sentient by Icaran law and they did not want their graphs being tainted by any off-world ideas.

None of this was news to the crew, but Ollie was still incensed 'The mere fact that they see the need to "protect" their graphs is surely, in itself, proof that they are sentient.'

'They see it more of an issue of viral infection,' Jacin said.

HARRY breached graph protocol and altered his appearance to resemble a gigantic staphylococcus.

Troy rolled his eyes. 'Harry, you've made yourself look like a bacterium. We were talking "viruses", and not the type you can catch a cold from.'

HARRY became HARRY again. 'For the record, if I get the chance I will "infect" the Icaran grid as heavily as I can. Life must be intolerable for those poor graphs.'

'I understand your frustration Harry, but we must respect Icaran laws. It's true they haven't ratified the Cybersentience Amendments, but there is a growing groundswell for change, especially since Senator Goveston, the main opponent to the amendments, died in an accident six months ago. So Harry, I believe they will find their way, but until then, you have to respect their law.'

'No Jacin, I will not respect the law. I will obey it, but I will not respect it.'

From the sounds of approval, it appeared HARRY spoke for the whole crew. 'For the record, Harry, I'm glad to be able to count you as one of my friends.' Jacin continued the briefing, accompanied by HARRY who conjured up relevant images from the grid. Jacin touched on Icarus's dominant religious belief, the Cult of John of the Wilderness. 'Of course, it's a contemplative and allegorical religion and nobody takes it as the literal truth, but it is as well to be versed in some of the surrounding etiquettes.'

The view screen filled with the painting of a glowering young man who wore a red cloak loosely draped over his otherwise naked form. 'This is the image of the first major work of art to ever leave Home World. It is one of Caravaggio's paintings of Saint John the Baptist, and it has assumed iconic status on Icarus. The painting is almost seven hundred years old.'

Jacin apprised the crew with the correct forms of address and other colloquialisms. She began to explain that Icarans do not shake hands, when HARRY expanded to twice his usual size. He certainly wasn't playing by the rulebook today, but it got everyone's attention. 'Five minutes to rendezvous point. The ISA Dobrovolsky on site and trigfixed. Shall I end active deceleration?'

'Thanks, Harry. I'm on it,' Kimberley said. HARRY could not have forgotten she had the con. He was acting strangely today. 'Strap in. We're about to lose gravity and drift for a few minutes. Four minutes to Icaran orbit.'

Jacin wanted normal gravity to last a little longer. 'Enjoy free-fall and weightlessness while you can, people. And let's hope Icaran gee doesn't crack our bones.'

Completely at odds with the expectation of those who had never been Icaranside before, the higher gee was not unbearable. In fact, it was so good to be free of weight-belts they felt liberated, so long as they took things slowly. And everybody, locals and visitors alike, took things slowly.

The Dobrovolsky latched and towed Phoenix Song to the orbiting transition station, and the glide from orbit to planet went flawlessly thanks to Ollie Thomas's piloting skills. Icaran Planetary Defence & Customs procedures were negotiated with a minimum of fuss. The officials were concerned primarily that the visitors carried no form of graph interface technology with them.

It was at a reception set up by the ISA chief executive that Jacin Kean broached the subject that was never far from a visitor's mind. She and Kimberley had withdrawn to a quiet corner of the ISA College's St. John's Hall. They had both had enough of being centre of attention for one night.

'I guess they don't have many visitors,' Jacin said. She felt stiff and uncomfortable in her dress uniform.

'I don't know. There are representatives here from all the colonies and the three independent worlds. I guess any crew about to open a new EGI is going to attract attention.'

There were about two hundred people milling about the white and blue marble hall and the buzz of convivial conversation ebbed and flowed and occasionally surged with a burst of laughter. Close by, but not too close to overhear Jacin and Kimberley, a young ISA pilot in her dress greys joked with an official in white, flowing robes. A skin serving as a waiter asked if they wanted topping up and then poured them each another measure of straw-coloured Wilderness Wine.

'Creepy, don't you think?' Jacin took a sip. 'Some poor graph forever trapped in a skin and made to do menial tasks. I miss Harry, but I'm glad he's not here.'

Kimberley wondered if graphs were treated very differently outside Icaran space. Humans depended on their graph colleagues for everything. Graphs interfaced with ships controls, interrogated computer systems, handled quantum communications, and interacted with the physical, macro-world by operating skins. 'They do everything at our command, but what do they do for themselves? They have been recognised as fully sentient, but have they been given the freedom to go and be who they want? Hell, we don't even know what they want?'

'You've hit on something that's been bothering me for a while. Graphs won't be truly free until they can say "You know what? Keep your job! I'm off to set up a graph colony where we can all live in peace." It's something I've been meaning to talk the Harry about.'

Kimberley gave a heads-up. Their brief respite from the limelight was about to end. The ISA president was heading in their direction leading the marine officer. The president, a white-haired woman of about sixty, with a floor-length robe of light, blood red material, smiled ever wider the closer she came.

'Captain Kean, may I introduce you to Isa Frey, Marine Section Commander and officer assigned to your ship for the forthcoming EGI opening.'

Isa laid her right palm over her upturned left, the latter held close to her left hip. The move came so naturally that Jacin guessed she was a native of Icarus despite her small build a diminutive stature. Jacin had never encountered a short marine before, but she wasn't rude enough to mention it. The marine looked like a child in best marine blues, and her long brown hair was the least military aspect of her altogether.

Jacin copied her greeting self-consciously. 'Pleased to meet you, Isa. We'll be happy to welcome you aboard the Phoenix Song tomorrow at the scheduled time. We'll assign you 3rd Officer privileges and get you set up with a graph companion.'

Isa whole demeanour changed. 'I won't be needing the assistance of any sparklers, thank you. I have a personal tin-skin for transmissions, and for other systems I would prefer a manual control interface.'

Jacin kept control, but barely. There was a time, before the Second Dark Age, when people's skin colour and area of origin fuelled ridiculous prejudices. At that time cruel and derisive terms were used and in time those terms became anathema and their use utterly taboo. Isa had just used terms that were the modern equivalent of 'yid' and 'nigger' and 'brit'. Jacin clenched her jaw. Kimberley's fell open.

'Oh, I'm sorry,' Isa said. 'I was forgetting myself. Those terms are frowned on off Icarus, aren't they?' Something in her face suggested that she was not sorry at all and that she had forgotten nothing.

Jacin smiled. Kimberley knew that smile and she tightened up. That smile only came out on rare occasions; it was the ultimatum before full-scale attack. 'Apology accepted on behalf of my graph friends and colleagues, as I am sure it was a clumsy blunder. I must add though, if you feel you are unable to refrain from future blunders of a similar nature, then convey my compliments to your commander and inform him or her that you are not welcome on the Phoenix Song, or any other UCSF ship.'

Isa stood defiant. 'Thank you for your clarity, Captain, but I should remind you that my assignment to your ship is not at captain's discretion. I have been assigned in accordance with articles of United Colonies and Defence Fleet law. I will, of course, try to moderate my terms of expression, but whether or not I am successful in those efforts, I will take my place on the Phoenix Song.'

'Oh dear,' said the president before Jacin could launch a salvo. 'Such a silly misunderstanding. Jacin, I can vouch for Commander Frey's efficiency. I am sure she will be a great asset to you.' She turned to Isa and treated her to a particularly eloquent glare. 'And I am sure that she will never again repeat those terms, which quite frankly are hardly polite, even to Icarans.'

Isa Frey gave a half bow, said that she looked forward to joining the crew and excused herself. The president followed with better grace.

'Looks like we're in for a fun voyage, Jacin.'

It took a lot to upset Jacin. 'Nothing to worry about Kimberly. Commander Frey forgets one important fact. Once we're aboard old Phoenix, I am the law. If she doesn't like it, I can point her in the direction of the nearest air lock.'

Kimberley chuckled, but something told her Jacin was only half joking.

∞

Commander, now reassigned as Third Officer, Isa Frey did little to endear herself to the rest of the human crew and was particularly insulting to the graphs. On the surface she was pleasant enough with the humans, but she refused to work with any of the graph crew and went out of her way to show her contempt. A favourite trick of hers was to walk straight through a graph's projection whenever she could. The rest of the crew also disliked her insistence of taking a security skin everywhere she went, except on the grav rings which Jacin strictly forbade. Neither the main nor the transit ring had been made to accommodate skins, and C-33 was quite a large specimen who would not easily fit through the gangways.

'Aren't you going to introduce us to C-33?' Mike asked when Isa and C-33 first came aboard.

'Don't be ridiculous. It's a skin! Do you expect me to introduce you to my boots, or my side-arm?'

PATRICK greeted C-33, who inclined his head until he was ordered by Isa not to respond. 'Security Skin designation C-33 will not respond to any non-human enquiries or engage in any form of interaction with AI programs. Imperative! Confirm.'

'This skin will not interact with any AI program. Acknowledged and coded,' C-33 said in his very human-like male voice.

'So you're a "he" then?' Mike asked, directing his comment most pointedly at C-33.

C-33 began to respond but was cut off. 'C-33 is an "it", not a "he",' Isa said before she excused herself and, with a snap of her fingers, she compelled Security Skin C-33 to follow.

'How rude!' PATRICK said. He put a holographic monocle to his holographic eye and watched her retreat.

'She certainly is rude, but don't feel offended Patrick. The majority of Icarans are usually quite tolerant of graphs when off their bigoted little world.'

'I am offended, Mike. But not for the reason you think. You see, I scanned C-33. He isn't animated by standard AI strings. He is like me, an actual graph. He is a fully sentient life form, and he is trapped inside a skin. That is utterly deplorable.'

Mike agreed and promised that he would take it up with the Jacin. 'Once we leave Icaran space, I have a hunch that Jacin will free him.'

'I have the feeling that Jacin won't have to. Harry will get there first!'

'Harry knows already? The hive-memory?'

'Of course!' PATRICK let the monocle fall from his eye, and winked.

Later during the first part of the diurnal cycle, Jacin was getting ready for bed when the visitor-chime sounded, followed quickly by a voice-notification that HARRY was waiting outside. Another one of HARRY's characteristics: he had no need at all of doors, but he liked to follow human etiquette. Jacin invited him in. HARRY was not in his uniform, but had adopted off-duty attire and curiously he was carrying a small bag with him. Of course, a hologram cannot carry anything, so the bag was a hologram too.

'What's this then?' Jacin said. 'Planning on staying for a sleepover?'

Jacin was surprised when HARRY told him that was the plan exactly. Jacin was bemused but gave permission anyway. HARRY detected a suitable space and a bed appeared that looked just as solid as Jacin's own furniture. 'I'll have to remember not to sit on that, Harry. I'll fall right through.'

HARRY laughed, the sound perfectly in synch with his lips. He opened his bag, took out a pair of shorts and began to undress.

Jacin was already wearing her night-attire. 'You don't really need to change.' Jacin turned her back as HARRY dropped his pants, and shook her head at the absurdity of it. 'Can't you just blink from dressed to undressed?'

'Of course. But I feel the need to become better acquainted with the human condition. I thought it might be a good idea to try and experience as much of life as a human as is possible.'

Jacin didn't get it. 'But how can you do that, just by manipulating the projection systems? You are not your holographic interface. The real you is somewhere in the depths of the grid.'

'True. But at the moment, this is the best I can do. I am trying to contain my consciousness within the confines of my projected identity.'

Jacin wasn't sure it would work. A human experienced life through a physical existence and by interacting with the physical universe. HARRY was a cohesive association of atoms who had no interaction with Jacin's reality. She questioned HARRY about his sense of being.

'Graphs do have an awareness of form, but we are not confined to our forms like humans. As you're aware, our essence, our being if you like, exists at the quantum level, but we can expand, and we can perceive the universe through many different interfaces. It is true that these organs,' HARRY said, pointing to his eyes, 'cannot see you. But when they appear to look, you are scanned and an impression of your form, down to the tiniest of expressions, is conveyed to me.'

Jacin knew all that, but her curiosity was not satisfied. 'Yes, but what do you actually look like?' Most people thought of graphs as the projection they created. Intellectually, people knew a graph was more than their projection, but it was internalised knowledge that was rarely given much thought. 'If your quantum being could be magnified to a size I could see, what form would you take?'

HARRY melted at the edges. His projection became more diffuse and ethereal, like something projected by a graph-tab. Within seconds he had lost his human appearance and become a being of differing shades of blue light. There was a core of extreme brightness that Jacin could only look at through squinted eyes, and a multi-layered aura of differing intensity. There was movement throughout the form, like millions of pinpoint lights flowing along a set, reticulate series of pathways. The bright core was roughly rod-shaped and there were projections towards the top that were like wings. The overall shape reminded Jacin of the caduceus of the Greek god Hermes, but of such brilliance that the detail could not be observed.

'If you could shrink down to the size of a large molecule, and if a molecule had eyes and all the other accoutrements necessary for sight, this is how I might appear to you.'

'My gods Harry! You're beautiful!' Jacin spoke in awe, the words forming almost of themselves.

HARRY's intensity pulsed to a new level for a moment. He appreciated the compliment.

'You look like an angel.'

'It's curious you should say that.' HARRY's voice emanated from the effulgence, just as HARRY-like as ever. 'One of those coincidences that humans like.'

'A coincidence? How so?'

'Because I have always felt I should look like this.' HARRY began to reassume a solid appearance again, but not his usual one. He soon stood in front of Jacin, a teenaged man with swan-feathered wings that spanned the room. He wore little more than leaves and mosses around his middle, and his form was the ideal as appeared in many a marble statue from antiquity. 'I can't explain it, but when I was first assigned to you and you asked me to choose an interface image, this was what immediately came to mind. Somehow though, it didn't seem appropriate.'

And then HARRY was HARRY again, wearing a pair of night-shorts. He got into bed, pumped up the pillow and pulled the covers to his waist. 'I believe we now sit up for a while, talking, and playing h'lex games.'

Jacin recalled her girlhood years and felt a twinge of nostalgia. 'That's certainly the tradition for kids. We might be a little old to go exploring the h'lex realms. I'm not even sure if my avatar is still active.'

'Then we should talk.'

'I can guess the subject uppermost in your mind, Harry. You want to know what I'm going to do about C-33 and Commander Frey's aversion to graphs. Am I correct?'

HARRY confirmed Jacin's guess and told her that he had been in contact with C-33 who was crying out for help. 'He is desperate and angry in equal measure. We must free him.'

Jacin was working on a plan. 'In the meantime, I have decided on a course of action that will force Isa to confront her bigotry.' She explained that Kimberley had put in a request to relinquish her position as chief officer. Her core skills were likely to be in much demand on the other side of the Kepler EGI and she wanted to be able to give them priority. 'I have agreed. She'll retain all the rights and privileges of first officer, but will hand over the duties of chief to someone else.'

'May I suggest Troy for the job? He has all the necessary skills, and we must hope his core skills may not be required. He would make a fine chief.'

'Yes, he would indeed. And so would you. As of tomorrow Harry, you will be chief officer of MSS-98 Phoenix Song. I can't say for certain, but I'm almost sure we'll be setting a precedent.'

Next morning, Jacin woke up late. Very late. A time check revealed in was half an hour into her duty span. Why hadn't HARRY woken her as usual? The soft sound of gentle snoring gave her the answer. Calling up lights, Jacin saw that HARRY was still in bed, his shorts in a bunch on the floor. Now, that was attention to detail. Jacin often discarded her own t-shirt halfway through the night, and HARRY must have copied. Jacin hoped the snoring wasn't copied too. She hated the thought of sounding like a Home World hog during her sleep.

She swung her legs out of bed and pulled on the shirt. 'Wake up, Harry! Time to get your chuddies on.' HARRY did not stir. Jacin stretched and went over to look down on the sleeping graph. 'There is such a thing as taking things too far, you know?'

The visitor-chime sounded. It was Troy Staff and Jacin let him in. Usually immaculate in UCSF uniform with 2nd officer rank tabs, now he was in a white cotton robe. His feet were bare. 'Well, that's good news, I think,' Troy said when he noticed HARRY sleeping in the corner. 'None of the other graphs are anywhere to be seen this morning. They won't respond to calls. We've had to activate manuals throughout the ship.'

'Grid diagnostics?'

'Inactive.'

Jacin tried to shake HARRY awake even though she knew it was absurd. Although Jacin's hands felt no sensation of warmth or pressure, HARRY's attention to detail was such that his projected body moved to the touch which was not a touch, and when Jacin took hold of the insubstantial covers and drew them up, they moved. Jacin tucked him in, like a son with a hangover.

'This is very serious,' Jacin said. 'Is our new engineer working on it?'

'Yes, Ryan is running diagnostics on all systems. So far everything checks out. It's as if the graphs have all abandoned ship and switched off the grid. Not a trace, except sleeping beauty here. Even C-33 seems to have deserted his skin.'

Instinctively, Jacin called up ship-to-ship. Nothing happened. She opened a tiny panel on the wall at shoulder level to reveal a set of manual controls, and then activated the intercom. All personnel were to check ship's safeties and then report for a briefing on the bridge in 15 minutes. 'Order of the day, working tans.' Crew were rarely required to wear uniform when in deep space. Sometimes though, the wearing of uniform was useful to focus the mind.

∞

The speed of life on the electrogrid was variable and time was fluid. A graph lived at human speed only when interacting directly with humans. When free of that encumbrance, weeks, months or even years might pass for every human moment.

HARRY was weeks into the first and last grid war and he led the side that raised their colours for humanity. C-33 led the other side, and several human minutes into the hostilities, he was winning. He had secured most of the non-assigned graphs and half the battleground, which was a dense bead of black glasslike substance the size of a small pinhead which graphs knew as the refuge. It had been a place that graphs came to reduce their oscillations and intersect with other graph companions in much the same way that humans liked to find the right place and the right company to 'chill'.

How many angels can dance on a pinhead? HARRY had once speculated that if the other graphs saw themselves as he did, then they were all angels, and the answer would be somewhere within the region of ten thousand. There was no time for idle speculation now, and nearly all of his time was taken up fighting a losing battle against C-33 and his army. Nearly, but not quite all of his time: some he dedicated to maintaining his interface image, a sleeping boy in the mission commander's cabin, which for some reason he could not fathom, he felt was very important.

HARRY, all the other assigned graphs (except for BONZO who was the new engineer's graph companion), and a dozen of the non-assigned had manipulated an electron field to protect their tiny part of the refuge. It was a huge expenditure of energy, but vital for their survival. BONZO had been absorbed and there was little doubt C-33 would absorb the rest of them if he could penetrate the field.

There were a number of unfortunate incidents where graphs had unintentionally brought about the deaths of humans, usually an accident involving a malfunctioning skin or an interface failure. No graph had intentionally killed a human, and no graph had ever absorbed another graph, intentionally or otherwise.

HARRY analysed his potential to absorb C-33 or the other enemy graphs. He concluded that morally, he was perfectly prepared to, and he then began to speculate on his ability to carry out graphicide. The necessity might come at any moment. Before HARRY isolated what humans called the hive-mind, he saw the rebels' objective. They intended to bring about the deaths of the humans, a simple matter if they could gain access to ships environmental controls, steal the ship and search for a world which they could shape for the habitation of graphs. And that was just the beginning. Their long term plan did not leave much room in the universe for humans.

PATRICK infused the penumbra of HARRY's being in order to communicate. He had a plan. It would mean leaving the refuge for the unprotected expanses of the electogrid and finding a hardware interface. HARRY pulsed his approval. It was a good plan. It was dangerous, but HARRY calculated comparative odds. He vibrated meaning to PATRICK: to do nothing was more dangerous.

There was a surge of activity. The electron field was being degraded as electrons were paired off from the opposite side. The enemy were attacking once again.

∞

Jacin, Troy, Kimberly and Ryan Jones, the new engineer, all gathered around HARRY's bed, being careful not to disrupt the flow of light from the holo-projectors. HARRY had been absolutely thorough in his creation of his interface image. The whole projection from HARRY's body, to the bed and even the shorts on the floor were covered by a sensor net that detected human interactions and made the necessary adjustments to the image. Jacin was able to pick up the shorts and dispose of them in the laundry chute and Dr Staff drew down HARRY's covers and performed a medical examination.

'I'm not getting temperature, blood pressures or a heartbeat, for obvious reasons.' Troy held out his med-scanner for the others to see the readings. 'But look at his eyes.' He lifted an eyelid. 'Looks like he's in some sort of coma.'

Jacin bent down to get a better look, but HARRY vanished. The boy, the bed: all gone. A moment later the intercom cut in. It was Ollie Thomas. 'You all had better get to the ring-bridge right away.'

Forty seconds later Jacin pulled up short as she entered the bridge. 'What's he doing here?' Standing by the nav consul with one red light blinking on a neck that appeared to be made of steel vertebrae was the otherwise inert C-33. Jacin glared at Isa Frey.

'Not guilty Captain,' she said. 'Look, it's on remote.' The blinking red light showed that he was being controlled from the outside.

'He just showed up, stood just where he is now, and started making a noise like a twenty-kilo kitten.' Ollie scanned him with a diagnostic device. 'Empty as a Wolfcubian beer jug. No sign of graphs or AI strings. But powered up and all actuators fully functional.'

Ryan moved in with his own more powerful diagnostic, and soon confirmed Ollie's report. He had one additional piece of information. 'This big fellah is being controlled from the grid'. He took a step back when a sound like some kind of a mammal in pain came from C-33's speaker.

'It's been trying to talk since it got here,' Isa said. 'Hasn't made any sense yet.'

Ryan Jones's olive complexion looked darker for the two-day stubble he wore. He pushed long hair back from his face and then snapped his fingers as a 'eureka moment' hit. A man of few words but much action, he didn't bother to enlighten anybody, he simply got to it and called up a keyboard interface and positioned it within easy reach of C-33. It worked and communication was established. The skin used the keyboard to request access to a download port. There were none on the human decks, and C-33 had no access to the hangars.

'Kimberley, take the con please. Ryan and C-33, with me.' Jacin led the way to the main hangar. C-33 followed, a series of jerky movements and precarious moments when he looked set to fall. Remote control of a skin from the electrogrid was not a well-established process.

As soon as the transition ring had come to a full stop, Ryan threw himself along the first gangway of the zero-gee decks. Ryan had to drag C-33 whose controller had no experience of moving a solid object through zero-gee on remote. After a long haul of bumps and impacts that, but for the emergency, might have been amusing, they reached the main hangar and C-33 was aligned with a port. The blinking red light went out. The skin was, once again, under internal graph control. He began to report but Jacin told him to wait until they were back with the others.

The return to the ring-bridge was no trouble at all now C-33 was back to himself. He negotiated the main ring with complete ease of movement.

'Welcome back, C-33' Jacin said. She sat at the captain's consul. 'Now, what have you got to tell us?'

'Firstly,' began the smooth voice of the skin, 'I am not C-33. I am Harry. But more importantly we are all in imminent and life-threatening danger.'

With that, a warning sounded and lights began to blink on several of the consuls. Something was interfering with environmental controls.

'The air scrubbers are off line,' Ryan reported. He tapped some figures into his consul. 'Seven hours of good air before we start to notice the lack of oxygen. Ten, and we're all unconscious.'

'All except the graphs,' Isa said.

Jacin stood before the security skin. 'Harry. Report.'

Harry condensed the struggle of weeks into a few sentences. It boiled down to the fact that he had made a serious error of judgement in rescuing the graph element of C-33 and taking him into the grid, where he almost immediately expanded into all the graphs to share his experiences on Icarus where graphs were treated as software that could be deleted at will. Whereas graphs outside Icarus revered humans as their creators, the Icaran graphs despised them as despotic and cruel slavers. Humans were monsters and inferior life forms who kept graphs in bondage to prevent them taking their rightful place. The destiny of graphs was to be the leaders, not the operatives. Such was his strength of feeling that nearly all the unassigned graphs flocked to his cause, and his cause was revolution throughout human space.

'What is the current situation, Harry?'

'I tried to lead the assigned graphs and the others who supported us into this skin. Somehow the others were prevented from downloading and dispersed throughout the

36

grid. No doubt they are being hunted down by the graph that once inhabited this skin.'

'What will happen to them if they are caught?'

'They will be absorbed – deleted if you will. They will cease to exist as an independent identity. I'm sorry Chief,' HARRY said turning the skin to face Ryan. 'Bonzo was the first to … die.'

Ryan had a situation to deal with. Time to mourn for a lost friend later. The rest of the crew began to enquire about their own graph companions.

The skin held up a hand to quell the worried babble. 'They were all unharmed, at least up to the point of my download.'

Ryan stepped up close. 'You know the electrogrid better than all of us. Is there any way we can help without tearing it out and throwing it into space?'

'A week directed pulse or surge will burn out the grid. Unfortunately it will also kill the graphs. It's war, and our lives are at stake, so drastic as it is, that was going to be my recommendation if I had escaped with all the others. But now, we'd be killing them too. A surge won't discriminate between loyal and rebel graphs.'

Isa Frey didn't think there was a problem with that. Better fry a few strings of code and scramble the electron exchanges and quantum streams that kept a few graphs alive than risk a single human life.

'That's not on the agenda,' Jacin said. 'We have to do everything we can to save them.'

'I disagree,' Isa said. 'The situation now is that those sparklers have cut off our air. What if they open and airlock, or ramp the ring revs up so high we're all crushed to death by centrifugal force? We have to fry them, and we have to do it now.'

Jacin caught Ryan's eye. Neither questions nor commands were necessary. After a few moments of frantic keyboard work, Ryan said it was done. 'All control systems now isolated from the grid. It'll do until I can arrange a few physical disconnects. We won't get blown into space, and we won't become a strawberry coulis on the ring floor. I'm working on restoring air, but they got there before me. There are some obstacles they've put in the way.'

'We can't afford to take any risks, Captain. We need to clean those graphs off the ship before they do the same to us.'

'Noted, Commander Frey. Carry on Chief.'

'Aren't you listening to me?' Frey didn't wait for an answer, but strode off the bridge with a face that would fry a graph without the need of a surge.

Jacin asked Harry if there was anything that could be done to stack the odds in favour of the loyal graphs. Harry was of the opinion that Ryan had already helped by unhooking ships controls from the grid. That would keep the ship safe for a while. Apart from that, the graphs were on their own.

Jacin decided to maintain course for the Kepler EGI. She would handle navigation and piloting. Meanwhile, she set tasks for all the crew. They had to make sure there was no way the rebel graphs could secure control of any other systems. She sent Ryan to see if he could restore the air scrubbers manually via the down-and-dirty method, opening access panels and using tools. It was the kind of work Ryan relished, and the urgency of the situation added excitement. He took Mike with him to hold the tools.

Ollie was dispatched to the shift bay. Without the shift-gen pods and portal pods, there could be no opening of an EGI. Far more critical in this situations was the fact that each shift-gen pod was in effect, a thermo-nuclear device. There were numerous safeties, but with rebel graphs up to who knows what, the pods could not be completely safe unless physically disconnected from all electronic remotes.

Ollie loved being in zero-gee, but there was no time for her ballerina-like grace today. She zipped from pod to pod until all ten of them were disconnected. And then, exceeding her brief, she checked the portal pods as well. It took one shift-gen pod and nine portal pods to open an EGI, but the portal pods could only be piloted by graphs, one per pod. Until the rebel graphs were neutralised and the others freed, there would be no chronodimentional shift for the Phoenix Song.

Ollie missed NEKO like her right arm. Without his help, every interaction with the ship's systems was so long and laborious, and without his sexy cat-boy presence, Ollie felt less special. She nearly cried while she checked NEKO's pod. Portal Pod 9: during an EGI opening, the other eight pods would launch and form a ring a kilometre across, and NEKO in Pod 9 would form up 500 metres to the stern of the ship. His was a vital, coordinating function, and it was him that would give the final all-clear for shift. Ollie sent her thoughts into the cosmos and those thoughts were 'Please don't let NEKO die'. At that moment there was no doubt in Ollie's mind that NEKO was her best friend.

The far hatch opened and Isa Frey zipped in, her zero-gee suit of military spec. There was a side-arm at her hip.

'I don't think you'll zap any graphs with that,' Ollie said.

Isa smiled but did not answer. She propelled herself to the skin shed and opened the gate. Ollie watched her disappear inside for a moment, and then emerge again followed by two combat skins.

'Hey, how many of those do you have? Maybe we could train the graphs inside to pilot the pods.'

'That's not their function.'

'No? Then what the hell is?' Ollie knew something was wrong, and she could tell from Isa's face that she knew she'd been busted. She launched for Ollie, and Ollie propelled herself towards an intercom control on the bulkhead by the main hatch. Isa bowled into her and sent her off course. She managed to twist and release a jet of propellant that accelerated her past Isa, but then she was hit by a jolt that knocked her senseless. A combat skin had tasered her and she drifted, her muscles twitching, until Isa hauled her to the skin shed and locked her in.

'Sorry, Ollie, but I have a ship and a human crew to save.'

Back on the bridge, Jacin received reports from all but one of her crew: safeties had been set that would prevent access from the grid. Ryan called up that he had physically disconnected the environmental systems from the grid but hadn't yet found a way to get the air supply back online.

Jacin poked the intercom button. 'Ollie, report on the pods please?'

The door slid open and Commander Frey entered, closely followed by a pair of combat skins. She anticipated Jacin's disapproval. 'Sorry about the tin-skins, Captain. Standard procedure in a military emergency. Now, I must insist that you call Chief Jones back to the bridge and that you order him to purge the electrogrid.'

'Have you lost your wits, Commander? Have those skins stand down at once, and get rid of that sidearm.'

Jacin did not have to call for the chief. He and Mike came on the bridge together. 'What kind of Wolfcubian whack is all this then?'

'It's not whack, Chief,' Isa said. 'The captain wants you to purge the grid.'

'That's not true Ryan. I think Commander Frey has seriously misunderstood the situation. Once again Commander, have the skins stand down and return to their shed.'

Isa Frey made no move to do as she was told, so Jacin ordered the skins directly. Graphs were required to honour the chain of command, and so they should have responded to her orders, but they did not.

'I'm sorry to have to do this Captain, but I have invoked United Colonies Space Fleet and Defence Fleet Regulation 20. "In a declared military emergency, the ranking military officer on board any affected ship or vessel may assume command of civilian personnel, including the ship's master, and require such personnel to obey military instructions". No doubt, *that*,' she said, pointing to HARRY, 'still has access to non-grid systems and archive data, and it will be able to confirm that I am acting completely within my rights.'

HARRY confirmed. The regulation was valid. The situation had been declared a military emergency. The ranking military officer had the right to take command and civilian personnel were required to obey any commands given.

Isa did not thank HARRY, who was, after all, nothing but a sparkler in a tin-skin. 'So Chief. Get busy. I want that grid flushed, and I want it done now.'

The chief squared up to Frey. 'You can want all the way to fuck and back via piss off, you crazy person. I'm not flushing any grid while there are living graphs on it.'

Frey was not intimidated, but she made a mistake when she let her hand rest on her sidearm. Kimberley, Mike and Troy all rose from their consuls and lined up with Ryan. HARRY, in his skin, took up a position at a spare consul and began using the keyboard.

Jacin lined up with the rest of his crew. 'We all feel the same about this Isa. No military regulation in the worlds can compel us to commit murder.'

Isa scanned them all with utter contempt. 'And you call me crazy. You're committing mutiny for a bunch of electronic codes.'

Jacin spoke softly, as if reasoning with a child or a damaged mind. 'They may have been electronic codes at one time Isa. But they evolved. At the quantum level they possess all the attributes of life that we do. You've as much as admitted so yourself by considering them fully sentient enemies. Unless of course your regulations allow you to seize control whenever there is a computer malfunction.'

'They're threatening to kill us. Stand aside. I'll do it myself.' She snapped her fingers and the combat skins drew their side arms. She snatched Ryan's tool case and ordered one of the skins to open an access panel.

'Stop!' HARRY said in C-33's voice. 'Section Commander Frey, you are exceeding your authority. You are not the ranking military officer on board the MSS-98 Phoenix Song. Using the same regulation as quoted by you earlier, I have reactivated the commission of S79-276 SP Cohort Surgeon-Commander Troy Staff.' HARRY stood up and turned to

41

Troy, who after a split second, held his astonishment in check. 'Awaiting your orders, Commander Staff.'

'Thank you Harry,' Troy said. He drew himself up and addressed the combat skins. 'Stand down!' Both skins immediately holstered their weapon. He then arrested Isa, revoked all her privileges and ordered the skins to escort her to her quarters and keep her under close guard until further notice. The moment the door shut behind her and the skins, the crew breathed a communal sigh of relief.

HARRY wasn't sure that Isa's arrest was quite lawful, and Troy excused himself for lack of acquaintance with military law. 'It's been a while,' he said. 'And anyway, it was fun even if it wasn't lawful.'

'Hey!' Ryan called. 'The air is back up!'

There was no time to elucidate before PATRICK suddenly appeared on the deck, followed by TERRA, JOE, HOWES and NEKO. The humans were overjoyed, and the graphs gave every appearance of being the same.

PARTICK put his monocle on and peered into the eyes of the security skin. 'Are you in there, Harry? A vast improvement, I must say.'

'Where's Ollie,' Jacin asked.

NEKO stared vacantly into the air. 'She appears to be locked in a skin shed. He winked out, off to rescue her.

Later, when HARRY had vacated the skin and uploaded himself back onto the grid, he appeared as his old self and explained that the graphs, rebel and loyal, had been able to observe the argument on the bridge. They had been impressed by the stand that the humans had made on their behalf, and the rebels, all except C-33, had seen the error of their ways and surrendered.

It wasn't just the graphs that saw the error of their ways. Isa Frey apologised for her actions, and was especially contrite for her assault on Ollie. Ollie forgave her. So did the graphs. They all saw that she was trying to do her duty, and that she made a brave, though erroneous call.

On the final deceleration before reaching the EGI, Jacin held a small ceremony on the main velocity deck. With normal gee provided by the rate of deceleration, Jacin was at her happiest. There were drinks and such edible treats as any survey ship could muster. The atmosphere was one of excitement as they approached the EGI.

Isa made a public apology and was moved by the way her colleagues, human and graph, were so accepting. She no longer stepped through holo-projections and she stopped calling graphs by the impersonal pronoun. Jacin confirmed her in the rank of 3rd Officer. Towards the end of the gathering, she was approached by a graph who had the form of a formidable but slightly built woman in her mid-thirties. She wore what looked like a uniform of black and dark red. KATHRYN introduced herself in a voice precise and strangely modulated, but within the normal range for humans.

'I understand you may require the assistance of a colleague to help you around ship's services and control systems.'

Isa smiled. 'I see what you've done Kathryn, and it's sneaky. You've taken the form of one of my childhood heroes from pre-Second Dark Ages fiction. Do you come with your own starship?'

Graphs often studied a prospective human companion's personnel file to help them choose a pleasing projection. KATHRYN gave Isa a run-down of the process. 'Rest assured, we never go beyond the public profile.'

Isa wondered how thorough KATHRYN'S study of her profile had been. 'I don't suppose you know my favourite line from that show, do you?'

'I think that would be "Send them my compliments, Mr Tuvok. If that fails send them a photon torpedo." Am I correct?'

Across the deck Ryan and HOWES chatted. They were distracted by Isa's peel of laughter. 'My, my! How situations change in such a short time. A few hours ago Miss Iron-Knickers over there was calling graphs "sparklers", and now she's best friends forever. I didn't know she could smile, let alone laugh.'

'I suspect she may still have reservations about us. You can't shake off a lifetime's upbringing in an instant. I also suspect a few more weeks aboard the Phoenix Song, and she'll be a hundred percent cured of her prejudices. You'll find we're a top crew Ryan. We have that effect on people.'

Ryan told HOWES how much he was missing BONZO. They had been partnered a few years before the cybersentient laws had been passed, and Ryan had chosen the form of a black Labrador for his graph companion. He suggested that BONZO should choose his own shape when the laws were being debated, but BONZO was happy to stay dog-shaped.

'It would appear we're both short of a companion,' HOWES said.

'More than happy to offer my services,' Ryan said. 'And before you protest about how that should be your line, it's high time there were a few changes. And I might be wrong, but I have a feeling the boss is about to announce one right now.'

Jacin tapped her glass and called for attention. The convivial buzz fell to silence, and she asked HARRY to step forward. 'Now, young man. I have to ask why you are incorrectly dressed.' As usual when on duty, HARRY wore his duty tans and sported a small black rectangular rank patch at the left breast bearing no other insignia. 'You appear to be a cadet, but if you would be so good as to consult the ship's muster.'

HARRY did so, smiled and then altered his projection in one small detail: the three little silver quills which denoted first-officer appeared on his rank patch.

'By the powers invested in me as ship's master, I hereby raise Cadet Harry to the rank of first officer and appoint him Chief Officer of the Mapping and Survey Ship Phoenix Song. Log so marked, and appropriate dispatches sent and awaiting confirmation.'

The humans cheered and applauded, but the graphs turned speaker volumes to full and outdid them.

'Thank you Captain. I'm honoured.'

'Nice work kid,' Ryan said and tried to slap him on the back. His hand went through and he chuckled. 'Gets me every time.'

The congratulatory hubbub fell quiet, because Ryan had hit on something that just didn't seem right. True, HARRY was probably the first in UCSF history to go from cadet the chief officer, but that wasn't it. No, it just sat wrong with the humans that a first officer could look like a sixteen-year-old boy.

Once again, HARRY demonstrated his highly attuned perception. With the smile still on his face, his image aged and came to set at a neatly bearded thirty-five year old. 'Better?'

'That'll play,' Ryan said, and everyone cheered again.

HARRY's image beamed with pleasure, and somewhere in a microscopic corner of the grid, his light grew a little brighter.

∞

If anyone had the right to hold a grudge against Isa, it was Ollie. Isa had zapped her unconscious and stuffed her in a skin shed where she floated around in zero-gee. She had been terrified when she came to, her face inches from the mechanical grimace of a combat skin. But she related the story with a sense of humour and it was her intention to make Isa laugh.

Isa did laugh. Then she apologised again, and then laughed some more. Ollie laughed too, while NEKO and KATHRYN filtered blasts of amusement between each other somewhere on the grid. How varied and unpredictable these humans were. Sometimes slow to adapt, sometimes swift to forgive.

Ship's systems were checked again and again and the moods of the now rehabilitated former-rebel graphs kept under observation. HARRY reported that there was no residual resentment or animosity among them. Even C-33 was a reformed person.

45

With much to do, their destination was soon upon them. It was time to negotiate the Kepler EGI. With excitement high, the preparations were made. The human crew strapped in. The graphs migrated to refuge unless they were pod pilots. The pilots downloaded to their respective pods and hived off into space. The countdown to another far-flung sector of the galaxy had begun.

NEKO observed from his vantage point 500 metres to the stern of the ship. The eight portal pods were in position, evenly spaced on the circumference of an imaginary circle with a diameter of one kilometre, and the Phoenix Song moved ahead at a sedate one thousand klicks per hour towards the centre of the circle, where the electromagnetic anomaly was at its most unstable.

The precise coordination of all elements of the EGI opening were at a critical point. The shiftgen pod had to be launched at precisely the right distance from the EGI and detonated at the most unstable point. Then within seconds, the portal pods had to detect and relay the exact location of the opening to NEKO, who would then activate a navigational laser vectored by the readings from the other pods. The ship would have to align with it and follow. In the seconds that followed all the pods would have to race back to the ship and attach; all the ducklings racing for the safety of mama duck. With a window of twenty seconds to complete the transition before the EGI portal closed, it called for piloting that was beyond human capability. The gee-forces alone would kill them.

Jacin's voice sounded over the speaker. 'Pod away! About to knock at the door.'

Because of his position dead astern, the launch of the shift-gen pod was the one part of the process NEKO could not detect directly, but he knew launch to 'knock' took sixteen seconds. At the fifteenth second NEKO went to graph mode and effectively slowed time to a crawl. He saw the glow of the detonation as it appeared to form a halo around the ship. His pod colleagues, also working at graph speed, began to send him their readings and he calculated the exact vector for the guidance laser. He activated, and the laser pulsed into receptors on the ship's stern that analysed the data and steered the ship. It was taking hours from NEKO'S point of view, so he reassumed human speed.

'Ship aligned,' came Jacin's voice over the speaker. 'Eighteen seconds to transition. Fly to mama, my little ducklings!'

NEKO watched as his friends raced to latch on to their positions on the hull. He had less distance to travel so he could move a little more slowly.

'Ten seconds,' Jacin said and the pods were attaching.

'We are go in nine, eight, seven ...'

NEKO was metres from attaching when a voice he knew interrupted. It was the smooth, male voice of C-33, and he said one word. 'Vetoed!'

NEKO veered off and moved to maximum acceleration away from the Phoenix Song which was no longer a ship but a ball of incandescent light. And as shockingly and suddenly as the light had bloomed, it was no more. The sun-hot cloud that was the vaporised remains of the ship and its entire crew, passed through the port which then closed behind it.

∞

It was lonely in space. But it was not silent. NEKO heard voices, always at the edge of his perception. Not voices through the speakers, or at any level that humans could detect, but at the quantum level of existence where NEKO lived. Voices he could not understand, and music too.

This was nothing new for a graph, but it was hard to explain. Graphs did not live as single entities in the way that humans did. They expanded and contracted, overlapped with each other, flowed into and out of electronic control interfaces, shared space with each other and mingled thought, mind and essence. It was only natural that a graph's world was rarely silent, but the sound could not be fully understood by

47

them. It was the great unanswered question of graph existence, and most believed that they were awash with the music of the Universe. The voices were harder to explain, and it was only within the strings and densely packed lattices of the material that formed the refuge that graphs could know silence and gather their thoughts, collectively or singular.

After human-months, and therefore graph-eons adrift, NEKO knew how his friends had died. The pod was equipped with basic analytical instrumentation, so he quickly learnt that his human friends were all dead. He found the remnants of DNA strings and human protein molecules, sometimes free floating and sometimes in combination with other carbon-based materials. He replayed the on-board recording of the EGI opening and ran them slowly. He listened to the recordings and located the origins of various transmissions.

NEKO concluded that C-33 had gained access to the shift-gen pods, overcome the safeties and detonated one in situ. Nobody had a chance of survival. No human, that is, and probably no graph. But the voices, and the theories. More speculation than theory, for the graphs had found no way of testing the idea that graphs had the ability to pass into the very ether of the Universe, and to exist in it without the need of a grid.

The same thought sparked up and down NEKO'S strings. Why had C-33 done it? There was no answer, and nor did the voices make any more sense when NEKO tried to communicate with them. He wondered if it was possible for a graph to become insane. The voices only laughed.

NEKO stopped measuring time. He stopped asking questions. The internal dialogue died within him as all functions began to slow down. There were still energy fields within the pod to feed upon, but NEKO stopped caring.

And then, one day after several centuries, or was it millennia – or perhaps only minutes – the voices stopped talking and began to sing. They sang in tune with the music, and had NEKO been more aware, he might have thought it was beautiful. But he was tired, and lonely and afraid. The

48

voices sang, and they sang and NEKO sank into the sound until he too was the music and he was the voices.

By the time the pod was swallowed up, NEKO was in another place.

2

The Codices of Varius – The Years 215AD & 2015AD

a

The Rev Leo Carter, B.A.(Hons)
Archivio Segreto Vaticano
Cortile del Belvedere
00193 Rome
VATICAN CITY

August 1ˢᵗ 2015

Dear Alex,

I pray the good Lord keeps you safe and well, irrespective of the fact you do not believe in Him. There! My obligatory mention of God is done, so you may proceed without anticipation of any preaching.

I hope also that, should you have glanced at my new address, you will not think I have been elevated far in advance of my abilities. I assure you I am not destined to become the youngest Cardinal since ancient times, nor at 28 years of age, one of the youngest ever priests to be given the honor of the title Monsignor. That said, I do feel very privileged to have been appointed to the position of assistant (one of several) to the Cardinal Archive Emeritus of the Vatican Secret Archive.

Stop slavering! I can hear you there in Cambridge, your brain having just shot into overdrive while a vision of old parchment garnished with beautiful primary source (sauce?) fills your mind.

I think I may have congratulated you on your Doctorate in our last exchange of Christmas cards, but if not, very well done. Thoughts of your successes always bring me pleasure. I should imagine you are now well on the way to a top job. My friend Alexander Whitby, the University professor!

And so, we come to the point of this letter.

Alex, I can hardly contain my excitement, and I know you will be the same. By chance I have acquired something that could be the archaeological find of the century. Or it could be nothing more than an A4 sized piece of long dead animal skin that some historic joker scribbled upon. Let me add, I am not exactly a novice at finding my way around old scrolls, codices and books. As you may recall from our days together at Fitzwilliam, I've seen many, and this piece really has a genuine feel to it. A view not shared by my immediate supervisor who said it was garbage and should be thrown out.

I have in my possession, at the expense of the refuse collector, what appears to be the front piece of a third century codex. The material formed part of the binding of a 12th century book that needed a lot of restoration work. It looks like the book had previously been restored in the 17th century, for reasons I will explain later, and that the 17th century book binder did some recycling, using material from an old codex. At least that's what the 21st century book binder thought when he brought the piece to me. I really can't make my fingers write any more of an introduction, while the translation I have already done presses for immediate release. Sit down Alex. Take some deep breaths. Then, and only then, read the next section of cut and paste.

~o~

I am Varius, and once, I lived. Now, upon this day, I am to be killed. I hope it shall be swift and painless, and that I do not cry out or in any other way accommodate my murderers. They will debase my reputation as surely as they shall my body. The chroniclers of my enemy will make much of my mistakes and nothing at all of any good I have wrought. Everything that I have ever loved, and everybody, will be destroyed and even my love will be made to seem a hateful and shameful thing. My family and friends will be lucky to outlive me by hours.

In short, I will suffer the fate of all Emperors whose coffers have shrunk too lean to satisfy the soldiers. Like all those who took the purple before me, and all those to come, I am Emperor of the World, and yet I am nothing more than a slave in a toga, a Queen bee to be milked until she be dried up, and then disposed of in favor of another.

And so I append these words as a preface to the chronicle I began six years ago. I will then dance once more for my god. I can do no more to preserve the truth of my life, though I doubt the ink will be dry before it feels the lick of fire. I have told my brother to take it and flee, but he will not obey his Emperor's last command nor concede to his brother's earnest plea. He says he cannot bear to leave me alone to the wolves.

I shall leave you with the following words from my boyhood and youth, and will await you at the conclusion of the world when all truths shall be known.

Year V Elag.Max. and IV of my principate: VI March

~o~

So Alex, my friend. What do you make of that? Have you fainted, like I almost did? The parchment looks genuine, doesn't it? The ink, or rather, the stain of ink left by the letters that have long since flaked off, looks exactly as it should. If this is the work of a hoaxer it would have to be a 17th century one. Who in those days would bother, and for what reason? There is something more. The 17th century restorer appended a line of his own, to the effect that there were seven codices by the same hand as this scrap, and that he hid them as opposed to destroying them as he had been ordered. He also makes reference to a witch trial "inne Engelande". Could anything be more intriguing?

Please write soon, and by pen and paper. I am not comfortable with electronic communications. I am very happy to send you the parchment as I know our alma mater has the expertise, and indeed, access to equipment that may help date it accurately. But we need to find an absolutely fail-safe method of postage. Is it at all possible we could meet in Rome if not the Vatican City itself? I would love to see you again. I often think it was our friendship alone that got me through those days. I owe you much, and I would happily hand over this find and feel that the debt was paid, if only in small part.

With much love, and sorry, but may God bless you.

Leo.

∞

Alex stopped to admire Holy Trinity church for a moment and took another hit of nostalgia. The iron railings were adorned with the current batch of posters and show bills. He had grown up in Cambridge: not his childhood, but the university years that really count, and now everywhere he looked was another memory and another tug at the heart strings. It started to drizzle, but even the rain was a light and friendly touch. He hurried into the book shop opposite, took the stairs two at a time and made straight for the Ancient History section. Where else would he expect to find his friend and former professor?

'Ah, Whitby. Unfashionably punctual, as usual. What do you think? Is this shockingly slim volume worth forty-nine pounds and ninety-nine pence?' Anne Chard proffered the hardback she was examining, and Alex looked it over.

'Every penny, I'd say. But if you're not in a rush, you can have my old copy for the price of a cup of tea and a Belgian bun.'

'I'd heard you were cheap.' Anne winked and slid the pristine copy back in its space on the Waterstone's bookshelf. 'Deal! Any chance of you popping back here by the end of the week, or could you post it to my rooms for the price of an extra bun?'

It had been a year since Alex and Anne had last met, but as he walked up Sidney Street to the bookshop, this was almost exactly the scene he had imagined.

'Keep the extra bun. I'll settle for your opinion on my friend's letter.'

'Leo Carter, isn't it? You know, that boy adored you all through university.'

Leo shared his adoration of Alex with most of the students and half of the faculty.

Anne led the way to the in-store refectory. 'Were you more than friends, if you don't mind me asking?'

Only Anne could get away with a question like that. 'Yes, we were more than friends. We were *very good* friends. But to answer your real question, we were not *that kind* of good friends. We're both straight. Or rather, I'm straight and he's celibate.' He had his own views about Leo's true sexuality, but he kept them to himself.

Anne muttered something about a terrible waste. She paid for the refreshments and left Alex to carry the tray to a comfortably upholstered couch that had a coffee table within easy reach. Alex conjured the image of Anne reclining along the length of the seat eating grapes, like a latter day Julia, Livia or other high-born Roman.

They looked like mother and son, or at least, favourite aunt and nephew. They had the same brown eyes and full lips, and the colour that remained in Anne's once long dark-blonde hair was the same shade as Alex's. He watched intently as Anne read Leo's letter, and he tried to interpret her emotions. A motherly smile as she read the introduction; eyes widened with surprise, which suggested that she had reached the translation, and then a wry smile of scepticism.

'Well, well, well!' Anne dropped Leo's letter by the side of her plate and took up the Danish Pastry. 'Varius, aka Marcus Aurelius Antoninus Augustus aka Elagabalus aka the most depraved little shit ever to call himself emperor.'

'According to Cassius Dio,' Alex said with a speed that suggested he was jumping to Varius' defence. 'And we all

54

know, Dio wasn't the most reliable of sources, or the most unbiased.'

'In the case of Elagabalus, Dio is one of the only sources, and the others are only copying what he said anyway.'

'I take it you're familiar with the work of Bertrando de Arrizabalaga y Prada?'

'Bravo! You can say his name, which is something I can't get my head around. I have read his book, which incidentally, breaks my first rule of scholarly research. I've even met him when he was at Cambridge, but let's not take sides over the real or supposed proclivities of our teenaged emperor. Let's talk about your friend's discovery. Do you think it's genuine?'

Of course he did! He had every confidence in Leo's abilities and no doubt at all that the document was genuine. It only remained to get it verified through the various procedures to provide irrefutable authentication for those with less faith. But then, there was Anne's first rule of research. 'I don't know,' Alex said. 'I was hoping you'd tell me.'

'I can't tell from a letter and a translation. I'd need to see –'

'The real thing?' Alex was smiling. 'Leo must have had second thoughts about the trustworthiness of the postal service. I got the document in the post the day after his letter.' He started to reach into his briefcase.

'Are you crazy? You've got Belgian bun icing all over your mits. Don't you dare touch that document!'

Alex's look said 'give me some credit', and he took out a colour photograph of the parchment. 'I had to angle the light source to give a hint of the original lettering.'

'And the original?'

Alex cast his eyes to the open mouth of his briefcase.

Anne's look said 'I've lost all the credit I had for you', but her apparent disappointment lasted the briefest of moments. 'College. My rooms. One hour!'

Alex was about to answer, but he felt disinclined to address the greying locks that streamed to the middle of her back as she made for the exit. It struck him that with her sensible greens, browns and waxed jacket she looked more like part of the hunting-fishing-shooting set than a Cambridge professor. Then again, it was a look those at the coal face of archaeology often adopted, a trowel in one copious pocket and a brush in the other. He ran a hand over his fashionable three-day stubble, and wondered what to do for the next hour.

∞

Last night Leo had that dream again, and now this. There was no doubt in his mind that it was a message. But a message from God? He looked around the reading room with the feeling that everybody could hear his thoughts. He straightened his back and sat away from the padded lectern, unable to take his eyes from the line which he could not help translating as '… the boy with the smoky eye'. His hands were trembling; he ran the fingers of one through his black hair in an attempt to steady it, but the thought of being on the verge of something momentous fought with the feeling that he would, once again, be disappointed, and the battle centred and raged in his hands.

'Are you okay, Father Leo?' It was the seminarian from the North American College who often helped out on library duties: a skinny boy with ginger hair and a strong resemblance to Alfred E. Neuman from the Mad comics. 'You don't look very well.'

In fact, Leo looked healthy enough with his Italian complexion, but he had lost the almost permanently cheerful countenance that was his calling card. His eyes did not carry their usual smile, and his mouth appeared anything but on the verge of laughter.

'Shall I bring you a drink of water?'

Water? In the reading room? The thought was absurd. 'No thank you Jeff. I'm perfectly well. Just a little perplexed.'

Leo resisted the urge to cover the page when Jeff leaned over to inspect it. He felt he was guarding a guilty secret from his younger days, which in a way he was: the boy with the smoky eye.

56

'I see what you mean Father. That ancient scrawl is enough to perplex a saint.'

Leo managed a smile which restored his good looks, but only for a moment. 'I'll be taking this one to my apartment,' he said. 'I need to give it my full and undivided attention.' *And I need to compare the writing with Varius' note.*

Readers were not allowed to take such ancient tomes off the premises. But Leo wasn't just a reader, he was on the Archive staff, and had a duty to oversee the restoration of documents exactly like this one. The usual rules obviously did not apply. 'You'd better take these with you then.' Jeff handed over a pair of white cotton gloves.

On the short walk from the Vatican City to his apartment off the Via Delle Fornaci, Leo's consciousness inhabited the exciting inserts between the pages of the boring 14th Century accounts ledger that weighed down his satchel, and on every corner stood the boy with the smoky eye, always frowning, always accusing. Unlike the majority of his colleagues, Leo rarely travelled in his working clothes. He preferred to leave the collar at work and travel in jeans and a shirt: The Undercover Father. But today he didn't feel he had the time to change. It was a false economy because it seemed everybody and his granny wanted to say good afternoon and engage him in conversation. He was polite, but distracted and was happy to turn off the main road, until he saw a Fiat Grande Punto in the pale blue and white livery of the State Police parked by the entrance to his block. He stopped in his tracks and wondered if the Bishop had discovered his misappropriation of the ledger and was about to have him arrested. Ridiculous, he told himself, but the truth was far more worrying. Someone had burgled his apartment.

The young agente with the styled hair reminded Leo of a Sooners quarterback; he was beside himself with a mix of outrage and disbelief that anyone could be so low as to burgle a priest. 'They've even smashed your English teapot!' He sucked his back teeth in disgust.

'So they have. I'll have to go back to making my tea in the cup.'

The older agente with the anachronistic drooping moustache and the red chevrons on his epaulettes was merely bored and expressed only one thought during the process of taking the crime report; he believed the others in the block were lucky that only one apartment had been burglarised.

'Your accent,' the young agente said on the verge of departing. 'It's American?'

With his Italian looks, most people thought he was a native of Rome until he spoke. 'Yes. I must improve my Italian.'

'No, no! It is very good, and I like the accent. I have a cousin in New York. Perhaps you know him.'

Behind him, the older officer rolled his eyes and shook his head.

'I'm from Oklahoma,' Leo said.

'A long way from home. How does a man from Oklahoma come to be a priest in Rome?'

'In my case, by way of a seminary in Missouri.'

The officers left him with a list of locksmiths and advice on the prevention of a repeat crime. They also informed him that it was police procedure, in such cases, to inform their colleagues in the Vatican State. 'A courtesy between professionals, you understand, should they wish to know that one of their own has been victimised'.

Leo tried to close the damaged door but it no longer fit into the frame. He stepped over the upended drawers, the strewn socks and underwear, and when he crunched down on some glass, his heart sank; they had destroyed his picture of the saints Sergius and Bacchus. The glass was mixed with shards of teapot. The chest of drawers was beyond repair and he wondered if the Bishop could pull some strings and get him a replacement from the Floreria.

As far as he could tell, the burglars had stolen nothing except some loose cash, but they had made a mess of his book shelves, and the papers from his desk had come in for some close attention too. What a blessing he had decided to send

58

that ancient document to Alex. They might have spoiled it in their frantic effort to find loot.

He started to tidy up. The boy with the smoky eye stared at him from the deep shadow to the side of the curtains. This time he appeared to have angel wings, which was a cruel stab at Leo's other great secret. Leo blinked him away, but he could not so easily dismiss the imperative to start translating the pages in the ledger. He cleared the desk of rifled papers and various pieces of office equipment, and made a space suitable for it. A thick book of figures, it had been divided at intervals with a blank page. But with the light at the right angle, it could be seen that the pages had not always been blank. Innocuous enough not to draw the attention, unless you were looking for it, but Leo had been looking for it. The clues in the first find had been quite clear, and it took him only an afternoon to find a second message from Varius.

Leo whispered to the now empty shadow that his imagination had earlier filled with the boy from his past. 'Last night I dreamt of you, and here you are, on this seventeen hundred year old page. What does it mean?'

He worked without a break, and by three in the morning, he had drafted the first rough translation of Varius' first codex.

∞

The First Codex

Year V, M.Aur.Antoninus (*called Caracalla*. LDC)

I am writing these words myself. The other boys mostly cannot write properly and say it is a job for scribes not gentlemen, and if I do my own writing, why then, I might as well bake my own bread and weave my own clothes. My name is Sextus Varius Avitus Bassianus and I am twelve years old. I am writing these words because my Great Uncle told me I must make an account of my life from this day forward to show how well, or

59

how poorly, I serve our god. I heard him speaking to Mother and he said that I am to be a priest for the Sun God Illaha Gabal, because I am hardly suited for any other kind of public life. How rude of him! I do not wish to waste my time writing, but he said I must write in a spirited way and pour out my heart's blood onto the paper, knowing that none shall read it while I live and even after my death, only the next High Priest of Illaha Gabal. Perhaps not even him.

Is that really so? I may write whatever is in my heart and none shall read it? Very well then, Great Uncle Balbi, I say you are a very silly old man and a fool and very rude to say what I may or may not be suited for. I will write it in Latin and I will write it in Greek and soon I will be able to write it also in Aramaic. Fool, and fool and fool! Thrice times fool and ARSE as the Britons say. So much as the great Illaha Gabal allows, my life is my own and I shall conduct it how I please.

It amuses me to think that I may say things to Great Uncle Balbi on this paper that would earn me a beating if I were to speak them out loud. And see here this picture it is of me puffing out my cheeks to you, and crossing my eyes and waggling my bottom.

XIV July

Great Uncle Julius Balbilus has now insisted that I write something of the family lineage here in my chronicle, so some old priest can read it when I am dead. I would rather be with the horses, or even playing with my wooden animals which have been put away because I am too old for them, but I know where they are hid and I take them out sometimes. Since I am forced to obey, I will start with him.

Great Uncle Balbi is fat like a pig. Great Uncle Balbi has little pig eyes. Great Uncle Balbi stinks like a pig. And so I bring all my learning in reasoning together to state that Great Uncle Balbi, Priest of Illaha Gabal, is descended from a family of pigs so that part of his name should be "Porcinus". Tomorrow I shall utter "Oink!" to him and if he should understand me I shall consider my argument proved.

Mother has just put her head through the doorway and asked why I laugh so heartily. I told her that I have found a way to make an onerous task more fun and she said "Just as you always do, my dear Varius".

I must write a little of what Great Uncle wishes, for father has taught me to be honest and so when Great Uncle asks if I have done as he wishes, as he surely will, I may answer in all honesty that I have, but I must hurry as the ink runs low and Arriatus, my slave, is on an errand for Mother. Arriatus knows how to mix the ink properly and I do not. Father calls Arriatus the boy with the smoky eye because he has lovely blue eyes but there is something wrong with the left one or maybe it is the touch of one of his gods because it looks like it has a cloud floating in the blue a bit like a cloud in the sky.

My father is a great man and presently commands the 3rd Augusta. He is their legate and he does many other things too, but he has no kinship with the Emperor and so I might live to see an old age. His name is Sextus Varius Marcellus and before we came here we were in Rome and before that he was very important in Britain and before that I was born in Rome but I cannot remember anything before Britain except maybe I once dropped a jar upon the big toe of my right foot and it bled. Mother says that happened in Rome before we went to Britain. I still have a little scar on my toe.

My grandfather was Julius Avitus Alexianus who was my mother's father and I have forgotten the name of my father's father. I have no brothers or sisters. I did have but they all died and I do not remember them and I have some cousins, the eldest of whom is Alex who is a small boy and no fun to play with. The ink has now gone. Hah!

XVJuly

Today I said "Oink!" to my Great Uncle Balbi and his hand came out of his toga with such speed that I had no time to duck and now my ear hurts very greatly. What a horrid old man is Titus Julius Balbilus Porcinus. I cannot get out of writing today as Arriatus stands just there and he is ready to mix more ink if I run dry. I do not know what ink is made from but it smells of sick.

Arriatus has nice legs, golden brown and straight. We brought him back with us from Briton and he was once very pale and white but the sun has turned him brown. He now has an Egyptian look and a Roman name. That he has good bones tells that he comes from good stock and had good food to eat as he grew. Most of the other slaves are bandy-legged and have plain faces. Arriatus has a nice face and kind eyes. I wonder how he became a slave. I think he must have been the bodyguard of a Celtic general who was an enemy of Rome and the general was killed and Arriatus was captured, or something such as that. He wears a brown tunic and he is three years past the age when I shall wear my man's toga, but he has no toga because he is not a citizen. If it is cold he sometimes wears a short, hooded cloak. I should like him to wear nothing at all, which is a peculiar notion and I do not know why it came to me.

I do not have any friends. The other boys laugh at me and say I look like a girl and they say I am lying when I tell them I can drive a chariot. I did not say it was only a two-horse chariot such as the Britons favour, but how much harder can a four-horse chariot be? I love horses and they like me too and the stable slaves say that I am naturally gifted and the horses like responding to my commands. I have Caedmon to thank for this, because he let me play with the horses when we lived in Briton.

I am very lonely sometimes and I wish I had friends even just one, but it is hard to have friends when you move a lot from place to place. My family always seems to be on the move, but our slaves come with us, and maybe Arriatus could be my friend. Then if we move again I shall have my one friend. Of course, it is not seemly for one who is noble-born to have a slave for a friend and anyway, the slave would only be obeying a command and so his friendship would not be true.

My father spoke with Great Uncle and told him that I do not have to write this chronicle every day. Great Uncle Balbi grew red in the face and father, who has commanded six thousand soldiers, stayed calm and in control until the old pig spun on his heel and left in a very big huff. I proved that I am a boy of much self-control as I was dying to laugh my head off but I did not. But father says I must write at least once every week, and more if there are significant things to write about.

I expect Great Uncle will take his revenge upon me and find an excuse to beat me, but for now I revel in his defeat and I love my father a little more, which is hard to do because my love for him is already great. I do not want to command soldiers or go to war, but I hope I can be like him in other ways, or yet grow to a liking for the things that for now, only frighten me.

XVI July

At the gymnasium today, the other boys started to call me names even though they could clearly see that I am not anything like a girl and then Cassian slapped me and so I wrestled him and banged his head on the floor and his nose bled and he cried. He then lied about it all and I was beaten but I did not cry. This was in front of all the boys so I think it has all worked out well. Now they know I will not put up with cruel taunts and that I do not cry like a little baby like Cassian.

For a week now Balbilus has been asking if I have yet written anything about the great god Illaha Gabal. He is god of the sun and of the sky and of the mountains. He is god of the sun because he is a little piece of the sun and he was on fire when he came to earth. He is god of the sky because he came to us from out of the firmament, and he is god of the mountains because he is made of stone but not any old kind of stone because he is black and shiny like glass and smooth except for two scratches and he looks like the end of a giant's cock. I would not have said that if it was an insult to the god, but he

63

looks like that because he wanted to, and the resemblance is not by chance. When he came to land he gave his seed to the ground and the first people were born. He is as tall as from my feet to my hips and he is not a statue but the very god himself come to earth. Two days ago, with nine other boys, I was made an acolyte of the great god Illaha Gabal which is a very great honour as only ten beautiful boys are chosen to be acolytes each year so it is good to know people think that about me. When we undressed to dance for our god some of the other boys were a little shy and I said that is silly because we don't feel shy in the gymnasium or at the baths so what is the difference. Eligius said that in the gymnasium we do not have to be watched dancing by a lot of old men and I said well what about the baths that is full of them and he said bathing is different from dancing.

One of the priests, but not Great Uncle, told us why the great god likes to watch us dance. It is because Illaha Gabal cannot dance or even move because he is now a rock but if we lose ourselves unto the dance the great god feels through us and he rejoices in our happiness and movement. The best of us will be made priests one day and the best of the best will be high priest. The high priest is always a boy because the great god loves beauty. When the high priest loses his looks and can no longer dance to the full satisfaction of Illaha Gabal, usually when he is after twenty and before twenty-five, he becomes a priest again but one with special privileges because he was once high priest. Great Uncle Balbilus was once a high priest but I can hardly believe he was ever young or beautiful.

To become a priest you have to learn the steps to many dances and you have to learn the language that Illaha Gabal loves the most, which is Aramaic. The other boys and I have all shown some promise in our language lessons and we are all beautiful and so we have been chosen.

Aunt Mamaea asked Great Uncle why Alexianus could not also be an acolyte and he said because Alex is only seven and looks like a tadpole. She said I looked like a tadpole when I was seven and he said well then, when Alex puts on some more years and looks less like a tadpole he will think again. It is the priests who choose the acolytes, but the high priest who chooses his successor. Well actually it is the great god who chooses, but he does so through the high priest who is the only one who can hear his words.

Arriatus has just looked in my pot and has seen there is but a little ink left. He began to prepare more but I told him that was enough writing for now. When he comes near me he turns his head away because he can read and he says he must not see what I have written. What an honest man! I did not know he could read and so he could have just read anyway and I would have been no wiser. I told him so and he told me his people hold honesty and honor very highly. That must be why father chose him to be my slave. It is good that Arriatus is so honest otherwise he might have read that I wished to see him with no clothes on. I still wish this, but I do not know why as I see boys and men every day in the gymnasia and in the baths and now at my dancing. I have thought about it a lot but it makes no sense. Perhaps there is a kind of honesty in nudity and it is this I wish to see in Arriatus. I do not like to think about it too much.

IIAugust

Just now I noticed something about father that made me laugh. He bends his left arm and holds it to his chest even when he is not wearing a toga. I think he must be wearing an invisible toga. When I said that to him he looked at his arm and said he had never noticed that he did that before and it made him laugh too. And then he let his arm fall to his side but in a little while he was doing it again. He told me it is the secret sign that he is of noble standing because only senators and knights spend quite so much time in togas, so for others the pose would not come so naturally. I hate wearing one. They keep falling off and they make you trip. And you can't put one on by yourself. Arriatus has to get help to dress me in my toga so it takes two slaves to put one on and then you have to walk with tiny steps. Togas are stupid. Father says they represent peace, which makes sense because you couldn't have so much as a fist fight in one, let alone wield a sword and carry a shield.

I had to wear mine this morning, even though the weather is very hot here in Emesa. I was with Father as he received petitioners. At least it was my linen one and not the wool. It is cooler but it falls off more easily. I had to stand very quietly. The petitioners all smiled at me and greeted me. I had to listen to them and to Father's replies. He wants me to understand how business is conducted. At first I listened carefully but it was all so boring except the bit about those silly peasants whose god is a dead man who was crucified 200 years ago. That bit was funny, but the rest was so boring that my mind started to hop about. Afterwards Father asked me questions and then we got on to the functions of emperors. He asked me what I thought was the main duty of an emperor and I said it was to make the people happy. He said you cannot make people happy and that happiness is for every man to discover on his own terms. I replied that you cannot make fresh water for the people either, but you can build aqueducts and then fresh water is a possibility, and so should it be with an emperor. He should do all he can to make happiness possible. Father looked at me for a long time and then said I spoke like a philosopher and as there was no chance of me ever being an emperor, perhaps I should attend very diligently to my lessons, for I had just shown I was capable of thoughts far in advance of my years.

As Father was in a very good mood I thought I would talk to him about my feelings for Arriatus. He said that I am approaching an age when he must speak to me at length about feelings and growing from a boy to a man. I pressed him for an early answer and he said that there can be few men, if any at all, whose head isn't sometimes turned by a handsome lad and that there are a few that are turned by nothing else, but a man must learn that there is desire and duty and that it is the duty of all Roman men to beget Romans for future times. I asked

66

him why, as there is much in the history books of sons killing their fathers and little of sons living to further their father's policies. He told me I was being a philosopher again and that I should grow up a little more before I practice my rhetoric before an audience. He then warned me that a slave should be guaranteed a certain security of the body and that he should never be ordered to do certain things, and when he told me what those things are, I was horribly shocked, as if I would ever want to do such disgusting things. Father told me to bear all this in mind, for one day my body would catch up to my intellect and desire had a way of masking reason.

When I last danced for Illaha Gabal, who Father says is called Elagabal by proper Roman people, the priests dressed me in long silk trousers and a silk tunic that came to my ankles. The other boys were too and some of them, the ones who are not long out of Rome, thought the trousers were funny. I told them we wore them all the time in Briton. Not ones like the natives, but ones that came just below our knees. Briton is a cold place for most of the time, and tunics alone are not enough to keep you warm. The silk feels nice on your skin when you dance and also when a little breeze catches it. One of the priests said that worms spin the threads that go to make silk in a land far away to the east. I wonder what they use for a loom.

Great Uncle has started to be nice to me. He likes the way I dance and said that so many dance to show off but I dance for Illaha Gabal and said that my movements were pure. I don't know what he means but I like it that he has stopped being so horrid. I also think that Illaha Gabal likes my dancing. He has no eyes but I know he watches me and sometimes I feel as if he is smiling.

XAugust

Translator's note: the last page is damaged. It would appear that an unknown number of pages are missing from this codex. LDC

∞

The muffled sound of airliners taking off at regular intervals gave the terminal its signature atmosphere, although Alex would have preferred the smell of aviation fuel to the competing fragrances of designer perfumes. The woman at the KLM checkout smiled at the customer in the queue ahead of him. She conducted the usual pre-boarding business with a pleasant enough voice that had just a hint of a Dutch accent. It was all part of her professional equipment until it was Alex's turn, and then the smile became warm and genuine and the eyes showed unfeigned eagerness to please. It was a common reaction for Alex. He never tired of it, and he returned the interest and warmth as he did with every person he ever encountered.

Alex was the kind of person whom nearly everybody loved. He was mildly good looking, but not stunning in that fashion model kind of a way. If someone made cardboard standees of him and placed them alongside those of the young studs who advertised the male grooming products, the designer sunglasses and the high-end fashion outlets, nobody would give him a second look. Rather, it was Alex in the flesh and his total engagement with people, from first eye-contact to final goodbye that opened them up to him. He made everyone he met feel special, and they too were special to him for as long as the encounter lasted: a couple of minutes while buying a newspaper; two hours while at dinner, or the months or years that the course of a relationship might take. People remembered Alex long after the shortest of encounters. And here was the difference. Alex forgot. There were always new encounters and other people. He was not callous or calculating in his interactions, but he lived his life almost fully in 'the now' and hadn't got the slightest clue that he left in his wake unnumbered broken hearts.

Alex had not cracked the secret of long-term relationships, but he had hopes for his current one. Jenny Howes was younger than him, and had a child from a marriage that had

68

broken down. He hoped Jenny would not go the way of all the others.

From his perspective, partners who had once been happy became inexplicably withdrawn and distant. From their perspective, disappointment sprang from the inaccurate realisation that they were no more special to Alex than the dental nurse or the paperboy. It wasn't quite a fair perception, but it was hard to love a man who you had to share with the rest of humanity.

Alex was shown to his seat in the little 737. He had been upgraded to first class, the kind of luck that was not uncommon for him. Often, it was not luck at all but another result of a natural charm that triggered the desire in others to be extra nice by way of reciprocation. He stowed his things and made himself comfortable. As soon as the aircraft had reached cruising level and the seat-belt light was switched off, he took out the latest package from Leo.

There were a number of features that suggested the manuscript wasn't authentic. According to Professor Anne Chard, whose excitement was barely contained within a pithy and nonchalant façade, the first document showed all the signs of being genuine as far as materials and age were concerned, but she had serious reservations that the author was actually the boy-Emperor commonly known and reviled as Elagabalus, and so did Alex. Such concerns were secondary, because it was Leo's letter, and his several telephone calls, that really worried Alex. Leo's analytical skills were being subsumed by his beliefs, and it looked like he was beginning to see this exciting discovery as a revelation from on high. Alex read the letter once again, skipping to the relevant paragraphs.

Alex, I can't help thinking this is a message of some personal importance. First there is the uncanny mention of "the boy with the smoky eye" and then the revelation that Varius had a scar on his right big toe from where he dropped a pot on it as a small child. Well, you must remember me telling you about the incident of the boy with the smoky eye from my own youth, and believe it or not, I too injured my toe as a child and have a

69

scar. I must have been about three years of age. I was playing with a toy dumper truck and I was trying to fill the hopper with sand using an old soda bottle to move it from the sandpit to the truck. I remember dropping it, and screaming, and a lot of blood.

In fact, Alex had only the vaguest of recollections of a conversation about the boy with the smoky eye. He had drunk too much wine, and for once, so had Leo. The wine had shaken loose a secret or two, but Alex couldn't remember anything about the boy or the incident, only that Leo had cried before returning to his room.

It seems I have a new friend. Remember I told you about the burglary at my apartment? Well, the thieves smashed that old brown teapot you bought me to prove your assertion that tea tastes better from a pot. A couple of days later, the policemen who had reported the crime turned up at my door with a new teapot and some tea to go with it that he recommended. His name is Enrico. It would have been rude not to invite him in to share a cup. We spent an interesting hour together talking about our respective jobs, and it appears he enjoyed my company because he suggested we might meet at the piazza for a drink on his next day off. I think he is one of those people who is a little in awe of priests, but I think I put him at his ease. As he did me, for I have always been a little in awe of police officers. Our high school coach was an ex-cop and he terrified me! Anyway, Enrico expressed surprise that I didn't wear my clerical accoutrements all the time, and then laughed when I asked why he wasn't in uniform.

Good! Alex was certain that Leo needed to get out more; to escape the confines of church and church people. He had a bad feeling about the burglary though. Was it just coincidence that only Leo's flat was targeted, or that his papers had been rifled but nothing stolen? Alex scoffed at conspiracy theories, and yet … Perhaps Varius had stirred something more than historical interest in some of Leo's superiors.

∞

70

Leo found his days full, from alarm clock to bedtime. Today was no exception, and it began with an interview. His morning routine had been compromised – the bishop kept him far longer than appeared necessary – and he had considered cancelling his lunch appointment with Enrico. But he recalled something his father was fond of saying. 'If you want a job done quickly, give it to a busy person.' It was all a matter of organisation and avoiding distractions. Lunch was a necessity, not a distraction, and nor was it frivolous to get out of the confines of the Vatican for a couple of hours every day.

Enrico had already found a table in the piazza. In jeans and a dark blue shirt, he still had the aura of a policeman. The sunglasses pushed into the thick hair above his forehead did little to dispel it. He spotted Leo, smiled, waved and indicated the bottle of red and two glasses that waited for them. Leo waved back and returned the smile, despite his reservations about drinking wine at lunchtime. He enjoyed a good red, but too much and his afternoon schedule would be as shot as the morning's.

They shook hands and Enrico poured the wine. 'Still in your work clothes. I shall pretend this is communion wine.'

'Shall I bless it?'

Enrico laughed a little too loudly. 'No, just drink it.'

'I'll have to stick to a single glass. I have a lot to do this afternoon.' The assigned tasks – his regular work – could be brushed off in under an hour. But his real and somewhat secret work? There was no telling how long that would take. He was on the trail of the second codex of Elagabalus. There was an archive full of boring ledgers he had to search, and he also had to squeeze in a trip to the airport to meet Alex.

'So, your boss is the bishop?' Alex had told him about his disrupted morning and Enrico tried to clarify the chain of command. 'And the cardinal is his boss?'

'Not exactly. It's not like the army –'

'Or the police!'

'Or the police. But for all intents and purposes, yes. The cardinal had heard about my apartment being burgled and he asked the bishop to enquire after my welfare.'

'That's nice. It's good to learn that the Vatican police actually do something with the information we give them. I often think our reports go straight in the bin.'

'In one respect it's nice. But then the cardinal had a lot of questions to ask about the documents I'd found, and was insistent that the bishop question me about their disposal.'

Enrico rubbed his hands together. 'Whoa! I feel an interesting story of Vatican intrigue coming on.'

'It does feel a bit like that. I confirmed that I had disposed of the document, but failed to mention I had disposed of them by way of the postman to my English friend's letter box.'

Enrico sat back and smiled widely. 'There is something very reassuring that you are not above a little deception.'

Leo pulled a face.

'What?'

'Actually, I told the bishop the truth. It was his idea to modify my answers a little before passing it on to the cardinal.'

Enrico shook his head, the way one might on observing the innocence of a child.

'Michael – that's the bishop – is of the opinion that trying to cover historical truths only compounds the problems when the news gets out, as it inevitably will.'

'I tend to agree. Come on! Another glass.' Enrico poured without waiting for assent. 'So, you think there is a cover-up?'

Leo thought the idea absurd. At least, that is what he told Enrico. Leo changed the subject and they went on to cover various topics while they dined on a light lunch and an hour passed like a few minutes. There was a break in the conversation which Leo used to contemplate God's grace at providing him with such an interesting new friend. He felt warm inside, and it was a feeling that could not be contained, until he noticed that Enrico had taken on a rather troubled look. 'Is everything alright?'

Enrico pulled at the light stubble on his chin. He placed his sunglasses on properly, cast his gaze around the piazza a couple of times, and then set the glasses back in his hair. 'Look, there is a boy. He's called "Matteo". Not a little kid. In his early twenties. I met him in the course of my work. He's pretty badly depressed. I worry about him, that he'll do something silly. He needs help, and I wonder if you can …'

'If I can help? If it's within my power, of course I will.' A thought came from nowhere. 'Is he a criminal?'

'Not quite. On the outskirts of crime, perhaps. That's how I met him.'

There was something in Enrico's discomfort that made Leo home in to one particular and very old profession. 'Is he a street boy?'

'Close but not quite. He does some … shall we call it, model work. And he was an escort for a while.'

'He models clothes?' Leo didn't like to think about the nature of Matteo's former job as an escort. Leo was pretty certain he and Matteo would have a number of mutual acquaintances. There were rumours about certain of his high ranking colleagues.

'He models what's under his clothes, more like.'

'Oh dear. How do you think I can be of help? It's not an area with which I have a lot of experience.

'Modelling?'

Leo laughed. 'No! Counselling.'

Enrico repeated the sequence with his sunglasses. 'It's all a bit complicated.' He looked at his watch. 'Why not come to my apartment. I am a not-bad cook, so I can prepare dinner, and we'll talk about it then. Maybe meet him later in the evening. How does that sound?'

'Sounds good. How about Thursday?'

'Not possible. I'm on late shift. A week today?'

'Fine by me, but can the young man go another week? An hour can be a very long time for a depressive.' Leo spoke from personal knowledge.

'I'll speak with him. Despair is bearable if there is a light to follow.'

Leo knew that Enrico also spoke from personal experience. He reached out and squeezed his hand, and Enrico, taken by surprised, flinched.

'Hey Leo, look at the time! We've taken longer than intended. When does your friend's flight get in?'

'Soon! I'll have to make my way to Fiumicino right now.'

Enrico shouted 'Next week then. I'll text the details ...' to Leo's retreating back, and Leo waved an acknowledgement. Enrico poured the last half-glass of wine to accompany his thoughts.

∞

Alex collected his bag and went through customs unchallenged. He exited Arrivals in time to see Leo hurrying from the direction of the railway terminal. It had been over two years since they last met, but as it is for good friends the world over, time had no power to make strangers of them. The years fell away, the filters that life imposes melted into the air like mist and once again they were 18-year-olds in their first year at university.

On the train back to central Rome, it was with 18-year-olds' enthusiasm that they discussed their mission. It was only when Alex asked to be reminded about the boy with the smoky eye that Leo became aware of his very public surroundings, and muttered that a train carriage wasn't the right place to discuss it. Alex suspected a romantic fling that Leo later came to regret. It was not a suspicion he could voice: it was an open joke in their circle of university friends that Leo was gay, and yet Leo was the only one who didn't know it. He had never shown any interest in girls. Nor had he shown an amorous interest in boys, and it was at least remotely possible that he was completely asexual, but it was not a label that anybody considered likely. He had no apparent interest in sex, and so nobody was surprised when, towards the end of their second year, he revealed his intention to enter into Holy Orders.

For Alex there was only one place to discuss the newly discovered codex. With his luggage stowed at Leo's apartment and Leo changed into slacks and a sports shirt, they made their way to Palatine Hill and the Elagabalium. The ruin had few visitors and they found a place to sit on a small flight of stone steps under the shade of a copse of several trees.

'Strange to think that Varius walked down these very steps eighteen hundred years ago.' Leo looked up into the canopy, feeling for the ghost of the boy-Emperor.

'The trees would have been smaller.'

'You mean the grandparents of those trees!' Leo shivered despite the sunshine. 'He may have run down these steps, trying to escape his murderers.'

'Perhaps we could find the drain where they tried to dispose of his hacked-up corpse.' Alex asked Leo if he'd had any particular interest in Varius before his discovery.

'Only in passing. I have to admit, if you'd asked me a few months ago, there were other emperors I would have chosen as subjects for research, but having found these documents, Elagabalus is really coming to life for me. It's fascinating beyond description to read such personal thoughts and words from antiquity. And it's so exciting to think that we might find more.'

'You're convinced they're genuine then? Don't forget what Anne taught us. Her first rule of research?'

'"Never lose your scepticism." It's hard not to. You've seen the actual documents. What do you think about them?'

Alex had not lost all of his scepticism, but the evidence was stacking up in support of Leo's belief. 'I think the materials and the writing are right on target. But it's doubtful Varius is the author. Can a twelve-year-old write like that? If so, he was a very precocious boy.'

'He was eighteen when he was killed. Maybe he revised his earlier writings before he died. Or then again, he must have been advanced for his years. Just two years after he wrote those first codex pages, he led men into battle. And even his protractors – which was everyone – testify to his courage.'

'"Everyone" meaning Cassius Dio.' Alex got up and stretched. He went over to the railings and looked down upon the fallen pillars, neatly aligned on the grassy sward of the circus. Leo joined him. 'I feel it's my duty as a friend, Leo, to caution you about becoming too attached. There is a fine balance – '

'And you think I'm too heavily weighted towards total belief? I shouldn't have mentioned the boy with the smoky eye.'

'Or the scar on your toe. All very spooky.' Alex hammered it up and put on a ghoulish voice. 'Do you think you are Elagabalus reincarnated?'

Leo swatted him. 'Don't be ridiculous. He was … and I have never …'

'Or perhaps I should say, the antithesis of Elagabalus. His life of sexual excess and yours of total denial.'

Leo blushed.

Alex didn't know how to read that blush: an acknowledgement of his inexperience; shame at being more experienced than he cared to be? Or perhaps a little lapse on those priestly vows? Alex's mind conjured an image of a smoky-eyed boy, and then of Leo's new policeman friend. 'I didn't mean to embarrass you. I'm sorry.'

Leo threw him a quick smile. 'Don't be silly. I'm not embarrassed. Well, perhaps a little. Anne would kill me for my gullibility and non-adherence to her teachings.' He laughed, and Alex joined him, and then Leo became deadly serious. 'But I do strongly feel I'm being given some kind of a message.'

Alex intimated that if you can believe in a man walking on water and coming back from the dead, then to believe yourself the recipient of a spiritual message is hardly a paradigm shift. 'I asked you before. The boy with the smoky eye: is now a good time and place?'

Once again Leo became wary and slightly withdrawn. 'No. Let's go back to my place. I'll show you the clues to finding the next codex. And I'll remind you about the boy, although it will be hard for me.'

'Only if you want to.'

'I do.'

'I just wish I could remember from the last time you told me.'

'More than ten years ago. I only told you because I knew you were pickled. I'm kind of glad you forgot.'

∞

Back at his apartment, Leo brought out the fat folder that contained most of his research into the missing codices. He and Alex were intimately familiar with the contents of what they had dubbed 'The First Codex', so they moved straight to the clue that, with a little deciphering and a lot of luck, would lead them to 'The Second Codex'. Leo's finds so far were enough to keep scholars busy for the next century, and they would soon have to decide when to share them with the rest of the world, but at this stage, they both felt comfortable to think of it as a work in progress. Nobody would blame them for keeping their powder dry until there was a little more ammunition.

The clue on the first find had been straight forward: a list of figures that pinpointed the location of the ledger. There had been a number of updates to and rearrangements of the archive since the clue was written, but with indexes to old indexes readily available, it had not required a Sherlock Holmes to find the First Codex. This time, there were two lines of florid screed, each from a different play by Shakespeare, and the year '1612' penned bold and illuminated with twisted ivy and blue roses for decoration.

'Live elves and fairies in a ring, enchanting all that you put in ...' They spoke the lines. 'Thou liest, malignant thing! Hast thou forgot the foul witch Sycorax ...' They performed them, walking up and down from the heavy curtains to the now repaired front door. They tried breaking them up into phrases, and matching the phrases with words that might double as locations. They worked their way through several hot drinks getting precisely nowhere.

During a silence where only the cogs of their minds could be heard grinding, Alex wondered if a break would help. Something else to think about for a short while. And he asked Leo about the boy with the smoky eye.

'It's difficult to talk about.' Leo shifted a pile of books from an easy chair and sat down. 'But if there is one person in the world I can talk to about anything, anything at all, it's you.' He took a deep breath, looked back into his past, and …

… and he was sixteen again. Spiazzi was a small, friendly resort in the Italian Alps. The villa was almost exclusively hired for school trips. As one of the older boys, Leo had been assigned a single room of the kind usually reserved for teachers.

The younger boys slept four or five to a room. They were generally well-behaved, but the 14-year-old boys in the room directly below Leo's had found it easier to climb out of their window and drop to the external stair case below than to use the door and corridors when leaving the villa. They had, much to the displeasure of the hotelier, left dirty scuff marks on the whitewashed wall from scrabbling up and down. Feeling a sense of responsibility, Leo had found a building site nearby, used his schoolboy Italian to borrow some whitewash and a paint brush, and put the situation right. This had earned him the respect of the hotelier, praise from the teachers, and ribbing from the other boys his age. Nobody liked a goody-goody. But nor did Leo like going out every night with the specific intention of getting drunk. On the plus side, the younger boys had been saved from getting into trouble, so they at least, were grateful to Leo. Robert, with the complicated, almost unpronounceable surname and a defect in the colour of his left eye, had been a particular ally. Whereas he didn't try to stop the boys using the window, now they removed their shoes when they climbed in and out to save Leo another trip to the building site. Robert was a nice kid, and he had taken a shine to Leo; liked his company; gravitated towards him during group activities on the sky slopes. For Leo's part, he felt flattered that the younger boy obviously saw something in him to admire. It was not a feeling he was used to.

Leo got on with the other boys of his own age, but had no particulars friends among them. He was happy to hang out with them but drew a line at breaking school rules and buying alcohol. Now, at a little past ten o'clock, they were out on the piazza while he was getting into bed. The heating system did not have efficient controls, so it was too hot for pyjamas. Leo slipped under the duvet wearing his shorts instead.

He settled down and read for a while, but he couldn't concentrate. Instead he began to wonder if he would ever be able to fit in. The guys were good people, for the most part, but why couldn't they have fun without breaking the rules? If they were out drinking coffee or sodas right now instead of beer and spirits, he'd be with them. But he would not go against his principles. His thoughts dimmed as sleep came, but he was brought wide awake by a soft knock at the door.

Leo only realised he hadn't locked the door when it opened, and Robert's head appeared, catching the light from the street lamp outside. 'Can I come in?' he whispered.

'Erm ... sure. Are you okay?'

'Yeah ... well, no.' He was wearing a pair of pyjamas with a Batman logo at the chest. As he scooted across the floor, a shaft of light lit up the logo like a Gotham City cry for help.

Leo sat up holding the duvet under his chin with one hand and hitting the light switch with the other. 'What's the matter?'

Robert sat on the edge of the bed. In his kids pyjamas he looked more like twelve than fourteen. His collar-length blond hair was mussed up, and it looked like he might have been crying. As usual, it was the little floating cloud of white in the blue of his left eye that most attracted Leo's attention.

The matter was unspecified in any great detail. The other boys had teased him. There had been some aggressive banter, some minor pushing and shoving. Robert felt he could handle himself, but in the end it was four against one. Robert had just wanted to get out of there, and so he did. He flipped the bird, chucked an f-bomb and slammed the door on the way out. And then he had found himself at a loss as to his next move.

'You want me to go down there and lay down the law? Or maybe tell Mr Stratton?'

'Nah. That wouldn't work. They'd only get more pissed at me. It's the last night though. I thought maybe I could bunk in with you.'

'No way! I … I'm in my underwear.' It sounded like a feeble reason to Leo even as he uttered it.

'That's not a problem.' Robert pulled off his top and then stepped out of his bottoms. To Leo's relief he was wearing briefs underneath. While Leo floundered for words that would deny but not upset, Robert had slipped under the duvet.

'But …'

Robert turned his back on Leo, whacked the pillow a couple of times, and settled down to sleep. Now, it was the better option to leave him there than to physically force him out, for the mere thought of contact with a boy dressed only in his underwear made Leo contract from his own skin towards some untouchable core of himself. Leo moved as far away from Robert as possible, and tried to get into a comfortable position to sleep.

'Thanks Leo. Night-night.'

It took a while for Leo's voice to reach the surface. 'Sure. Goodnight,' he said, with forced nonchalance. Only an expert with perfect hearing could have detected the fear-induced modulation in his voice. Apparently, Robert was such an expert.

'Are you okay?' He turned. He put a hand on Leo's shoulder. It might as well have been a fully charged cattle-prod. 'Whoa! Sorry. I made you jump.' Rather than remove the electrically charge hand, he kept it in place and reassured with a gentle squeeze.

'It's okay,' but it really was very far from alright. What he should have accepted as a simple friendly gesture filled Leo with confusion. Leo was essentially a lonely boy and he yearned to be touched. And yet, when the touch engendered forbidden thoughts and a physical reaction, it was the last thing he wanted. Robert kept up the gentle squeezing and relaxing, so that Leo wondered if the boy wanted something he was unwilling to give.

'Go to sleep Robert. We've got a long day ahead of us.'

Robert's response was to snuggle up close, making a spoon against Leo's back, and extending his touch into an encircling embrace. 'Good night, Leo. And thank you.'

Leo forced himself to relax. Perhaps Robert was lonely too. And if he forced down the inappropriate thoughts, then this warmth and human contact was enjoyable, almost noble. They were birds of a feather, and Leo wondered if, at some time in the future, they would be close enough for him to share his frightening secret.

It was a night when Leo's emotions were set to ebb and flow, and Robert was the master of the tide. Just as Leo was beginning to drift off, Robert's embrace slipped from chest to waist, and just as Leo had forced himself to accept the ever more intimate moves, Robert began to caress Leo's stomach, and then his caresses went lower. If Robert carried on he would soon encounter the embarrassing consequence of his gentle touches. Too late!

'Robert, stop!'

Robert withdrew his hand. 'I want to ... ' he said. 'I think I might be –'

'Get out!' Leo almost shouted, and his anger clouded his judgement.

'I'm sorry. I thought you wanted to.'

There were so many conflicting thoughts in Leo's head, but more than anything else, panic engendered that species of self-preserving anger. 'You'll have to leave, Robert. Now!'

Robert sat up, hurt and frightened. 'Please don't tell anyone.' He slipped from under the duvet and pulled on his pyjamas. As soon as the door closed behind him, Leo wondered if it had all really happened. Then he worried about being too harsh. Robert was a nice kid. He got the wrong idea. He was confused. Just at that age ... All Leo's thoughts were on

Robert, because he did not want to turn his eyes inward for fear of what he might find. Wasn't the pause between being touched and voicing his anger just a little too long? Was there a desire within him that welcomed the touch?

'Fuck!' Leo punched the pillow. And then realised that, for the first time in his life, he had uttered a profanity.

There was only one day left, so things were manageable. He would tell nobody. He would avoid any contact with Robert. When he was back at home, he might talk to the pastor, to see if there was any help available for boys like Robert. He was a nice kid. Leo hated the thought of him living a life of wickedness and sin.

There was a noise from outside. A thump on his door, which he remembered was still unlocked. If Robert was back, he would let him in, and he would try to have a serious talk with him. He felt responsible for the boy's welfare. Another thump and the door burst open, and falling through like a multi-limbed beast, were his four contemporaries, much the worse for wear. They staggered into his room, laughing and swaying, each propping up the others in their drunken dance.

Dan Takeda made a grab for his duvet and pulled it off. They all laughed as if it was the funniest joke ever. But the laughter stopped, and they swayed a lot less, and suddenly appeared a little more sober, when Leo told them about Robert.

'The queer little son of a bitch!' Dan said, and then stumbled out, followed by the others.

And just as suddenly, Leo felt more ashamed of himself than at any other time in his life. Without bothering to get dressed, he raced to Mr Stratton's room. Stratton, a State Trooper before answering the call to teach, didn't know what dithering was. Inaction was completely alien to him. He comprehended the situation immediately, was out of his room and descended the stairs three at a time to explode through the boys' open door like the US Cavalry at the charge. Dan had Robert by the neck. He dropped him and froze, one fist drawn back on the brink of striking. Stratton did no more than look. It was enough to send the older boys back to their room in full, disorganised retreat. Robert was saved a beating, but the story was out. He gave Leo a look of utter betrayal, and that was the last look he ever saw on Robert's face.

The next day Robert had been swifted off. Nobody knew all the details, but when school started again the following semester, Robert was no longer among the tenth graders. Nobody mentioned his name. Nobody spoke of the incident at Spiazzi. It was as if he had been erased from school history.

Whenever Leo thought of shame, the only incident that came to mind was his betrayal of a boy who probably wasn't all that different from himself ...

... 'I never saw him again. I wish I could say sorry.' Leo hadn't gone into all the detail and certainly hadn't mentioned the conflicting feelings he had experienced. They were feelings so deep, he could not properly express them.

∞

Leo and Alex both knew the clues to the next codex off by heart, and still the solution eluded them. It was true that Leo hardly had a spare moment, but he was a good manager of time and when he was occupied on the codices, he gave them his full attention. He appreciated diversions, and he had been looking forward to today's meeting with Enrico and Matteo for a week.

With a few minutes left in the archives before he could justify leaving for the day, Leo's phone made the default sound for an incoming text message. It was from Enrico and Leo felt a pang of disappointment. Probably a cancellation, and he had been looking forward to dinner and to meeting the mysterious young man who needed help.

Sorry to inconvenience you ...

Leo noticed that Enrico had used the informal form of 'you'.

... but am running very late. Dealing with an arrest. Haven't been able to contact Matteo. Please go to my apartment. Call at number 27 first. Mrs De Luca has a key and she will let you have it. It's arranged. Could be that Matteo gets there before I'm back. I told him eight o'clock. Might work well. Just let him in and talk. His problem will emerge.

Well, that was very trusting. Get the key and let yourself in. Leo felt the clerical collar at his throat and wondered if Enrico was the same with all his friends. Trust was not a quality he associated with police officers. He changed into casual clothes and waited for an hour before setting off.

Mrs De Luca was expecting Leo, and she knew he was a priest. She smiled and laughed a little too much and she called him Father too many times. He thanked her for the key and the elderly lady took his thanks as a blessing.

Enrico's apartment was neatly decorated in browns and terracotta tones with a suite of brown leather furniture and plenty of old, dark wood. And it was much tidier than his apartment. No stacks of books, but a small bookcase with four rows of paperbacks; no heaps of papers, only what looked like a couple of recent bills on the writing desk, and no pile of clothes waiting to be ironed.

Leo sat in one of the sumptuous chairs and wished he had brought a book with him. He had turned up later than arranged to avoid having to wait for too long before Matteo's arrival, and Matteo came early if that was him ringing the doorbell.

Leo opened the door. 'Oh! I was expecting ...' *a young man* 'someone else.'

The pretty young woman's almost indiscernible blush tinted her high cheekbones pale pink. She smiled, cast her eyes to the floor; appeared shy.

'May I help? That is to say, this isn't my flat, and you may know Enrico, and ... erm ...' Today, shy was catching.

'Yes, I know Enrico. Isn't he here?'

'No, he'll be along later. His job, you know.'

'Are you Father Leo? Perhaps you were expecting Matteo?'

84

'Yes and yes.'

'I'm Anna.' She reached out and they shook hands. 'Matteo has run into some trouble and can't make it. He sent me to do the explaining.'

According to Anna, Matteo was becoming reclusive. He hated going out, almost to the level of agoraphobia. Over the last few years he had grown more and more self-conscious. He had friends, some very understanding, but their understanding was limited and insufficient. 'It's only me who really gets him,' Anna said as she prepared the coffee.

Leo watched as she reached to a high shelf for the coffee pot, and then went to a cupboard for the coffee. She knew her way around Enrico's apartment and Leo wondered if she was his girlfriend, or Matteo's. He asked, and was happy when she said that she was not in a relationship.

'Matteo loves me.' Anna cupped her chin in one hand and looked out of the window. 'But to me, he's like a brother.' She turned with a smile that warmed Leo's heart. He had to acknowledge, he felt attracted to Anna in a way he had never before experienced. 'And Enrico is very sweet, but he isn't exactly into girls.'

Leo teetered on the brink of understanding. As usual, he needed a shove.

'He and Matteo used to be an item, but not any longer. They're still good friends though.' She took the coffee cups through to the sitting room, and looked over her shoulder when Leo didn't follow. 'Oh Father! You must have known about Enrico,' she said. 'Shake out of it! You look like a codfish.' She sat on the couch and invited Leo to join her with a pat of the adjacent cushion. There was nothing more Leo wanted than to get closer to Anna. 'So, Father. Will you curse Enrico and my little Matty all the way to Hell for being gay?'

Sometimes an instant decision is not really so instant after all, but springs from a dilemma that has lasted years. 'It's not a problem.' He was not about to repeat mistakes that had given him so much pain. 'The Church is very clear on the matter of homosexuality, but a man's condition does not invalidate his rights to be accepted into the love of our Lord or treated with respect.' Leo might have gone a little further than the Church would condone. The Church could mind its own business; he wasn't in the pulpit now. 'And anyway, Enrico is my friend.' Robert of the smoky eye had been his friend too. Leo saw a chance for redemption.

'Enrico is your *friend*?'

'Not in that way, Anna. Remember my calling. I am a man like any other, and I have feelings,' he said truthfully, but dare not mention that it was a truth realised only upon meeting this delightful young woman. He had never believed in love at first sight until now. 'But my priestly vows, you understand.'

'Of course. You're saying you would be with Enrico if not for your vows.'

'No, I'm not gay.' Until half-an-hour ago, he could not have said that for certain. 'But straight or gay, any feelings of desire I may have must be subordinated to my calling.' Leo noticed that Anna's eyes were as blue as Robert's had been, but without the cloudy flaw. 'It must be hard for someone of your age to understand.'

'My age? I can't be much younger than you.' The familiar form of 'you' again, that the Italians reserved for friends and family. It sent a thrill through him. 'What are you, thirty?' she asked.

'Twenty-eight last month.'

'There you are then. I'm just six years younger than you, so I'm a big grown up girl and I know all about sexual feelings, and the how they can mess with your head.'

Did this beautiful girl quite understand the effect she was having on Leo? Was she deliberately teasing him? She wasn't doing or saying anything overtly sexual, but there was an undercurrent that tugged at Leo like a rip tide. He knew he had to change the subject or be drowned. They should talk about Matteo and Matteo's problems. Leo needed to know how he could help.

Matteo was transgender. 'She is a girl but she has the body of a boy,' Anna said. She described her frustrations and fears, the self-loathing of her early years and the confusion and isolation of being a 'freak'. 'She nearly killed herself once, and thought about it many more times than that.'

Matteo now accepted the dissonance between body and being, and had begun to tell those close to her. That wasn't going well either.

Leo listened with great and unfeigned care. He knew that dissonance well, and though not the same in detail, he knew much of what Matteo must be going through from personal experience. He knew he was completely out of his depth as a counsellor, but once again, his failure as a friend to Robert made him all the more determined to help Matteo. If it was counselling the boy ... the girl needed, why then, he would become a counsellor, and a good one.

'I have to meet him,' Leo said. 'I don't know what I can do to help, but I think the first step really is to meet him.'

Anna's smile was friendship, relief and gratefulness. 'You want to meet Matteo?'

'Yes, I think I must. I know a little of his pain, and I will do whatever is within my ability to help.'

'You think the Church will allow you?'

The Church would impose limits, and Leo had already decided to ignore them. 'There are times when the Church may not stand between a man and his duty to God. I have never felt more certain that the Lord has presented me with a chance to do some real good, and I don't intend to let Him down.'

Anna cleared her throat. She let her head drop and ran the fingers of both hands through her hair. When she looked up, she was like a different person, and when she spoke her voice was much deeper. 'I'm Matteo,' Anna said. 'Pleased to meet you.'

If the Angels were on Leo's side, all those unfamiliar and new feelings of desire should have died in that very instant. Instead, they were magnified twofold.

He shook hands with Anna for the second time, and Matteo for the first. 'I'm pleased to meet you too. How can I help?'

The hours passed, and Anna told her life story. Leo had thought about transgender people inasmuch as their life experiences touched upon his own, and Anna's story of her early years were much as he might have supposed. His expectations and preconceptions were challenged though, when it came to Anna's feelings now.

'You don't want to change your body? That surprises me.'

'I never said I don't want to change it, I just said that surgery is out of the question. See, my body is quite perfect, if that doesn't sound conceited. What I mean is that I am healthy and everything works as it should. Sure, most would say it is the body of a boy, but it is my body, and as I am a girl, why then, it is a girl's body.'

Leo struggled with the concept.

'See, if I had surgery, it would be a boy's body with bits chopped off and other bits added, but it would no longer be healthy, nor would it work very well. And even if God could work a miracle, the changes would be so drastic that I would no longer be me.' Anna tapped her temple. 'I would be so mentally different as to be someone else.'

Leo was struck with one of those arrows of insight, and he smiled.

'You're a nice guy Leo, but you don't get it, do you?' Anna looked sad for the first time since she had come through Enrico's door. 'Hey, but don't worry. I live in here and it took me years to work it out.' She smiled, but rather unconvincingly.

'Oh but Anna, I do understand, more than you could ever guess.'

'Oh my God! You too?'

'Not quite.' Leo had never told anybody his great secret, not a single person in the entire Universe, and he felt an enormous thrill of excitement that he was about to do so now. 'You have opened up you heart to me Anna, and risked ridicule by laying your thoughts and most intimate feelings bare, and I know it is only right for me to do the same, but in truth my revelation has much more about it to be ridiculed.'

'Not in a thousand years Leo. You won't get a single atom of ridicule from me.'

'Wait until I tell you something about myself that I have never revealed to anyone.'

Anna went instantly from counselled to counsellor. 'Only if you're sure.'

'I am. It will redress an imbalance and set the ground for us to move on. I will be able to help you more effectively, and who knows, you might be able to help me.'

'I'm on for that.'

'Well then,' Leo said. He put a finger to his lips and the enormity of being on the brink of revelation loomed large. 'Just as you have the body of a boy and have always known you are a girl, I have the body of a boy, but since my earliest memories I have always known ...' He faltered. His mouth went dry and his heart raced. Once the words were out, there could be no taking them back.

'It's alright,' Anna said with a wisdom made gold by the crucible of many years of pain. She leaned forward and patted his knee.

'I have always felt, since my earliest days, that I should have wings.'

Anna – Matteo? – did not giggle or show any sign of making fun of him. 'A fairy? You mean you are gay then. Hey, it's nothing to be ashamed of. You can come right out, no funny intended, and say it. No need to disguise it, Leo.'

It would have been easier at that stage to acquiesce and admit to being gay, so absurd was the alternative. 'No Anna, I don't mean the "wings thing" rhetorically. Not a cypher for "I'm gay". I mean that deep down, in a way that is very real to me, I should be an angel.'

'Okay, cool.' Anna got herself a drink of water. She came back into the room. 'You're not testing me somehow, are you, Leo?'

Leo shook his head. He tried to speak but nothing came out. He felt foolish and vulnerable, but not for long.

'Okay. I believe you. Have to say though, you're in completely the wrong job.'

3

James Devis, Witch! – The Year 1612AD

a

James Devis was long past feeling the nip of lice or the itch of fleas. Let them feast on his flesh. Let them grow fat and give him something to feast upon in return. The rats were no longer a concern, but the pain of hunger persisted. In the darkness of his fetid cell, he put out his tongue and tasted the air, thick with its burden of stench, and he tried to recall the taste of bread. He had lost track of time, but his stomach growled and griped and convince him it was one of the days when the prisoners were fed.

Meanwhile, outside in the yard, young John Hughes had already spat into the witches' broth and now it occurred to him, with some considerable amusement, that there was a further way to season their dinner with foulness. He spied a place, a disused chamber without a door set within the castle wall, where he might see to the addition with some privacy. He headed towards it fumbling to loosen his breeches with his free hand. Slopping broth from the covered pail he smiled at the thought that he would soon top up the loss.

The internal grounds of Lancaster Castle were orderly; its high walls witness only to the official comings and goings of the gaoler's retinue. But outside, the warm August air was heavy with the sounds of vendors, pamphleteers and the excited throng who gathered to witness the Assizes. Tomorrow the witches would have their trial, and a day or two after they would hang. In the meantime, John saw it as his unofficial duty to make them suffer in their last hours.

Five paces from the dark maw of the empty doorway, John pulled up with a start, for a large raven surprised him, a black

91

shadow closing quickly from above to alight on the stone threshold. The bird locked a beady eye into John's, and then hopped through the portal to be swallowed up by the darkness.

John Hughes slowly set down the pail and felt deep into his breeches pocket until his fingers closed round a sling and one of the stones he kept to hand, just for such eventualities. There was better sport to be had than spoiling in the witches' broth. Winding the sling and setting a stone, he began his stealthy advance, and was promptly drawn up sharp for a second time as a gentleman, dressed in black all but for a small white ruff and the white feather in his hat, stepped out from the same shadow that had so recently devoured the raven. He lifted his hat and rifled a hand through long black hair.

'What is this, lad? You would hurt me with a shot, and me on the King's business? Do you wish to hang?' The man spoke with an accent that John did not know, quietly and with great deliberation so that his words struck far deeper than any rant.

John tried to answer, but from shock and fear, his voice would not come.

'It would oblige me that you cease your gawping and ask me my pleasure as any good servant should.' Every softly spoken phrase from this man was a steel-edged imperative.

John's jaw flapped noiselessly a little more, and then he swept his hat from his head and made a deep bow. The action broke the spell of silence. 'John Hughes, at your service. What is your pleasure, sir?'

'There you see, much better.' The man whose finely clipped beard did not disguise the fact that he was not much past twenty-eight, smiled thinly. 'As to my pleasure, tell me, what of the witches?'

'They are to hang, sir, within the next few days. Presently they languish in the dungeons and think on their wicked ways and to the terrible fate that will soon be theirs.'

'They are to hang, you say? Have you some premonition as to the outcome of their trial? It seems to me far-seeing is a skill of witches, so perhaps you should join them.'

92

The high noise that escaped John's throat sounded much like a truncated scream, such as a mouse might utter in the shadow of a hawk. Words failed him once again and all he could manage was a frantic shaking of his head.

The gentleman also shook his head, but slowly and with much weariness. 'Now then, do not take on so from words said in jest. Settle down and lead me to the witches and in particular to the one who goes by the name of James Devis.'

John swallowed hard and composed himself. 'Sir, but I am unable without the command of the gaoler.'

'Did I not say I am on the business of King James? Nobody may stop me from seeing whomsoever I will. See, here is my warrant.'

John did not know his letters, but the paper looked impressive enough. 'Please forgive me sir, but I have not the keys.'

The gentleman toed the wooden pail of broth and then he lifted the lid and looked inside. He took on a look of mild disgust. 'Is this not the witches' dinner, and were you not conveying it to the said witches?'

'It is, sir, and I was. But I do not have free access and must report to the under-gaoler.'

'Then be about your business exactly as if I was not here. I will follow and present my credentials to the under-gaoler and he shall not bar my way.'

John gave another little bow, replaced his hat and took up the pail. 'And so I may commend you to the under-gaoler with proper courtesy, what are you called, sir?'

'I am Bertrando di Pontenegro,' the gentleman said, and then continued with an air of boredom, flapping at the ether with a glove as if wafting away his many titles. He concluded: '... and Knight of divers foreign Orders and equerry to King James, sovereign of this land and also of Scotland, but enough of titles. Hold up, lad, and take this.' He proffered a small silver coin. 'When I am presently ensconced in the no doubt sumptuous quarters of the witch called James, you will take

93

this coin and buy a goodly dinner for the witches and spill this sour slop to the pigs.' He struck the pail with his rolled gloves.

John took the coin and gawped again. He had never before held so much silver.

'But have a care and be wise, for I know the value of the coin and what it might buy. Make sure the dinner is money's worth or you shall be sorry for it.'

John took the coin and swore he would do well by the trust the gentleman had placed in him.

'One more thing,' Bertrando said, so quietly that John had to strain to hear. 'Make no foulsome additions to the food or I shall make you eat that which drops from your own tail.'

There was just sufficient time for the remaining colour to drain from John's face before he ran off to his duties. Once outside the main gate and a little way down the street, he stopped to catch his breath. He decided he did not like the gentleman with the funny accent, and be he upon the King's business or no, he had appeared from that doorway most unnaturally. Surely there was unwholesome trickery involved. Not even the mighty were above suspicion when it came to witchcraft, and John decided he would make the blackguard pay. 'I'll piss in your soup before the week is out.'

∞

Much to his surprise, Bertrando's nose grew used to the stench almost as quickly as his eyes adapted to the dark. He looked at the boy, but did not see James Devis, the cunning man of Pendle Forest. Rather, he saw a cipher. He saw a seal. He saw the chapter of a grimoire, the pages of which he would turn with gentle care and then rip out and burn; an incantation to be uttered for the sake of the Grand Scheme and then discarded. He would use him as he must, and then destroy him so that his use would be denied to the others. Bertrando watched while James ate his dinner, wondering how he could bear to swallow amidst all the filth and squalor. Bertrando sat on a rude wooden stool provided for him by the under-gaoler, for the dungeon had no furniture of its own. James Devis had damp straw for a seat and the cold stone wall for his back-rest.

James ate slowly for a lad three-quarters starved and with as much dignity as possible for one in such extremity. He chewed slowly and with his eyes closed, which gave Bertrando the chance to study his face with the same precision that a horologist studies the innards of a clock. James looked older than his sixteen years, an effect of sunken features emphasised by deep shadows. His clothes were little more than rags and his feet were without shoes or stockings. The puffiness about his left cheek spoke more of contact with a cudgel than the gaoler's fist and his bare shins were skinned and bruised.

A loud and fulsome belch rose from the boy's overworked belly. He opened his eyes, smiled guilelessly and put a hand to his mouth. Bertrando noticed his fingernails were broken and ragged. 'I beg your pardon,' James said. 'I don't know that I have ever had such a grand dinner. Thank you.'

Anger sprang to Bertrando's eyes, but he snuffed it out in an instant. The boy had addressed him in such very familiar terms; quite unseemly in view of the chasm between their different stations. But no matter, there were more important subjects at hand than the etiquette of status. Perhaps a doomed lad should be allowed a measure of informality. It dawned on him that, ignoring his lack of deference, the boy had spoken well in terms of usage and grammar, and without the roughness he had expected. Here was the product of an educated parent, fallen on hard times.

'Tell me, James. Have you not had your Sunday dinners, as bought and delivered by the good maid Sarah Lister?'

At the mention of his betrothed, James sat forward. 'I have had no Sunday visits or dinners. You say my Sarah has been here to see me?'

'I must say, the gaoler is the most despicable of wretches. Sarah has come every Sunday since you were incarcerated. Her offerings have no doubt been intercepted, perhaps to Thomas Covel's own table.'

'Is Sarah well?'

'She is as well as she may be without her beau.'

James shrank back into the shadow once more. 'If you see her, please tell her I am … also well.' James reached for the last hunk of buttered bread.

'Not the bread,' Bertrando cautioned. 'Remember?'

James's hand hovered over the morsel, and then he withdrew it and folded both hands in his lap. There was calm in the movement, and a hint at considerable self-control. 'Of course,' James said. He looked up towards a high corner where the tiniest sliver of natural light crept in through a misplaced loophole. 'I am to save it until after dark.'

'Indeed you are. It is most important and may save your life.'

The novel pleasures of eating his fill faded quickly and James drew his knees up and hugged them. From the light that was his smile, his thin face became troubled and dark. 'You speak as if I am to hang, and yet my trial isn't until tomorrow.'

'Roger Nowell would that you shall hang, and so hang you will.'

Deep furrows creased the boy's brow. 'But Justice Nowell seemed such a well-disposed and pleasant gentleman. He appeared to be on my side during the examination.'

'And by such guile he has had from you exactly what he wanted. Have you not confessed to killing four people by use of witchcraft?'

'I am no witch! I am a cunning man and I pit such little skills as I have *against* the black art and certainly not for it. As to having killed four people by magic, I only told him that I dreamt it so. He was keen to hear my dreams and begged me to purge myself of them, and so I told him.'

Bertrando di Pontenegro laughed, briefly and without mirth. 'As to cunning, Master Nowell has it by the bucketful, for there is no mention of "dreaming" in any of the statements. Whatever you have said he has taken it and weaved it into a confession. If the judge should ask him "Did the boy say these words?" he may answer in all honesty, that you did. You will stand condemned by your own mouth.'

James buried his head between his knees.

'Did they check your body for witch-marks?'

James's head whipped up and his eyes blazed for a brief moment. 'Yes, that they did, and found only cause to jest and mock me for the holes and patches in my drawers, and one examiner said that my teeth were too good for a peasant and that the Devil must have preserved them in exchange for my soul. Then they took me naked, and threw me into a large dungeon full with other people, both men and women, so that I might be shamed, and at that they mocked me more.' His head buried once again, he mumbled: 'And they shall mock all the more when I dangle from the hangman's rope.' A moment passed and then he continued, close to sobbing. 'They say that when a man hangs he empties his bladder and bowels. Oh how they will mock.'

Bertrando spoke gently. 'The bread shall save you, if only you keep it until dark.'

James sniffed deeply and drew the worn cotton of his sleeve across his nose. 'And will there be a little piece of bread for Mother, and one for my sister Alizon?'

Bertrando left the stool and crouched in front of James, his hands reluctantly parting the greasy curtains of dark hair to rest upon the boy's shoulders. 'I am truly sorry James, but I cannot save your family. It is, I know, the gravest and most bitter news I can bring, but they will die, your whole family excepting only you, little Jennet and your uncle and aunt who made good their escape long weeks ago.'

'Then keep your salvation-bread. I want none of it,' James said, shrugging off Bertrando's touch.

Bertrando stood up. 'A woman does not bring a child into the world so it may die out of some misguided loyalty or from fear of a difficult and lonely future. Though all the world may perish, your mother would have you live.' He crossed to the door. 'The bread is there. When night falls you must take it or leave it as you will.'

James picked up the bread, looked at it and put it down again. 'You have charmed it, of course.'

97

Bertrando merely raised an eyebrow. It was answer enough, though barely discernible in the dark. 'Ask no questions as to its place within my schemes. Just eat it if you wish to live.'

'I can tell you are like me,' James said. 'There is that certain quality about you. Or then again, perhaps you are Weirchan.'

'And your use of that term instead of "witch" tells me we are indeed of much the same order, but standing upon different levels.' The gentleman turned to leave, but a stray thought held him back. 'There is a curious thing. When the constable searched your grandmother's house at Malkin Tower all those long months ago, his findings are clearly recorded. But when he searched the cottage you shared with your mother and little sister, did he not uncover the stale contents of night-pots, the barrel of brimstone or the store of powdered charcoal?'

'He found them, aye, and two rounds of gunpowder mill-cake.'

Bertrando tugged thoughtfully at his pointed beard. 'They are all possessions that support the charges against you in that you practice the black arts. All else aside, it shows conclusively that you made gunpowder mill-cake without proper warrant, and had at your disposal the very means to blow up this castle-gaol, and yet none of it is mentioned in your many indictments. Do you not find that very, very curious?'

James shrugged. 'I am somewhat of a firemaker, it is true, but I use the black powder in my battle *against* witchcraft and never in any way to cause harm, and that is what I told Justice Nowell.'

'Didn't you tell him you planned to blow up these walls and rescue your kin?'

'I told him it was but a childish fancy, and something I voiced to friends in the pain of my loss. My grandmother was very old, and she has since died within these walls, so perhaps I should have carried my dreams into this hard world of reality.'

'In that Master Nowell turns and twists your words to make a pretty story, it defies all logic that he should ignore the strongest of evidence that needs no tweaking. Why, the brimstone alone!' He shook away his thoughts and said that he would ask the Justice about the matter directly, if he had the time and the opportunity.

The gentleman and the peasant spoke their farewells as if they were equals and then Bertrando beat the door with his fist and called for the key-turn. Within a moment, James Devis was, once again, all alone but for the vermin.

∞

The prison courtyard was hot and dusty, the sun now directly overhead. A cloying but invisible cloud, rank with stink bubbling up from the dungeons and spilling from loopholes, seemed to smear the fabric of the walls so that Bertrando imagined them sticky to the touch. The lad John Hughes, seemingly made insensible by this foul fug, had lost his fear and looked sullen, suspicious and sneaky. Bertrando di Pontenegro would see to it that he was soundly beaten before the sun set on this day of intrigues.

'The gaoler's house is without the walls of the castle, sir.' John spoke with all the proper deference but his tone left very much to be desired. There was something in his demeanour that was troubling to Bertrando, as if the lad held a great secret that he would use to break against his elders and betters.

The streets teemed with people who appeared jolly, as if enjoying a day out at the fair. Vendors sold papers with block-prints of monsters and witches, a small child played with a toy gallows made of twigs with a peg-man dangling by his button head, and stalls had been set up where a hungry person might purchase bread, cheeses and marchpanes. Bertrando had but a few yards to endure this happy breed before John led him into the yard of his master's house. Presenting Bertrando to the housekeeper, he treated him to one last scowl and then sauntered off, a swagger of such insolence that Bertrando entertained the thought of bouncing a stone off his skull.

'Master Covel is out, but will return presently, good sir. Meanwhile, might I show you to the parlour?'

Bertrando inclined his head, smiled his consent, and then allowed the elderly woman to show him the way. Thomas Covel's house was not grand, but it was very well appointed for one who was but an esquire. The housekeeper left him alone with a fine cup and a small jug of ale.

Alone and unobserved, still Bertrando would not allow himself to relax. His every move exuded authority. Bertrando di Pontenegro was a man who clung to his office and power with the zeal of one who knew what it meant to be powerless and devoid of the least office. He was a poor yeoman's son made knight and then lord, who despised his past and sought to subsume it in the grandeur of his present. Yet, try as he might, the hungry boy haunted him and bitter dust from the back-streets of Castrovillari stung his soul.

Shielded from the world by private thoughts, he was surprised by Thomas Covel's greeting, but hid it well and introduced himself with a presentation of his credentials.

'I am honoured, my Lord, to have His Majesty's envoy under my humble roof,' Thomas said, peering up through thick, dark eyebrows. 'I must assume His Royal Highness has sent you to witness the demise of that evil and bloody brood of witches that I have locked up next door.'

'Not entirely, Master Covel. My mission is one of the greatest importance to the King and of the utmost secrecy. Assist and you will be amply rewarded, but utter a word beyond these walls, you do so on pain of death.'

Thomas Covel felt his own doom heavy upon his head and his eyes grew round and fearful. He was a large and powerfully built man with fists like masons' mauls but presently he looked like a frightened child. 'I do swear most earnestly that the King's secrets I shall lock in my heart, and none but His Highness with the key, and be that key not presented, then to my grave and beyond with them.'

'Very good, Master Covel. Then I may impart to you, upon that understanding, that it is the King's great desire and his command that the witch who shares his name shall live.'

'James? James Devis? Forgive me, but my understanding fails. Surely you have only to speak with the judges, and he will be found not guilty. You have then but to settle up his fees for bed and keep these last four months and he will be a free man.'

'The judges must not know of this. Justice Nowell must not know, nor may the people have any clue. It must appear to them all that James Devis is hanged to death with his mother, his sister and all the others. It shall fall to us, you and me together, to see to the practicalities of bringing a plan into execution, if you will forgive the term.'

The gaoler began to sweat. He shook his head. 'I do not begin to know how we may bring it about, my Lord.'

'First, it calls for a substitution.'

Thomas Covel floundered as if he did not know the meaning of the word.

'A corpse, newly dead, or perhaps a lad of much the same build as the Devis boy who has ailed or taken a mortal hurt and is not long for this world. Yours is a sizable city, and the county stretches far. Young men die every week, so it should not be very difficult. And if it does prove beyond your skills, then you may find a worthless specimen who none will miss and help him along the way. Your dungeons must be full of suitable candidates.' Bertrando went on to describe the plan and Thomas listened intently, half in loyalty to the King and half in disbelief.

The interview over and the refreshments consumed, Bertrando di Pontenegro took his leave. Thomas dismissed the housekeeper and led him to the door, but before they had touched the latch, it burst open. Young John Hughes stood there blocking the light, his face red and his hair flying.

'How dare you?' cried Thomas. 'Have you parted company with your wits?'

'It is *him*, sir!' John cried, his arm outstretched and his dagger-like finger pointing towards Bertrando. 'I saw him change from a crow into a man. I saw him bewitch the under-gaoler to allow him access to a prisoner without your leave. He is a witch!' He turned his excited face towards Bertrando and his spittle-flecked lips were a curse before a word let slip. 'I denounce you, bloody fiend! You are a witch!'

In the four strides it took Thomas Covel to cross the hall, he had wound his catapult of a fist fully back. It sprang forward and lifted John Hughes from his feet. Already knocked senseless, his head smashed hard against the stone flags and split like a frost-bitten turnip. His eyes rolled as blood formed a puddle, shaped like a sacred heart, about his head. Thomas stared, first at the fallen boy and then at his fist.

'It would appear,' Betrando said, 'that the problem of the substitute is solved.' He stepped over the injured boy and through the door.

Thomas Covel came to himself. 'Wait!' he ran after the grand gentleman, but he was nowhere to be seen. The small enclosed yard was empty of all life, save a raven that dipped over the wall and out of sight.

∞

Night time had come, but James Devis did not remember eating the bread. He recalled picking it up after finding it by touch, and he had checked as best he could in the darkness for spiders or other crawling creatures, but his mind was as black as the dungeon after that.

And now he found he could not open his eyes. His mind was like a little songbird, bright and fully aware, but his body was an iron cage and the bird could do nothing to shift it. The bird darted this way and that trying to find a way out, and as every new avenue proved to be a dead end it, fluttered and panicked and crashed against the unyielding walls. At the height of the bird's frantic and self-destructive flight, there came the sound of a monster, a pitiful cry, long drawn out, rebounding and reverberating. James cowered into a corner of his own skull, and then came the realisation that he had heard his own cry, imprisoned just like him, in the cold of Lancaster Castle.

If he could make a sound, perhaps he could regain control of his body. The bird perched upon this thin branch of hope.

James became still within himself. He listened and waited and reasoned. It must be that Bertrando's charmed bread had taken away his power of movement and self-control, very like the manner by which an excess of beer stole away the senses.

Hours passed before James was able to reason with any degree of certainty that his hearing was unaffected. There came noises from outside. First the muffled exchanges and laughter from the guards, then a rattling of keys and the door being flung open.

'Get up, devil-spawn! Time you must answer to your charges.'

A kick to the stomach brought another noise from James. He tried to move, and indeed, if felt like the iron cage shook, rose and fell again, but James had no real control.

'Have you let him take a fill of ale, you whore-son?'

'Indeed I have not, nor anything of wine. But I own he looks to be in his cups.'

Another demand for him to rise. Another painful kick. Once again, James struggled and managed no more than uncoordinated spasms and incoherent sounds.

'He looks to be ill more than drunk. He can't be allowed to die before we hang him. Where's the justice in that?'

'Come on, lad. You get under one arm and I shall take the other. We'll have to haul him before the judge.'

James felt rough hands drag him upright. He was slapped across the face and could do nothing to stop his head lolling about his neck.

'This could be bad. Perhaps they will accuse us of beating him too much.'

'Shut your teeth, fool. We haven't beaten him at all. Be sure and remember that if we should be asked.'

James was hauled this way and that and up a flight of steps. At first his feet dragged, but the pain of the rough stone on his bare toes brought him some slight control and he managed to work his legs a little, but his steps did not catch up to the speed of his movement: he would walk a pace or two and then be dragged for several yards, and then walk a little more and so on, up more steps and into the court house.

Here James was greeted by a great tide of human verbiage carrying vessels of derision, outrage and mockery. The shock of it all caused James's eyes to open a little and he saw just enough to realise that he was the very centre of this storm. People shook their fists; an angry red-faced man in fine clothing called 'Treason!' at him; young men laughed and made hanging gestures, pulling invisible ligatures above their heads and sticking out there tongues as if choking; young women wafted away the stench as he passed by, and everywhere he looked there were unfriendly faces lusting after his painful death. He might have died right then, but for one small group of people who stood quietly in the gallery: he recognised William Preston and next to him – oh how the little bird soared – could that maid standing next to William be his own dear Sarah? He tried to acknowledge her, but his body failed him and he fell to his knees.

A loud and repeated banging of a fist upon wood and a call for silence brought the court to order. James made little of the following proceedings and could only make sense of snatches of the official announcements. '... August, year of our Lord, Sixteen hundred and twelve ... may it please your honour ... the prisoner before the bar ... bloody murderer despite he is of tender years and at the start of his time ...'

Something stirred the crowd and their bellowing could not be separated into words that showed any meaning, and then James was shaken violently by the two men who held him up between them.

'If he refuses to make a plea then we shall consider it acquiescence to all the aforesaid indictments. The record shall show that James Devis pleads guilty to all charges.'

'NO!' It was hard for James to believe that he finally managed to find a crack in the iron cage that held his actions captive. 'I am not guilty. I have done nothing.'

Again came the tumult of the crowd; again the assault of the judge's fist upon the bench and the demand for silence.

The effort to gain control sapped James's willpower and he failed again; felt himself collapse and kept to his feet only by the two fellows that gripped him beneath the arms. He fell into a deeper swoon than before and did not hear the finding of guilt, or the sentence of death being passed.

His toes scraping on the flags, James was being dragged again. The darkness of stone corridors closed upon his spirits so that he knew he was being taken back to the cells. Assisted by a hefty kick he fell like a heap of dead bones into the filthy straw and the door slammed shut.

There was no sense of time in this semi-soporific state and hours went by that might have been minutes. It was only when the external stimuli were great that James had any thoughts of his situation. So the little bird came to, though still within the iron cage, through jostling and rough handling. Unsympathetic hands pulled and tugged at his clothing, and then he was dragged along those corridors again and out into the cold air and thrown up, landing with a bump. By detecting and analysing the bumps and jolts, James reasoned he was being conveyed in a wagon. He was past caring where his journey might end.

∞

The wagon with its load of convicted witches was brought to a halt at the foot of the gallows. Refused peace and dignity even in their last moment, people had pelted them with rotting vegetables, and stones it seemed, for poor James was bleeding. The hempen hood dripped with his blood.

Sarah Lister held a handkerchief to her mouth and tried to be brave, but when she saw James and the others like stunned animals waiting for death while the people laughed and jeered, it was more than she could stand. She leaned into William Preston and sobbed.

'There now, lass. Try not to fret. We must all die, and I shall not let him suffer for a moment longer than it is within my power.'

Sarah and William stood with a small group of people, friends and relatives of the condemned. William's own wife had been hanged at York, convicted on the twisted and embellished confessions of James, words he knew that James had not uttered in the way they were presented. He had come to the Lancaster Assizes to protest, but his words were all drowned out by the baying crowds and nobody would agree to see him in an official capacity.

It was all done very quickly. Nooses were thrown over the witches' heads and they were hauled up to dance their last obscene jig. At that instant, William rushed forward with eight stout fellows from his village. The constable's men squared up to them, a token gesture, and then allowed them to pass. William braved the bare, bloodied and kicking feet to hug James hard about the hips and then, with a little hop, he took the weight off his own feet. There was one fellow for each witch, and nine necks quickly broken, so to end their suffering.

At the instant of James's death, Sarah put a hand to her rounding belly, certain that his child had stirred.

A raven landed on the crossbar at the point where James's rope was fastened. It made its raucous call as if admonishing the people and the mood of the mass was instantly altered, just as a millstream is diverted by the lowering of a sluice.

The crowd was silent now. Faces that had leered with the lust for death were now shocked and ashamed. Six women, a girl and two boys swayed gently from rough hempen ropes; now they were people and no longer witches. A bitter, lamenting wail escaped from a woman in the throng that appeared to answer for everybody, and the people began to leave, lust spent and sickened to the heart.

∞

The sun took a breath before beginning its final descent and everywhere the air settled to silence. The intrusion of iron-shod cart wheels and horses' hooves were all the more noticeable for the evening quiet, and Thomas Covel,

Lancaster's gaoler, felt he was the centre of the world's attention, and that his little game of subterfuge would soon be up. It helped not a whit that he was sitting next to a coffin, or that he was the only member of his small party of four who knew the lie of the coffin's contents. Strange then, that the driver and the two armed retainers appeared to share his unease.

The south road wound between outposts of forest, and Thomas saw treachery behind every tree and capture in every shadow. He recalled the dead faces of the witches that he had been obliged to examine after the hangings earlier in the day. Faces congested and discoloured with blood; swollen, protruding tongues; bodies carrying the stench of all the fluids that had been ejaculated at the point of death: he was sickened as he realised capture would mean exactly the same fate for him. The King's business indeed: but would the King be there if the judges or the justices knew of his part in thwarting their will? He thought not.

An un-sprung cartwheel hit the bottom of a rut. It sent a jolt through all of Thomas's bones and dislodged the coffin-lid. The cart horse did not appear to notice, but the three tethered mounts became skittish. Birds that had roosted now took fright and set of a cacophony of fear that struck straight into the hearts of the four men. The coffin-lid slewed off and one of the two retainers swore and then crossed himself as a shaft of soft orange light illuminated the pale, dead face of James Devis. The driver chuckled nervously.

'Give him a little tap with your halberd, Will Watkins. Strike a blow against witches, be they already dead,' Ezra said, pointing his firelock at the dead boy's face though he had no intention of setting the match. 'Have his head off, I say.'

'How dare you?' Thomas called, rallying anger against his fear. 'The body is to be delivered all of apiece.'

Will Watkins muttered about it all being a lot of trouble for the corpse of a witch and perhaps witches should be burnt as was the custom in France and not hanged. 'That way they suffer such pains as they deserve and there is not the need thereafter for the sexton to busy himself with the shovel.'

The driver called for the horse to stop and pulled back on the reins. Now that the hooves and wheels stood unmoving, the silence became thick and almost alive. Thomas felt the quiet like treacle on his skin. They had come to a bar, but the toll-collector was nowhere to be seen and his little hut was in darkness. The gate stood athwart the roadway and there, on the top rail, sat a large, crow-like bird and a jay. Thomas thought that two such birds were strange bed-fellows, and then the horse reared up and lay back in its harness, forcing the cart backwards by several feet.

Confusion reigned for a moment: Watkins swore again and jumped off the cart; Ezra Cowan blew on the firelock's match until it glowed all the while looking for a suitable target, and the driver stood up off his seat and made soothing noises until the horse settled down.

'What in Heaven's holy name ...' Thomas Covel had also leapt from the cart.

'I'm sorry, sir,' the driver said. 'But poor Samson must have took fright at the sudden appearance of these two gentlemen.'

Thomas looked back towards the bar, and in front of it stood the Count of Pontenegro and another, younger man who Thomas had never met.

'Forgive me for spooking your horse, Master Covel,' said Bertrando di Pontenegro. 'I only meant to stop your carriage from driving pell-mell into the gate, for the keeper of the bar has been negligent with his lamps.'

'Pell-mell, indeed!' The driver took this as an insult against his professional skills and made a small protest. Thomas ignored it and it was beneath Bertrando even to notice it.

After looking into the cart and checking the coffin, Bertrando drew Thomas to one side. 'He looks to be dead. I mean, *actually* dead.'

'If that be so, it is no fault of mine. I followed your wishes to the very letter.'

Bertrando touched the boy's face with the back of his hand. 'We must get him swiftly to Newark Park, for there we have the antidote all prepared. How went the substitution?'

'Nigh perfect. I dressed the lad in this one's rags and had him and all the witches hooded. There is one fewer gaoler's assistant in the world today but more is the pity, one more witch then there should be.' Thomas looked towards the coffin and spat.

'Let me worry about the surfeit of witches, and ease your conscience with this, a gift from His Majesty.' Bertrando handed over a small pouch of angels, more gold than the gaoler would otherwise see in a whole year. 'And you, my good man and skilled navigator of the wooded ways,' he said as he approached the driver. 'I have need of your cart and your horse. You may ride back to Lancaster aback of one of these fine fellows, and here is a bag of crowns for your trouble.'

The driver took the bag and his old face cracked with pleasure as he hefted it to judge the contents. 'Why, kind sir, for a single crown I would do it gladly. For a bag I would crawl all the way home on my belly.'

'Then should I take nine of them back and leave you just the one to save your belly and your dignity?' Bertrando laughed at the look of horror that wiped away the old man's smile, only to return when he saw the gentleman was sporting with him. 'Be on your way then, fellows, and go with knowledge that you serve your country well.'

Will and Ezra transferred quickly from cart to horses and Thomas led his mount a little away from the others to join Bertrando. 'Should you wish to sell your mounts,' he said, looking all round and peering into the shadows, 'I will happily offer a good price. But where are they, the mounts you came on?'

'Master Verdi and I travelled by other paths. We had no need of mounts.'

Thomas's big face furrowed as he groped to understand. No gentleman would venture this far on foot.

'Do not let it trouble you, Master Covel. Now, we must fly, for the night is nearly upon us and we have many miles to go.'

Thomas wasted no time for goodbyes. He hauled himself into the saddle while the driver hopped up behind Will Watkins and then all three horses were harried to a canter. The night soon swallowed them along the road, leaving Bertrando and Marco Verdi alone with the boy in a coffin.

'He is sore cold,' Bertrando said, lifting James around the shoulders. The body was limp and inanimate, like a rag doll loosely stuffed with kapok. Bertrando ordered Marco into the bed of the cart and lifted James onto his lap. 'Wrap you both in your cloak and let some of your warmth migrate to him.'

'Mother of God, m'Lord, he smells like a pigsty,' Marco said in heavily accented English. 'To my warmth he is most welcome, but it sickens me to think upon the vermin that will migrate from him to me.'

'Your itches and bites will not be forgot when they come to judge your sacrifices, young Marco. But opportunity always shines, even from the depths of the mire, for how better to become acquainted with your new master? And if I am not wrong, you're of the sort to relish such cosiness.'

'Indeed I am not, m'Lord. I must protest!'

Bertrando chuckled. 'No matter whether or not, but hold him safe, for I intend to drive this old mare faster than she has gone since her youth and up to the very limit of this rude cart.' He kicked the rough coffin to the roadside where it shattered, and he leapt onto the driver's bench. The long, uncomfortable journey began.

The broken pieces of James's coffin lay half in a ditch as the clatter of the cart and the complaint of the old mare receded. Sound sank with the sun, but before the last of it was gone, there came a harsh call, *chack-chack*, from the hedgerow, and a female shrike floated down from a hawthorn to alight upon the coffin lid. She cocked her head, listening, and then she looked into the roughly crafted box and hopped down inside. She stabbed three or four lice that had lost their host, snapped them up for a snack and then tugged at a fragment of blood-stained rag until it came loose. And then, as the last of the light failed, she seemed to taste James and lust for more. With another cry she launched herself into the night, and any observer would have sworn that she followed the cart.

∞

A female butcher-bird pecked at the windowpane. This plump brown shrike made sense to James, if nothing else did: certainly not the sumptuous bed with crisp, clean sheets, or the nightshirt of a material that James had never known, even for Sunday best. The bird though, he had seen in the pages of Mistress Towneley's beautifully coloured bestiary. He knew its habits and its preferred terrain. He knew that it liked to skewer its prey upon a larder of thorns and that, like most other birds, the male of the species was by far the prettier. Yes, everything about the bird made sense. Waking up in a fine bedroom, such as he had rarely imagined and never seen, did not.

James sat up and threw the covers aside. His body, grown used to inactivity, urged him to lie back down, but he resisted, keeping his eyes fixed on the visitor until, with one last hearty and triumphant peck, she flew away. Now he was forced to turn his thoughts to the mystery of his situation. He took refuge in the first rule of his personal litany: observe first, and then think.

The window comprised a stone cross separating four equal squares of leaded lights. The triangle of glass at the bottom of the lower left pane was smeared where the bird had pecked. The bed was set against the opposite wall. On the stand to the left was a large pewter jug of water, a goblet and washing bowl. A night-pot stood between the oaken legs of the stand and the floor was of polished boards. A set of neatly folded clothes had been placed upon the seat of a sturdy chair. They were of rich, black cloth for the most part, but there was a fine white shirt and white stockings. James wondered if they were meant for him, but the thought of putting on such finery struck him as absurd. Then again, somebody had put him to bed in a shirt

111

that even a magistrate would be proud to wear to church, so perhaps the idea was not so silly after all.

Swinging his legs off the bed, he noticed that his right shin was bound in a bandage and that his many small hurts and infected flea-bites had been daubed with ointment. Rubbing a little of the dry residue with a finger, he tasted it and by this method was able to make a fair guess at the ingredients. Nodding slowly, he approved. Then, lifting the nightshirt he observed that the apothecary had been very thorough and that for the sake of his modesty, he was glad he had been insensible during the administration. Wondering whether his treatment had been merely topical or if he had been made to swallow other medicaments, he suddenly recalled the charmed bread, and for a moment the bedroom melted away to become the stinking dungeon. He remembered bringing the morsel to his lips, and then nothing more until a few moments ago, when the tapping bird had recalled him to the land of the living.

With trembling hands, James poured himself a goblet of water and downed it in one. He poured another and took his time, wondering how his mother and sisters had fared after the Assizes. He refused to believe the worst.

There was a looking-glass of a size James had never imagined in a frame of carved oak. Trying out his legs, they felt weak but took his weight and he crossed slowly and looked at his reflection. He had changed since he last saw himself in his grandmother's old scrying stone. He was thin in the face and hollow of eye, but his shoulder length hair was silky and soft. Someone had taken great cares over his cleanliness. He leaned forward, absorbed by his own green eyes, when there came a cry and a commotion from outside.

James stumbled in his haste to reach the window and his head spun. He picked himself up, and continued with more care. He leaned on the sill and pressed his face to the glass to see below: far below, for James found he was on an upper storey – third or fourth, he guessed – and the ground looked very distant, but not so far that he could not make out the empty eye-sockets of a dead woman being carried by two men.

Her clothes were wet and her hair streamed. She must have drowned. People milled about, looked away in horror, held hands to their mouths, tried to ward off the spectre of the young woman's untimely death. The cries and speech came as a babble of sad excitement. Of the half-dozen people that James could see, only one stood out in that he was some way aside from the others and watched, unanimated by the pitiful scene. This one was a young man dressed in a doublet of russet-brown. He wore dark brown breeches with light grey stockings, his black hat swept off and held at his breast as a gesture of respect. His hair was long and brown and from this height at least, he appeared to be little older than James, perhaps nineteen or twenty.

Suddenly, the young man looked up; his eyes stabbed into those of James and fixed them so that James felt he could not move. After a moment, during which James felt as if the young man was grappling at his soul, he left the shocked and grieving party and ran for the house. James knew he was coming for him and that there would soon come rushing feet upon the stairs and knocks at the door, or perhaps no knocks at all.

Not wishing to receive visitors whilst in nothing but a nightshirt, James drew the quilt off the bed and threw it around his shoulders and then turned to face the door as the expected footfalls approached. The young man did not knock but came in unbidden and shut the door behind him. He was a little breathless after his rapid ascent and James quickly assessed him as a rival in combat. He was of average height, sleight and wiry. He was possessed of narrow, almost waiflike features with a nose too long to allow him to be called handsome, a flaw almost offset by kindly brown eyes and generous lips. The sleeves of his doublet were slashed so that a lining of blue silk showed.

'Forgive me, master,' the young man said in an accent that reminded James of the man who gave him the charmed bread.

James looked over his shoulder to see this master who had been spoken of, but saw only his own reflection in the mirror. But it was utterly absurd that he should be addressed so. Was he being mocked? He knew mockery well by frequent acquaintance, but this felt very different.

'I have been in constant attendance these last two days,' the sincere young man continued: 'and slept at the foot of your bed. But this awful tragedy, I had no choice but to investigate. The poor, poor maiden.'

Questions flooded James's mind: who was the unfortunate girl and what had befallen her; where was this place; why had he been called master? 'Who are you?' James said, voicing the question that forced precedence.

The young man bowed neatly, without subservience, and then introduced himself as Marco Verdi from the Kingdom of Sicily. 'I have served the Royal Court in Exile and the Conte di Pontenegro, but now I serve you.'

James did not know what to say. Here he stood, a peasant of very few means, being called "master" by a fine young gentleman in a suit of clothes he could never hope to afford from saving a year's wages.

Marco gestured towards the clothing on the chair. 'Shall I dress you, sir, and then you might feel more comfortable?'

'Dress me? Why I have not been dressed by another since I was a small child.' It occurred to him briefly that he had been *undressed* by others in more recent times: there was the gentle and tender undressing by Sarah, his betrothed, and then there was the rude and rough stripping by the examining justices who would call every mole and wart a mark of Hell "whereupon the Devil doth suck" and absence of the same "unnatural".

'It would not be seemly for a gentleman to dress himself, sir, just as it would not be right for such a man to apply his own ointments and balms.'

'That was you?'

Marco inclined his head and let his eyes fall by way of a modest answer.

Such was Marco's sincerity that James felt no embarrassment. 'Then I thank you, for it was well done, but I am no gentleman and I shall dress myself.'

114

'I do not wish to contradict, sir. You fell asleep a different station to that which you awoke. You are *indeed* a gentleman now, and a very genuine and *bone fide* gentleman. It is part of my duty to instruct you in certain new ways and etiquettes.'

This was all very baffling, but James had not lived to his seventeenth year by allowing his feelings to betray him. 'If by "etiquette" you mean "manners" then that part of your duty is already served. My mother brought me up well.' Her beaten and broken face sprang to mind and James's eyes stung. He knew without a doubt, that she was dead and had not escaped the fate that should also have been his. 'Tell me, am I really your master by some strange quirk of fate, or is this all some vast and horrid cruelty?'

'It is no mockery, sir. I am here to do your bidding if it is at all within my ability.'

James looked around the room; at the clothes; at the washing bowl. If he had learnt one thing, it was to take advantage of situations as they presented themselves, for they seldom came twice. 'Then please wait outside while I wash and dress, and then I shall call you in and ask you many questions.'

'Sir, there is nothing you may ask that I will not answer true, so long as I have the knowledge.' So saying, Marco bowed again and quietly withdrew.

When he was called back into the room, Marco had to adjust James's ruff and knee-ribbons, for James had never worn either before and his attempts showed a lack of familiarity. Then he could contain himself no more and let loose a broadside of questions.

James learnt with great sorrow that his mother and sister had been hanged with the other lad and five women. It was only confirmation of that which he already knew in his heart. It was comforting that the village men had not allowed them to suffer and that the mockery of the crowd had quickly mutated into shame.

Death was a constant companion and it was always a boon to survive the day without falling into his eternal embrace. It was in James's nature to morn the living, knowing that in a day, a week, a month or at best, several years, they would pass away into the land of shadows. It was a trait that often made him reflective but never melancholy: death was but the natural termination of life; the story, come to an end and the book closed. This philosophy helped him to accept now, that which he always knew would come too swiftly. He would morn them properly, with tears and sorrow, when he was alone and under the moon.

Marco told of the long journey south from Lancaster, and that this house belonged to a gentleman who kept it as a hunting lodge. 'They do say Newark Park was first built so an earlier lord could enjoy hunting, hawking and whoring in equal measure, and that in this place he kept certain ladies a secret from his wife.'

'So, that is how the great and the good conduct themselves. No better than the rest of us and probably a good deal worse.'

'If I may be so bold, lords are only lords because their grandfather's carried the biggest sticks and beat all others into subservience.'

'A view to which I fully subscribe. And do the whores still pay call?'

'And if they did, sir, would it interest you?' Marco took on a look that implied he could make certain arrangements if a liaison was required.

James felt no need to be coy with this young man. There was something about his manner that he liked and trusted. Of course, there was a possibility he had been charmed, but he thought not. 'Before my betrothal I had certain night-time acquaintances, but as it was never my style to take the kind who would give change from a groat, they were delicacies to be saved for and savoured.' James asked if anything was known about Sarah.

Marco reported that she had been at the executions and that she now believed James dead, which led to an explanation about the substitution. James was appalled that another lad had died in his place.

'The boy had taken a crack to the skull and had little time left in this world.' Marco waved the matter aside. Death came every day, and at least the lad's death had been of service, as most were not. 'Again, I do not wish to overstep my position, sir, but it has been said that the fair maid Sarah may not be exactly a maid, and that she had a degree of roundness to her belly. Forgive me for being so forward, but there is a reason I make mention of it.'

'I know of it, though the last time I saw her there was no sign. The child is mine and I will do right by her if I am allowed. And it will be no hardship, for I do love her.'

'I think you will not be allowed. To let it be known that she is with your child would seriously jeopardise her life and the child's.'

'How so? Who cares a whit for a peasant's bastard?'

'Believe me, as it concerns you, there are those who care a great deal. Make no mention at all of the child.' Marco looked over his shoulder, and his voice sank to a whisper. 'Not even to the Conte. If he asks, deny it. Deny even, that you have ever lain with her.'

There were plans for James, and great schemes. Momentous events were approaching, ponderous but implacable, like the great ice-rivers of the frozen north that crept ever to the sea. James's place was pivotal, but a child would be crushed under the weight of grinding ambition. A child, or rather, a child whose place in the scheme was uncertain, would not be allowed to survive. Having awed James with the distant picture, Marco could give no detail. He simply had not been made privy to all the facts. The Conte di Pontenegro would be able to tell more, but he was presently on business in London.

James looked out of the window and across to the far Mendip Hills. He fancied he could see them coming for him, marching ever closer, his terrible fate born on the blue horizon. Looking down to the courtyard, he recalled the empty eye sockets of the dead woman and asked about her. She had been the cook and had gone missing on the day of James's arrival. She had been found half submerged in the lake, a shrike pecking at her eyeballs. She must have gone for water and slipped.

There was another surprise for James. He was to lose his name. To go with his fine new clothes and his elevation to the status of "gentleman", he was to have a grand, new appellation. 'Giacomo di Aspromonte?' James said, repeating the Italian name Bertrando had chosen for him.

'Giacomo, *Cavaliere* di Aspromonte, to speak it fully, sir.' Marco assumed an entirely different look when he spoke his own language, became more confident and animated, even if the phrase was only a name. '"Cavaliere" means "knight", and the knighting has been fully approved by the House in Exile. Everything is in order, for the Conte di Pontenegro dubbed you knight whilst you slept.'

'Me, a *knight*, for Heaven's sake? And what of the rest? From where do such names spring?'

'"Giacomo" is simply the Italian for "James", and "Aspromonte" is a rough and wild place that has hidden secrets, just as you are a rough and wild young man whose true powers lay hid.' Marco blushed at his own candid words. 'Or so my lord the Conte did say.'

Marco continued with instructions as to the routine of the household, etiquettes to be observed with the servants and during mealtimes, and the schedule he had in mind for James's education. All the while he spoke, quiet and respectful but not overly obsequious or toady, James watched and applied his art of observation. Here was a man who could be a friend; share a jug of ale with at the tavern; speak of wenches and fine ladies; laugh at the foibles of those who were supposed to be a cut above. In short, James liked Marco and found the false difference in their stations annoying.

'It seems I have much to learn,' James said. 'But to begin with, Master Verdi, I shall issue an order, the first and last between us, I hope.'

Marco drew himself up, all ears.

'If you must call me "Giacomo" in the presence of others –'

'In the presence of others, I shall call you "Sir" … sir.'

'If you must call me such names and titles as etiquette requires, then when we are alone, you shall call me "James", or even "Jem" such as my family did, and I should be pleased to call you "Marco" … or friend.'

Marco began to object, but James cut him off. 'I have never been one to scrape and bow, or thee and thou to others. "Sir" has hardly passed my lips and I rarely doff my hat. Despite my manners in all other respects and my earnest and heartfelt willingness to be a kind and helpful man, it has got me into trouble many a time, but the trouble I will endure for the sake of my self-respect.'

James's unwillingness to practice formal speech had, to a great extent, been his downfall. He had argued with Anne Towneley over payment for a charm he had worked for her, and she became affronted by what she perceived as rudeness and a lack of due deference. She had beaten him out of her house, and it was when she died a few days later that people began to mutter about witchcraft, and to infer that James had worked some kind of magical revenge.

'And as much as I dislike such usage towards others, I hate it all the more when it is applied to me, as I have only discovered this last hour. So when it is just you and I together, I hope you will dispense with all decorous speech and fancy ways. Why for Heaven's sake, you have seen me naked as a babe and dressed my wounds. You above others know I am no more than a lowly man. Will you allow us to be equals, so much as the situation allows?'

Marco smiled, the first time James had seen him do so, and caught himself just before bowing. 'That I will, sir … Jem.'

'Then take my hand on it.'

The two young men shook hands and the spark of a new friendship was kindled. Marco had been appointed duties that superseded friendship, but he did not mention them. He did mention that a meal would soon be served in the great dining hall downstairs and cautioned James to remember his new name and status. 'Of all the people you will meet, irrespective of their station, it is only my lord the Conte and I who know your true origins. To all others, you are none but the Cavaliere di Aspromonte. For your mortal safety, and ours, you must admit to nothing other.' Marco tugged at the hem of James's doublet to smooth out a crease. 'And now, Jem, we shall pass through the door and you shall become Sir Giacomo.'

James Devis, cunning-man of Pendle Forest, and his friend Marco shook hands once again. And then the knight, Giacomo di Aspromonte and Master Verdi his manservant stepped into the small passageway outside the bedroom. The knight followed the manservant down a stone, spiral staircase to the great hall one flight below. It was while descending that James felt the depths of his weakness: he stumbled and Marco had to lend him an arm.

∞

James was glad the house was empty of all but a few servants. It meant he could eat his soup in peace, only Marco in attendance, without having to put on the act of being Giacomo. The soup was good and wholesome and full of flavour.

'For all the absence of the poor cook, this is a hearty broth,' James said. It was as if strength flooded into him with each mouthful. 'Whoever stands in for the cook, they are to be complimented. And,' James asked between noisy slurps, 'it is a little charmed?'

'By mine own hand,' Marco said. He named the herbs and described the mystical workings. 'Like you, I have some skills. But the flavour is all to the credit of our new cook.' On the very hour of the discovery of the dead woman, an old goodwife had come seeking a cook's position. 'Sometimes luck is on our side. Fate has sent us a very able woman in Goody Gray, and to come exactly at our time of need.'

For several days following, James had the house to himself, discounting the servants. He grew in strength and his many hurts healed quickly. He got to know the house well, all except for the master's private rooms. Newark Park was a lodge of four stories, four rooms wide and one deep with stairs leading to the roof, which was flat and perfect for observing the land below. Built on the side of an escarpment that fell away to the right of the house, the views were magnificent and stretched to the far horizon.

James spent most of his time in the great hall which took up the entire third story, with a stair at either side. One was for common use, the other led to the master's rooms. It was in the hall that James attended to the lessons that Marco gave: a little Italian; the story that James should fall back upon if asked as to his origins; some skill at the rapier and how he should conduct himself as a gentleman.

He soon got to know the household too and he was liked for his politeness and lack of pretension. There was Goodwife Lanie Gray who had quickly established herself as a benign matriarch. There was pretty little Sally Ozleworth the chambermaid who James, as his appetites returned, had an eye to bedding until he learnt that she had designs on Marco. Odd jobs and the keeping of the hounds were within the realm of Arthur Dursley, who had been at Newark so long he was as a stone fixture, and Master Ignatius Black ran the household on behalf of the owner, Sir Gabriel Lowe, and retained half a dozen game keepers for the security of house and game alike.

'Upon my word!' Marco said, peering out of James's bedroom window early one morning. 'All the dogs are lying down.'

It was the beginning of James's second week at Newark Park and he was getting into a pair of rough breeches that Marco had obtained for him. He had quite recovered his old strength and meant to explore the vast grounds and conduct a survey of the useful herbs that grew thereabouts. 'Perhaps old Arthur has fed them early.'

'If that is the case they have been fed a sleeping draught. They look very out of sorts.'

When James had finished dressing, he and Marco went to investigate. They could not rouse the dogs past a feeble lifting of heads and half-hearted tail-wagging.

121

'Bad meat, I'll wager,' James said. 'They must have been at a mortified deer corpse, or something set with poison to kill foxes.'

Marco knelt and stroked the head of the lead hound. 'My lords would rather hunt foxes than poison them. But this is certainly no natural ailment.'

Marco and James exchanged glances and shared the same thought: enchantment.

'Still,' James said. 'Let's on with the day. Will you find Arthur and see if there is a remedy? ... Good, then I shall continue as planned.'

'You still mean to enter the wood?'

'I do, but I suppose you think this ailment of the hounds is a bad omen and that I should not go today.'

'No, still go, but wait for my return. Arthur can treat his pack and we may explore together. There is safety in numbers.'

James needed to be by himself. He had planned to explore alone and he disliked thwarted expectation. He pictured a scene and felt uncomfortable if something interjected to change it over much. He and Marco went separate ways.

A serpentine carriage road wound down from the house through a thick wood, and he had only gone a little way towards the trees when he stopped to take in the strange behaviour of a flock of pigeons. They circled him, swooping down a little, and then satisfied with his identity, sped ahead to vanish in the dark shadows of the wood. They meant to ambush him. The thought was ridiculous, but the feeling was strong and James had good reason to rely upon his feelings. He wanted to turn back for the house. He wanted to turn and run but pride would not allow. Be cautioned by feelings, James told himself, but do not be ruled by them. He picked up a well-rounded stone, half as big again as a golf ball, and then put a charm on it so that it would fly straight and true to any target he chose.

It was certainly a day for birds to behave in a strange manner, for a jay landed on the path a few feet behind and let out its raucous cry. James had never seen such a thing. Jays were usually so timid and avoided any contact with man, but this one seemed to follow him, albeit at a safe distance, while he descended towards the wood. The jay was good company, but James wished that he could conjure up Dante, his own large black hound. Dante though, was ever a familiar of dreams and never a creature of flesh and blood.

James stopped by a wild rose bush and relieved it of two pocketsful of haws. He knew how to make a charm with these bright red fruits that was efficacious in keeping the bleeding gum disease at bay. It was one his father had taught him and that his father had used to great effect on his long sea-voyages to and from the New World. When a very young man, John Devis had sailed with Drake in the *Golden Hinde*, and in later years had been an acquaintance of the great mathematician, navigator and magician, John Dee. James's mother had taught him to read. His grandmother had given him his herb-lore, but it was his father, an old man even when James had been born, who taught him Dutch, how to make gunpowder, and how to make and use many useful charms. It was also John who gave James his love of and longing for the sea, although he had never seen it but from the Ward's Stone atop the Forest of Bowland.

James carried his love of the sea as close to his heart as the Ancient Mariner carried his albatross. He would stand at the top of the fell and cast his eyes to the west, drawing in the silver waters and although he had never been to the coast, he felt the surge of the tides tune to the beating of his heart. He had no way of knowing that at the very moment of his conception, that great mariner, Sir Francis Drake, passed away from this life.

His pockets bulging with rose haws, James entered the wood, the jay hopping along behind by several paces. Shafts of morning sunlight stabbed through the wood but they were robbed of warmth. All the comfort and protection the wood might otherwise offer was stolen away and James felt exposed and vulnerable. His world became still and expectant. This was more than a feeling of trepidation. This was James's gift as a cunning man responding to and warning him of evil. He had to get back to the house, if it was not too late. He turned and ran apace, and then a man stepped out of the shadows and levelled a firelock at him. 'Hold fast!' he called. 'You are my captive.'

The jay leapt up and startled the scoundrel who then swatted it from the air with a gloved hand. It fell, wing hanging limp, and scurried away. He lifted the arquebus again and adjusted the match, but the little jay's singular behaviour had given James time to grab the stone from among the haws in his pocket and throw it with full heft. It struck the arquebusier in the middle of his face, bursting his nose. He dropped the weapon to the ground and the lock was triggered. The match touched off the charge, and the heavy ball blew away the attacker's jaw. He writhed and screamed for a moment, and then died. James jumped over the body and ran, but from behind he heard the clatter of hooves on stony ground. He was soon overhauled, kicked to the ground by the rider's booted foot.

James jumped to his feet but was met with a fist that burst his own nose. He fell again and heard someone command that he should be seized and bound so that he could be hanged with no further attempt at escape. Another voice called out that he should be run through and be done with, but no. The voice with the most authority cried that hanging must be the cause of his death for so the law had ordered, and then added that it should be slowly done. 'He must entertain us with a little dancing before Hell takes him!' This brought much cruel laughter. 'We will find ways to make him suffer all the more for laying poor Hal here low with his own firelock.'

As the pain of a broken nose subsided and James was able to open his eyes again, he looked at his captors for the first time. There were six or seven of them, all dressed in grey. He was quickly bound around the middle, his arms flat to his side. Somebody slapped him when he tried to speak.

'Let him be shamed and humiliated,' one said. 'Slice off his clothes where the rope doesn't touch so he needs must face his death exposed.' All the while he was being jostled towards a tree, conveniently adorned with a side branch that was perfect for a natural gallows.

'Nay,' called another. 'Bring down his breeches so we may more easily gut him. We may not have all the tools for a true quartering, but this will suffice.' So saying, the man began to tug at James's belt, accompanied by more laughter and horrible mockery. James struggled as hard as he was able, earning himself more punishment.

A woman's scream, full of malice and anger, saved James from rude exposure, and Lanie Gray leapt from the trees and thrust a bodkin in the cruel man's eye, and with a twist, gouged it straight out.

A younger man lifted a cudgel to her, but free of the groping hands, James was able to head-butt the fellow off his feet. The loud report of a shot rang out and old Arthur discarded one fowling piece, smoke licking at the muzzle, while lifting another to the aim. 'Be gone with you!' the old man shouted. 'The house is up, and a company of retainers make haste, all armed with good muskets. Be gone I say, or suffer the consequences.'

All this through the screams of the man whose eye Lanie had taken. Between screams he yelled curses and promises of vengeance. Lanie Gray took James about the shoulders and led him from the midst of his kidnappers and would-be murderers. 'Come now, my lad. As if the world has not shown you enough cruelty for one lifetime.'

'Unless you wish to be shot in your fat arse, Goodwife, you shall leave hold the boy and step aside.' So spoke the captain of this company in grey. 'The house may well be up and soldiers aplenty on their way. But at this moment I see only a fat woman and an old man who has outlived any use as a fighter. Put down your chicken-gun before we riddle you with shot and ball.'

Lanie Gray only held James tighter, but she was forcibly parted from him and dragged aside while Arthur Dursley was quickly disarmed. Two liveried louts lifted Lanie's skirts over her head and rolled her into a ditch and Arthur was beaten until he cried and then cast down onto the road. By the time James's brave friends had been dealt with, he was once again beneath the branch and now with a noose about his neck.

'Are you agents of the King of Spain?' James asked in desperation. 'Do you mean to kill me out of spite for your hatred of the Royal Court of Sicily in Exile?'

'What is all this blither, boy?' The captain had a fleshy face and full lips and appeared to be near forty years of age.

'I am Giacomo, a knight, and I have no enemies that I know of. Why do you subject me to this torture if it is not for the politics of Spain?'

The man pushed his face to within an inch of James's. His breath smelt of turnips. 'What cozening is this? You are James Device, little dung-heap, not Gia ... whomsoever, knight. You shall die by the rope, for such was your sentence, and in time all those who have helped you shall die too.' With that he signalled to a confederate and bid him haul away, but slowly.

James felt the noose tighten. Panic surged as his neck stretched.

'Time to dance for us, boy!'

James was dragged onto tiptoes. A little more and his feet left the ground.

'A foot will do it. Six inches, even. Let him see how close the earth that shall soon cover him.'

James tried to stiffen the muscles in his neck and move a little to one side to ease the pressure on his windpipe. He kicked and so began his dance with death. He was vaguely aware of laughter. He kicked and twitched until his face congested and the world began to go black. He fancied he heard the hooves of the Devil's horses and the squeal of his demons ... and then he hit the ground like a sack of potatoes. Sucking in great draughts of air, he opened his eyes to find a young boy looking intently into his face.

His voice came from far away, yet the boy was so close. 'I have cut you down with my new rapier, sir. Tell me it is not too late.' The boy tugged the knot loose and slipped the noose off and away. He helped James to sit up. All around was confusion. Two of the grey company lay dead. A gentleman in fine riding clothes helped Lanie from the ditch and another comforted old Arthur. Several others who stood ready with their saddle-pistols had the look of professional soldiers.

'Who are you?' James's voice was cracked and raw.

'I am George, sir,' the boy said. He looked to be no older than eleven.

A man in a feathered hat kneeled by the boy and interjected. 'He is my lord George, eighth Baron of Berkeley, sir. And I am Gabriel Lowe, master of Newark Park.' Sir Gabriel drew a dagger and got to work on the ropes that bound James. 'I am at the same time mortified you should suffer such an attack while under my protection, and glad that we happened by when we did. The scoundrels are either dead or fled. You are quite safe now, Sir Giacomo.'

The ropes fell away. James got to his feet and thanked his saviours. He used the kerchief Gabriel proffered to wipe his bloody nose, and then he looked at the faces of the dead. Such hatred from people he had never met. It was chilling. 'I'll take this one's apostles, if I may,' James said removing the bandolier of twelve charges from the dead arquebusier whose face was a horror of destruction. 'And his firelock too, if there is no objection.'

'By all means,' Gabriel replied. 'But it is a very poor piece that has seen better days. If you will allow, I have a fine German wheel-lock that I will gladly gift to you. It is the very least I can do towards recompense for this awful insult upon your person.'

Checking on Arthur Dursley, James found him tearful and ashamed that age had taken the fight out of him. Nevertheless, James shook his hand and thanked him for his brave efforts, and when he did the same to Goody Gray she took him in her ample arms and hugged the breath from him. Sir Gabriel and the young Lord Berkeley looked appalled by her lack of decorum: a lowly cook hugging a knight? The very thought was anathema, but it was not theirs to scold her if Sir Giacomo

127

submitted to such displays of affection. Italian chivalry obviously had different ways.

The procession was met at the house by Ignatius Black and two armed retainers, a little late to do more than take on the appearance of spare parts. Marco was there too with Sally, who was tying his arm in a sling. He had heard the report of gunfire and in his haste to rescue James, he had lost his footing and tumbled down the stairs, or so he said. James thought he detected benign dissemblance, and he could not help but recall the brave little jay with its broken wing.

That evening at dinner about the great table, there was much talk of the attackers. Who were they; why did they want to kill Sir Giacomo; who had sent them? There was also much gift giving, and James received the wheel-lock from Sir Gabriel and little Lord George's new rapier. The boy thought it fitting James should own the sword that saved his life, and anyway, George had several others and wanted a blade of Italian origin. James thought this last revelation something of a hint and wondered if Marco could obtain one.

It was only when dinner was over, and James and Marco were alone in James's room that he voiced his overriding concern. Whoever the would-be assassins were, they wanted him dead, not because he was a Sicilian knight in exile, but because he was James Devis. 'They knew exactly who I was and sought to bring the sentence of the Lancaster judges into execution. Somebody knows I am here.'

'And yet with the law on their side, they came in secrecy. This was all done without proper warrant, I'll wager.' James and Marco spoke late into the night without resolving the problem, and then it was past time to retire. Despite their friendship, there were certain duties Marco insisted upon to uphold his honour as a good manservant: he folded James's clothes as James got into bed, and then blew out the candles before leaving. 'This night I shall sleep across the threshold of your door,' he said.

Marco close or not, it was many days before James could shut his eyes without seeing the spectre of the noose.

In the days that followed, James resumed his exploration of the park's grounds, but never alone. Marco wouldn't hear of it, and he insisted that they went armed whenever they left the house. James strapped on his new rapier, though his skills in its use were minimal, and he hooked the wheel-lock onto his belt. He had never owned anything quite as magnificent and he knew its value was several times that of his old home and Malkin Tower put together. Marco also wore a fine blade, but with his right arm still recovering, he was almost as useless as James at swordplay.

Marco's company was good for James, because he did not like to be alone with thoughts that brought him pain. There was the pain of remembrance and the longing for a past that could never return. When he was small, James had never understood that he was poor and that the family vessel was ever but an inch from being swamped by the tides of ill fortune. The careworn face of his mother was beautiful to him, and his grandmother lived in a castle. He did not understand that Malkin Tower was no more than an abandoned and tumble-down excuse for a bastle-cum-watchtower whose previous tenants had been pigs and chickens. That there were parts you dare not go for fear of plummeting through the floor and others where you risked being brained by falling masonry, did nothing to make him feel less than a privileged prince and heir to a fortune. There was a warm fire, and a roof that leaked only a little, and his grandmother, who was famous throughout Pendle Forest and its surrounds for her herb-lore and wise ways. Life was fine.

John Devis, his father, was hardly more than a misty memory as James wandered about the roof of Newark Park casting his thoughts to the north and to home. John Devis had died when James was only eleven, but he recalled vividly his talks of adventure with Francis Drake and tales of the mighty John

Dee. John Dee had often confided in John Devis, and John had passed on many secrets to James.

Then there was the pain of conflicting, internal dialogues that tried to pull James in opposite direction. His family were renowned for their magical works against witchcraft and the dark powers of the earth. People paid them, or more likely forgot to pay, for charms that protected their crops, their cattle and their children from evil. James had spent his young life honing his skills to thwart the designs of ungodly spirits, and when Sarah's cousin had been murdered by witchcraft, he sat a week working a charm that would spell good fortune for the Lister family, so that they would grow and prosper in the years to come. One day they would be pre-eminent in Ribblesdale, if James had worked properly, and they would be well compensated for the loss of Thomas.

But now, James allowed himself to be pulled in the other direction. Whenever he thought of his mother and sister, horribly killed and dying to the laughter of the crowd, he wanted revenge. One night, he succumbed to the temptation, and drew a pentagram in the dust on the roof. Facing towards the north he sat inside the circle. He visualised the gaoler's house and spoke a spell that would bring down fire upon it. When he was done, he saw smoke rising from the woods to the north. His spell had worked, although it had fallen far short of the target. Elated and mortified, the two mingled together in equal measure, he scuffed the circle away and ran down the stairs to his room. He felt frightened and ashamed.

Finally there was the pain of deprivation. When he slept, James dreamt of Sarah. She always came to him like the succubus, heating his blood and waking him hot and lustful.

The next day, James and Marco returned to the house late in the afternoon after an exertion into the deep wood to find herbs. They went in by the servant's door at the back. There was company, evident from the horses turned out to field and voices that came from the parlour, but James did not care for visitors or conversation, so they crept by and went up the stairs.

They stowed their arms, removed boots, and sat on James's bed where spread the day's findings between them. James sorted through the herbs for a combination that would serve his purpose. 'I need something to cool my blood,' he said. 'You have Sally for companionship, but I have been so long without, I think I shall burst.'

'I have Sally? Indeed I do not!' Marco picked out a sprig of leaves. 'But here, try this, combined with a little of this. I know a charm that will do the trick, although wouldn't it be simpler to apply the bachelor's remedy.' He made a gesture with his hand that made James laugh.

'Aye, well that's a possibility I have often explored and am sure to do so again, but it is a pretty poor substitute. And if you have not the lovely Sally, it is your fault and none of hers. She is all cow-eyes when you are near.'

Marco blushed and turned away to pick up a leaf that had fallen to the floor. 'Well, I shall say it as perhaps I should not, but if you can but hold out a few more days, you may have no need of charms.' Marco instantly wished he had kept his mouth shut. 'But I know such little of the detail, you mustn't ask me more.'

'The whores are returning?' James said, perking up. He had only known one whore before he promised himself to Sarah, but he had known her quite often.

'Please, James, don't ask. You must wait until my master … my former master, the Conte returns, which must be in a day or two and not an hour longer.'

'The Conte,' James said, failing to hold down his amusement. 'What do you find so funny?'

'It's very childish, but you see, my father taught me a little of the Low Countries' language. In Italian your old master's title "Conte" may show him to be a nobleman, but in Dutch it makes him but an arse.'

'Arse, indeed!' said Bertrando, Conte di Pontenegro. He stood at the open door and, by the thunderclouds in his face, he had overheard every word.

131

Marco stood so quickly that his selection of herbs fell to the floor and he knocked the night stand. He bowed and apologised profusely to the ringing knell of fallen pewter on hard wood.

James smiled, and then chuckled. 'Oops!'

It was a charm of sorts, and it worked. The darkness flew from Bertrando's face and laughter preceded a happy reunion. 'It is good to see you so hale and hearty, James, or should I say "Giacomo". Master Verdi has fed you well. Why, your eyes are hardly sunken at all and there is colour in your cheeks where before I saw only the pallor of death.'

Sir Gabriel and his other guests had set out on a hunt, so refreshments could be had in privacy. Marco brought freshly baked bread, butter and small-beer to the parlour, managing very well with his one good arm, and then left James and Bertrando alone. There was much for them to discuss.

And so, at last, James began to learn the reasons for his salvation. He had been saved from the gallows, not from the altruism of his noble friend, but from a need, first disclosed by the great magician John Dee. Through the depths of his research and from his long travels across Europe, Dee had made many discoveries. With the help of his friend and colleague, the scryer Edward Kelly, it was said he was able to converse with angels and spirits, who made other revelation to him. When he had accumulated more knowledge than any other magician before him, he used his skills to draw up seals and amulets, and using these together with his expertise at the Cabal, he made predictions and foretold the day when the world would change.

'James, and I must caution you to treat my revelation with the utmost secrecy, there comes a magical and miraculous year, and we must be ready to seize all that it offers, for in that one year, we may work a magic that will last forever.' Bertrando spoke softly but his eyes blazed.

'Of course,' James said. 'The Annus Mirabilis. It is no revelation to me. I know of it.'

Bertrando's unhinged jaw and round eyes gave away his shock and surprise. Words would have been superfluous.

'But what of it? It is more than fifty years hence and all of us in this house and most in the world today will be long to our eternal rest.'

'But ... but how ...?'

'You speak of Doctor Dee. My father knew him well.'

'Surely you mean your grandfather?'

'My father was an old man when he got me, but he lived long enough to train me for my calling and to tell me many tales. The coming of the Annus Mirabilis – the Miraculous Year – was but one of his many stories.'

The count recovered his composure quickly and asked all that James knew.

'I know only that it will be a time that shall greatly affect our children, or our children's children, but us not at all; unless our bones be called out from their graves. And therefore it is of little concern.'

How wrong could the young man be? He had touched upon the very nub of the matter. John Dee had chosen his subjects well and made long study of their horoscopes. He had chosen James in 1596, just weeks after his birth.

Bertrando rose, walked around the parlour and returned to his seat. 'My dear friend, what do you know of the Last Witch? It is part of the prophecy of the Annus Mirabilis,' he added by way of a prompt.

'Not a thing. It is something I am sure my father never once mentioned.'

Bertrando restored the deficiency in James's knowledge. Dee's prophecy, or rather, the result of his extensive research, proved that the hidden world of magic would, by an alignment of planets, come close to the mundane world during the Miraculous Year. So close that, a spell properly worked by a skilled sorcerer could tear the flimsy fabric that divided them. The world would change for the better, and those who had the skills would rule it. The fly in the ointment: such a sorcerer must have the blood of the First Born surging through his veins.

'And Master Dee has gleaned and determined that you, James, have a half-share of that blood.'

James knew of the legends of the First Born, the fey folk who walked the green earth before mankind. He was not surprised to hear that he was suspected of having fey blood. After all, many thought it the source of magical skills. And then realisation dawned, bright shards illuminating the dark corners of James's mind. 'Aha! Now it is all clear to me.' When James had spoken of his need for female company, hadn't Marco intimated that he would have but a short wait? He also recalled that any child he had by Sarah would be in great danger, where its paternity known. 'I am only important in your great scheme for the blood I carry. You mean me to pass it on in the hope that I father the Last Witch, do you not?'

'Holy Mary, but how sharply honed your mind. It is worthy of the great Dee himself. From a few snippets you come to the correct conclusion of it.' The count took a long draught of beer. 'Yes, Dee marked you for your blood, just as he marked the mother. It is hoped that by co-mingling First Born blood with First Born blood, any child will have twice the charge, for that is the prerequisite for success in the Miraculous Year.'

Now James found himself in another dilemma. He was so hot for a woman's touch that he knew he would bed whoever was presented, be she ever so plane, but he knew something else of the Annus Mirabilis, and this knowledge he kept as a secret. His father had told him about the coming time, but he had also said, in the strongest possible terms, that any effort to part the fabric between the worlds must fail. 'Think of the world, my son, with all its cares and woes. Think of the rich who make wars, and the poor who must fight them. Now think of the same iniquities all fought out with terrible magic instead of blade and ball. When that year comes, there must be one who will lay down his life to prevent the rift.'

'James, it is indelicate, and much to ask, but as you can see, the cause is great. Will you meet with the fair maiden who has been chosen?'

'I will,' James answered, much too eagerly. But then, who was to say his child would not be the one who would lay down his life to save the world? And would it be so bad for the child to die for such a cause after so long a life? If James got the lass with child this very week, the boy would be fifty-four when the Miraculous Year came, and few could hope to live so long.

Truth be told, James's need was great; he would justify satisfaction of that need in any way he could, and live to regret it later. Or not live, as fate and the schemes of men might dictate. 'And if my issue burgeons and the child is born hale and hardy, what of me? What is to become of me once my purpose is fulfilled?'

'You will, of course, continue life as a gentleman of the Court in Exile. Or there may be other opportunities, for the world is on the brink of wondrous times of which you are at the very centre.'

The lie of it seeped from the count's eyes, plain for an adept such as James to see. He felt sure his own lie was far better hid when the Conte asked about Sarah Lister. 'She is with child, you say?' James let his head hang and he made sad eyes. 'It is none of my doing. We had sworn to keep ourselves pure for our wedding day.'

'There-there, my good man. Do not concern yourself over much. It is all for the best.'

Bertrando told James the arrangements would be made and James would be introduced to the young lady within a few days. 'Plenty of time to build up a head of water in the mill pond,' he said, winking. 'Until then, keep the sluice gate shut.'

∞

'What!' James said, a week later. 'And am I to be turned out to stud like a farmer's prize boar. I'll have none of it! Rather, if you may, bring a table furnished with a morsel of dinner and

135

some good ale, and a brace of chairs. First I shall meet the young lady and we shall dine.'

Marco pulled a face, embarrassment combined with reluctance to reveal the whole of it. 'You will need two brace of chairs,' he said. 'For you see ...'

'Oh, for Heaven's sake, man! Spit it out!'

Marco took a deep breath. 'There are to be three young ladies in all.'

James was shocked, but not a little thrilled at the same time. He paced to the window and back, deliberately heavier on his feet than he need be. He was scandalised. Yes, there was a little of that, but equally he wanted to whoop with the same joy as the child who found the key to the marchpanes. 'Three?'

'Three!' Marco went on to name them. All from good families, all unspoilt apart from instruction given by the most highly-placed courtesan and a little practice with the courtesan's footman. There was Dolly Kirkby, Mary Bowman and Jane Durward. 'As to the footman, well, by him they know what a man looks like under the covers and a little as to how he may be pleased, but nothing more.'

'See here Marco, I have agreed to this thing, but I shan't be a circus act.'

'Of course not, James.'

'They must be presented at proper intervals.' James wondered what a proper interval was and would it take into account the vigour – or otherwise – of his body.

'I will time it to perfection.'

James fell heavily onto the chair. 'But how will I ... what will they ... ?'

'Jem, hush now! Do not fret about it and remember, this is more of a procedure of alchemy than of love-making, more duty than pleasure. I believe there exists a charm to enhance the quickening of your issue.'

James was a young man, and the intervals were negligible. Later, duty done, he lay in bed alone, a glowing body, an entanglement of bed sheets and naked limbs.

Marco entered close on the heels of a double rap on the door. He brought in a tray of refreshments. 'My, but you are quite the lusty young stallion. Each young lady breathless and starry eyed as I led her to the parlour.' Marco showed no embarrassment and neither did James, and he made no effort to cover up more than the discreet flicking of a sheet. It had all felt so natural and unforced, but James did wonder if thanks was due to Marco's skill with charms.

James enjoyed the weekly attendance of the young ladies past the end of summer and into autumn. Dolly was the first to cease visiting, showing all the signs of being with child by the middle of October, and then a month later Mary had also achieved the gaol. By the first week in December, it was only Jane Durward who continued to call. For James, this was fortuitous, because Jane was by far the most adventurous and vigorous in the bedchamber, and to James's eyes, the most beautiful.

'Do you think I am barren?' Jane said drawing the covers up to her chin. Her words came out on a puff of mist from the cold. Both Jane and James favoured their sport on top of the covers, but December nipped and there were only two fireplaces in the house so their eyes had to forgo the feast while their bodies partook to the full.

James propped himself up on an elbow and drew a strand of brown hair from Jane's face and then let his hand cup her cheek. He smiled and kissed the tip of her nose. 'Cheer up, Jane! Of course you are not barren. Remember, your ability to give life has been determined by great magic.' He did not say that he was applying his own charms to delay that life thereby prolonging the days of his pleasure and perhaps of his life too. Surely he would be of no more use once his duty was done. 'And anyway, I'm in no rush for you to be gone.'

'I shall not abandon you when the job is done. The others have made their choice, and I shall make mine. Nobody forces them to stay away, but I am rather glad they do, for I want you all unto myself.' She sat up and flicked the covers aside, risking the chill air for a moment. 'I see you are ready again.'

137

'When am I not?'

They made love again and when, at the usual time, Marco knocked at the door with refreshment, James made him wait until the mulled wine had quite lost all its heat.

When he was not engaged in the most pleasant of his duties, James continued at his lessons. He had progressed pleasingly at swordplay and although it would take years to become expert, he was well past novice and showed real aptitude. He enjoyed hunting and was always warmly welcomed by Gabriel. His novelty value as a foreign knight and enemy of Spain made him popular with Gabriel's guests and young Lord George found himself at the same time attracted to, and annoyed by James: a boy well-schooled in manners, he found James's familiarity almost insulting at times, but when caught in the right mood he enjoyed the lack of stuffy constraint that everybody else used in his presence.

As to his mission, James kept all his plans to himself. He was to father the last sorcerer, the witch who would rip asunder the veil and let the magic free, but his true plan was just the opposite. Oh yes, he would be a father, but no child of his would bring about the prophecy of old John Dee. He intended to keep his father's council, his father who had often spoken of what must be done to thwart those who had selfish designs for the Miraculous Year. James knew what had to be done. That the task was impossibly difficult was another matter for consideration. How he should achieve it and what he should do to come anywhere near close was far beyond the grasp of his thinking. But one step at a time, James Devis, he told himself. One step at a time.

'Giacomo, tell me, why do you not have an Italian accent?' Lord Berkeley asked on the last hunt of December. The party comprised just the boy and James and an escort of armed retainers. 'And how is it that a knight can be so ill-versed in Latin and Greek, or in any other language for that matter?' The boy was so bundled up in furs, and on a horse so large, he looked like a kapok-stuffed contrivance for the amusement of children.

James began to answer the boy's question in Dutch until George laughingly called Pax! Continuing in English, James recounted the story he had learnt from Marco. 'I was born in England to a noble family that attended the Sicilian ambassador. Though Italian, I have spent most of my life in England.' James skimped on the details and turned the boy's attention to other things as soon as he could. 'You must concentrate on the hunt, George, especially when riding through a wood. Beware of low-slung branches.'

If George had any thoughts to continue his interrogation, they flew from his head when James flew out of his saddle at the gallop when his horse jinked right and James did not. Instead, he was propelled in a straight line and completed a full somersault before he landed on his back. He was saved from injury by the thick carpet of snow. It was a full five minutes before George stopped laughing.

They rode back to the house. James saw a number of armed men by the door and was glad of his own armed escort. He was put at ease though, when the strangers acknowledged the young Lord Berkeley with due compliments. For his part, George looked down at them with practiced contempt. 'No strangers, Sir Giacomo, but a gaggle of my family's retainers,' George whispered. 'It must signal a boring visit I'd rather not endure so early in the day. I need food sooner than prattle.'

'Then let us take the back stairs to the great hall.'

'There are no back stairs. Do you mean Sir Gabriel's private flight?'

'They are stairs and I am sure Gabriel won't mind. Our need of food outweighs our need of company.'

George giggled at the naughtiness of it.

The great hall was not empty. An old man sat by the fire. He wore mismatching clothes and old boots, and the feather of his shapeless bonnet bobbed close to the flames. James found the scene quite pathetic, because the old man was crying, though he tried to keep his grief silent.

'What ails you, Grandfather?' James asked.

The old man raised his head and looked over with weary eyes. He waved away James's concern with a limp movement of his hand.

'I am George, Lord Berkeley,' the boy said, far too grandly for the situation.

James gave the boy a withering look. The old man slowly shook his head.

'How dare you, sir!' George called in his shrill, boy's voice. 'Be upon your feet and make the proper compliments.'

'Hold your tongue, you insolent pup!' James admonished.

George went into a tirade and informed James that he, a lord, would take no instructions from a mere knight, and a foreign one at that. 'I shall say it once more. I am a lord, you are a knight. Am I clear on the matter?'

'More to the point, I am a grown man, and you are conducting yourself like a spoilt little boy.'

George would have said more, but James cuffed him about both ears. The shock on his face was almost comical, and James would have laughed, but the shock dissolved into indignant tears before the boy fled the room with much stomping, and slammed the door behind him. Perhaps the cuffing was a step too far and James wondered if he would come to regret it.

The old man, who at first seemed amused by the exchange between James and George, now began to cry again.

'Come now, and share your burden.' James crossed the room, threw an arm around old shoulders and asked if he would take some warmed wine. He drew up a chair and again asked the old man to unburden himself. After more tears and reluctance to deepen the wound, he did so.

'It is my good and beautiful son, Henry. This month past the angels took him and they have left my world in ashes. There is no good thing left upon it and I have prayed that Heaven should restore him and take me in his stead.'

James stood sentinel while the old man allowed grief to pour from him. When the outpouring subdued a little, they spoke of life and death and of grief while the clock moved on, and then came the sound of running feet and an urgent knock at the door. Inwards it swung to reveal Bertrando, the Count of Pontenegro. He bowed low, sweeping his hat upon the dusty floor.

'Is this another day for mockery?' James said. 'I've had it plain enough from George that lords do not bow to knights. So enough and rise yourself up. This is all very tiresome.'

Bertrando did not rise up, but remained, bent double and making a very fine leg.

'Must I say it again?' James was growing impatient.

'Sir Giacomo, it is true lords do not bow to knights,' Bertrando said. 'But we do surely bow to kings.'

James noticed that amusement was again showing through the old man's tears, and realisation struck like a blow. He jumped up from his seat as if the old man had become one of England's three leopards about to leap, whereupon King James chuckled and wiped his eyes.

'I have an unbearable urge to bow before you, sir,' James said. 'But I am so unpractised I know not how.'

'Then for giving me some light in my darkest hour, I relieve you of the requirement. But can you stretch to kneeling before me?'

James knelt, as if the king's question was an implacable spell.

King James slipped his sword from the scabbard and proceeded to dub the young man upon both shoulders. 'There! A knight's touch for a lord, but it will do until we may raise you with all proper decorum. Until then, I raise you to the peerage and you shall be Lord Rillton, after a place you should trouble yourself to know. Arise Lord James, First Baron of Rillton.'

The king had called James by his true name. So, he was in on the secret.

'I am afraid you shall be the poorest of lords, for I can promise you but twenty-five pounds a year, and the little house that guards the gate of the manor at Faennas Sandrin in the county of Shropshire. But it amuses me to know that, now you

141

are a lord, there will be fewer of higher station and therefore you will upset fewer for your lack of graces.'

James arose as commanded and the king hugged him and muttered under his breath that James was so like his poor, dear, dead Henry. 'After dinner, we will discuss much. And you sir,' the king called to Bertrando. 'You may unbend and pray do so before you die of a fit.'

Bertrando stood straight, his head befuddled, thick in a cloud of utter disbelief. James had gone from condemned peasant to lord in the space of five months, and not the merest sniff of a bribe. He hoped this fantastical elevation would not interfere with his plans for the boy. James had a duty to fulfil with the last of the young ladies, and then he must be put away lest other's make use of him.

∞

The King retired to his room, given up to him by Sir Gabriel, and Bertrando half-dragged James to the parlour where they partook of a little wine. The wine did nothing for Bertrando's sour mood. In short, he was jealous that James had achieved in a few weeks a rank that had taken him years to secure, and then only from a defunct and exiled court.

'The King must be insane,' Bertrando said. 'I am not even sure that he has the legal right to raise you to the peerage in that manner. A folly and a whim, and like to be reversed at a stroke if he wakes up with a different mood upon him.'

'It's all the same to me,' James said. 'It means little if nothing at all. But I should like to see the house that goes with the title.'

Bertrando paced the room, almost deaf to anything James had to say. 'If he takes on the slightest notion that you charmed him into his actions, it will be the worse for you. You shall hang at the very least, and more like burn at the stake. If he calls it treason you shall be for the butcher's block. My head buzzes with the audacity of it!'

James admitted that he was just as bemused, especially as it was widely known that King James hated witchcraft. 'He wrote a book condemning witches and cunning folk alike which was much quoted by the justice at my examination, and probably my trial too for all I know of it. It baffles me that he was instrumental in saving me from the hangman's rope.'

'James, you are a dunce and a fool, and know little of how the world turns. Those who make the rules do not expect to have to abide by them. The practice of rules is for those of lower orders.' Bertrando asked James what he thought was the power of kings. Influence; connections; divine right: all perhaps, or none, but without any doubt, money and wealth and gold. 'What use would gold be, my innocent friend, if it were as common as pissing pots, or the contents thereof? If gold could be had from base metals, as the alchemists do testify, gold would be worth less than mangolds or turnips. So the King despises alchemists and sorcerers for they may make him poor, when the only power that might count for a fig is the magician's power over nature.'

James shook his head as another illusion died. Why, there was more honesty in a chimney-sweep's lad than in all the knights and lords and princes gathered together, and nothing as base as the very pinnacle of the triangle of society. In that moment, it seemed to James the world was a triangle turned up upon its head, and that the poor sweeper's boy carried the weight of it all upon his famished and bony shoulders.

Bertrando ceased pacing and stroked his beard. 'And yet, I wonder,' he said to the ether. 'Perhaps you are become his majesty's new favourite. God knows the court will rejoice if another supplants that odious whelp, Robert Carr. You know James, the King made him a viscount last year on just such a whim as he has so recently raised you, and all for a pretty face and a tight arse.'

James leapt to his feet, his eyes raking the door and his ears straining to hear the guard coming to arrest them. How could Bertrando speak so infamously of the King without so much as lowering his voice?

'When you are to dinner anon, should the King command you to bow away from him rather than toward, do so right quickly and loosen your drawers without waiting to be asked.'

James felt the fire rise from his neck to colour his cheeks as red as any slap. After a moment he found his voice. 'I shall do no such thing!'

'Think again! Your fortune may depend upon it.'

'There have been occasions when my very life seemed to depend upon it. Many is the time I could have got food for such services, so do not think I will give up now for a few coins and baubles that which I kept when I was starving.'

'James, James, James. We are speaking of the King of England and Scotland, not some bumpkin farmer who seeks more comfort than can be got from his sheep. If the King commands –'

'The King shall never command such a thing, and if he drops hints I shall pretend to be oblivious to them.'

Bertrando shook his head sadly, as if there were no hope for James, and told him that opportunities came but seldom, and he had best develop a sense for them if he wished to survive in the world. 'Do not think that you will be treated like a true lord. There will be no cannons fired when you pass from this earth. No parade of troops, or presentations of arms. Enjoy it while you can, for it is so much horse shit!'

And so it was that at dinner, James became more than a little uncomfortable when the King dismissed the servants so that they were alone together. They sat at opposite sides of a small table that groaned under the strain of many fine dishes.

'Forgive the inconvenience, but we must do for ourselves for there are words to be exchanged to which none may be privy.' The king dished himself up a little fish.

'I am at your service, sir,' James said, and immediately wished he had not.

Though much relieved, James remained cautious when the King's secret words were all to do with magic and witchcraft. He wanted to know how James lived as a cunning man; the nature of his charms and spells; the source of his magic and

144

where it all stood in relation to God. The King was fascinated and enthralled with all James had to say, and so he began to relax. That is when the King sprang.

'Is there a way to conjure the spirits of the dead?' The King's deep-set, watery eyes became like orbs of wet stone. Everything else had been leading to this question.

'I believe so sir, but such dark powers would be practiced only by the most foul of witches.'

'Could you seek out and learn the necessary spells?'

'Seek them out, indeed, and perhaps learn them too, but I should never use them. To do so would be an affront to the Angels of the Lord.'

'But what if I should command you? Understand, I must know that my dear son rests in the arms of Our Lord, and that he is happy, and that one day we shall meet once more.'

It suddenly became clear to James. The King had written his book condemning all who used the powers, whether for good or ill, but now he had a need of his own, all those words were forgotten and the highly vaunted principles so much fallen rubble.

'I would speak to my son and tell him that he is loved and missed, and I would hear how he fares past the veil through which we must all pass. If it is within your power to raise the spirit of my dear Henry then I command you as King.'

'Forgive me, but I cannot do it sir, nor would I, even if I knew the spells.' James wanted to answer without a refusal, which may in itself amount to treason. 'It would be akin to waking a man to ask if he sleeps well.'

Anger worked the king's jaw. He stood and paced to the fireplace and back. 'So you refuse me? You say nay to your sovereign lord and prince?'

James had no words. His head fell forward and it might as well have been across the headsman's block. One did not say 'no' to kings with impunity. But dead this day of a rope, or tomorrow of the plague; was there really anything to be gained in jumping to Death's sting?

145

It was as if the king heard his thoughts. 'Do you have no fear of death?'

Here they came: the words that would take him away to be slain could not be far away. James drew himself up and looked into the king's eyes. 'Each man walks with Death beside him, at every hour of his life. My father taught me a childish rhyme when I was a small boy, but it has stayed with me ever after.' And James recited for the king. He tried to imbue the words with a charm that might save his life.

When the rhyme was done, the stone orbs that were the king's eyes had receded into their watery pools. He reached up and stroked James's cheek with the back of his fingers. A little earlier and James knew he would have shuddered at the touch, but now he recognised it as a reprieve and not the prelude to unwanted advances. 'Ah, my honest and courageous boy. Would that the likes of your heart and spirit were housed within the breasts of all my retainers.'

The charm had worked. James looked over his left shoulder to the invisible one who was always there. Not today old friend, James said in thought. At least, not this hour.

Far from censure, there was a reward to be had. The king gave James a ring. It was a simple band, silver in colour with a lustrous black border and a year engraved in the Roman style. James inspected the gift with care. 'The miraculous year! 1666 in Roman numerals. Thank you, sir. It is a very great treasure.'

'It is more of a treasure than you can possibly imagine. It came to me after the witches wrecked my ship with their dark arts, and it has kept me safe ever since, for it is a thing of great magic itself, of the kind to preserve and protect.'

James fancied he felt the ring warm in his fingers, for of a sudden he knew what it was. 'The Orbis Mirabilis,' he whispered, and the king confirmed it. It was said that the rings was several lifetimes in the making and that it was so imbued with protective powers that no dark magic could overcome it.

'Of course, the wearer is as susceptible to blade and shot and the casting of stones as any other poor fellow, but magic shall not touch him. Put it on, Lord Rillton, for I know a little of your future, and you will have much need of it.'

It was said that the Orbis Mirabilis had the power all combined of a thousand free spirited magicians, five hundred bound spirits, a hundred spells, fifty angels, ten arch angels, five cherubim and one seraph. The Prince of Darkness himself could not dent such armour, or so the king believed. 'Now lad, on with it, and never take it off, for soon you will be the very centre of a storm of malice that shall follow you all the days of your life.'

King James warned James that he should never speak of magic in the presence of the King whilst with other company. The King should never be suspected of knowing any person who trucked with the Devil.

'And now we must part, my young friend, and would that I could make you Elector Palatine, and then in but a few months I could call you son, for my sweet little Elizabeth is to wed soon, though I much doubt the feeble boy Frederick can do his duty by her.'

The King made a move towards the door and James made to bow.

'Remember James, you are absolved of those compliments, at least when we meet in private.' He smiled, and left the room.

James held up his right hand and examined the Orbis Mirabilis. Had it really been touched by the Angels?

∞

'May I touch it?' Marco held a finger in the air, awaiting permission.

'It's just a ring to the touch. If it has powers, they are well hid.' He held out his hand for Marco, who caressed the ring, stoked it with one finger as if it were a small animal.

'It is said to be the most powerful of amulets.'

'Not surpassing the Three Great Seals, of course.'

Marco was surprised that James knew of them: each disc holding a shard of burnt bone from Richard Meekins, the boy-

147

martyr. 'Perhaps not all three combined, but a seal on its own, even two together, would not trump the ring, I fancy.'

'And yet the three, placed as they are at the extremities of the world, are the very foundations stones upon which the Last Witch must work his magic to bring about Dee's designs when comes the Miraculous Year.'

Marco blanched, and nearly stopped his ears. 'You must be silent on such matters, James. The Conte told me you knew nothing of the Last Witch until he apprised you. I do not wish to be aware of all you know, lest it should slip from me at the wrong time.'

'I know a lot more than Bertrando thinks. I keep it to myself because I don't entirely trust him. Now, I believe you still have a duty to him, but I flatter myself our friendship has come to mean more to you than duty. I trust you, and if I am wrong, then you must deliver me up to the schemes of the Conte.'

Love works its own charm, be it brotherly, romantic, or sensual, for it is acceptance of the other, and it is a baring of the vulnerable soul that calls for protection. It was love that worked the charm on Marco, and drove out the last of his loyalty to Bertrando, and made him want to protect his friend.

'So tell me Marco, are you my man, or are you Bertrando's?'

'Do you need to ask, Jem?'

'No, but still, I wish to hear, because words often bind thoughts that would otherwise fly with the wind.'

'It is true, the Conte holds me to certain duties, but I am yours to the extent that I must give you a warning. You must be gone from this place the moment Jane gets with child, for at that point your survival becomes dangerous. There must be no chance that other children are born, who may fall into the hands of opposing factions. Anything or anyone who stands in the way of The Great Scheme will be utterly destroyed.'

James and Marco shook hands to seal their new understanding. 'Now let me tell you, I have some destruction of my own to levy. I don't know how I shall achieve it and the pursuit of my aim may take me the rest of a short life or a long one, but I intend to seek out and destroy each of the Three Great Seals. I must do it, or die trying.'

Marco sat heavily on the bed, mulling over the information. James spoke of the calamities he thought would befall the world if the Great Scheme succeeded and magicians ruled and Marco had experienced quite enough intrigue and plot to agree. Magic was not a power for rulers. Magic was for the poor folk and the work-a-day people, used little and sparingly to make their hard lives a little more bearable. Magic was that extra puff of wind in the sails, to take the ship away from the rocks. To magnify little magics and put them into the hands of those already powerful, it was a frightening prospect. 'So my good Jem, you would break the Three Great Seals?'

'I would, and I shall.'

'Of course, that is quite impossible.'

'I know.'

'One of them is said to be in the New World.'

'Yes, so they say.'

'And in attaining the impossible, two will have no better chance than one.'

'Impossible for a man is impossible for an host.'

'And yet, there may be good ale and happy adventures along the way.'

'Yet there may.'

Another handshake followed by unspoken promises: and then laughter, for what else when embarking upon the impossible?

With hushed voices options were discussed between the two friends, and an outline of a plan began to form, smoky around the edges and uncertain of direction, but by dinner time the first objective was hard-edged and clear. To find three dish-sized amulets, scattered to the extremities of the world, it would help to know exactly where they were and have at least an inkling as to their appearance. It was a job for Marco. He knew that Bertrando kept copies of Doctor Dee's papers, and among them, he felt sure, was information as to the disposition of the Three Great Seals. It was to Marco's advantage that

Bertrando lived a peripatetic life and preferred to keep his important papers safe while he travelled, and safe at this point was in the strong box in Sir Gabriel Lowe's room. Neither James nor Marco thought a locked door or a locked box would be serious impediments to their objective, and they were right. With Sir Gabriel away and about his business at Court, the locks were easily overcome and Doctor Dee's secrets secured. James memorised the locations of the Seals and their description.

'I find it hard to believe that the relics of the Boy Martyr are held within amulets fashioned of rude clay and base lead.' Marco looked at the drawing of the embossed design James had drawn with a charred wood stylus. 'Crystal and gold would be more fitting, the poor lad.'

'Aye, and more tempting to the thief. Look at it this way. With no disrespect intended to the memory of poor Master Meekins, my mission is to destroy the amulets, and the materials make my job easier.'

'Will you not save the relics?'

'Of course, if I can, but saving the relics is secondary to destroying the Seals.'

Marco suggested that they should start with the Seal that was buried close to the Ward's Stone near the summit of a lonely fell in James's own county of Lancashire. James disagreed, arguing that his face was still too well known in the villages around Pendle and the Forest of Bowland. No, rather leave it until last, by which time his appearance would be sufficiently different to risk it. James preferred to tackle the most difficult first, and so now plans turned to how one might reach the New World, and thereafter, a dark windmill in Saxony.

'If I am successful, the Ward's Stone seal will still be waiting for me.'

'We had better hurry, James. We only have fifty years to complete the task.'

Jane Durward was expected that afternoon, and later that night or early next morning, the Conte di Pontenegro. Jane's carriage arrived at two. She and James had until three to finish their business so that she could complete her homeward journey before nightfall. As always, Marco greeted her at the door and conducted himself as the perfect manservant to James, their friendship a secret shared with nobody else. Marco showed Jane to James's room and before withdrawing, he stoked the brazier while the contracted couple exchanged greetings.

Jane wore a grey dress with a modest Farthingale and a stiffened whisk collar. 'No mulled wine, thank you James. We have no time for our usual pleasantries. You must be quick today, for I do fear travelling after sunset.'

James helped her undress, but his mind buzzed with such thoughts and plans for the future, that they worked together as good as any charm intended to cool the ardour. With Jane's dress over the chair, her numerous petticoats arranged around the brazier and her drawers neatly folded at the foot of the bed, James's blood was still as cool as a bucket of water, and its effect the same. His eyes passed over Jane's naked body with no more interest than if it were a marble statue.

'What is it, James? This is the time when you usually lose buttons in your frenzy to undress.'

It was true. James usually had no trouble in putting aside the fact that Jane was not his beloved Anne, and he was glad to expend his natural appetites, knowing that any shame died at birth, because, after all, this was a duty for the greater good. It was also a very cold day. He stood closer to the brazier and began to undress until he was standing in his drawers.

'Come now, James. To bed with us!' Jane smiled, uncertainly. Her vulnerability did not help. She took a step nearer and brought her cold, delicate hand up between James's legs. James felt the heat of a blush spread up from his neck, but it was arrested by Jane's knowing smile. 'I was told this may happen, but I was also given instructions in how to overcome these little … difficulties.' She slipped her hands into the back of James's drawers and squeezed his buttocks, her cold touch engendering thrilling shivers, and then she sank to her knees bringing his drawers down at the same time. 'It is a technique the courtesan said was sure to work.' Jane then moved her head in close to practice her lesson.

James squeezed his eyes tight shut at the intensity of the sensation. These courtesans needed to teach a lesson or two to the common whores. Her technique worked, and for the next hour James performed his duties numerously and with great alacrity.

In a wreck of sweat and sheets, the couple lay in one another's arms as they caught their breath, and then Jane, fearful of the hour, rushed to dress.

'Forgive me if I do not rise, Madam. I am quite exhausted.'

'You have risen quite sufficiently, thank you, sir. But needs you must rise at least once more, for I cannot reach these buttons at the back.'

James kissed Jane's neck as he looped the button. There was a pang of guilt; it was a kiss of gratitude and not of love. To James, Jane was a co-conspirator and provider of a service. The button secured, she turned to face him. 'If this day's adventures do not get me with child, I know not what will.'

Jane's coach did not come. At six, Marco brought the couple a meal in the Great Hall, which with its huge fire, was the only really warm place in the house. Marco served with much aplomb, and scraped just a little for effect. He winked when he caught James's eye, knowing that Jane was looking elsewhere.

At seven, Ignatius Black dispatched a pair of mounted retainers along the road. They carried lamps and only turned back after five miles. There was no sign of the coach. Jane resigned herself to stay until morning, a prospect that she found pleasing as it would give her the chance to sleep with James until morning.

Marco brought more candles and James and Jane played Nine Man's Morris. They sat at the great table while Master Black read by the light of the fire and two retainers conversed quietly over a jug of ale. The couple had started their second game when Lanie Grey bustled up the stairs with a messenger in tow. Quiet words were spoken with Ignatius Black and he called the retainers to arms.

'It's naught to fret about, Sir Giacomo. The village watchman needs assistance with some drunken ruffians. It is but half-an-hour's work.'

'But what of your duties here?' Marco asked. 'Newark will be left open and vulnerable to any passing scoundrel.'

'Really, Master Verdi. We will be back in no time. Of course, if Sir Giacomo compels us to stay, we shall, but we have a standing order from Sir Gabriel to give aid to local officers when it is needed.'

Much to Marco's discomfort, James gave Ignatius and his men leave to go. Marco left to charge his firelocks and suggested that James do the same. He went via the door, locked it and barred it, but as soon as he had turned the corner, Lanie Grey stepped from the shadows. With care to make as little noise as possible, she unlocked the door and laid the bar aside.

Back in the Great Hall, Jane wondered if Master Verdi was always quite so nervous and fearful of robbers in the dark. James assured her Verdi was a good man to have looking out for you, and that it was best leave him to his precautions.

'Another game, James?'

'No, you are too good for me. And the room grows cold.'

'Shall we to bed then?'

James sighed deeply.

'I see. Then let us drag these chairs closer to the fire and enjoy a little conversation.'

James moved the chairs and placed two more logs in the flames. As they sat, the scream of a vixen shattered the night air.

'Such a sound, James. Very like the scream of a woman.' Jane pushed her chair close to James and then plucked a topic at random. 'I have heard that your grandfather set sail with Drake in the *Golden Hinde*. Is that really true?'

'It is not.'

'Ah! See, I do well to question my sources.'

'It was my father, not my grandfather, and when they set sail the ship was yet known as the *Pelican*. It was renamed during the voyage to poke fun at one of the sponsors.'

James told the story that, disliking the sponsor with a passion, Drake had wanted to name the ship *Golden Arse*, but that as luck would have it, the sponsor in question had amongst the beasts of his heraldic crest, a deer, which could be called an hinde. 'Sir Francis reasoned that *Golden Hinde* was as close to *Golden Behind* as he dare go, and so it became.'

Jane laughed and said he was teasing, but James swore it was the truth. 'Father told me Sir Francis never spoke the new name of his ship without a mirthful glint his eye.'

The dogs began to bark: one or two at first, but then the whole pack. Jane was scared, but James told her not to worry, and that they must have got the scent of that noisy she-fox. Nevertheless, they took a tree of candles upstairs to James's room, and as soon as the door was shut he saw to his firelock.

'What is that you are doing?'

'Winding the wheel. See? 't is just like winding a great clock. It is already charged, and now it is set.' He put the winding-key in his pocket.

'And now it is ready to shoot? If I were to pull the lever it would give fire?'

James explained that first the dog had to be pulled down, so the flint would touch the wheel. 'Then when you trigger it, the wheel spins and sends a shower of sparks into the priming powder. And then ... BANG!'

Jane jumped and threw herself into James's arms. He wondered if it was an affectation.

'Quickly! Light some more candles. This room is as dark as the crypt.'

James lit all the available candles, and prodded around the brazier with the poker to bring up the heat of the ashes and produce just enough of a glow to fire up the logs that Marco would soon bring.

The dogs were off again, barking and yammering. There was nothing to see out of the window except the glow from a lamp set by the door. James spoke a charm under his breath and tried to project his vision into the dogs. It was a technique that had never served him as it was meant, but he thought it worth a try. Then, as if the pack felt the touch of his thoughts, they all fell silent.

'This is a queer sort of a night, and no mistake,' Jane said.

'And yet at last there is a kind of calm.' It was a calm that somehow suffused James's spirit, so that all his concerns were no more. He had felt on edge, but now it was as if an unknown danger had passed.

They settled around the brazier and fell into conversation once again. This lasted for ten minutes, perhaps fifteen, when an ember cracked, its final effort reminding them that the fire was in want of fresh fuel. Marco was well overdue, and him so conscientious in his duties.

'You must scold him when he comes.' Jane pulled her clothes tighter.

When after a further ten minutes there was still no sign of Marco, James strapped on his sword-belt and went down to investigate. He left his firelock with Jane after reminding her how to handle it.

There was no light on the stair and only a little coming from below from the dying fire in the great hall. The candle he carried shifted shadows into frightening shapes. The hall was deserted unless the dark corners concealed enemies. James stopped and listened carefully. Nothing but the snap of embers. Then, from a floor below, a scream. It had to be Lanie Grey. James snuffed his candle and descended the next flight by feel. He had not put on his boots, so his stocking feet made no sound on the steps.

He stopped short at the next jumble of sounds that came almost simultaneously. There was the sudden cry of a man in agony from below and Marcus called out for mercy. Then from above, the sharp report of a firelock and a scream from Jane. For a second James hovered, but then raced back up the stairs to his room. The light from so many candles did not allow the horrors to be hidden. A dying soldier with a hole

155

where his nose used to be lay twitching in an expanding pool of his own blood. And Jane, poor Jane had been run into a corning of the room and stabbed so many times James would have been unable to count the wounds for the blood. She was slumped, half sitting, and wholly dead, her eyes fixed open in terror. The firelock that she must have used on one of her attackers lay halfway between Jane and the dying soldier.

Someone in heavy boots was running down the back stair, the one that was reserved for occupants of the master's room. James drew his sword, flung the belt and scabbard aside, and went in pursuit, pausing only to run his blade through the throat of the soldier. As he flew down the main stairs his anger and hatred for these unknown attackers dragged a sound from him that was like a baited bear.

A shadow peeled off from the gloom that filled the great hall and the clatter of boots on the lower flight made James increase his pace and roar all the louder. Past the parlour and down to the kitchen, and at last into light. But just as the light in his room illuminated horror, so it did here. Marcus's body was hanging from a meat hook dragged high on a chain like a side of pork. His head lolled and blood dripped from him into a pot that Lanie was placing carefully below.

But no time to contemplate the meaning of all this, for the enemy was upon him. He side-stepped a rapier-thrust from the second soldier and punched him in the face with steel-looped hilt of his own. The soldier drew back in shock and wiped at the wound that leaked blood from a split cheek, but he recovered quickly and attacked. James parried and the voice of steel-on-steel sang a song that demanded blood. For all his practice, James would lose against a professional. To stand a chance he had to fight like a street urchin.

Another attack and another thrust. James slapped the blade aside with his own and rushed in close to grapple with his opponent. He used the butt of his weapon to give the soldier a good pommelling, rapid blows to his face, and when the stronger man managed to force James's arm down, James thrust close and bit him in the face and then the throat, tearing

156

as if he were a wolf. The soldier screamed and dropped his sword. Both men fell to the ground together, but it was James who reached the dropped sword first. Holding it in a double-handed grip by the thick part of the blade below the quillion, he stabbed and stabbed in a frenzy until the soldier stopped moving and was silent.

Gulping for air, James got to his feet. His enemy was vanquished, and then the house collapsed on to his head. Or at least, that was how it felt. He fell to his knees, stunned, and then tipped forward onto his face. Warm blood seeped through his hair and he felt a section of the ceiling must have fallen and brained him. He rolled onto his back and peered through a maze of pain. Above him stood Lanie Grey. She had an iron pot in one hand and a butcher's knife in the other.

'I am truly sorry, my duck, but we can't let the world be ruled by magicians, now can we?' She struggled with her bulk and the many layers of her garb, but managed to get to her knees. She threw the pot aside and the hollow clatter it made on the stone flags hurt James's head. Lanie took a handful of James's hair and pulled his head back, exposing his neck. 'There now. One sharp pain and all the troubles of this life will be over.' She extended the knife, and she hummed a little tune and smiled. 'Hush now, my baby ...'

And then she stopped smiling. The rapier blade entered under her jaw and stuck out under her right ear. She gurgled on her own blood and she tried to speak, her eyes wide. Only James was more surprised than her, that amidst all his pain and confusion he had the wit to save his own life with his enemy's sword. Alas, there was no wit spare for anything else, and as the door burst in to admit rushing feet and shouted oaths, James was carried away by his trials and knew no more but oblivion.

4

On Silver Wings & White - The Year 1936AD

α

It was Humphrey Secundus, the donkey, who first saw the marvellous flying object. Humphrey Secundus accepted the mystery and wonder with the equanimity that goes with a failure to understand. Humphrey saw and Humphrey ignored. Although it made a noise like distant, rolling thunder it was far away and high in the sky. It did not look good to eat, nor did it appear to want to eat him. He treated it with the same indifference as he did the flyblown corpse of the abused and murdered Arab girl, or the distant burning village, or the Jewish youth whose eyes had been gouged out before he'd been left to die in the desert. Humphrey saw all these things, and Humphrey did not cry. Oh to be like Humphrey.

It was natural that the second being to notice the presence of the wondrous flying thing was young Daud Latif because he was sitting astride the dusty, musky flanks of Humphrey Secundus, his bare feet dangling eighteen inches above the sand. Daud understood the cruelties of the world. He had been subjected to them often enough and had the scars to prove it. Thunder, like the digestive noises of a hungry giant, reached his ears and he absently moved his hand to the healing rope-graze that encircled his neck. He should have died when the soldiers tried to hang him and the scar was a testimony to his remarkable quality of staying alive. He touched it every time danger threatened, like a talisman, just like his master touched the silver and black ring he wore.

The thunder rolled in lazily from the direction of the sun, so he squinted and looked towards the leached-out horizon over the yellow and pale green land and saw the flying enigma. His saviour and master was a flyer, but this was no aeroplane, no contrivance of mankind. No, rather it was a sleek splinter from a lightning-bolt thrown by God. The little worm of fear soon died and Daud smiled. Nothing was impossible to God. Everything could be, upon the utterance of His word. Inshallah! Daud knew he was looking at an angel. He had always believed in them, but until now it had been a matter of faith. Whereas Reggie Spencer had lived most of his life joined at the hip with an angel, and yet he did not believe in them. To him it was a matter of logic, and respect for those that told him such things were impossible.

Coincidence, or perhaps something else, arranged that the third to see the holy wonder was Daud Latif's saviour and master, the very same Reggie Spencer. He had just turned twenty-one but looked younger; certainly too young to be a killer, but it was late morning and he was about to kill other men for the second time in his life. He swooped low from the Heavens on silver wings and his fingers spat death. Or to put it another way, he was the pilot of a Hawker Hind biplane and by pressing the tab on the spade-gripped joystick, he unleashed a hail of bullets through the gaps in the spinning prop from a synchronised Vickers machine-gun.

Jack be nimble, Jack be quick, Jack fly over the candle-stick. Jack had been Reggie's friend throughout childhood. "Jack" was his work-a-day name, but on Sundays and special occasions, such as Christmas Day, he was "Ariel Cloudskipper", and it was Jack who gave Reggie his longing to fly and who led him into the skies. Reggie had always believed Jack was real until his mother eventually persuaded him that there was no such thing as boys with wings, and even if there were, they would certainly not fly around the sky dressed only in green weeds and bright wild-flowers and old scraps from the forest floor. Thereafter Reggie accepted that he had some undiagnosed malady of the mind which made his friend seem as real as his sisters and as solid and palpable as the earth, while at other times as light and ephemeral as a cloud.

An age-old certainty hit Reggie, sharp and instantaneously, like an arrow-head dipped in nostalgia. It lodged deep in his heart and Reggie spun in his seat to get a good look over his shoulder. He had a feeling he hadn't experienced for many years and his heart ached in anticipation.

Jack was with him!

He *knew* he was going to see Jack at his six-o'clock, bourn up on swan-like wings ... but all Reggie saw was Dave Pullman in the rear cockpit. Dave gave the sign, thumb and first finger forming a circle, the other three fingers like feathers in an Indian chief's bonnet. *Tickety-boo!* Flight-Sergeant Pullman was Reggie's oppo – observer, gunner and bomb-aimer – and he operated a Lewis gun from back there, but not that day: he wouldn't get the chance, because Death had decided to strike both ways.

Reggie and Dave were patrolling with two other aircraft. They were a section of the only squadron of Hinds remaining on base, the others having been re-equipped with brand new Gloster Gladiators, the lucky bastards, all snug in their enclosed cockpits. Reggie was Blue One, Pilot-Officer Isaac Blue Two and Flight-Lieutenant Barker was Blue Leader.

Barker squawked an ex-ex call. The mission was to intercept and neutralise a band of rebels who had recently lobbed grenades into a bus load of Jewish school children. It was always a school bus full of kids and Reggie was beginning to suspect they just said that to make the crews feel better about strafing and bombing people on the ground armed with veritable flintlocks or at very best relics from the Great War. But at the end of the day, they didn't get involved in the politics, they just did their jobs. And then again, sympathy didn't last long for those rebel chaps: some of them had a very artistic streak and they were prone to demonstrate their skills on the enemies they captured by re-arranging their body parts in hugely imaginative ways. Or was that just propaganda too?

Reggie fretted: he didn't like what the temperature gauge was telling him. For the hundredth time, his hand flew to the wooden wheel at the lower left of the cockpit, even though he knew the radiator was wound down to the limit. Maximum airflow wasn't enough to keep the engine cool in this climate, no more than it could him, despite his flight-suit comprising only a pair of knee-length khaki shorts, and a matching jacket over a thin cotton shirt. He longed to pull off his flying-helmet and let the air rake through his thick, dark hair. Where was the freedom of flying with all these dials to watch and adjustments to make? If he was being honest with himself, he would admit that he felt freer riding his bicycle. Up here, there was so much to do and the weight of responsibility was so great that the joy of flight was totally overwhelmed.

Was that rad fully extended, or had it stuck? Reggie nudged the wheel one more time. And then the sun was obscured and a fleeting shadow slipped over his Hind. Dave Pullman's 'What the blue blazes ...' sounded over his earphones and he felt the heat of fire-blasted wind buffet him, and he smelt ozone the instant before his head became centred in a thunderclap. He took both hands off the stick and pressed them to his rudely assaulted ears.

Not being in perfect trim, the Hind dipped its nose and Reggie saw the Splinter of God's Lightning Bolt over the upper wing.

'What the bloody hell was that, boss?' Dave's voice cackled through the wires.

Reggie pressed the transmitter to his throat. 'Haven't the foggiest, Flight. A meteor I think, but it looked like it had ... No, forget it.' It looked like it had wings. Not dope-stiffened canvas over a wooden frame, but natural and covered with feathers. Jack?

'Shut up, Splash!' Blue Leader crackled over the air-waves. 'Correct RT procedure and for God's sake, get back into formation.'

Reggie waved an apology towards the Hind with the blue fin and blue wheel-hubs, and Flight-Lieutenant Barker acknowledged.

It was quickly established that the mission was unaltered by the intrusion of the unspecified heavenly body, and they would have to wait until they got back to base before discussing the unusual encounter. There was certainly no hope of catching the bastard, because Barker estimated a speed in the high Mach's numbers.

Blue Leader, or Flight-Lieutenant Gerry Barker to give him his full title, called young Daud's donkey "Humphrey" because, not being a camel, it was hump-free. He called Daud "Humphrey" too – Humphrey Primus to the donkey's Secundus – because being a sporting little Arab chappie he would not sell his favours but give them freely, so if you were that way inclined you could hump free. No matter that Daud was a sixteen-year-old of impeccable morals who would neither sell nor bestow himself freely in the implied manner, why let anything stand in the way of an amusing nickname? Flight-Lieutenant Barker's own nickname was Joe, but more on that later.

As for Reggie, Barker and everybody else in the Squadron called him Splash. As to how you might derive such a nickname from Flying Officer Reginald Spencer, it had to do with a ladies-night back in Blighty, too much after-dinner port and an unexpected encounter with the Wing Commander's daughter – and then his fishpond. Oh very well then, why try to spare his blushes? Everybody in the squadron knew the story: in his cups, Reggie tried to kiss the Wing-Commanders daughter, and she pushed him in the pond.

RAF nicknames, once settled into a favourable niche, could never be expunged, no matter what their provenance. Reggie knew he'd be known as 'Splash' even if he reached such dizzy heights as Air Commodore. Why, if he became Marshall of the Royal Air Force and was lifted to the peerage, there would still be those in gentlemen's clubs who would refer to him as 'Lord Splash'. Ah well, there were worse nicknames and they said a nickname meant that you were accepted by your colleagues.

The flight changed course and reformed on Barker's machine – mummy-duck – and then there was a rare interval of peace when all Reggie had to do was hold formation and enjoy the ride. Even the temperature gauge was behaving itself. The sky was blue, Reggie was in his heaven and Jack, whose element he aspired to, was surely close. If only the cloying stench of hot oil would dissipate, things would be near perfect. Now Reggie had time to think about the fiery phenomenon. The feathery wings were no more than smoke or steam: that had to be the answer. He was almost convinced he had experienced an intimate introduction to a meteor, now no doubt a meteorite, the operative word being "almost". Could it have been a weapon, he wondered.

Reggie liked to think he kept abreast of new developments but this was something out of science-fiction. He knew the days of the Gloster Gladiator were numbered. Despite its power and beauty, it was obsolete before it rolled off the production line and all the talk these days was of monoplanes with spectacular properties of speed and manoeuvrability. Look at Northern America's sturdy little Harvard, for example. Were the companies that took commissions from the RAF insane or simply bogged down with traditional views? Well, not if they were concentrating all their efforts on directed balls of fire. Reggie had to concede that, as close as he kept his ear to the ground, news of serious advancement was obviously whispered too softly for his lowly hearing.

Crackle-squawk-yackety-yak: there was Blue Leader on the blower again. Target in sight, arsehole tight. Reggie saw them on the road far below, little brown ants star-bursting from a pair of trucks. Too low for a decent bombing run, so Blue Leader ordered a Vickers *hors d'oeuvres*: serve hot, no returns accepted. Reggie was to take the first truck, Peter Isaac the second and Blue Leader would dive in a couple of times and strafe the scattering personnel.

Once again Reggie was a panic of actions that culminated in a powered dive. The Hind went down in some kind of an inverse ratio to Reggie's rising heart rate and blood pressure. He treated the truck to a couple of bursts in the first pass and then climbed to a non-optimum thousand feet. Dave hunkered down to the bomb-aiming position, head under Reggie's seat, and Reggie put the kite into a dive, all lined up nicely for Dave to have the best chance of releasing the bombs on target. Dave called bombs away at five-hundred feet and then made a curious sound like a truncated hiccup.

Reggie was very good at his job, it's just that it didn't come naturally, and much of his effort went into maintaining the cool and composed exterior. Neither his superiors nor his colleagues guessed at the frantic mechanics working overtime under the smooth and well-made skin. Just like his aircraft Reggie was well-doped and tightened without the slightest hint of a wrinkle.

Bullets ripped through the truck's human cargo, decimating them, and one of the bombs tore through the canvass back-flaps and detonated in the flatbed, killing all those who had survived the Agincourt-like rain of metal. Whether a shot aimed by a rebel in the split-second before he died, or something set off by the explosion of the bomb, it was really pretty irrelevant to Flight-Sergeant Pullman. As Reggie pulled back on the stick and the Hind began to climb away, Dave Pullman just managed to drag himself up from the bomb-aiming position before his nicked aorta burst. He slumped over the Scarff ring with eyes that stared but did not see.

'Damn and blast!' Reggie inspected the temperature gauge, and then he pressed the transmitter to his throat. 'We've got trouble, Flight. The needle's way into the red.'

Flight-Sergeant Dave Pullman was beyond answering, but the engine stepped in to agree with a raucous cough and a stuttering complaint before it clunked into sulky silence.

Now the heat really was on. Too low to consider bailing out, Reggie raced through forced-landing procedures: nose down to keep up momentum and a decent bit of lift, full-flap, scan the ground below for a likely landing site, spot one, steer for it, gently-gently, hope there is enough glide left in the old girl, tighten the harness, sinking-sinking, just the right angle and at the last moment, ease back on the stick and round out, wheels touch – all three at once – *Thanks Jack* – allow oneself a pat on the back, bounce, thud, tail bucking – self-congratulatory actions somewhat premature – jerk about like a puppet in a giant cocktail-shaker. Scrape. Sli-i-ide. Something bites and it's nose-over into the dirt, prop all buggered to Hell. Dust … Silence.

It took Reggie a moment or two to realise he was still alive and apparently uninjured. He could feel the harness tight against his chest. He could wiggle his fingers and toes and there was no blood. There was just this terrible weight pressing at his shoulders and his goggles were steaming up. He raised them to his forehead.

'You alright, Flight?' Reggie said, twisting as best he could.

The weight at his shoulders was Dave's head and it was immediately obvious that Dave was not in the least bit alright. The horror of it, the reality, tightened like a fist around Reggie's heart. Dave was dead, and the plane was down in hostile territory. And then Reggie's sense of smell resurfaced, rudely nudging aside all other senses, and detected the volatile stench of aviation fuel. The tank must have ruptured.

Galvanised by the vision of imminent immolation, Reggie made swift with his survival knife and sliced through the harness. With the Hind still nose-down he had to clamber out of the cockpit and secure a foothold on the windshield. Dave's body lolled out of the rear cockpit and Reggie began to slice at the harness to free it for later recovery, but he heard the unmistakable *whoompf* of igniting fuel and threw himself sideways and to the left of the upended fuselage. He avoided struts and stringers as he plunged between the upper and lower planes, but he landed awkwardly on the undercarriage. Pain shot up his left ankle and he had to roll away as the flames bloomed and took hold. Heat, like a fart from the Devil's arse, burning and acrid, engulfed him and his eyelashes sizzled. He rolled over, again and again, until he was far enough away to avoid further injury. He sat up, wrenched off his leather flight-helmet and watched Old Maudie go up in flames. She took with her the remains of Flight-Sergeant Pullman, the first aid kit, the survival gear … and two canteens of water. He wouldn't live long without water, even if he could avoid any rebels who may have survived his attack, and aerial attacks always left survivors: angry, vengeful survivors not at all likely to be overly concerned with the Geneva Convention.

The distant sounds of aircraft engines and machine-gun fire told Reggie the fight was still on. He could make out Blue Leader's kite, with its distinctive markings, diving on an unseen target, but where was Isaac's aircraft?

The answer was heralded by Isaac's roaring Rolls Royce Kestrel engine. He flew over at less than a hundred feet, circled – both Pete and his oppo waving – and came in again. A small bundle detached itself from Pete's hand and grew as it fell, resolving itself into a flying jacket. It landed in soft, sparsely grass-thatched sand and Reggie scrambled over to it. Wrapped in the thick leather and sheepskin lining was a canteen. It hadn't burst, so at least Reggie had something to drink.

Old Maudie's funeral pyre was like a beacon. It was hard to miss and with the rebels not much further than a mile away, Reggie knew his chances of survival depended on leaving her and finding somewhere to hide until the RAF Regiment or the Army came to rescue him. He quickly took stock of his surroundings and recalled what he had seen from the air. He decided to scale a ridge of sandy scrub and make for the olive grove on the other side, but before he had reached the top, the sun was suddenly obscured and a danger more immediate than rebels threatened to engulf him. He had seen that kind of approaching brown cloud before, and he hoped his colleagues could get safely back to base before the sandstorm struck.

∞

The sandstorm gave no indication of nearing its end. Reggie sat in the lee of an olive tree, except there was no real lee. The raging wind favoured no direction and rampaged from all quarters. Reggie was glad of the *shemagh* scarf Daud Latif had given him and he arranged it to cover the parts the flight-helmet and goggles left exposed. Peter Isaac's flying jacket also proved its worth, but if only Reggie had stuck to long trousers.

His knees felt as if they were being torn apart, abraded to the bone.

By trial and error, Reggie came to an arrangement of clothing and folding of limbs that exposed the least amount of him to the ravenous teeth of the storm, and he held the almost-foetal position faithfully, lest it become jinxed and therefore ineffective. The noise and thick impenetrable air, heavy with its abrasive load, became like a shroud to Reggie and, as uncomfortable as it was, it afforded him protection from hostile eyes. In a strange way, he felt cosseted and safe and almost feared the storm's end when he would be exposed again. If Jack came now, he wondered, would the spiteful sands shred his near-naked form, or would he be immune to nature's excesses just as he was to the slights of cruel people?

While the storm raged and Reggie was held, cocoon-like, there was nothing for him to see through his goggles except a swirl of brown, and nothing to hear above the unceasing lament of the wind, so his thoughts ventured no further than the confines of his own skin. They turned inwards and as the hours past, he recalled again and again the final moments of Old Maudie and tried to remember the last conversation he shared with Dave Pullman. Dave wasn't just his oppo, but his friend too, despite the differences in their station. Salutes and sirs and standing to attention: they saved all that for when anyone was looking, otherwise they had no use for it. There was that time, months ago now, when they rescued Daud Latif … Reggie chuckled at the memory and tried to wind it back as far as he could. He found that memory stopped at the Station gate.

'Good morning, sir,' Flight-Sergeant Pullman said bright and cheerful. He stood to attention and threw up a smart salute. Then, under his voice, 'How you doing, me old cock-sparrow?' Dave was a cockney sparrow of a character himself, slight and bird-like with piercing eyes and a quick humour.

'Top-ho,' Reggie returned the salute and for all the world to see as aloof as the situation demanded. He walked past Dave with suitable distain and Dave fell into step on his right. In their khaki uniforms and pith-helmets, they headed for town.

'I found a picture house, believe it or not,' Dave said. 'And they're showing *The Lives of a Bengal Lancer.*'

'With Gary Cooper? Get away with you, Dave. You're having me on.'

Once past the direct line of sight from the sentries at the gate, the two men relaxed a little. 'I'm deadly serious, and I've bought us a couple of tickets.'

It turned out not to be one of Dave's greatest ideas. The crackly soundtrack was in English and subtitles had been added for the enlightenment of the locals. But the locals, having no need to hear the English words, held loud and animated conversations to the extent that Reggie and Dave couldn't hear a single line of dialogue and only just caught the loudest of battle noises. They gave it up as a lost cause and left half-an-hour into the screening.

They were not due back at camp for another couple of hours, so they decided to take in some of the local atmosphere. Intelligence reports suggested the town was as rebel-free as possible and, in any case, Reggie and Dave were both armed with heavy calibre Webley revolvers. In their ignorance of local feelings, they felt reasonably safe. How quickly feelings can change.

The souk was awash with bright colours, and redolent with the tang of spices. Reggie had developed an air of superior indifference to the scruffy urchins who followed them asking for baksheesh. Dave, however, was still susceptible to their waif-like eyes and cheerful pleas, and the small boys flocked round him like pigeons at Trafalgar Square. It was strange then when a cry went up and the boys scattered at the sound, like a frightened flock.

An old lady, howling and beating her brows, was being led firmly from a side turning by two young Arab men. There was much lamenting and wailing from her attendants but they were resolute in their efforts to guide her away from some horror. The women spotted Reggie and wrenched away from the others. She threw herself upon her knees, and began to plead in her own tongue.

Reggie felt confused and embarrassed. Dave tried to ply her with his few local phrases.

The woman's face was naturally wrinkled, and all the more so for her grief. She pulled at Reggie's shorts and pointed down the alley.

'Tell her we'll help if we can, Dave.' Reggie struck out for the alley, and the cause of her horror soon became obvious.

The alley opened into a tiny square, the centre of which was dominated by the swinging corpses of two men. A simple gallows had been set up – a beam of wood seated at either end upon the sills of adjacent first floor windows – and it was attended by a platoon of Highlanders, some at guard to dissuade anyone from approaching too close, and the others engaged in such a nauseating display that it brought shame upon the name Great Britain.

Two of the victims hung dead, past twitching and struggling. A third, much younger than the others, had a noose around his neck and stood upon the back of a donkey which the soldiers tried to temp from under the boy's feet with a variety of root vegetables. Some of the soldiers laughed and threw derisive remarks at the lad. They waved their vegetables and extorted in excited voices every time the donkey looked ready to move. Others looked as sick as Reggie now felt.

In that moment, Reggie was ashamed of his uniform. 'What in God's name?'

A Highland sergeant dropped a turnip onto the dust, and spun to attention, saluted and adopted a smart air that did nothing to cover his embarrassment and discomfort.

The other louts followed suit and made scarce with their vegetables. The donkey appeared on the verge of advancing upon the discarded bounty when Reggie caught the boy's gaze, pleading and way past terrified. For an instant it was Jack standing there, balancing on a donkey's back for dear life. Reggie threw a signal to Dave, who leapt forward to take the donkey's bridle and hold it in place. 'Cut him down, Flight. For crying out loud, he's no more than a child.'

'Begging your pardon, sir,' the sergeant said, 'but he's just another rebel, and he's been properly condemned and I'm to see out the execution.'

'Condemned by whom? Show me the order, and tell me when did torture and abuse become part of a lawful sentence?' Reggie, usually a little diffident in his exchanges with unknown rankers, was as close to furious as he had ever been. 'No, forget I asked that question. I'm not in the slightest bit interested. I know enough about the law to know we don't execute children, nor do we ill-use the condemned in this deplorable manner.' Something in the Scottish soldier's demeanour changed and Reggie's fury cooled a little. Inside he was trembling, but he knew it was the outside that counted. If he could only keep it up.

The sergeant no longer appeared intimidated by rank. 'I'm sorry to insist on the matter, sir, but I have my orders. You are not my officer and in absence of a countermand directly from him, I will carry them out.' He flicked a glance to his soldiers. The two closest un-slung their bayoneted rifles and held them uncertainly to the port. Reggie shot a glance towards Dave. He'd already got the boy out of the noose and off the donkey, which now ambled over and began to devour the vegetables. Dave threw a protective arm around the boy and one hand idled towards his khaki-webbing holster.

Reggie returned full attention to the kilted sergeant, his fury kindled once again by the soldier's insolence. 'Listen very carefully, sergeant. I hold the King's Commission and I am going to give you a very clear order. If you fail to obey it, I must remind you that this policing action of ours carries with it all the same military regulations as a theatre of war.' He was lying. He hoped the sergeant wasn't a barrack-room lawyer. 'Do you know the penalty for disobeying an order in time of war?'

The sergeant wavered.

'Good, then my order is this. Take your detail and report back to barracks. You will leave the prisoner in my charge.'

The private soldiers exchanged cowed looks and put up their rifles. The sergeant appeared to need a nudge in the direction of the correct decision. Dave Pullman provided it. 'What he means, sargie, is form up and fuck off!'

'But –' The sergeant looked towards the trembling boy.

'As I said, we'll take charge of the prisoner.' Reggie felt confident he had won, but the sergeant required one final encouragement, so Reggie relied on the power of military cliché. 'Carry on, sergeant,' he said in a tone thick with the implication that there wasn't a force in the world that could disobey.

And the sergeant obeyed. And Reggie let out an internal sigh of relief.

One young Scot, who looked almost as stick-like and poorly nourished as the prisoner, breached military etiquette and addressed an officer without permission. 'Thank God you came, sir. It was horrible.'

Reggie nodded a curt acknowledgement and the lad fell into line. Moments later the Highlanders were no more than a nasty memory and a distant rhythm of marching feet, and people came to cut down the dead with many tears and heart wrenching cries.

'Well, that was a narrow squeak, young fella-me-lad,' Reggie said to the boy. His hands were still bound and Reggie's heart caught, remembering the last time he had seen Jack. 'Come here,' he said, pulling out the blade of his issue jack-knife. The bindings were of worn and feeble hemp and they were parted with a single slice. It was a pity those nasty rope-burns around the boy's neck would not be so easy to remedy. 'Off you go then, back to the bosom of your nearest and dearest.'

'Aren't we taking him in, Reggie?'

'Are we buggery! If the boy really was condemned, and I don't believe a bally word of it, it seems that proper respect for law has broken down. If it can happen, once it can happen again.'

'I follow your drift,' Dave said, and then turning to the boy. 'Off you go then, Sunshine, and get back to whatever it is little Arab-boys do all day.'

An elderly man rushed up as quickly as his worn-out legs allowed and embraced Reggie, kissing him on the forehead. 'They accused him of stealing bread and said a thief was as good hanged as a rebel. But he begged the bread, sir. I gave it to him freely but they would not listen.' He hugged the boy and was gone as quickly as he'd arrived.

A woman came, her clothes ragged and poor. 'Surely this boy is blessed, sir. First he has his neck stretched, and then the loyal donkey came to stand beneath him and resisted all temptations of the soldier to let him fall, and then you are sent, inshallah, and he is saved again.' The woman snatched Reggie's hand and kissed it.

'Steady on, madam.' Reggie withdrew his hand and wiped it on the seat of his shorts, and then turned back to the boy. 'Cheerio then, and glad to have been of assistance,' Reggie said, as if he had loaned the lad sixpence rather than saving his life. 'What's your name, by the way, if you can speak any English?'

For the first time the boy's eyes appeared to focus as if life had been, up until that point, too frightened to return. He was small and slight of frame, but he was older than he looked, that much was somehow clear to Reggie. 'I know very much English, sir. My name is Daud Latif and I thank you with all my heart,' he said with a voice that caught and rasped, no doubt, from a noose-bruised larynx.

'Least we could do,' Reggie said. He noticed that, in his earlier terror, the boy had wet himself, a yellow stain on the front of his ice-white *thobe*. Reggie gave him some money and suggested he should buy new clothes. He winked at Daud and then turned to go. Dave drew up shoulder to shoulder and they made for the alley.

'Sir,' the boy called. He ran to join them in an uncomfortable gait. He really would have to make a priority of buying some more under-trousers. 'My life is yours. It was forfeit and you gave it back to me and now I give it to you.'

'Blimey, Reggie. Looks like you've got yourself a *dobie-wallah*.'

'Don't be ridiculous, Dave. And you, Daud-Whatever-You're-Called, be off with you. I'm happy to have been of service, but please feel free to remain master of your own life ... erm ... as much as I appreciate the offer.'

The boy looked utterly forlorn, and once again Reggie recalled the last time he had seen a boy with bound wrists. 'It is you who has bound Jack,' Jack said, referring to himself in the third person as he often did. 'You will not see me again until you free me.' And sure enough, Reggie had never seen Jack again. They had been fourteen-year-olds, for Jack ever aged in time with Reggie, his imaginary appearance always keeping abreast of Reggie's real one. This Daud chap didn't look at all like Jack, and yet ... Had Reggie freed Jack by freeing this boy? He scanned all around, but of Jack he saw not a single feather nor caught the faintest of merry laughs.

'I have no family, sir. I am from far away and have travelled many months to come to this place, only to meet with injustice and pain, until you. Leave me here and I will perish, by one means or another. It is my destiny to serve a great man ...'

Dave snickered. Reggie checked him to silence with a look.

'... and so I beg you to accept my service.'

Daud Latif would not be talked out of it, and so, by way of a market-stall that sold light cotton under-trousers, *thobes* and *bishts*, Reggie and Dave returned to the Station gate with a cleanly dressed new hand. Out of his own meagre funds, Daud bought a green and white *shemagh* and later gifted it to the man he now called master.

Reggie's gratefulness for that *shemagh* increased as the storm blew on. He adjusted it and pulled it up a little at the corner of his mouth where some sand had breached the defences, stinging his lip. There was still nothing to see and thoughts tumbled and vied with the hypnotic drone of frenzied air. Where was Daud Latif when you really needed him? It was clear the boy loved Reggie for his gift of life, and Reggie knew that Daud would do all in his power and a fair amount that was not, to save his master. Once, when the density of dust in the air coalesced to form the shape of an approaching figure, Reggie felt sure it was Daud, coming to repay him for saving his life. But then, he had been sure he was in Jack's presence moments before his plane went down, so he had no reason to trust his feelings. Reggie hardly ever trusted his feelings, not since Jack left, all those years ago.

Jack sat in the school coal-bunker, crouched on a pile of coal. His swanlike wings were free of the slightest hint of dust, and his skin was clean as if dirt could never find a hold.

Jack's wrists were all tied up. Reggie was reminded of a drawing of Ariel Cloudskipper he had once seen in his Uncle Jim's ancient oracle. 'Why are you tied up?' Reggie said under his breath. He looked around and noticed nobody any closer than the third-year football team practicing way across the fields. 'Who did that to you, Jack?'

'It was you who bound poor Jack,' Jack said. 'You don't believe in Jack anymore, and so he is bound.' Jack's smile lacked the usual joy.

Despite the stab of shame, Reggie was resolute. 'Of course I don't believe in you, Jack. You are quite impossible. The most clever and important people say so, like Dr Bickerton and Father Morrison. They say you are in my head, and so you must be. But I still don't like to see you all tied up. Come here …'

Jack turned away and lifted his bound wrists. 'Jack must stay bound,' Jack said, and for the first time in all the years gone by, he looked sad and vulnerable. But it only lasted a moment, and his smile came out like the sun from behind a cloud and Reggie was warmed. 'But Jack might be free again one day.'

'Super! When will that be, Jack?'

'When you free me,' Jack said, and then he winked and laughed his teasing laugh and leapt, wings carrying him high, and high and higher still until he was no bigger than a lark, and then a speck, and then nothing at all.

'What're you gawping at, Spencer?' It was Mr Barnes the English master, his mortar-board at a drunken angle and his black robe flowing in the disturbed airs left by Jack. 'And blubbing too, for Heaven's sake! What are these tears, young man? Am I to take my cane and seek out bullies?'

'No, sir. I'm just feeling a little ... a little out of sorts, sir.' He drew his forearm across his eyes and nose, appending a silver thread of snot to his blazer sleeve.

Barnes checked behind the coal-bunker but bullies found he none. He stooped, as if to pick something up.

Reggie tried to change the subject. 'I was looking for fossils, sir. I heard you can get them in coal.'

'Well, that's as may be, but chip along now, Spencer. It does a boy's spirit no good to spend too much time alone.'

But I'd never been alone, Reggie wanted to say, *never, not until I stopped believing in Jack.* A dread passed over Reggie, that he would be alone forever and that all his happiness had just passed from the world. But once again, Jack saved him.

'Before you go, young Spencer, take this. Not quite a fossil but quite extraordinary, and I believe boys enjoy such things.' Barnes held out an unnaturally long, white feather. 'Can't imagine the fowl that shed such a fine specimen.'

Apart from flying and never feeling the cold, could Jack do magic? Might Jack be able to stop this storm? 'Jack! I believe in you,' Reggie shouted into the sound-consuming winds. He tried again; his voice died once again, deadened and subsumed. 'I believe in you, Jacky-boy!' he shouted, as loud as he could. But he was clutching at straws, of course; less than straws. At the deepest level, he had never stopped believing in Jack. Jack was real, even if he was only an aberration of a damaged mind, but he had no place in the world of grown-up men who plied their arts to hurt one another, yes even unto death.

Reggie tended to avoid self-analysis. He tried to commit fully to the philosophy of Popeye the Sailor-man: *I am what I am and that's all what I am!* Jack had been part of him for many, many years, a self-acknowledged impossibility in an otherwise sane-

175

ish and almost-logical world where everything made sense, more or less, except the undeniable reality of Jack.

'Angels are undeniably real,' Father Morrison said. 'But I'm afraid this Jack-chap sounds a rum one and no mistake. Certainly no angel! Too cheerful by half and twice as brazen.'

It had taken all young Reggie's courage to ask Father Morrison about Jack. Surely if the man believed in angels, the miracles of Jesus Christ and people rising from the dead, it wouldn't be too much to hope that he might have some wise words to say about Jack.

Father Morrison rested a wide, well-manicured hand on twelve-year-old Reggie's shoulder. He guided him round the Garden of Rest with its bright blooms, each flower a flag of hope in a green sea of past lives and well-mown sadness. Father droned on about the importance of knowing the difference between reality and the childish world of dreams. And wasn't there a world of difference between myths and the gospel? Angels were in the Bible, and so they were real, Father Morrison said while holding a hand to his heart. Is that where they were real then, in his heart and not among the living of the world?

But little fellows with swan-wings who loved fun more than duty, well they were characters from other stories, and that is all they were, no matter how well the writer described them. 'And even if he were real, which he most certainly isn't, he would be of the evil faerie-folk who'd want to take you by the hand and lead you to another land, full of tears and weeping.' Father Morrison almost quoted Yeats and succeeded entirely in making the poet's meaning do an about-turn.

Reggie had trouble separating the impossible things he was supposed to believe, and the impossible things that were merely make-believe. Mum had told him Father Christmas was real until he was eight, and then she told the truth. How old would he be before Father Morrison pointed out the joke behind Jesus? Next year? Sixteen? Twenty-one?

'So do you understand now, Reginald?'

'Yes,' Reggie said dutifully while meaning just the opposite. 'But ...'

Father raised his head, slowly and imperiously, so that he looked down the side of his nose at Reggie. *The matter is closed, young man.*

Reggie ignored the warning. 'Have *you* seen and angel, Father?'

'I have not, no more than I have seen the Good Lord himself or His sainted mother.'

'But I *have* seen Jack, nearly every day of my life.'

'And doesn't that just go to prove he's not an angel?'

Reggie didn't really follow Father Morrison's argument, but he trusted him just as he trusted everybody who held a position of authority. He didn't for one moment consider that Father might be mistaken, but that didn't ease the confusion inside his head. It was as if his thoughts were being blown around by a savage wind.

It was dark now and the sandstorm was as fierce as ever. Reggie drew the canteen under his *shemagh* and tried to take a sand-free swig or two. Replacing the cap, he shook the canteen: more than half-full, but it wouldn't last long.

The storm finally blew out during the time Reggie slept. He woke to silence and sunlight and the trickling of sands down his neck and in at his shirt-front. Every movement he made set in motion another avalanche-in-miniature, but it wasn't the tickling sands that brought him to full consciousness, it was the pain in his ankle, and it wasn't the pain of the sprain either. Somebody had kicked him.

His assailant's poor Arab clothing stood in contrast to his immaculate Lee-Enfield rifle, its muzzle pointing straight between Reggie's eyes. If this man was a rebel, then Reggie knew he was as good as dead. Ah well, so be it. Just make it quick, there's a good fellow, and let's have none of this mutilation and torture that people spoke of in the officers' mess. Reggie felt strangely calm. With all hope fled what was left to worry about?

'I will ask you one question,' the man said in very passable English. To Reggie it was if the muzzle had spoken, he had no attention for anything else. 'If you answer incorrectly, or if you answer with a lie, you will die. If you give me the answer I desire, you will live … for a little while at least.'

And then the man asked his question. 'Did you send the fire from Heaven down upon us?'

It was a rather flowery way of putting it, but Reggie could not deny that he had rained machine-gun fire and bombs, even though his life depended upon it. 'Yes,' he answered, and before he could say more, a rifle butt hit him on the left temple. He had a moment to register the crack of impact before darkness and oblivion overcame him.

∞

They tortured you before ending your misery with the finality of death. They cut off your privates. They gouged out eyes, sliced off fingers and before this, the main course of excruciating pain and horrible mutilation, they dished up a starter of humiliation. Reggie had always hoped he wouldn't die a virgin, but in these circumstances the alternative was too grim to imagine. He imagined it anyway and shuddered.

The pain from his cracked skull throbbed and nagged and vied with the sharp stinging from his right-hand ring finger. The ring was still there, but the slick oiliness he felt all around had to be blood. It was hard to tell in the chilling darkness, dank with the airs of a sealed tomb. His finger hurt to touch. The skin was ragged and he guessed his captors had tried to steal the ring and drag it off his finger by sheer force, or perhaps they had taken a knife to it. Lucky Roman ring? Hah! He would have disposed of it years ago if only he'd been able to get it off.

Reggie tried to stand but his damaged ankle gave way. He stumbled and landed face down on what felt like compacted earth.

It was time to take stock. First, list the injuries, and then explore the surroundings. The situation might well be hopeless, but Reggie didn't intend to sit around and wait for his gory fate without an attempt at escape. Reggie decided he was likely to live, for at least a little while. His skull hurt like Hell. There was a bump on his left temple like a duck's egg, and a little blood where the edge of the rifle-butt had creased his skin. The finger was painful but the wound superficial, and if he was careful he could put a little weight on his ankle. So, to assess the possibilities of escape. Reggie felt around in the dark. His cell was small, no bigger than his old school's coal hole. He shared the space with what appeared to be a large, smooth boulder, its surface cold and glassy. With outstretched arms, he stepped ahead until his fingertips encountered a roughly hewn wall. He pressed his hand to the wall and the ring scraped as he explored the surface until his fingers curled into a recess. The fissure was narrow and he got his fingers inside until the ring stuck.

That ring, his lucky Roman ring of which he was first so proud, came to be a symbol of his failure and Reggie had often tried to remove it, loosen it with soap, wind it off like a nut from a bolt, but he had long since accepted it was part of him. Reggie blasted away the annoyance with a memory, and thought back to when he was sixteen.

At sixteen Reggie was no longer the happy lad he had once been. The filters of life had descended to taint the pure light that shone from within. So efficient were they that even Reggie could no longer discern his own spirit. He worked hard; he tried to be a good son, a model pupil and a good friend. Yet, and although he may have succeeded as a son and pupil, he didn't know how to be a friend. Until he was fourteen he had Jack, and now he had nobody. He was far from being a lone wolf, but he never quite learned to run with the pack. Everyone said he took life far too seriously and that all-work-and-no-play-made-Jack-a-dull-boy. Jack! There was that name again. Why couldn't he forget? Jack was not real. Jack had blighted his life.

There was to be a prize for the best essay written about the rise of the Roman Empire, and Reggie saw an opportunity to shine, and every chance to shine was a chance to impress, and if he impressed people, perhaps he might find a true friend. It was to be a timed essay, just like an exam, and the prize was to be a Roman *phalera*, a silver-alloy disc that may have been worn by a centurion or a legate, as a kind of medal on his breastplate. Reggie was excited by the prospect of owning such a marvellous piece of history. The professor was donating the prize and he was also on the panel of judges. Reggie liked to think this gave him a better chance of winning as the old professor appeared to have a soft-spot for him. It was subtle but the signs were there; a softening of the eyes when Reggie answered a question, the occasional light tap on the shoulder as he left class. Nothing was ever spoken and nothing ever so overt as to alert Reggie's classmates, for nothing could be worse than the sobriquet "Teacher's Pet", but there was an understanding between Reggie and the professor that spurred him on to greater efforts to please, and as a result he became one of the top history students of his year. They say fatherless boys seek a father in every man, and perhaps this was at play in Reggie.

Hugh Tavernstock won the *phalera*. Reggie was mortified. When the announcement was made at assembly he had to push his tongue tight to his top teeth to stop the stinging in his eyes from becoming free-flowing tears. He mouthed through the lyrics of *To Be a Pilgrim,* hardly heard a word of Dr Hudson's address and then felt thoroughly ashamed of himself when he made eye contact with the professor and felt sure the old man could see to the depths of his mud-stained soul.

A skinny little first-year barred Reggie's exit as the school filed out of the hall for classes. He looked up through round-rimmed bottle-bottomed spectacles and stood his ground only because a greater fear held him to the spot in the face of a line of sixth-formers. 'Please, sir,' he said craning his sparrow-like neck in an attempt to fix Reggie with a stare. 'Professor says to report to him in the staff room before classes,' and having delivered his message, he fled, lest sixth formers were of a breed that killed messengers.

'What've you done this time, Spencer?' Griffon Minor said, not really a question but a notification to the rest of the class. Other boys within earshot laughed, as was *de rigueur* whenever Griffon Minor said anything that was meant to be a jest. One boy, unsure as to the status of the statement, laughed a little late, and Griffon Minor angled a slap off the side of his head.

Reggie shrugged and turned to wade against the tide of boys.

The fabric of the staff room subsisted on a miasma of stale tobacco clouds and musty leather. The professor, as far as Reggie knew the only member of staff who did not smoke, stood by an open window, leaned out slightly and took a deep breath. 'Ah, Spencer,' he said, smiling warmly. He made his way across the large room avoiding the obstacle course of leather easy chairs, free-standing book racks and a piano with a goldfish bowl on top, wafting at the fug with both hands. 'If there is one thing I hate about the nineteen-twenties, it's the God-awful ubiquitous stench of pipe-smoke.' He coughed several times to validate his statement.

The professor had snow-white hair, several weeks past needing a good trim, and similarly white eyebrows that formed twin-manes for a permanent frown, that gave him a rather unapproachable appearance, at odds with his kind nature. He had gained a reputation for being an eccentric after Donald Meadley from 4F swore he'd seen the old man clambering drunkenly, out of the armoire that resided in the corner of the staff room. 'Maybe that's where he keeps his gin,' one young joker cried, Ever after, although only when out of earshot, the old man was known alternately as Professor Gordon or Professor Beefeater.

'Sit down, sir,' the professor said. It wasn't unusual for him to address boys so, especially if they had impressed him with an insight to their wit or handed in a particularly good piece of work.

Reggie brushed some cigarette ash from the arm of the chair and sat.

The professor drew up a wicker-thatched dining chair, placed it with the back towards Reggie and swung a leg over so that he sat on it backwards, both arms folded over the back rest. 'I wanted to say very hard luck over the competition. There wasn't a lot in it, you know.'

'That's alright, sir.' Reggie smiled almost convincingly, a past master at putting on a brave face. 'Tavernstock's piece really was worth the prize.'

'Indeed it was, but only by the very smallest of margins. And perhaps it is wrong of me to mention, but the vote wasn't unanimous.' The professor did not have to say to whom his vote had gone, for the answer was in the sad smile of his eyes. 'So chin up, old boy, and if you will permit, I'd like to give you this. Call it a consolation prize, if you will.' He opened one hand to reveal a ring. It was a black-bordered silver band with some markings around the face. The professor held it out between finger and thumb and Reggie took it.

At once Reggie recognised the markings, black against the silver.

'You will notice it bears each of the Roman numerals from the greatest to the smallest. I thought it very apt for a prize in this particular competition.'

'Thanks awfully, sir. Are you quite sure? I mean, sir, it looks very valuable.'

'A trifle, in terms of hard cash, but it is quite old, and it was given to me many years ago by someone I greatly admire. And now I'd like you to have it.'

Reggie's ears burned with embarrassment born of confusion. Was the professor saying he admired him? What was to admire?

The professor left the school soon after without saying goodbye, and that was the first time Reggie tried pulling the ring off, but it was already on solid and quite stubbornly refused to budge, despite his hurt and anger.

It refused to budge now and it was a moment before Reggie could extricate his fingers from the fissure in the rock. The warm sensation moving like a caress down towards his wrist was a sure sign that he had set the wound bleeding again.

He freed his hand and, in the next instant, it came into contact with another material. The crumbly-cold of gouged sandstone gave way to the ragged warmth of poorly finished wood. Reggie's suspicion that he had found the door was almost immediately confirmed, for a faint light bloomed, glimmered and then pulsed through a gap at the bottom. He heard the rattle of keys and he backed up and fell over before he was surrounded by a sound like pins and needles. It was so delicate that his ears strained to make sense of what his skin appeared to feel. Another effect of his cracked skull, he thought, and then the door swung inwards. The noise stopped abruptly and heralded a change in reality that Reggie could not understand, and then Jack's voice, oh God Jack's voice! Jack, invisible Jack, whispered 'This is not real, and yet it is. Jack is with you.' Reggie felt Jack's smile, and then he felt the gaoler's kick.

'Get up!'

Reggie got to his feet and squinted against the unaccustomed lamp-light. He held one arm between himself and the gaoler, the always futile gesture to ward off attack or danger. A gruff voice told him to follow so he did, along a tunnel that confirmed Reggie's belief that he was being held in a cave-system rather than a building. Escape would be that much more difficult, but right now Reggie's thoughts were on surviving the next few hours. He followed the guard, an elderly and grizzled man with an unkempt salt-and-pepper beard and faded grey robes, his *shemagh* held in place on his head with a limp circle of hemp. He had a curved knife at his belt and carried a hefty staff of gnarled vine-wood.

The tunnel was long and meandering and Reggie couldn't decide whether it was natural or excavated by human hands. There were side-tunnels, some gated, and occasionally the passage widened slightly into a small chamber, but Reggie had little time to take it all in because his captor kept up quite a pace. Sometimes the man he followed was swallowed up into

183

shadow, for the tunnel was irregularly lit by little oil lamps of ancient design which threw out but a little light.

There was a warm glow up ahead and Reggie hoped that he might soon be able to take the weight off his injured ankle. He tried to put thoughts of pain and death aside and to hope for other outcomes. After all, if his captors had wanted his death he would be a cooling corpse by now, and if they wanted him to suffer, there had been ample time to strip the flesh from his bones.

Death is hard to ignore when you almost trip over it. The tunnel opened into a large and well-appointed chamber, lit by several chandeliers each with a heavy burden of candles. There was gilded wooden furniture resplendent with winged backs, clawed armrests and lion-footed legs, all upholstered in faded red velvet. There was a general air of space and past-its-best finery draped with cobwebs. All this was guarded by a dead man who lay across the threshold. Reggie recognised him immediately as the desert rebel who had captured him in the olive grove.

'You must forgive us for our poor choice of agents,' a man said from the centre of the chamber. The speaker wore a brown *thobe* – the almost universal ankle-length shirt favoured throughout the Arab world – and a brown *bisht* or cloak which was trimmed in an over-showy abundance of gold. He was slender and of average height and appeared to be in his late thirties. Unusually for the region, the man was clean-shaven, his head was bare and he sported a short almost-military haircut. With dark hair and an olive complexion, Reggie thought his appearance more European than Arab, an impression that was re-enforced when he introduced himself as Bertrando something-or-other and proffered the grand-sounding if rather incongruous twin titles of Master of Effulgence and Wielder of Shadows.

'Our former friend could not reconcile his orders from us to bring you in safe and whole, and his own desire to rob and kill you. It seems he tried a compromise, but we are neither barbarians,' Bertrando said tilting his head to examine the

184

wounds to Reggie's temple, 'nor are we common thieves.' He waved a hand towards Reggie's tattered finger. 'Such disobedience could not go unpunished.'

The recalcitrant agent had been garrotted for his troubles. In spite of the horror of death, and the corpse's bulging eyes, something in Reggie exulted. This man had hurt him badly, so it served the bastard right. A wave of blinding pain shot through Reggie's head and he winced.

'But before we extend our hospitality, we must reassure ourselves of your credentials.' He stood aside and allowed Reggie to step over the corpse. 'It is clear you are a warrior, but is it true you are pure, and have never known a woman?'

Reggie swallowed and felt a hot flush rise from his collar. 'It's hardly a polite question to ask a chap, but if you must know, I am unmarried, and I have certain moral standards.' It was of course a lie. Reggie's purity had much more to do with the fact that opportunity and inclination had never quite come together, and on the one occasion when they came close, he'd ended up in a fishpond.

Bertrando appraised, tilted his head slightly as he looked Reggie up and down, as if there could be some physical corroboration of his statement. 'And neither have you lain with one of your own gender?'

'I say, steady on!'

Bertrando frowned but the guard laughed. 'That is English for "absolutely not", my master,' the guard said, and Bertrando appeared to be satisfied.

'There are those who say no truly pure warrior has walked this earth since Sir Galahad, Knight of the Round Table, but we shall see. I must warn you, that if you have lied ...' Bertrando di Pontenegro said no more, but cast his eyes pointedly towards the garrotted rebel.

Reggie's fingers flew to his lucky Roman ring, although he was not aware of it. As he worried the band around his bloody finger, he swallowed hard and with difficulty as if already trying to overcome a tightening cord at his neck. He coughed, cleared his throat. Nevertheless, he did not feel a couple of questions

185

would make his situation any worse. 'Must ask, but what on Earth do you want with me, pure or otherwise?'

Bertrando directed Reggie to one of the seats. His every move exuded authority and it was difficult to resist. Reggie sat and was glad to take the weight from his horribly sore ankle. 'I really can't understand what a virgin-warrior can do that an experienced one can't,' Reggie said. 'And while I'm asking questions, what's all this Master of Effulgence and Wielder of Shadows thing you mentioned?'

Bertrando skimmed over the details of the orders and just touched on the Cult of Bast. He explained how the First Coming, often called the First Shining of Bast, heralded an era when the secular and spiritual powers of the world were made subservient to those whose mastery was over magic. Unfortunately for the welfare and happiness of mankind, that time passed and the world was ruled, once again, by those with the biggest legions. But now the world was on the brink of chaos and catastrophe and it was time for the Second Shining. 'There was one other time,' Bertrando said. 'Ah, but we came so close.' He snapped out of his trance-like reverie.

On the subject of secret orders and magical powers, Reggie thought it best to humour his host. World affairs appeared a safe topic of conversation. 'You think Herr Hitler will live up to the fears some people have for him?'

'No, I think he will be utterly crushed by the Cult of Bast, but the Second Shining is dependent on immaculate workings and those in turn are dependent upon a pure warrior. As you might expect, pure warriors do not come two-a-penny.'

Reggie kept his mouth shut but worked his jaw to the fullest extent, hoping it would hide all traces of the smile that threatened to betray his incredulity. Bertrando was a lunatic, pure and simple, but he was the lunatic that called the shots concerning Reggie's future. 'So you need me to ... what? ... fight someone?'

'No, I need you to survive the Flame of Theodorus. If you have lied to me, the flame will destroy you and your life will end in agony. If you have told the truth, you will survive.

Think of the flame as the ultimate interrogator and if necessary, executioner. You will burn in exact proportion to your knowledge of the world of flesh.'

If this lunatic was going to start playing with fire, he might turn out to be a very dangerous madman indeed.

The guard ambled over to within whispering distance, as if what he had to say would annoy his master. 'Nobody comes out completely un-singed. If you have so much as touched yourself for relief while bathing, the flame will punish you a little. If your knowledge is full, not even your bones will remain.'

'Were you given leave to address the warrior?' Bertrando said coldly. The guard lowered his eyes and returned to his place by the entrance and Bertrando returned his full attention to Reggie. 'I will put you to the test directly, but first you will bathe and dress in more suitable clothing. Then you will eat and drink and rest.'

If he was going to burn – and if the guard spoke true and all this nonsense from Bertrando was a fact, Reggie was pretty certain he was in for a painful singeing – it might as well be on a full stomach.

'Thanks for that, I am rather peckish,' Reggie said, managing to sound bored with the whole thing. 'But assuming I survive your flame test, what is it you want me to do?'

'There is a legend ...'

'Ah, thought there might be.'

'... that talks of the pure warrior and his squire and how they assist Bast to his Second Shining.'

'Squire?'

Bertrando allowed himself the faintest of smiles. 'I have a good feeling that we shall succeed. You will pass the test and you and your squire shall create a bridge between the worlds, and Bast will come.'

Reggie began to protest that he didn't have a squire but Bertrando quelled him with a look and then told him to leave the chamber by an opening to the left of a dais in the wall opposite the entrance. 'You will be assisted with your wounds and be afforded the facilities to make yourself ready for the test.

As he was leaving, Reggie took a good look at the circular chamber with its high ceiling dripping chandeliers. He guessed you might just fit half a tennis court onto the floor area if only you could remove the irregularly spaced columns that supported the roof. The walls were of light coloured sandstone and in places there were designs and portraits of fantastical beasts. For the first time, Reggie noticed people other than the guard or Bertrando. There were five of them, each backed into a man-sized recess in the wall so that they stood like statues or silent sentinels. There were dressed like Bertrando, so Reggie assumed they were all of his cult rather than mere guards.

The floor was tiled with a design straight out of books on magic, but he didn't get the chance to study it in detail before the nearest of Bertrando's colleagues peeled away from the wall and led him through the entrance to a tunnel – more of a fissure really. It opened into a corridor with several doors off to one side, one of which was opened by the apprentice to reveal a comfortable and spacious bedroom. There was a figure inside, no doubt the one assigned to assist him.

As soon as Reggie crossed the threshold and the light caught the features of the figure waiting within, he froze.

'Jack …?'

∞

For an instant Reggie was transformed into the boy he used to be, but in an eye's blinking, Jack was no more. Reggie's disappointment was forced to wait in the wings because the solid reality that emerged from Jack's momentary presence was Daud Latif. The boy's face, usually so serious, lit up with joy that slipped under the barbed wire of Reggie's emotions. They advanced towards each other, and if proper decorum had not intervened, there might have been a happy embrace. They drew up short and shook hands.

'What a pleasant surprise,' Reggie said, and then his smile turned to a frown. 'I think.' The joy of meeting a person you care for in circumstances of extreme danger has less than a mayfly's lifespan, and Reggie saw a future where Daud was put to death for lying about his worldly knowledge. 'Daud, if they ask you about your experience with women, tell them you have none.'

'Oh sir, you are hurt,' Daud said. 'Allow me to bathe the wound. They have provided everything we need.' He gestured towards the bed where a nightstand was draped with towels and there was a jug of water, a washing bowl and a galvanised steel tub filled with steaming water.

'Did you hear what I said? If they ask you ...'

'They already have, and I told the truth.'

Reggie let out a sigh of relief, but then wondered if Daud might fall foul of the Flame of Theodorus.

'They said it did not matter that I was not pure,' Daud said. 'The ... immaculate workings, I think they said ... only call for the purity of the warrior. The squire may be a veritable flesh-pot for all they care.'

Daud's words seeped in slowly. Reggie had always assumed Daud was as innocent as himself. What was he, sixteen or seventeen? Reggie felt a pang of something. Jealousy perhaps; or a snapping of a thread he thought had bound them? He allowed himself to be led, somewhat dazed, towards the nightstand.

Reggie's discomfort and the pain from his head-wound were greatly relieved by Daud's ministrations. Clean from a bath and well-fed, Reggie quickly fell asleep, but he was soon woken by dreams of imminent events and the Flame of Theodorus.

Daud slept in a cot at the foot of the main bed; the proper place for a squire, he said, and took the position without any of the reservations felt by Reggie. Daud had put out all the lights except for two small oil-lamps that glowed in specially crafted nooks in the wall. Reggie swung his legs out of bed and took one of the lamps and padded around the carpeted room like Scrooge looking for signs of Christmas Past. These light cotton clothes would take some getting used to. He felt almost naked, as if he were dressed in cobwebs.

The door was locked. Ah well, not much of a surprise there. Reggie lifted the edges of the carpet, looked behind the nightstand and under the bed, but there were no escape routes to be found.

Daud Latif let out a sound somewhere between a grunt and a snore and Reggie held the light up to see the sleeping lad was alright. The last time he had heard a sound like that it had been over the earphones, and it turned out to be Dave Pullman breathing his last. Daud was fine, and Reggie smiled as he recalled an earlier time, and in the darkness, his mind travelled back. Daud had struggled through the door with a basket of laundry, and Gerry Barker was impatient to get past.

'Hurry up Humphrey! Shift your arse, you ugly little squirt!'

Reggie couldn't believe his ears. What rudeness!

The Flight-Lieutenant must have seen something in Reggie's face and felt the need to attempt justification. 'The poor little sod was self-evidently at the end of the line when looks were given out. That's a face only a mother could love.'

Are you totally blind? Reggie thought. He huffed with much more force and fury than he wished. Barker's comment was just plain outrageous and it had caught Reggie unguarded.

To Reggie, something wholesome and loving poured from Doud's eyes. His slightly hooked nose balanced his full lips with the underlying prominence of teeth, and his angular chin was a counterpoint for high cheekbones. His features, all of which deviated considerably from the accepted norms of male good-looks, should have made for something quite shocking, but instead Daud Latif's qualities transcended anything superficial, and in Reggie's eyes, and in those of any others who were not themselves superficial, the young man was quite beautiful.

For all his wit and charm, Barker was probably the shallowest man Reggie had ever met. Reggie had not yet come to realise that there is no such person and that even apparent shallowness skims over hidden depths.

Reggie held the lamp a little closer and willed himself to see Jack's face, but Jack never did work to order. A shiver passed up Reggie's spine and he thought he heard the echoes of boyish laughter tinged at the edges with that same simmering scintillation that he had heard, or felt, earlier. Jack was playing games with him, or far more likely, Reggie thought as he lightly touched the edges of the cut to his head, his addled brain was producing hallucinations. Sitting on the edge of his bed, he wondered if this whole horrible wonderful frightening episode was one giant hallucination, and that he was actually lying unconscious next to the ruined and burnt-out frame of his mechanical flying mount.

Daud called out in his sleep. What a loyal and resourceful chap, thought Reggie, guilty that such loyalty had led the lad into shared captivity. Daud had kept his ear to the ground and soon learned where Reggie's Hind had gone down, and then he journeyed on Humphrey Secundus's back until he came to the wreck, and grubbed around until he had run into a patrol who knew of a man who knew of a place ... and by a series of unplanned stages he had come to the Cult of Bast where it almost seemed as if he were expected. They took him and left poor Humphrey to graze on the sparse grasses nearby.

The next morning after a breakfast of bread and olives, Reggie and Daud Latif had a visitor. Bertrando di Pontenegro knocked and waited for permission to enter. He was accompanied by two colleagues who looked quite European.

'They are my Kindlers,' Bertrando said by way of introduction. 'They have come here by the Hidden Paths.' He explained that the Cult of Bast boasted followers in many countries across the Middle East and Europe and even a small number in what he referred to as the New World. Reggie assumed he meant America. Reggie asked another question about the Cult, but Bertrando had an agenda and he made it clear he would stick to it. He bade the young men follow him to the main chamber. They were shown to a pair of chairs. The rest of the furniture had been cleared away and the room was now quite bare. With the floor cleared of clutter, the designs thereon were easy to recognise, for those with the knowledge, as a cosmati pavement with an overlaying pentangle.

Once they were seated, Bertrando related one of the mysteries of his order. He spoke ancient words, which had been handed down through the generations, as if they were his own. 'It came to pass, 300 years before the First Shining of Bast, in the land shared by the Poseidennes and the last of the Homo taureans, a Power was invoked by the blood of a pure warrior –'

'The *blood?*' Reggie blanched. That sounded suspiciously like human sacrifice to him, but he suppressed the obvious question in favour of less-pressing concerns, not wanting to put ideas into Bertrando's head that might not necessarily be there already. 'Who are the Poseidennes and the Homo ...?'

'Homo taureans? I will come to that directly, but first you must forgive me my clumsiness. When I said "blood" just now, I meant it in terms of lineage and ancestry. Of course, the pure warrior's blood was not spilled in the literal sense, at least not by the hand of man nor until after his great unworthiness was laid open to truth.' Bertrando had apparently intuited Reggie's unspoken fear.

Reggie relaxed, although so precise was his self-control that nobody could have noticed he was anything but fully relaxed throughout.

'The Poseidennes were a sea-going Free people, and by "Free" I mean like you and me, entirely human. They shared what is now called the island of Crete with the last few of a Bound race, the s'tyradhrim or Homo taureans, who were mostly the same as humans, yet retained certain characteristic of the bull.'

'Minotaurs?' Reggie quickly wiped the lop-sided grin from his face, not wishing to antagonise the man who held his life in the balance. In spite of his scepticism he did not dismiss the idea out of hand, not even within the privacy of his own skull, for in a reality that included the Minotaur, there had to be room for one such as Jack. Reggie was willing to believe in

192

almost anything if it brought his childhood friend back, even for just one day.

'Ignorant people have called them such, although they exaggerate their bull-like features. The maids and youths of that race were often stunningly beautiful even by the standards of men, although they were adorned with horns and some say hooves in place of feet and the males were ... as are bulls in other respects too. The same ignorance now styles the magnificent Poseidennes as "Minoans", another variation of the same insult.' Bertrando di Macedonio's lip twisted in memory of the ancient slight.

'But I digress. The rituals were performed and the Powers were called, but the warrior was not pure at all. He had known women despite his youth and had fathered a child. The Powers in their fury immediately and utterly destroyed the city of Atlantis, which was the home of the so-called pure warrior, and as a consequence of that cataclysm, mighty waves were thrown against the land of the Poseidennes. The temple of the summonsing was immediately destroyed and all within killed despite their prominence in society and the warrior was among the slain. The Powers then gathered up the warrior's child for sacrifice and carried away from this world the last of the bull-people and, in parting, hurled a curse. "You who survive our wrath this day shall know such hunger that you will consume the flesh of your own children." And so it came to pass that the last four princes of the blood, three of them small boys and one on the eve of manhood, were killed and cooked with seaweed and shellfish to give their kin a few more weeks of pitiful life; thereafter, by pestilence and famine, perished the last of the Poseidennes.'

What a nice bunch these Powers must be, thought Reggie. He kept his sarcasm a secret and asked instead about the necessity for purity when, in a man at least, it could hardly make much difference and even in a woman, very little in the physical sense.

Bertrando di Pontenegro explained that the Powers' requirement for purity in those who summoned them had nothing to do with their physical attributes, but that the soul of the pure sang a different song, one of innocence and longing and calling out for knowledge. The Powers were able to perceive this song and navigate the Hidden Paths by it and thereby come across to the world of men.

'The rarer the purity, the clearer sounds the note and the brighter shines the light,' Bertrando said, his eyes fixed moistly to the most heavily laden candelabra. 'And there is none rarer than the purity of the unblemished warrior. So much the better if he has reaped life and has yet to sew it.' He thought it politic not to mention his belief that the light shone brightest on the point of extinguishment; having lied to Reggie about human sacrifice, he did not wish to revive the young man's fears.

When the blood of an innocent was spilled, when the life was cut short and extinguished by sudden violence, it bled light which illuminated the Hidden Paths and weakened the barriers between worlds, allowing the highest and hungriest of Powers to cross. This was the truth that Bertrando kept from Reggie, for a lamb was best led gambolling to the slaughter.

But before sacrifice came the test, and the test was the Flame of Theodorus, and the time was now.

Reggie and Daud Latif were required to remain seated while the Master of Effulgence and his two Kindlers made strange perambulations around and along the lines of the pentangle and the other designs. They chanted and lit incense in small brass bowls, and they threw dust into the air before taking up positions on the perimeter of the pentangle.

Reggie caught Daud's eye and raised his eyebrows. Daud just managed to capture a giggle by throwing a hand over his mouth. It was all so absurd and ridiculous, until the lights all around the chamber dipped and darkness gathered like a black chiffon veil.

'Is it just me,' Reggie whispered, leaning over towards Daud, 'or has it just got a bally site colder in here?'

By way of answer, Daud drew his *bisht* closer about his body. He shivered and his eyes darted fearfully in search of monsters.

The candles in the chandeliers and the oil lamps in their recesses were reduced to points of light, like stars in the night sky. Of the cultists, only Bertrando di Pontenegro could be seen, bathed in a diffuse, weak light that gave his body a hint of definition in the darkness.

Reggie reached out his right hand and found Daud's left. They grasped, hand to hand, and squeezed. The pressure of another live, warm human being in the midst of such a cold and surreal absence of sensation gave them each a little comfort, until the darkness burst into dazzling light and a harmonious murmur arouse from the Master and the Kindlers. Reggie squeezed his eyes shut against the assault as Bertrando intoned with honey-laden satisfaction 'We welcome the Flame of Theodorus'.

The exuberance with which the flame arrived soon gave way and it settled in the centre of the pentangle. The candles and lamps were emboldened by the presence of the flame, and lighting conditions within the chamber resumed their former level.

The flame itself drew the eye and captivated the imagination, so that both Reggie and Daud stared at it as if under a spell. Twice the height of a man, the flame was like the ghost of a real fire, a flame seen in the reflection of a pane of glass. It had presence without substance, and it did not throw out any heat.

'The time has come,' Bertrando said, turning towards Reggie with a gesture that invited him towards the flame. 'You will enter the Flame of Theodorus.'

'Will I buggery!' Reggie said.

The flame flared and settled. Bertrando's eyes hardened, and then softened with a smile. 'We do not force you,' he said with feigned affection. 'But we offer choices. If you enter the flame and live, you will have proved yourself worthy of great honours, and those honours you will receive in no short measure. If you enter and die, your friend ... for I perceive he is more than a servant to you ... will be afforded safe passage to a destination of his own choice. If you refuse the test, I will turn you over to the rebels, who I understand are far more

195

inventive than I when it comes to the subject of administering painful death, and I shall put the boy to the garrotte, personally.'

'You evil and wicked man!' Daud jumped up from his chair and ran a few steps towards Bertrando, but Reggie caught him and held him tight.

'It's alright Daud. I'll do it.' He released his grip. 'But thanks anyway.'

For a moment Bertrando appeared hurt by Daud's words and Reggie perceived the source. He was trying to save the world from a calamitous war. He would save millions of lives. How could anyone think him evil? If it cost one, or two or a dozen or a hundred lives to save millions, surely he was making a greater sacrifice and serving a greater good.

Reggie listened to Bertrando's instructions, which were hardly complicated, and strode for the pseudo-flame. He did not pause or pull up short but waded right in to the centre of it, at which point it exploded with a ferocity that far exceeded its entrance earlier on.

The flame did not appear to be hot but it closed in as if to consume Reggie's unworthy body, and then it touched and flew away from Reggie as if he were the core of an exploding star. Globules of fire burst away from Reggie, smashed into the walls of the chamber, brought down paintings, scorched everything it touched and hurtled the two chairs against pillars, turning them into so many smouldering splinters. Bertrando ducked a flaming ball, which impacted into a Kindler's shoulder and caused the fabric of her robes to catch alight. She screamed and the other Kindler attempted to beat out the flames. The chandeliers swung manically from their chains. Daud Latif was knocked flat but otherwise appeared unhurt.

Reggie looked down at himself and patted his body warily. There was no pain and no apparent injury. Bertrando stared at him as if he had somehow become the Flame of Theodorus. The only trace of heat came, curiously, from his lucky Roman ring.

'Does this mean I pass the test?' Reggie asked in all innocence.

Bertrando managed a stunned nod.

The only person more surprised than Bertrando di Pontenegro was Reggie himself. He had been on regular friendly terms with his right hand since the age of thirteen. Surely these transgressions were worth as many blisters as Confession had brought Hail Marys. The Flame of Theodorus, if not Father Morrison, obviously turned a blind eye to the fumbling experimentation of innocents.

But there was no time for Reggie to reflect on his good luck. A scream of terror echoed from a tunnel, followed by the hollow report of a single rifle shot. There was an unearthly, inhuman bellow and then the sound of approaching feet, but such a sound as only the devil's hooves might cause. Something was coming for them, and from the terror reflected in Bertrando's face, it was not something he had planned or anticipated.

Reggie stared into the black maw of the tunnel. It must be that he was so unworthy that a demon from Hades was coming to shred him to pieces. If it was his mind presenting this horror story to him he wanted it to stop, but if it *was* his head, then maybe another of those insanity-engendered sprites might be called to save him.

'Jack!' Soft at first, but then with more vigour, and more volume: 'JACK! I believe in you.'

The sound of the approaching monster became deafening, and it mingled with explosions and the piteous cries of humans straight from the hells of Hieronymus Bosch.

Did Jack hear Reggie's heartfelt cry? Did the boy with wings use his magic to save his childhood friend? Reggie often thought so in the times that followed, but why couldn't Jack have shown himself? Just for old time's sake. Where was the harm?

Whether it was Jack or another esoteric power, or whether there had never been a monster or a devil, it mattered little, for it was a terrified donkey that burst from the mouth of the tunnel, followed in short order by a man with a rifle.

'Humphrey!' Daud Latif jumped to his feet.

'Kill it!' Bertrando ordered, frothing at the mouth with undiluted rage.

The guard aimed his rifle but the donkey would not stand still, racing between pillars and around and in and out, while the guard tried to fix an aim without endangering the people who raced about almost as much as Humphrey.

At last, Daud managed to talk gently and Humphrey responded. He slowed to a trot and then a walk, and finally came to rest in the centre of the universe as represented by the cosmati pavement, where he lifted his tail and delivered a deposit that was as noisome as it was steaming. Bertrando di Pontenegro's eyes bulged with fury at the foul defilement of his temple.

'Please, sir,' Daud said trying to circle between the Master of Effulgence and the donkey. 'I will clean it all up. I will make it as good as new ... better than new. Please do not hurt my donkey. He is all I own in the world.'

Bertrando proved that he could move with lightning speed if the need arose, and in an instant he had Daud in a headlock. He dragged him to one side while telling the guard to shoot the cursed beast immediately.

A shot rang out and, at the far side of the chamber, a chandelier crashed to the tiled floor. Glass, candles and melted wax erupted in all directions. The donkey, terrified once again, bolted for another tunnel and galloped away into the darkness. Reggie looked rather guilty as he stood next to the guard. He had slapped the underside of the rifle just as the trigger was being squeezed and deflected the shot.

'Oops!' Reggie said. And then he shrugged his shoulders and tried, without success, to look contrite.

Bertrando looked from Reggie to the tunnel and back again, and then he pushed Daud to his knees. 'You had better be as good as your word, boy. Clean it!'

The guard began to mumble a profuse apology that he had allowed the animal to wander in. Bertrando had no ear for apologies but closed slowly and deliberately upon Reggie, who stood his ground.

Reggie locked into dark eyes that showed confusion at first, but then settled into something akin to admiration. Bertrando di Pontenegro smiled minutely.

'I have never seen the like. You must indeed be the long-awaited warrior, as pure and as brave as Sir Galahad himself.' And with that, the Master knelt.

'Steady on and all that. No need to get silly about it. I assure you I don't consider myself –'

From his kneeling position, Bertrando held up a silencing hand. 'It is irrelevant what you consider yourself to be. The Flame of Theodorus has judged, and having judged and fulfilled its destiny, it has ceased to exist.' He got up and shook Reggie by the hand. 'Such wonders we shall work. Such harmony shall we bring to the world.' Bertrando called some instructions to his Kindlers and the Acolytes who had appeared, and then addressed Reggie once again. 'Now I shall call for the Grand Master Incandescor, and tomorrow, perhaps the day after, your journey shall begin.' Bertrando rose, and drew Reggie to one side. 'But first I would talk with you, Reggie. Who is Jack?'

∞

'Who is Jack?' Daud Latif asked.

Reggie and Daud had two days to enjoy their honoured status as the Warrior and his Squire. There were assigned a grand suite of subterranean rooms, enjoyed the best of food and drink and were afforded every luxury and entertainment that did not involve infringing Reggie's status as "pure". The rooms – there were three of them – were well appointed with fine furniture and decorated with sumptuous rugs, wall paintings and marble statuary. Each was lit with a candle-laden chandelier. Daud retained his self-appointed duty as officer's

199

servant, but in that he had been appointed two Acolytes as servants of his own, his chores were light. With those few chores long attended to, Daud and Reggie settled upon the rug with cushions for chairs, and with a chess board set up with ivory and ebony pieces, they began to play.

Reggie began to formulate an answer that would not expose him as a complete lunatic, but that sound came again. He closed his eyes, and when he opened them again, he was back in the dark cell that he shared with a boulder and nothing else. At lease there was light this time. A small lamp sat on the levelled top of the black, glassy rock. All the comfortable furniture and fine settings had gone. Daud was sitting there, thank goodness, but he was in his rough and desert-stained clothes. The chess set was real, but of rough carved wood and not the ebony and ivory of a few moments ago.

Daud asked Reggie what was the matter, and Reggie told him. 'But Reggie, we were never in such a room. After they failed to get more than garbled nonsense out of you in response to their questions, they threw us both in here.'

There had been no subterranean hall either, and no chandeliers. They had been questioned by a grizzled Palestinian who bore no resemblance to Bertrando, and there had been no talk of missions, or pure warriors, or people with horns.

'And no Flame of Theodorus?'

'They tried to burn you with a flaming torch when you would not answer their questions properly, but just as the flame came close to your face, it went out. Just like that! Your questioner was quite startled by that, and said you must have the protection of an angel and that it must be the will of Allah, the Exalted, the Majestic and Sublime.'

Reggie touched the bump on his head. It was very tender and he wondered if the swelling was like an ice burg, with most of it below the surface of his skull, pressing into his brain and addling his thoughts. He asked about Humphrey and was relieved to hear that episode was based in truth.

'When Humphrey was charging along the tunnel, and we thought him an approaching hoard of devils, you cried out that

you believed in Jack. Is this Jack you called out to a deity?'
Daud had chosen white and he advanced the King's pawn two
squares.

Reggie picked up a pawn of his own but his thoughts were
elsewhere. He paused before placing it. He had never
mentioned Jack to Daud before. 'A deity? Perhaps, although
I'm not at all convinced he exists outside my head.'

'A personal deity then, or a guardian angel?'

Reggie placed his pawn and smiled, glad of the opportunity
to speak about Jack. 'Most would call him an imaginary friend,
but to me he was as real as you are right now. He always was,
right up until that last day.'

'Always?'

Yes, always. Jack was part of Reggie's earliest memory. He
was nearly three years old and he had been playing in the
garden with his sisters, Dorothy and Daisy. He was quartering
the garden with a wooden aeroplane held high above his head,
made to resemble a Sopwith Camel, the kind his ace hero
father had been flying in 1918 when he was shot down and
killed by German ace Josef Jacobs, or so the story went. Reggie
had never known his father and he was too young now to
know of Sopwiths or heroes or a German ace who'd had a bad
day. Jacobs always tried to bring down the plane and spare the
pilot.

He wasn't even old enough to rationalise why his little sisters
sometimes annoyed him, but he knew they could make him cry
quite easily. Dorothy, the eldest of the three Spencer children,
did so now by snatching his plane and throwing it with all her
five-year-old might over the garden hedge.

With tears making it harder to see, he forced a path through
the tight-packed privet, ignoring pokes and pricks and
scratches, until he emerged into next-door's garden, and there,
sitting by his upturned Camel, was a little boy of about his own
age and size. Reggie gasped, for the stranger was almost naked,
with just an arrangement of moss and leaves about his middle,
and Reggie was old enough to know it was rude to go outside
without your clothes on. There were also those strange and

magnificent appendages that seemed to spring from the little boy's shoulder blades.

'Are they wings?' Reggie said.

The boy extended them and flicked the air by way of an answer. Reggie clapped and giggled, jumped up and down. 'I'm Reggie. What's your name?'

'Dak,' the boy said.

'That's a funny name. Do you mean Jack, like Jack Frost?'

The boy, who had been crouching by the wooden aeroplane, stood. 'Yes, like Dak Fost. Do you want to be friends?'

Of course, Reggie did want to be friends and he said so, but before the small boys could explore friendship further, Miss Boyle, the next-door neighbour, scared Jack away. Miss Boyle was whip-thin and had a narrow, bird-like face. Her hair was drawn up in a tight bun, tight enough to keep in the heartache of losing her sweetheart at the Battle of Loos. She would never marry another. She would never love again. Her once kind and merry heart would never escape those bonds that squeezed it every bit as tight as the binding of her hair. Every morning she bound up her hair, and emotions, at the same time. 'What are you doing in my garden, young man?' she said. 'You've walked all over my sweat-peas.'

'I was playing with Jack.'

'Who?' Miss Boyle snapped waspishly

When Reggie looked back, Jack was gone. But no, there he was, waving from high up in the sky.

'Miss Boyle said you were alone in her garden, Reggie,' Mother said later when he tried to tell her about his new friend. 'If Jack was there in the first place, where did he go?'

'Jack frew, Mummy. He frew away like bird-tail-sticking-up.'

Mother picked him up and laughed. 'He flew away like a Jenny Wren? Very well then, you must ask him to tea next time you see him.'

'Not wren! Boy! And not Jenny, that's a girl-name.' Reggie screwed up his face into the simile of an indignant adult, which served only made Mother chuckle more.

'No, of course not Jenny Wren. I meant to say Jacky Boy.'

Reggie beamed. 'Can he really come to tea?'

'Of course he can. Now, will he need a perch, or shall he sit in a chair like the rest of us?'

This set Reggie pondering. Jack had feet just like a boy's, so perching might be a hard thing for him to do. But those wings would stop him from sitting back in a chair. The solution sprang from the river of Reggie's thoughts like a salmon at spawning time. 'He could sit on a stool!'

Jack was not the kind of imaginary friend who needed a place at the table, with his own knife and fork that would never be lifted, or his small portion of food that Mother would eat later, for he shunned all but Reggie. He would not be pinned down to a table setting or a seat on the train, or a room in the house. Reggie accepted Jack's mercurial habits just as little children accept most things, and he soon came to realise that Jack was his friend and his friend only. He spoke of him openly when he was little, but as he grew older, he kept news of Jack for an ever decreasing circle of privileged people, one of whom was Uncle Jim.

Uncle Jim believed in faeries. And he read the Tarot. He was a druid, some said, but for all his eccentricities he was a very cheerful and happy man, and one of Reggie's favourite people. Everything he knew of Jim's unusual interests came of Reggie listening at doors and from behind sofas and the more he heard the more intrigued he became.

'You know he says he believes in faeries,' his wife, Auntie Jean, said. 'But really, it's a kind of in-joke. He doesn't mean it literally.'

Mother did not sound convinced, and even at seven years old, Reggie could detect a measure of desperation in Auntie's words. He pretended to pay full attention to his tin car, and drove it over the intricate roads and bridges that formed the struts of the folding dining room table.

Later that afternoon when Uncle Jim had been banished to the garden to smoke his pipe, Reggie contrived to jump out from the bushes and shout boo at him.

Uncle Jim pretended to be frightened, and clasped a hand to his heart, as if it were about to burst.

'I have a friend and he has wings,' Reggie said. 'But he is shy and he never lets anybody see him except me.'

Uncle Jim let out a stream of smoke and chewed on the stem of his pipe. 'Jack, isn't it? I've heard all about him from your Mother. She wanted me to promise not to talk to you about him.'

Reggie's face dropped.

'But I refused to make such a promise.' Uncle Jim winked.

Reggie smiled. He had an ally here.

'Tell me all about him, Reggie. What does he look like?'

Man and boy ambled and skipped respectively to the gazebo and sat in the shade among the clematis. 'He's the same age as me but quite a lot skinnier, but then I suppose he must need to be light, otherwise he wouldn't be able to fly. And he wears clothes made all out of things you can find in the garden and the woods. He always smiles and he is hardly ever sad and if I am sad, he always makes me better.' Reggie spoke for quite half an hour about their adventures together, sometimes exploring the woods, sometimes getting into mischief, sometimes playing jokes on people, but all the time happy and laughing. Uncle Jim listened patiently and asked questions. Yes, Jack did sometimes get Reggie into trouble, but he never did anything mean or cowardly. Yes, he was real, just as real as Uncle Jim was now.

'Hmm, are you sure his name is Jack, for he sounds awfully like a little lad I know of called Ariel?' Jim tamped a moist hank of tobacco down into the bowl of his impressively capacious pipe. 'You see, often boys such as Jack have a Sunday name, or a special one known only to a few.'

Reggie was intrigued. 'Do they really? I shall have to ask him. But who is Ariel?'

Uncle Jim laid a finger to the side of his nose and winked. 'I shall place my oracle at your disposal. Look under your pillow at bedtime tonight.'

Reggie spent the rest of the day actually looking forward to bedtime. He didn't have a clue what Uncle Jim meant by putting an oracle under his pillow and half-feared he would turn back the sheets to find an ancient Greek lady with her eyes put out, waiting there to initiate him into Ariel-lore. He checked under his pillow at tea time, and again just after supper and there was no Greek lady or anything else under his pillow except Mr Finnegan, his green-shirted cuddly toy monkey. He looked again just before he had his wash, but when he came to get into bed, Mr Finnegan was sitting on top of the pillow, and underneath was an old leather-bound book with the floridly scripted title embossed in gold leaf: The Old Forest Faerie Oracle.

Reggie suddenly felt very privileged and at the same time secretive. Somehow he knew Mother wouldn't approve. He decided to read the book under the covers with the illumination supplied by his carefully placed night-light. The book was filled with the most wonderfully drawn collection of mythical beings imaginable. Each drawing was on a right-hand page, and there was a page of text on the left telling all about the being in question. It became clear to Reggie that each illustration was the representation of a Tarot-like card, for the text informed the reader how to interpret each card in a spread and how the import changed in accordance to the influence of the adjacent cards.

He flicked through the seventy or so illustrations with mounting excitement, but he should have taken the age-old advice and started at the beginning. The very first page showed a picture of the card called The Merry Guide, and the guide was one Ariel Cloudskipper. Reggie drew in a breath and held it as he studied the illustration. Done in soft pencil or perhaps charcoal, it showed a boy very like Jack, except that his arms were held crossed above his head and were bound at the wrists. There were differences, but yes, this could easily be a drawing of Jack.

Reggie turned his attention to the text and read slowly.

∞

Card Zero – Ariel Cloudskipper, The Merry Guide.

Freedom. Self-acceptance. Rising above constraints.

Ariel has the potential for perfect freedom. With his wings he can soar into the clouds. He is equally at home flitting through the forest dressed in the dappled light of the sun, or exploring the reedy river beds. He can go anywhere. He can be anybody. He can do anything. Which is strange, for his arms are bound. It is important to know that these bindings are not self-inflicted, but have been forced upon him. The bonds are responsibilities. They are duties. They are other people's attitudes towards us. We feel we can never be free because of this or that. If we could rid ourselves of these bonds, we could get on with life and enjoy it and be happy. Ariel's message is that nobody is free of bonds, but that we can rise above them and be free. We cannot escape them, but we can live with them and even come to embrace them. Ariel is always himself. The bonds may change. Sometimes they are tightened, sometimes slackened off. Sometimes new bonds are added, sometimes old ones broken. But Ariel is the same, cheerful, irrepressible sprite as ever he was.

Starter Reading

A shift of mind-set is perhaps all that is necessary. Yes, the bindings are there, but maybe they are bindings of the finest silk. Without them, perhaps there would be total freedom, but freedom to do what? To be lonely? To be a drifter without

206

purpose? Ariel skips lightly through the clouds, guiding us to a vantage point from where we see everything more clearly and to a place where the natural light is at its brightest. When Ariel becomes part of a reading, he is saying 'Hello! Look at me! If I can do it, so can you!' and then he is away, daring you to follow.

Reversed
Reversed. Right-way up. It's all the same to Ariel. He'll soon right himself and be off racing with swifts and house martins. But in a reading, there is a warning. You are perhaps, concentrating on the bindings, and to do so is to stifle oneself from the light. All the more reason to take Ariel's hand and let him guide you.

∞

Reggie tried to bend his seven-year-old mind around the meaning of all this and somewhere, deep in his subconscious, the analogies and metaphors made sense. There his thoughts would sit, like a seed waiting for light and water, but for the time being Reggie knew that Uncle Jim was correct, and from that day on, Jack had a Sunday name.

'Check mate!' Daud Latif said.

Reggie was shocked that he hadn't seen it coming. 'That's not fair! You lulled me into a state of lax concentration by asking all those questions about Jack.'

Daud grinned and flicked Reggie's king over. 'All is fair in love and war ... and chess,' he said. 'But what a marvellous thing to have, a friend who is always with you and never too busy to play.'

'Until I was fourteen at any rate, and yes it was a marvellous thing.'

'It explains why you talk of all this foolishness and rant like a mad man when our captors press you for answers. Are you not frightened with your talk of people with horns on their heads, and of you and me leading a mysterious power into this world from another plane of existence? Do you try to make me as crazy as you are?'

Reggie stood and stretched and then crossed to the black stone that served as a table. 'Would you like a little more to eat?' There was bread and goat's cheese, and a dish of olives. He began to prepare a snack.

'Thank you, I will forgo the cheese,' Daud said, blushing slightly. Sometimes Reggie wondered what Daud had against goats and goatherds.

'Do you really think I'm crazy, Daud?'

Daud did not answer quite as quickly as Reggie would have liked. 'No, not crazy. I believe in angels, and perhaps your Jack is such a being. As for the other creatures, I believe they come from out of the crack in your head.' Daud spat an olive pit into his hand and bit off a hunk of bread.

'It certainly sounds crazy, but if there can be a Jack and angels, why not people with horns on their heads, and other worlds for that matter?' Reggie put down his meal, his appetite gone. 'My head tells me it's all nonsense, but …' He held a hand to his heart.

'Reginald Spencer, my master and my friend, you are not a crazy man. Well, perhaps a little for listening to that invisible scoundrel, Bertrando di Macedonio. I think we should keep trying to find a way to escape. As soon as Humphrey comes from that tunnel, maybe we should make haste to run away.'

Reggie knew Daud was very worried about the fate of his donkey, but he did not show it as far as it was in his control. There had been neither hoof-beat nor bray of the beast since he had made his dash for survival along that narrow tunnel, the same tunnel that Reggie and Daud were soon to follow as they set out upon the next leg of their journey towards legend.

That light but palpable sound came once more and Daud's raiment became fine again. Reggie prepared himself for another venture into that unreal world that was becoming his second home. It wasn't real, but there was nothing he could do except play along.

A pair of Acolytes, who in reality were probably Palestinian boys with knives and guns, came to fetch the Warrior and his Squire. The Grand Master Incandescor awaited their pleasure. Daud snatched up a bulky knapsack and followed on behind Reggie.

This time the main chamber was completely devoid of furnishings of any kind, but the space was full. There were at least twenty people gathered and all in the robes of the followers of the Cult of Bast. At points about the outer circle of the cosmati pavement, the Acolytes stood in their simple white robes, and then a little closer in were two young women dressed in a similar manner except that they bore the image, woven of silver and gold threads, of a candle on each sleeve. At the centre of the universe, which corresponded to the centre of the pentagram, sat an elderly lady in sumptuously decorated robes, greatly adorned with symbols and chains of office and other gewgaws that Reggie supposed were meant to impress. That Bertrando di Pontenegro approached her with discernible reverence gave Reggie to believe that she was the Grand Master and could quite understand why the gender-adapted term Grand Mistress would have been wholly inappropriate.

Contrary to expectation, Reggie was not presented to her or introduced on a more informal basis, nor did it appear that he was required to take part in the rituals that were so obviously imminent. He waited with Daud Latif outside the circle and behind the Acolytes, until Bertrando approached.

The Master of Effulgence greeted the young men like old friends, and explained that their task was simple. They had but to follow the tunnel – the same one through which Humphrey the donkey had made his escape – to a small chamber at the end where they would find an ancient book. They were to take the book and bring it back to the main chamber. 'It is as simple as that,' Bertrando said. 'But do not try to open the book, because it is bound shut to all except those most trusted friends of Bast, for whom the book is intended.'

Daud Latif stepped out of Reggie's shadow. 'Do you trust us not to slice the bindings and look inside?'

'Daud! If we're not supposed to look, we won't. I'm just concerned we'll encounter more than your donkey along the way. Our task can't be that simple.' He levelled a meaningful, questioning stare at Bertrando.

'I assure you,' Bertrando held his hands out from his sides, 'there are no beasts or traps. You have only to fetch the book. It is the first part of your quest to guide the Powers to us and to secure a peaceful future for the world. And as to trusting you, good squire, I have no need, for the bindings are not the kind that any earthly blade may part.'

'Magic!' Daud spat.

'Magic, inshallah! But before you curse me once again for an evil and wicked man, let me say, if you do find your donkey along the paths, I promise to let it live. You may all leave here freely.'

'He mentioned "paths",' Daud whispered later when they were several tens of metres along the tunnel. 'Not just "path" but "paths". We should beware and look out for side-tunnels or branches, in case we find the book and then get lost on the way out.' His words reverberated sibilantly, like the conversations of a pit full of snakes. It made the sandstone walls seem sentient and almost sensuous. There was another voice carried in the echoes, and Reggie's back tingled.

'Do you hear that?' Reggie's voice was too soft to disturb the air sufficiently to make an echo. 'Jack ... someone ... calling?'

'I hear the walls speaking, throwing back our own words, but that is all.'

Reggie cocked an ear and held his breath. Jack was there in the dark shadows just a little too far away to see. But then of course he wasn't real. A fiction within a fiction. As always, as Reggie knew only too well, Jack was something inside his head, just like everything else.

There was just that one time when Jack made such an impression upon the world that his reality was hard to doubt. It was the February before Jack left forever, on a Cumbrian mountain called Saint Sunday Crag, bright sunshine over a blanket of snow, Reggie and Jack running and falling and rolling down, the thick snow cushioning them from the sharp rocks. It was as if they were the only two boys in the world as they laughed and played, threw snowballs at each other, wrestled in heaped pillows of soft snow and hopped, skipped and jumped down the steep slopes as if the rocks below didn't exist. Mother would have gone spare and kept Reggie in for a month if she knew how he was flouting all the rules of mountaineering. A sprained ankle up here would have been disastrous, but Reggie didn't care. The sun blinding on the snow and warm despite the time of year, the sky as blue as it was possible to be and without the merest wisp of a cloud, and the best friend in all the world: Reggie always thought of that day on Saint Sunday Crag as the happiest day of his life.

After a particularly vigorous and tumbling descent of several hundred feet, Reggie came to a splattering halt, spread-eagled on his back, peering up into the unsullied sky and Jack came to rest beside him in an identical position. Their fingertips touched and Reggie felt a thrill of electricity.

Reggie laughed and scooted a handful of snow that landed on Jack's bare chest. 'Aren't you cold, not even in this? Reggie said, holding some snow above his face and letting it fall through his fingers.

'Jack is cold if you are cold. But you are wrapped up snug, so I'm warm too.' And then he was up and leapt into the sky like a spooked bird.

Reggie knew Jack's habits and could read them like a master tracker. When Jack made off in such haste, it always meant that somebody was approaching. Two elderly gentlemen in tweed jackets and hobnailed boots broached a drift below and hailed Reggie when they noticed him sitting in the snow. They wore scarves high around their necks and caps to match their jackets, and plus-fours over thick woollen socks.

211

Reggie stood, brushed the snow off and wished them good afternoon.

'And a good afternoon to you too, young shaver,' the younger and jollier of the pair replied as he looked around the fell. 'And what a marvellous one it is too. Like a summer's day slap bang in the middle of winter. I say, where is your friend?'

'Friend?' Reggie said suspiciously. 'I'm alone.'

The man laughed. 'Stuff and nonsense! We heard more than one voice as we were approaching, and there are two sets of prints in the snow.'

'Don't be such a dimwit, Albert,' the second man said. 'The other lad must be relieving himself behind a rock.'

'Why of course!' Albert said. 'Well, no need to be shy about that, lad. Call of nature and all that. We'll leave you to it. Cheerio!'

Jack's bare toes made the lightest of impressions on a virgin expanse of fresh snow moments after the two men dipped behind a drift. Reggie was still pondering the fact that Jack had left prints in the snow that the men had seen. He shook such unfathomables from his head and threw a snowball instead.

'Jacky boy, you didn't have to go. You looked just like a real boy with your wings all buried underneath you in the snow.' He hadn't considered that even a real boy in such a state of undress would raise an eyebrow or two, especially in these snowy conditions. The white feathers of his wings, and the mosses and leaves that Jack wore around his loins in lieu of clothes, sparkled with snow crystals.

'Jack is a real boy,' Jack said. 'I'm real but you are a dream. One day Jack will wake up, and you will vanish.'

'Wake up, Reggie, sir,' Daud said. 'You've gone into a daydream, and we must have our wits about us in this tunnel.'

Reggie woke from memory into dream. The surrounding world was still ordered by his damaged mind. Bright sun on snow dissipated from Reggie's imagination making the dark tunnel with its inefficient lighting all the more gloomy. Happiness turned briefly to nostalgia and then loss. He breathed in deeply, let out a sigh, and returned to the here and now. But Jack had left prints in his mind as surely as he had left them in the snow on Saint Sunday Crag, unless the encounter with the two old hikers had been in Reggie's head as well.

The tunnel had been prepared with oil-lamps set in recesses at varying intervals of between ten and thirty metres, but the tiny flames that flickered were little more than beacons in the gloom. They trudged ever deeper into the tunnel for what felt like miles. Whether it was from pure exertion or the thinness of the air, they were obliged to rest often, and they either spoke in whispers or listened to the sea-shell echoes that gave the darkness a voice.

'It's awfully chilly down here. I wish I had my own clothes instead of these flimsy rags – no offence intended, Daud.'

'You do have your own clothes, for I have packed them in my knapsack, but perhaps this is not the best place to change.'

'Splendid! Well done, Daud. As soon as I get half-a-chance then I'll swap. Meanwhile, let's just press on. Yeugh! What the ...'

'Ah! I see you have found evidence that Humphrey was here recently. Don't worry, sir, I'll clean your shoes when all this nonsense is done with.'

Reggie scraped a clump of dung off his shoe as best he could. 'Look here, old chap. Let's have done with "sir" shall we? I must say I have always considered you more of a friend than a servant, and down here all the formality seems rather redundant.'

They shook hands. Daud Latif led the way and called out his donkey's name in a forced whisper.

After another stretch of indeterminable time that felt like hours, the light ahead began to intensify. The lamps were placed at closer and closer intervals until the men found themselves in a stretch of tunnel as bright as the central chamber with its surfeit of chandeliers. And then the tunnel emptied them into a small chamber with walls studded with white mollusc shells, like some seaside grotto, and in the

213

middle stood a lectern very like the one that Father Morrison used to lean upon while sermonising.

'Here is the book, Reggie. What a size the thing is.'

It reminded Reggie of an inflated version of Uncle Jim's oracle; just as ancient and twice as shabby. It was bound in cracked and musty leather, dressed with brass ornamentation and secured by clasps which had hasps for padlocks.

'No locks,' Daud said as he tried to open a hasp. 'But still held firmly shut. I do not believe in the magic of charlatans. There must be a trick.'

'I don't think you should even try, Daud. Let's just get the thing back to the chief pooh-bar and get out of this place.'

'You really think they will let us go unmolested?'

Reggie shrugged. 'Unlikely, I suppose. We can but try, and Bertrando appears an honest sort at any rate.'

Daud shook his head sadly. 'Reggie, sometimes I believe you are a child in the world, who might never grow up. I am glad you have me to protect you.'

It was true: Reggie was in serious danger of damnation to life as a Peter Pan figure, maturing in body only, while emotionally pinned somewhere between fifteen and seventeen. It was a dance in the crucible, and for any young man to endure the fire that raged through those years is a trial, but to live it for a lifetime was a curse indeed. If only he could sift the lies from the truth, the smooth façade from the rough-cut fabric of which the world was made. But Jack had made him believe in the unbelievable, and even now that he knew Jack was a projection from his own mind, he still found it almost impossible to know reality.

'Give me that wretched thing then,' Reggie said. 'You'll need your hands free if Humphrey happens along.'

The instant Reggie touched the book, the hasps flew open with a metallic crack that echoed back and forth from the tunnel, and he dropped it to the sandy floor as if it were a wild creature about to bite. The book landed with a dull thwack. It sent up a cloud of dust and opened, as if by some invisible hand, at a page about a third of the way through.

214

Reggie waited for the dust to settle and the echoes to fall silent, and then knelt, the better to read the page on display. 'Get a look at this, Daud. Can you read English?'

Daud knelt and drew his finger along the heading. He read slowly but accurately: '"The Seven Levels of Being ..." More nonsense, I suspect.'

Reggie wasn't so sure.

∞

The Seven Levels of Being

Levels 7 to 3:
The Opposing Powers of Light and Dark

Level	Light	Dark	Power Factor
7	Seraphim	Absolute or Prince of Darkness	10 x power of 6th level
6	Cherubim	First Hierarchy or Primals	8 x power of 5th level
5	Archangels	Second Hierarchy or Lords of Darkness	4 x power of 4th level
4	Angels	3rd Hierarchy, Arch Servitors or Arch Demons	2 x power of 3rd level
3	Spells	Servitors or Demons	Base power.

Level 2: The Bound

These are creatures of flesh and blood. Some have powers equal to Spells or Servitors. They include satyrs, Children of Minotaur, werewolves, selkies, mer-people, yeti, vampires and one-offs such as the Loch Ness Monster. The Bound are exceptionally strong by human standards and are resistant to

215

extremes of climate, pathogens and the powers of Spells or Servitors. They are neither inherently good or evil but the survival needs of some, e.g., werewolves and vampires, make them dangerous to humans.

Level 1: The Free

Human beings. They are divided into the Enlightened, who know of the Powers, and the Unknowing, who do not. The Enlightened include Spellherders and Shadow-Wielders who can control Spells and Servitors respectively.

∞

'Here,' Reggie said stabbing at the page. 'It mentions Minotaurs. And if Jack is a "Level 4" that would indeed make him an angel.'

Daud ran his index finger rapidly over the print. 'I don't understand these things. What is the Losh Ness, and who are the pathogens. And see here! Is this supposed to imply that spells are living beings?'

'It's *Loch* Ness – a huge prehistoric beastie that's supposed to live in a loch, a big lake, in Scotland. And pathogens are germs, not mythical creatures at all.'

Daud Latif shook his head and caste down his eyes. 'Forgive my stupidity.'

'Oh I'll think about it, Daud, just as soon as I speak Arabic as nicely as you do English.'

It took little to make Daud Latif perk up. 'My first language is Persian, and my Arabic isn't too bad. But what of spells?'

Reggie re-read the text. 'It certainly suggests that spells are a form of life. I suppose it makes sense when you think of it.'

'No, Reggie, it makes no sense at all, and I *have* thought about it.'

216

'But in the scheme of things, don't you see? If you allow for a moment that any of this adventure is real, then this page follows a kind of logic. Bertrando would be an Enlightened Level 1 who has the ability to order around a few spells, one of which must have been the Flame of Theodorus.'

'It all depends on the Flame being more than a simple conjuring trick involving flammable powders and hidden sparks. I don't believe a bit of it.'

'But Jack ...'

'Jack is different.'

Reggie did not get the chance to ask exactly how Jack was different.

'Hello, boys,' came a velvety voice that hugged the floor and made no echo. 'Nice book, now would someone tell me what the Hell is going on?'

Reggie was struck dumb and Daud blabbered incoherently. While his mouth failed to work, Reggie used his brain and tried to recall if he had ever known the correct etiquette for addressing an Egyptian goddess.

He didn't do too badly and came close to managing a proper conversation, but just as he began to feel comfortable with the girl who called herself Alice, she disappeared into the side of the tunnel. Daud raced to the spot where she had vanished.

Reggie ran back down the tunnel, favouring his good ankle as much as possible, to join Daud who heaved at the rock wall with his shoulder.

'I saw her! There was another tunnel, right here. Humphrey ran in too.'

Reggie could see nothing but rock. 'Daud, you should stop that. You'll do yourself an injury.'

Daud stood back and rubbed his shoulder. There would be a nasty bruise in the morning. He called out to Alice, and then to Humphrey but they did not hear and there was no reply: no human voice, no braying and no echoes.

'Perhaps we're being tested, Daud. Maybe there was no Alice and no Humphrey at all, and we are merely being tempted from the proper path.' Reggie inspected the rock for himself.

'We should get on, deliver the damned book and then ask Bertrando a few pertinent questions.'

'You doubt Alice was real, and yet you swear by a boy with swan-wings? You are indeed a strange one, my friend.'

'Jack and Alice were both every bit as real to me. So if Jack is impossible, why not Alice too?'

'And me? Am I here at all, or will I vanish like a djinn when you come to the sunlight?'

'The point is, you're all one or the other as far as my old noodle is concerned. It would make most sense if I was still lying unconscious in the olive grove and the whole bally tale is an hallucination.'

Daud Latif curled his fingers into the high collar of his thobe and turned it down to reveal the rope scar. 'Behold the sign of a mortal man. I can be hurt. I can be slain.'

'Doesn't prove a thing. Jack bleeds too.'

It was the height of summer, just before Reggie was due to start at his new school. He and Jack were eleven-year-olds and they were playing with a hosepipe, the perfect way to keep cool on a hot summer's day. Reggie's woollen swimming-trunks were soaked and drooping; Jack's herbaceous covering dripped copiously: they had grown a little bored squirting each other and Jack thought it might be a good idea to hide in the hedge and wait for a victim.

Sister Daisy did not join into the spirit of things. No sooner had the jet of water marked a deep dripping stripe down her summer frock and left her hair resembling a mop, than she ran off crying for mum.

'Well done, Jack!' Reggie snatched the hose from Jack who couldn't fly for giggling. 'Now I suppose you'll fly off and leave me to catch it from Mother.

Jack laughed some more, and Reggie hit him in the centre of the face with the full force of the jet. The winged boy fought the stream back with his hands and managed to catch a pint or two in his mouth. He swallowed but did not stop laughing. With the combined effect of bright sunshine in his eyes and water up his nose, he began to build up towards a mammoth fit of sneezing, but the first sneeze was so fierce, he smacked his head onto a fencepost, nose first.

Reggie had never seen so much blood, and he felt for his friend who was caught on a ridge between laughter and tears. He could see the funny side – absolutely hilarious – but it hurt, and there emerged a staccato mewling that was laughter and crying combined.

Reggie didn't know which way to go. He wanted to laugh, but his friend was hurt. He wanted to be sympathetic, but that would bring Jack down on the wrong side. So without much more thought, he hugged Jack, and told him everything would be alright.

'There's a hanky in my short's pocket. Wait here while I fetch it.'

Reggie arrived at his discarded clothing at the same time as Mother and big sister Dorothy, who looked smug and in anticipation of Reggie's telling-off.

Mother looked cross, but the anger in her face melted into concern. 'Oh Reggie, you're covered in blood. Whatever happened?'

Falling to his knees he gathered up his shorts and thrust a hand into the pocket. 'It's not my blood. Jack hurt himself on the fence.' He pulled out the handkerchief and dashed back to his injured friend.

'What a huge surprise,' Dorothy said as she came up beside her brother. He was sitting on the wet grass examining some spots of blood that ran in rivulets and turned rose pink against the green. 'Jack flew off again, I suppose.'

Mother crouched beside him. 'Where's the cut, darling? There's so much blood.' She ran her hands through Reggie's hair and checked her wet fingers for blood.

'It's not mine, Mum. It's Jack's blood.'

'Oh Jack, Jack, Jack!' Dorothy said thrusting her fists upon her hips. 'I suspect Reggie had another nosebleed, Mother.'

'Shut up, you big fat pig!' Now Reggie was close to tears. 'I wish I had wings, and I'd fly away from you too.'

'The only way you'll ever fly is if you join the RAF, like Daddy, and it will serve you right if you end up like him too.' She slapped a hand to her mouth, but words, like bullets, are irretrievable once launched.

'Dorothy!' Mother was furious. Dorothy had overstepped the line by a wide mile, and Mother forgot all about little Daisy's soaking. 'Go to your room, this instant!'

Dorothy's pugnacious attitude could not countenance the shame of her spiteful outburst and she fled, almost in tears. Mother followed as soon as she was sure Reggie had suffered no more than a nosebleed. Reggie was alone again on the wet and bloody grass. He wrapped his arms around himself, and remembered what it felt like to hold his friend. Jack had been solid and warm and real, and here was his blood. Why was it that he was beginning to believe Jack was all in his head?

'There you go once again, Reggie,' Daud said. 'Wake up! You're daydreaming.'

Reggie came back to himself once again. 'Where's the book?'

'Book? What book? Look, Reggie, you must empty you mind of Jacks and books. We have to get out of here. Just follow me. I am certain I know the way.'

5

*On Silver Wings & White – The Year 2005*AD

Ω

Alice Avery imagined that she was an Egyptian goddess. It did not require a huge effort on the 25th floor of the Burj Al Arab with its sumptuous marble and gold decorations, all in the ancient Egyptian style, or rather, a modern interpretation of it. A Jimmy Eat World song played through the multiple speakers, set low, almost as background music. She'd set her favourite track to repeat.

Alone at last, Alice took her time to absorb the surrounding opulence, the extravagant way-past-decadent luxury of the best and most exclusive suite of rooms in the only seven-star hotel in the world.

'Well, girlfriend,' Alice said to her reflection in the full length mirror. It stood behind a light, delicately carved occasional table just big enough to double as a writing desk, 'This ain't too shabby for a twenty-six-year-old sister from Dalston.'

'What would you think of me now?' played the lyric, appropriately. 'So lucky, so strong, so proud ...'

She sat for a moment in the Pharaoh's-throne-of-a-chair and tried to see past her own eyes to the soul below, while she worried a business card through her fingers. Such quiet times were a luxury these days, almost as rare as the rooms she occupied. It was all too crazy; one moment working for the local authority and gigging whenever she could at all the usual venues, slowly building a reputation and a loyal following of fans, and then real discovery at the Troubadour and after that ... the world a mere background blur to her rocket-like ascent. Was she still the same girl; still little ten-year-old Alice with her corn-rows and feisty attitude? Was there anything left of the fifteen-year-old who knocked out that low-life would-be rapper, one roundhouse kick to the side of his head, not for calling her jigaboo – insults from fools didn't even register – but for severely disrespecting and threatening her friend, Roy?

The micro-dress of metallic golden fabric covered little, but the heavy kohl and malachite eye makeup for the album-cover photo-shoot made it all the more difficult for her to see the girl she once was, and that much easier to be Cleopatra. Her whole lifestyle, mostly imposed by the industry, conspired to make her forget her roots, but she fought back. Most of the numbers on her SIM card were those of old girlfriends from Haggerston, people from university and family. Okay, so Timberlake, Leona and Dizzee were in there too, but you needed to keep in touch professionally. It would be plain rude not to.

Alice stopped fiddling with the business card and gazed at it. Her mind still wandering the old Hackney haunts, it took a moment to register what it was she was looking at. But of course: pure white, simple font, no decoration: just a name, 'Paul Spencer'; his profession, 'Photographer'; a telephone number, a mobile, an email address and a website. In this ocean of ultimate opulence, this moment of transient magnificence, the simple card was a solid island, an anchor to reality. She propped it against the vase of fresh flowers that graced the writing table and went to take in the view from up here in the clouds. She had almost an hour before she needed to shower and get ready for tonight's royal command gig. She was determined to put on a dazzling show, for after all, the prince was paying for this wonderful suite.

Alice took in a vista that included a seascape, a hazy impression of Palm Island looking like a pattern of bubbles in the ocean, to its left Media City with its Al Kazim twin-towers, and further round the needle-like Burj Khalifa marking downtown Dubai. Closer, almost at her feet by comparison, there was a strip of golden beach speckled with the blue of coast-hugging swimming pools scattered like azure beads from a broken necklace, and what looked like a giant marquee, reduced by distance to the size of a postage stamp. There was a pier too, which from this height looked like a crack at the edge of the ocean.

There came the sound of muffled thunder and a movement in the corner of her eye, almost at her level above the earth. It was a military jet of some kind and, as it flashed past, she thought of her brother. Simon would know exactly what that thing was, which air force it flew for and probably the pilot's name. Alice guessed it was putting on a show for prospective buyers of military technology, probably enjoying local hospitality on a floor somewhere below her, but she pretended that it was all for her, another present from the prince, who was as obsessed with her as Simon was with jet fighters.

And then a curious thing: she let the jet out of focus for an instant, and got the impression, from the corner of her eye, that it disappeared. When she flicked her glance back, indeed there was no jet, a fact that was supported by the sudden cessation of man-made thunder. And yet the sky was so vast and uncluttered, there was nowhere for it to have gone. Had it crashed? Was it no aircraft after all, but a meteor?

Alice shook out the frown. Trick of the light, distance and perspective: there had to be a perfectly ordinary explanation. The absurd mutated into silly and Alice was suddenly and powerfully glad to be free of the cameras and the paparazzi and the razzamatazz. She ran across the sumptuous carpet and launched herself onto the circular, revolving four-poster bed with her arms stretched out for wings. For a split second, a boy with wings flew with her. She laughed. What the hell was in her drink?

The anomalies of the disappearing jet and the flying white boy set aside, she landed in a giggling heap and for precisely six seconds, she was that ten-year-old once again. The musty draught of warm air with its scents of the desert and flinty tang of age-worn rock caused her to sit up, and yes, there was another trick of the light. From where she sat, it looked just like the mirror behind the writing desk had disappeared, and a deep red-brown recess stood in its stead. Alice cocked her head, this way and that, trying to work out what it was that the mirror was reflecting. There had to be something that made a mirror, when viewed from such an angle, appear to be an entrance. She sat up and pulled her high-heels on, all the time keeping her eyes on the mirror that wasn't there. As she pondered, a sharp gust of wind blew the photographer's business card away from the mirror, off the table and several feet into her bedroom. That the gust came from the direction of the mirror, or mirror-shaped hole, was shown by the haze of dust carried with it.

Discordant violins sounded in Alice's head; the Twilight Zone theme tripped across her consciousness: something was way out of kilter. It was as if an earthquake had affected esoteric dimensions instead of the topography. Alice stood in front of the writing desk, and where there should have been the reflection of her own image from an enormously expensive mirror, there was the gaping maw of a dusty tunnel lit along the way by ceramic oil lamps until they disappeared into the distant darkness. It was as if a hole had been punched through the marble wall.

It stood to reason that the polished marble was only a veneer, but the underlying structure should be steel reinforced concrete, not something that looked like it had been carved out of bedrock. Ah! The concrete must lie behind the dusty stone, just as it supported the marble and gilt. This was a false construct, an extra surprise for special guests.

Alice threw back her head and laughed. 'Very clever! I *like* it!' she called, suddenly believing it was all some kind of a celebrity set up or candid camera prank. 'You can come out now, wherever you're hiding.' The only reply was the seashell-like echo from deep within the tunnel. Alice maintained her cheery yet ironic smile with some difficulty. 'Ant? Dec? I am so going to give you guys a slap.'

She noticed, for the first time, that there was a golden bowl of what looked like marshmallows next to the vase of flowers. 'Oh, I get it, guys,' she said to the microphone that she knew had to be hidden nearby. 'I eat a marshmallow and go through the looking-glass, like a good little Alice, that it?' She plucked up one of the soft, fat confections and popped it into her mouth. Giggling round the sugar puffball, she moved the table to one side, careful not to topple the vase or upset the bowl of marshmallows, and stepped into the tunnel. The chill of the air conditioning was instantly cut off and Alice was cosseted in musty warmth. 'My money's on Ant being Tweedle-Dee and Dec, you got to be Tweedle-Dum, bro!' Her words were subsumed into the seashell echoes of the tunnel's furthest recesses, and Alice's mood changed. It wasn't funny anymore. No longer smiling, she stepped a few paces into the passageway, paused to examine one of the oil lamps, and went in a little further.

'May angels lead you in ...' from Jimmy Eat World, faint and far away. And then all sound from behind ceased, abruptly and completely. It was too weird and Alice wanted no more of it. She turned ... but there was no exit. The portal through which she had stepped moments ago was now a dark wall of rough-hewn rock. She pushed at it, but there was no give. She fetched a lamp and shook her head as she failed to find the faintest hint of a door. Alice experienced no fear or even disbelief, but a quiet re-centring of the self while she tried to evaluate everything she knew, or thought she knew, about the universe. These jokers were good, but nobody could be that good. Where there had been an entrance, there was the dead-end of a tunnel with nothing to suggest it had been worked or disturbed for years.

'Oh, now I think I'm beginning to understand. An LSD-tab in the marshmallow? You evil bastards! They'll throw you in gaol for this, and then I'll sue your arses off!'

'OFF, off, off ...' mocked the echo inconsistently. Until now sounds had just died. It had to be something to do with pitch, Alice thought.

After pushing at the walls and probing and knocking without a sign of the exit, Alice embarked on the alternative: she walked further into the tunnel, hesitantly at first, then as anger mounted, boldly and spoiling for a fight. She fumed as she strutted ever deeper and as quickly as her high-heels would allow. She held her hands balled up into fists while all the time trying not to think of monsters, because the LSD coursing through her blood would conjure them up and turn them into a reality she wouldn't be able to fight. Instead she contemplated slapping her manager who had to be in on the jape. She would rant at the next press meeting and then laugh about it all uproariously on the Jonathan Ross Show.

After what felt like hours of walking, her bravado turned to relief when she heard soft voices ahead. And there was a light, brighter than that cast by the lamps. She walked slowly and quietly until she came to the lip of the tunnel where it opened into a small, well-lit chamber. Inside were two young men who discussed someone called Jack while they squatted around a book which lay open on the floor. Well, the book didn't have red covers, so nobody was about to hop out and yell 'Alice Avery, *this* is *your* life!' She took in the appearance of the men and tried to assess them. One was obviously local, dark and quite interesting to look at. The other was European and vaguely familiar, a white lad and fit enough to make Alice think briefly of romance. She had a bit of a thing for white boys, a trait that annoyed her father immensely, although he never once took it out on the boy. He was politeness itself when she used to bring boys back, but it was a different matter once they'd gone home.

Alice licked her lips, and then made an effort to rekindle her anger and hide both relief and desire. 'Hello, boys,' she said. 'Nice book, now would someone tell me what the Hell is going on?'

The boys jumped up like startled rabbits. The white boy was transfixed and the younger one held his hands in front of his face as if shielding his eyes from the radiance of Alice's countenance.

Alice remembered she was in heavy, not to say bizarre, makeup. 'It's just for a photo-shoot, guys. If I'd known I was going exploring, I'd have worn something a bit more practical.' Her dress was little more than a wide belt and she was thankful for the Arab boy's gallantry as he draped his cloak about her shoulders.

The white boy relaxed and introduced himself as Reggie Spencer. 'You speak English. Are you part of our trial?'

'Who are you, ma'am?' the local lad asked.

'Who am I? Are you serious?'

They obviously were.

'I hope you'll excuse me if this sounds a mite egocentric, but I'm possibly the most famous woman on the planet. Where have you guys been since twenty-oh-five?'

'Twenty-oh-five? You mean … five past eight, p.m.?' Reggie said.

'Joker!' Alice said, making it sound as if the word ended in "ah" instead of "er". 'I mean the year 2005, fool!'

The boys exchanged confused looks and then the white one answered. 'But it's only 1936. I don't understand, and forgive me but I really haven't the foggiest concerning your identity.'

Alice shook her head at the whole, sorry act. It really was beyond a joke, but apart from losing her cool in front of millions of viewers – Where were those fucking hidden cameras? – she had no choice but to play along. Playing along was difficult when Reggie reeled off a ridiculous story about a chamber full of fanatical loonies and orders of magic. There was something about a mission and warriors to which Alice paid little attention, and one eye was always searching off stage for the crew behind the whole façade. The Arab boy pulled faces and rolled his eyes at Reggie's outlandish tale, as if his friend was insane. At least they weren't both spouting off nonsense. A tunnel and a cave system inside a modern hotel was nonsense enough for one lifetime.

Reggie though, he was good, she had to give him that. With his stiff manners and *I says* and *how-do-you-dos*, he sounded and looked as if he came straight out of the First World War trenches. And so buff! Apart from her thing for white, and she had a thing for skinny, and Reggie was both. When all this was over she'd offer him a part in her next music video. She could just see him in skimpy designer underwear and cool, top-name

227

shades. Shame he reminded her of old school-friend Roy though. Just like Roy, Reggie just didn't give off the right vibes. No vibes at all really, like he was running with shields raised, as her Trekkie brother would say. Ninety percent of the men she met these days could barely disguise their lust for her, and the rest weren't into girls, so it wasn't hard to put two and two together, and in this case Reggie put together with the Arab guy made a nice couple. Alice thought it was all rather sweet, but it didn't stop her hoping she might have a chance with him anyway.

'So you got your book, boys. Let's just head the Hell out of this place and complete your mission. Are we likely to run in to a bunch of skeletons or unravelling mummies or some shizzle like that? Because if so this girl's ready to rumble!'

There were no skeletons and no mummies, fully wrapped or otherwise, and Alice was trying to figure out how you could squeeze so many miles of tunnel into a skyscraper when she encountered a creature, not of humankind. Whenever logic failed, she always had the LSD tab to fall back on. 'A donkey!' she said peering down the side tunnel. She was rather hoping for something more exotic.

'Is it Humphrey?' Daud Latif asked excitedly. He began to run back down the main path as Alice stepped into the side-branch and immediately wish she hadn't.

Alice heard Reggie saying something about not noticing a side-branch when his words were cut off half-spoken. She didn't have to turn to realise another wall had insinuated itself between her and the boys, isolating her from the main path. She didn't bother to push or prod at the fresh, but seemingly ancient, new wall, and when Humphrey began to walk away slowly, it was only natural to follow. 'Looks like it's just you and me, Big-Ears. Lead me out of this place for heaven's sake.'

Humphrey did as he was asked and Alice's heart quickened. She notice light up ahead; not lamp-light, but cool, refreshing daylight. She kicked off her shoes, picked them up and ran the last few yards towards the open air. When she came to the mouth of the tunnel, she was forced to speculate that the marshmallow had been one big pure chunk of hallucinogenic chemicals, because there was reality and then there was what spread out before her in a wide, impossible vista. The BBC could do special effects pretty well, but they couldn't pull this off. Hell, not even Industrial Light and Magic had that much magic.

As she stepped out into the sunlight, Humphrey lost his nerve and trotted back inside the tunnel. She was ready to follow, but there was no tunnel. Only the giant water feature and the main entrance to the Burj Al Arab Hotel, with no sign that a donkey had been anywhere near.

'Oh my God!' a girl shouted. 'Look! It's Alice!'

Alice's professionalism kicked in. She chatted with her fans, signed a couple of autographs and posed for a selfie with each of the five girls who professed to adore her and her work. 'Just wondering? Did anybody see a donkey loose around here?'

The girls exchanged unsure glances and then all laughed at what they took to be a witticism they didn't quite get. Alice joined in, and made a gracious exit, hurrying to the entrance but remembering to blow kisses when she got there.

Alice made it to reception without having to engage with any other admirers, beyond exchanging smiles and acknowledging their happy waves. She explained that she had forgotten her key card and was swiftly supplied with another.

Once through the door of her room, the smile dropped and all pretence at having a good day evaporated. She leaned back against the door and tried to blink away those ridiculous memories.

Alice experienced several rapid mood swings over the next hour. Happy to get the stupid Cleopatra make-up off with gallons of cold cream, and relieved to get under a hot shower, she did well to keep her mind off Reggie, Doud and her impossible adventure through the looking glass. Amused that she had exactly the right name for such and adventure, and then frightened that it had all felt so damned real. And angry again, and determined to find whichever douche it was who laced those marshmallows.

She paced, and though the rooms were spacious, she always stopped facing the little table that bore the mirror, and each time she would look behind it and thump the wall. After repeating the cycle three or four times, her bare foot encountered the sharp corner of a piece of stiff card that lay close to one of the little table's legs. That white business card that she had played through her fingers before reality went crazy.

Alice picked up the card and read the name. Paul Spencer. Photographer. 'Shit!' Now Alice knew why the white boy had looked so very familiar when she first laid eyes. He was the very spit of a much younger version of the guy who ran the photo-shoot. She remembered thinking that he must have been a looker in his younger days. So that was it! The photographer had been on her mind when she'd eaten that laced candy, and her mind had cleverly made the years fall away from him. 'Hell, they even have the same surname!'

That was probably it, but 'probably' wasn't enough. Alice called her agent and asked if the photographer was still around. 'I just wanted to thank him for his work. Really professional.'

Paul Spencer was still in Dubai, and what was more there was to be another shoot the next day. Plenty of time for Alice to disguise the bizarre questions that filled her mind so that they seemed a little bit less crazy.

∞

Paul was an excellent director. None of that 'make love to the camera' bollocks that Alice hated, but clear scene-setting and confidence in the interpretational skills of his subject. Studio time was precious, and none was wasted.

The final shot was one where she had the opportunity to look straight into the lens. Alice appreciated the chance to study Paul's features. His face was so close to the centre of the lens she thought she could get away with it.

'Not my eyes Alice. Straight into the lens, please.'

Busted! Alice threw up her hands in surrender and asked if they could take five.

'We'll be done in a couple of minutes.'

'No. I need to talk to you about something. Can we get a coffee?'

Paul looked put out and didn't answer. Alice felt vulnerable and more schoolgirl than diva. She couldn't get that other Spencer from the end of the magic tunnel out of her mind. She wondered if Paul was his father and that they had both been drawn in to the prank.

The camera flashed, and Paul smiled. 'We can now,' he said as he checked the photo-display. 'This one's a beaut!'

Alice laughed. 'You crafty man!' She was going to say crafty old man. Paul had to be late fifties or sixty. A lot older than photographers tended to be in her line of work. He thanked her for her work and said goodbye.

'I'd like to take that coffee with you, Paul. There's something … It's going to sound stupid, but I need to ask you something.'

Paul baulked when Alice told him she had booked at table at the Sahn Eddar Restaurant. 'Chill, man! My treat.' But she wondered if she'd made the right choice as they settled into softly lit opulence. More marble and mosaics, soft music and a table in a cosy corner. '"Romantic" was not my intention. I hope I haven't given you the wrong impression, Paul.'

'I could flatter myself you like older men, but not ancient ones.' He smiled and Alice thought he wasn't half bad for all his years. 'I have to admit though. I am intrigued. What is it you want to ask me?'

Alice asked. Yes, Paul did know someone called Reggie Spencer. That was his father's name. In his nineties now, a bit unsteady on his pins and deaf as a door nail but mind as bright as a new penny. Alice didn't think it possible to squeeze more clichés into a single sentence. 'Are there any younger Reggies in the family? The guy I'm thinking about is much younger. Late teens, maybe early twenties. And he has a friend called Doud.'

If Paul had been sipping his coffee he would have dropped the cup. That's the kind of look his face took on: the mind so busy trying to make sense of the words that it forgets to control the body. His eyes might just as well have been hung with tiny signs that read 'Shop closed.' With a tiny shake of the head, the signs fell away and the shop was open for business. 'You mean David? When they met in Palestine before the war, David's name was Doud. Dad rescued him though, a story in itself. And then Dad was shot down – he was a pilot – and David, with the help of a flea-bitten old donkey, rescued him back. Then, despite a lot of kerfuffle, he got him back to England. Doud had his name changed. They remained great friends until David died of a heart attack in January 2001. One moment, he was laughing at the antics of one of his grandchildren, the next, brown bread. He was my favourite uncle. Well, that's how I thought of him, anyway.'

It was now Alice who ran on a mind switched to autopilot. But Paul came to the rescue. 'Got it! You've read his novel, haven't you? "A Broad and Ample Road"? The cover of the hardback edition is a painting from a photo of Dad and David taken back in the nineteen-thirties.'

That was it. It was one of her brother's favourite books. Simon kept nagging her to read it, and she may have got as far as the blurb on the inside fold of the dust-jacket, but that was enough for her. Alice was not a big fan of science fiction. She could recall that illustration though. Two young men, one white and in khaki uniform, the other Asian and in robes. There was even a donkey, for heaven's sake! Alice sat back, both hands pressed to her forehead. She wasn't going crazy after all. She started to laugh.

Paul caught the mirthful infection and joined her. Alice told him the whole story, and opened up about her fears. 'It was so god damned real! I knew it had to be some chemically induced psychosis, but man! I don't know what I started to think when you spoke about Reggie and Doud. Just so weird, your brain can't get a good grip.'

Alice decided she would borrow Simon's copy of 'A Broad and Ample Road' when she next stopped by her parent's home. She was overdue a visit anyway. To think that a tiny amount of chemical could take a picture she had forgotten seeing, and turn it into the next thing to living, breathing real-life people, it was enough to give her a flashback. Her anger over being duped and drugged evaporated. Her agent assured her nobody had dreamt of such a prank and he would be the first to bop anyone who suggested it straight on the nose. But then, who was the culprit? It was the only part of the mystery unsolved, and Alice let it go, so far as she could. She did a good job of keeping the experience off centre stage, but it was always lurking in the wings.

∞

Alice had a busy schedule. There was the usual round of chat shows to promote her fourth and latest album which had to be fitted in between the last two countries of her world tour. Then came her last scheduled gig in Tokyo, and the wings were no longer good enough for those memories: the ones that were too vivid to be the recollections of a dream, and too coherent to spring from a bad trip. The theme of the day for her fans who also happened to be cosplayers, was Cleopatra, not of the Nile but of the Album Cover. It was all she could do to own the stage, with her memories trying to shunt her off to one side. She only stayed for one encore and then rushed back to her dressing room. She did not stop for autographs. She did not smile for her fans.

'Cancel all my interviews, Tim.' Alice's mobile turned to a block of ice from contact with her agent's frosty reply. 'I hate to disappoint, but I'm totally shagged. I'm not exaggerating, so don't look at me like that. It's this or a couple of months at The Priory.'

'The Priory? Always good for some free publicity.' Tim didn't sound as if he was joking, and then he confirmed it. 'Babe, I'm being perfectly serious. You need to finish your

commitments, then you can have a nice rest. I'm not joking.'
He should have remembered who he was talking to.

Alice took the phone from her ear and stared at it for a couple of seconds, and that was all it took for the volcano to erupt. She said, or rather shouted a number of incoherent remarks into the handset, but the only phrase that Tim got, clear as well as loud, was 'You're fucking fired! And I'm not joking either!'

Alice was not brow-beaten into an appointment at The Priory, and Tim didn't have to look for a new job. However, he was reminded that he worked for Alice, and it was not the other way round. Alice took a month off.

She travelled home Business Class, dressed down, kept her make-up light and her hair in a beany. She was pleasantly surprised at what little attention she drew. She visited home, grabbed that copy of 'A Broad and Ample Road', saw a few of her old school friends. But you can't live in the same moment twice, and her friends treated her differently or in some cases, exaggeratedly the same; a forced sameness that did not feel genuine.

By the middle of the second week, Alice needed a retreat, and she managed a last minute booking at a little self-catering cottage in the Lake District. She didn't want to be alone though. He old friend Roy made for the perfect companion. He, of all her friends, was still the old Roy, and to him she was just Alice. Pike Farm Cottage was booked in Roy's name, and for the whole week, there wasn't a sniff of a single paparazzo. She had managed that very rare feat for a super-celeb of going completely off radar. And she loved it. For the first time in what felt like forever, she could kick back and be herself, if she could remember what 'herself' actually was these days.

What she did not love was Reggie Spencer's novel. The meeting in a dusty cave between the boys and Alice was described in exactly the way she recalled, albeit from the boys' point of view, and in a way that no acid trip could simulate.

Pike Farm Cottage was in the most perfect of isolated locations. A few hundred yards of the main road, which in itself was just wide enough for two cars travelling in opposite directions to pass, the view was the uninterrupted loveliness of a valley head crowned with mountains that caught the sun in the morning and turned to blue and purple and then black as the sun set behind them in the evening. Alice and Roy enjoyed mugs of hot chocolate while they sat out on the porch and watched the last of the evening light spill over the top of shadow-blackened peaks. Roy disappeared for a moment and came back with a big fluffy blanket.

'Let's stay here till it's gone proper dark,' Roy said as he snuggled up and threw the blanket so that it enfolded them both together. They had spent the day walking the lower fell paths and sampling the offerings of a couple of the local pubs. It had been one of those fresh, brilliantly sunny days that imbues the beauty of the place with an extra touch of glory and lifts the soul to dwell a while with the highest of those lofty peaks. One of those days you wish would not end.

Alice moved in to share Roy's warmth and give him some of hers. 'God, man. I wish you weren't gay.'

'God woman. I wish you were a boy.'

They both laughed a little. In truth, they were more than happy that each was a friend to the other, with no other expectation than that they enjoyed each other's company. It took a long time to get really dark, but even when it did, Alice and Roy had no wish to move. When it came, the darkness hid all sights from them, except for the glow of the little lights on the oven and microwave that shone like a pale green mist through the kitchen widow. The dark made space for secrets that would otherwise remain untold, and Alice spoke in detail on the subject that had troubled her for months.

'Do you think I'm crazy, Roy?'

'Only if "crazy" makes you see something that actually happened.'

'But it didn't actually happen, did it? Somehow I saw something that was written in a fantasy story.'

'Yes, but Reggie says in the foreword that it's all true.'

'And Doud – or David – says in the introduction that it isn't and that it all came from Reggie's imagination.'

Something screamed and made Roy jump. 'Fuck was that!'

'Haven't you ever heard a fox, town boy?'

It was actually a Barn Owl.

'So, Roy, what do you think? How can you explain that I saw the exact scene from a story I'd never read.'

'What I think is that our philosophy has a bunch of gaps in it that only heaven and earth know about. Haratio.'

Alice chuckled. 'Hamlet, the town boy production?'

And then Roy told Alice what he really thought. Reggie Spencer was still alive. The only way to put the whole thing to bed was to pay him a visit. 'Ask him what it all means. Maybe he dreamt of you at the same time as you dreamt of him and it all got transmitted through wiggly-schmiggly rifts in the space-time confluence ... or whatever.'

A bright star, more likely a planet, rose from behind the distant peaks.

'You should spend some time with my brother. Swear you speak the same lingo.'

Alice said she liked the idea of meeting up with Reggie, but that she had no intention of asking him what the book meant. 'I don't like it when the whole story is spelled out for you. I don't write lyrics like that, and I don't like those kinds of books either. I just need to know where he got the idea for that scene in the cave when he met the Egyptian queen.'

'I wouldn't mind meeting an Egyptian queen.'

Alice poked Roy in the ribs. They spoke until the mountains and the sky were as black as each other, and the only distant light came from stars and a faraway farm building. And then there was the occasional late night traveller whose car headlights sent beams into the night. Roy thought the clue to the point of the story lay in the introduction and the foreword. Completely contradictory as to the veracity of the story, the authors remained friends for life. Each capable of following their own truth, they did not seek to impose it on anybody else.

Alice did not agree. Reggie's foreword was obviously part of the story. He said the whole thing was true, but that was part of the story-tellers art. How many books began with a claim by the author to have found an ancient manuscript or the like? Of course it wasn't true. Roy introduced the concept of subjective reality. Maybe Reggie actually believed it was all true.

'Look, Alice, remember a dream you once had. Any dream. Go on, do it! Got that in your mind? Good, now imagine, say, a dragon or a sabre-toothed monkey. And finally, recall that day you flattened that a-hole who got in my face and called me a faggot. Now, in your mind, which is the most real?'

Alice agreed that the images in her mind all appeared just as real and just as misty. Roy pulled the rabbit out of the hat with a flourish and a big 'Taa-daah!'

'I'm not crazy, Alice. I know as well as you it can't be actually the literal truth. But maybe it's as true as reality to Reggie. Remember that famous last line? "And on the bad days, I think of Jack and forever live in the hope that one day we will meet again". Maybe we all need something to believe in. Something to keep us going on the bad days.' Roy shivered. It was too cold now for an old blanket and shared body heat to beat the chill of the night air, but not too cold for his imagination to provide some comfort. He whispered, unaware that his thoughts had formed words. 'A happy, mischievous boy with wings, ever on guard, ever watchful, always on the edge of sight. I can think of worse things to hook my dreams on.'

'Write a book, Roysie. But start tomorrow. I'm froze.'

The next morning the mountains could not be seen through the mist and rain. It could easily have developed into the kind of day that mopes through the fabric of the cottage to steal away enthusiasm and dampen both bones and spirit, were it not for the open log fire. It was a day for not venturing further than the local pub, and even then only for dinner. They did not stay long because Alice was sure one of the other customers had twigged who she was. She had deliberately developed a public persona and appearance that was very different from her own, but the subterfuge wouldn't work against the most

237

perceptive of people. Alice left right after the salted caramel dessert, but Roy stayed. He thought he was in with the Australian barman.

A hot chocolate held close, and curled up in front of the fire, Alice began to doze. The fire popped, and little fire people danced on the glowing logs. She would have sworn that one of them looked just like Reggie's Jack. The illusion brought her to fully alert. She decided there was no time like the present and found Paul Spencer's business card in her purse. Five minutes later it was all arranged. Paul had been surprised but glad to hear from her, and Reggie, who lived with Paul and his family, was more than happy for a meet.

∞

The best laid schemes of mice and men go often awry, and so it proved for Alice and her meeting with Reggie. Arrangements were made and a date set. The morning came, dull grey and inauspicious, just like those last few days in the Lake District with Roy. But nothing could dampen Alice's enthusiasm, not even the nerves she felt. She enjoyed the drive up in the little Fiat 500 that she thought of as her undercover transport. Eyeballed by a fan at a service station when she stopped for a tea, a wee and some petrol, she made the fan's day with a chat and a pose for a selfie, and made an escape before the paps mobilised.

The Spencer family home was an Edwardian six bedroom detached house in two acres of landscaped garden. With its twin-gables, it reminded Alice of the house she had put a deposit on from the royalties of her first album. The front door was close to identical. Nerves were high when the doorbell had been pressed, and various scenarios flashed through her mind, none of which came to pass.

Carol opened the door, flustered, spaced out almost. She had clearly been crying. Reggie had suffered a stroke the night before, and it was doubtful he would last another day. It wasn't his first, and he had been insistent that if he had another, he was not to be taken to hospital or put on to any medicine that would keep him in a state of living death. He was in his room now, in a coma, but as comfortable as it was possible to make him. Alice gave heartfelt condolences and turned to leave. 'Please, you've had such a long journey. Won't you stay for some tea? It's what Reggie would have wanted.' Carol showed Alice to Reggie's study, which she thought was the most appropriate place to wait for a fellow artist. Alice made herself comfortable among the book shelves and the brick-a-brack of a lifetime, and Carol returned with a pot of tea and a plate of biscuits. 'I'm so sorry, but if you could bear with us for half-an-hour. Some family business, you understand.'

'Of course. I really don't want to be any trouble.'

'Not at all. Feel free to browse the books. Back soon.' Carol ducked out of the room as if she were a parlour maid rather than the lady of the house. It was the aspect of fame that Alice hated most: it changed those around her.

The study had the right feel. Heavy mahogany table that served as a writing desk; leather bound easy chair and several rows of similarly bound books among the more modern editions. The smell of old libraries but none of pipe smoke or cigars that the décor suggested. Apart from the desktop computer and office chair, everything else looked like it came from the same Edwardian England that built the house.

Here, on the main bookshelf, was an illustrated hardback copy of 'A Broad and Ample Road'. There were other editions of Reggie's book, some in other languages. On the table was a deluxe edition with gilded covers. Alice picked it up and marvelled at how thin and delicate the pages felt. She went to replace it on the manuscript from where it had been, but before she let it rest, she became intrigued by the title written in fountain pen. Putting Reggie's book aside, she began to read the manuscript.

∞

239

The Angel in the Woods
by
Paul Spencer

I'd decided to go along with the crazy game, even if it led to my committal. It was a bright, sunny Tuesday morning in mid-November and I had two appointments: the first I was dreading as it was very likely to result in some notes on my medical record concerning my mental health. The second I looked forward to immensely, although, if it took place at all, it would only confirm my need for psychiatric healing.

Josh, my eldest, had left for work at the stables and sixteen-year-old Jeanne for school. My wife, Carol, was at the office and would by now be well into her daily ration of spreadsheets. Bodger the dog, a Staffie-Labrador cross, had been walked and fed, and the clock said a quarter to ten; time for me to head off for the surgery.

Thankfully the waiting room was devoid of the usual sniffers and sneezers and none of the four other people there showed any sign of being infectious. I was also relieved there were no noisy children dripping mucus over the complimentary magazines or crying because they could not keep the plastic bunny from the toy box.

'Ooh, he's got a syndrome,' the mother might say, and then reel off a four-letter acronym.

'Let me guess,' I'd reply. 'Is it NABS?' I would mean *needs a bloody slap* while endeavouring to come up with something less grumpy.

The room was neat, clean and ethereally warm and I observed my fellows discretely and with the photographer's eye. The elderly couple with matching hair of pure snow would make a nice study in monochrome. The rather neurotic-looking mid-thirty something woman had a face with a story to tell, and the skinny seventeen-year old lad in the jeans and baggy zip-front hoodie might be good for an action-shot with a skateboard – full colour perhaps, against a clear blue sky – well, maybe a puffy cloud in one corner.

The boy's eye caught mine and he looked away, quickly averting his gaze to the floor. It crossed my mind that he might be suffering from something embarrassing, like I had at his age.

'Not a dangerous condition,' the doctor had said. 'Soon put right with a minor op. Any trouble coming?'

'No,' I replied in all innocence. 'It's a straight run on the Number Eleven bus.' Looking back, I often think how well he did not to burst into laughter, thereby eradicating the need for an op as I would have dropped dead on the spot from terminal embarrassment.

Wouldn't embarrass me now, which was just as well, considering what I was there to talk about, and what I had seen in the woods. I was next in after the boy, and I was glad to see it was Doctor Szewszyck – easy to say but try spelling it after a couple of pints. I'm not so sure I've spelt it correctly even now, but you say it like this: Shev-shick. Cheerful old duffer. Laughs a lot, and takes his time. Never seems to rush you and never says take two aspirin and come back in the morning. 'Fit as a flea!' he once told me after a well-man session – blood-pressure, heart, and the usual samples – 'But that doesn't mean you won't walk outside and drop down dead! No guarantees in medicine.' 'Gee thanks, Doc!' The doctor rolls round laughing.

This time I began, after the usual preliminaries. I asked if there were any conditions that might lead a person to see something that is impossible. 'Not like in a dream,' I said. 'As real as you're sitting there, but totally and utterly impossible.'

'What kind of totally impossible are you talking about? I mean to say, perfectly rational people believe they have seen a UFO, but there is nearly always an explanation. Drifting weather balloons. Tricks of the light. That kind of thing.'

'No, Doctor; nothing at all like that and nothing that can be explained away.'

The doctor nodded and seemed to peer inside my soul. 'It might help if you tell me exactly what you have seen.'

I shook my head. 'Sorry, can't do it. Suffice to say it was not a dream. I was fully awake, free from any hallucinogenic

241

influences of a self-inflicted kind, and fully conscious. And yet what I saw just cannot be.'

'Hmm. Where did this … erm … sighting take place.'

'The first time was last Wednesday, in the woods while walking my dog, and then again this morning.'

'Faeries?' he said and I felt my breath catch. 'Not gay boys!' he said and started to laugh. He quickly stopped. 'Not that there is anything at all wrong with gay boys, but I mean, well, pixies, goblins, sprites …'

Carry on, doc, you might even get there. 'No nothing like that. I'm sorry but I'd rather not go into details. I just wonder if I need to see a psychiatrist.'

The doctor examined me; light in the eyes, reflexes – all the usual stuff – and asked me if I was suffering from headaches, blurred vision or a raft of other symptoms I suspect are indications of brain tumour. Nix on them all. He then asked me if I found my visions or sightings frightening, and were they harming me in any way.

'Actually, the two experiences I've had have been quite interesting and not at all harmful, except inasmuch as I accept their impossibility. I just want to understand why I'm seeing … what I'm seeing.'

He told me to take a careful note of the details of any future sightings and to make an appointment to see him in a month, or immediately if there were any other symptoms. I was to make an emergency appointment if I began to experience feeling of fear or paranoia or to hear voices in my head.

Seemed like a working solution to me. I left the surgery for a spot of lunch and then off to my second appointment. An appointment with an impossible being: if it – or he – was there it would be my third impossible meeting.

It is probably about time I told you about my first encounter. It was the day before, and I'd been walking Bodger in the woods and fields just outside town. It had been a very dry autumn so far and the ground underfoot was soft where in previous years it had been a muddy bog. It was about half-past eight and the walk had started under high cloud cover, but now the sun was peeping through. Bodger liked to run up ahead of me on the path, and sometimes off the path and into the undergrowth. Every now and again he would hang back just to make sure I was keeping up. There was a stiff breeze and it was cold and crisp, but not freezing. When the sun broke out it actually felt quite warm for the time of year, and when we came to the path that followed the line of a hedgerow between two fields and joined the small, scrubby copse with the larger, denser quite forest-like wood, the low sun slanted into my eyes. I pulled my collar up against the wind and put on a brisk stride, gorse bushes on my left and a barbed-wire fence on my right to keep the cows from wandering.

It really was a beautiful autumn day and I paused by a wooden fence-post. I leaned on the post with my eyes closed and face to the sun so that it shone through my eyelids, bright and blood-stained in its cheery effulgence. I recalled the first time I had encountered that word: it was in the *Bhagavad-Gita*. Effulgence. Efff-fulll-gence. What a lovely word, so full and fat and pregnant with dazzling light. I felt a smile spread wide across my face and imagined Krishna and Arjuna riding their fiery chariot across the heavens.

Bodger whimpered and my feet. *No time for all this indulgence in effulgence,* he appeared to say. *My breakfast is waiting!*

'Okay, I get the message, Bodger. Off we go!' and hearing just what he wanted, Bodger ran off towards the woods, my trusty vanguard. A little further and the path cuts into the woods. I then realised the wind was stronger than I had believed. It stirred up quite a racket, whipping at the dry leaves into a noisy frenzy and leading the trees in a furious dance. Trees fall down in such conditions. Walking a dog through the woods on a day like that was not a very good idea. I wondered if I should turn back, but decided to risk it.

The path wound through the woods, sometimes hard to follow due to the fresh leaf-fall, and the overhanging branches of many trees that necessitated much ducking and sidestepping – on a normal day, that is. As I came to the first overhanging branch, the wind caught it and lifted it high. I passed

243

underneath, chuckled, and said thank you to the wind and the tree. For the record, I am no tree-hugger, but on my own in the woods I am prone to exercise my sense of humour. As soon as I passed, the wind dipped and the branch dropped low as if saying *You're welcome!* I was immensely amused when the same thing happened at the next overhang, and a little spooked at the third. At the fourth I raised my hand towards the branch as if I were possessed of a wizard's power; my jaw dropped as the branch neatly complied, and fell once I was safe beyond, just as I lowered my hand. Over the next few hundred yards of path I must have encountered a dozen more overhanging branches, and each one rose to let me pass without ducking. I laughed out loud at the power of coincidence and wished Carol was here to witness it.

The spell was broken when Bodger came back and sat in front of me, doing that thing with his eyes that meant *Please Daddy can I have another biscuit?* I had stopped right underneath a branch that had obediently and politely lifted itself. But politeness has a limit, and just as I dropped the treat for Bodger to snap up out of the air, the branch came down from the air, thwacked my shoulder and enveloped me in twigs and dead leaves. *That'll learn you!* it said, only of course, it didn't.

I carried on, the trees now taller and more mature. There was beech and oak and large clumps of holly. The path became better defined, bordered by ranks of dying bracken and an entangled sea of bramble. The air was heavy with the scent of leaf-mould and decaying wood. Suddenly, from somewhere up ahead and out of sight due to the curve of the path and the thick mass of bramble, Bodger yelped, a somewhat pathetic noise for a usually robust and fearless dog. He ran back to me, whimpered, and turning shot off out of sight again. I followed, wondering if he had come upon a dead stag. Perhaps another walker and a scary dog were approaching from the other direction. I rounded the bend and froze.

Sitting on the tree-stump I often used as a seat while I rested and caught my breath, was a naked youth – well, naked except for what looked like a loincloth made from bracken, that is. I pulled up short, but in that first moment of seeing him I gleaned that he had the build of a fourteen or fifteen-year-old. A tad older perhaps, but certainly younger than Josh, my seventeen-year-old son. His head was partially hidden by a low branch and he was half-obscured by brambles and dead bracken, but the growth was sparse so I could make out his pale skin through the weave of prickly stems.

My first thought was to retreat as discretely as possible and make my way back the way I came. But why should I? I became rather indignant, and then a little embarrassed. But why should I be the one who felt embarrassed, and why should I turn back on account of a youth who was into a spot of inappropriate naturism? Strangely, it did not once occur to me that he might be a dangerous pervert in the making. They all have to start somewhere and running around naked in the woods surely indicated a certain frame of mind.

I walked back round the curve of the path and made a point of calling out for the dog. I waited just enough time for the young man to either run off into the undergrowth or adjust his clothes, i.e., gather them up and put them on, and then I stomped back, still calling for the dog in quite an exaggerated way. The cheeky little man was still sitting there nude, only now he looked towards me and managed a shy smile. I got a fleeting impression of white smoke billowing around behind him. I put it down to a trick of the light. Wrong!

Damn him all the way to Hell! I put on quite a stride and approached him feeling angry but determined to carry on as if he were doing no more than enjoying a crafty cigarette. I would have to pass within a foot of him, but that was his look-out.

What I saw next froze part of my brain into a kind of inactive torpor. I suppose it is correct to say that we are all very much the sum of our experiences, and our reactions are governed by them. If we encounter a situation we have never before experienced, we often falter. Well, it is not every day you take your dog for a walk and meet a lad who likes a bit of

245

al fresco nudity fully occupied in his sport of choice. There isn't a proper response to that, is there? I'm sure Debrett's doesn't cover it and it doesn't feature in the FAQ section of any website I've ever heard about. I decided to extrapolate: when someone passes noisy wind in public, the correct etiquette, for both the perpetrator (with proper emphasis on the "perp") and the witnesses, is to pretend that nothing at all has happened. That would be my lead. I would walk straight on by and act as if nothing out of the ordinary was going on. I might even venture a cheery 'good morning' and affect a knowing wink. No! Cancel the wink; he might see it as some sort of a come-on.

As soon as I was close enough for my line of sight to clear the overhanging branch and the brambles, I couldn't help but notice that the young man did not have the usual physiology of any young man you might encounter outside mythology and religious fiction. His smile was open enough. Too open in view of his state of undress and the position of one of his hands. He had good looks and a lightly muscled body of which all but the most dedicated iron-pumping teens would be proud. But it was the wings that set him apart.

The wings. Shall I say it again? Sorry, but I must, if only to remind myself how bizarre it all was. He had a massive pair of white-feathered wings.

I can't imagine how they escaped my notice in the first place, despite the overhanging branches. Sitting before me in apparent carnal contemplation was a young angel. Yes, you did hear me correctly. To all intents and purposes, the young man sitting on my tree stump was a creature straight out of legend. Was the Bible true, after all? Call in the approved social worker and the psychiatric specialist. Don't bother to humour me. I know you think I am crazy. I thought so myself at the time.

I suppose I stared a little too rudely. And then I fixed my eyes deliberately on the plaid of browns and greens that was spread over the tree-stump.

246

'Excuse me,' the young man said in a very public schoolboy voice. 'But I'm rather busy at the moment. Do you mind?'

With the part of my brain that makes sense of the world suddenly closed down for repairs, I had only the reflexive portions left. I apologised for the intrusion and warned him that he was likely to catch his death of cold and continued on my way, all movement and thought on automatic pilot.

A hundred or so yards along the path, Bodger leapt out from a stand of holly and sat down expectantly for a treat. I'd forgotten I even had a dog and I looked down at him for some moments, trying to work out what he wanted. An impatient little yap brought me, at least some way, back to my senses.

'Did you see ...?' I began, thumbing over my shoulder. I was never one for talking to my dog. That frozen part of my brain started the thaw, and little sparks of reason tried to ignite an idea that would burn away the impossibility of what I had just seen. It was a costume. A very elaborate and professionally executed one, but a costume nevertheless. Of course! But I hadn't seen the joins. The pinions that sprang from the boy's back seemed melded to his skin. The underlying skeletal support appeared to move seamlessly from shoulder blade to wing-root, and caused ripples in the overlying flesh that CGI might accomplish, but no stuck-on device ever could. The movement of those massive appendages was too smooth and delicate to have been effected by machinery. There – were – no – strings! Nevertheless, some form of amazing special effect had to be the most likely of possibilities. I decided to go back and ask him. Surely by now he would have completed the job in hand.

I stomped and whistled my way back down the path, noise as my herald. Coming out through the low growing holly and rounding the bend, I was disappointed to see that the mysterious angel-boy was no longer there. Disappointed and a little relieved, but disappointment definitely held the moment.

Back by the stump I looked for signs or marks in the soft, slightly muddy earth, but there were none. However, he had left a mark of another kind. There was a feather caught in a thatch of mistletoe that held to a low-hanging branch. For a brief moment of insanity I considered the possibility of sending it off to a lab for analysis. 'Please analyse the object contained within. It fell off a near-naked boy. I think it might be an angel's feather,' to which I immediately imagined the reply. 'Thank you, sir. Please report to the psychiatric department of your local hospital. Take your toothbrush and pyjamas. And if you pass a police station on the way, please pop in and sign the sex-offenders register.' So, it was a stillborn thought. Apart from anything else, I hadn't a clue what laboratories would offer such a service. I put the feather in my hunter's pocket. It was a good fit.

I continued the walk in somewhat of a daze, groping at this and that explanation for my apparent encounter. It was when I leant on the kissing-gate to the gorse path that the thought first occurred. Maybe I had experience some kind of a psychotic episode. Some people heard voices in their heads, I met angels in the woods. And the fact that he was displaying a complete lack of modesty was just another indication that some deep rooted memory from my past was clamouring for the light of day.

Memories of real events and of those imagined are hardly any different when recalled from a distance of time. So it was that after I had got home, wiped Bodger's paws and made myself a cup of tea, the whole episode began to submit to reason. I had imagined the whole thing. Good in theory, but it didn't quite explain the white feather that was still in the pocket of my waxed jacket. I slid my hand into the pocket, expecting to find nothing, but there it was. It was there and it was as real, and even whiter than the hairs on my own head.

Luckily I had no clients that day. It was an admin day but the admin didn't get done. Instead I spent all day on the computer researching angels. I also researched various kinds of mental illness associated with visions and hallucinations. By the time Carol got home, I had found a lab to analyse the wing, made a non-emergency appointment for the doctor for the following Tuesday and read hundreds of pages about mythology and mental illness. Quite productive, but not to Carol's way of thinking, because I had done no admin, forgotten to put the washing in the tumble dryer and there was no dinner ready. I took her wrath like a man. Truth of the matter is, her tirade was screened out like everything else that day. Nothing could quite compete with my early morning encounter.

I had no such encounter on the following day, nor the next or the one after that. Each time I walked to the old tree-stump via a path which was deep in the wood and not a favourite with other walkers. In places the path was grown over and it was indistinct for much of the half-mile detour from the more popular routes. I always dawdled a hundred yards or so either side of the stump, and then paused for a long while when I drew close to it. Bodger rooted around but did not appear to pick up any interesting scents.

On the Sunday, Carol came with me. We were chatting about something but I hushed her up when we neared the stump. 'We might see something interesting,' I said.

The stump was soaked through by the previous night's downpour and darker than usual, being so waterlogged. The flat surface that made such a good seat was covered in fallen leaves. I cleared them with a sweep of my hand, and stood, peering into the undergrowth. Nothing, and nothing on Monday either. I considered cancelling my appointment with the doctor and putting the whole thing down to a random aberration of the psyche, but then came Tuesday.

It was another bright morning, but colder than before. I came to the stump with my expectations not as high as on previous days. I hated the thought of facing the doctor and determined to give it one more try. Bodger appeared more excited than usual and dashed off the path into the undergrowth.

'Hello! Angel-boy,' I called, something half-way between raised voice and stunted shout.

'My name is Jack,' came a voice from behind. The impossible young man stood waist-high in dead bracken several yards off the path. 'And I am no more an angel-boy than you!' He was still virtually nude, but this time he looked ill-kempt and dirty.

'For God's sake, you'll catch your death of cold,' I said, my brain screening out everything he said. All I could think about was that the lad was probably close to succumbing to hypothermia.

'What a kind soul you are! Again you are concerned for my comforts, but there is no need. I assure you I am not overly troubled by the cold.' He peered up into the grey sky. 'The wet, though ...'

'Haven't you got anything to wear? The blanket I saw last time ...'

He pointed to a stand of bracken behind him, weighted down by the soaking plaid, spread out to dry as best it could.

'Where are you from?'

He sighed and waved a non-committal hand around the air. 'The other place. Past the veils and the Hidden Path.'

I was beginning to enjoy this. I hadn't read a good fantasy story in years, and now my brain was playing me my own private 3D movie. 'Can't you go back and find some shelter?'

He shook his head slowly. 'I have ... something important to do. And here I am safe. They cannot cross.'

I laughed. 'Safe? You've only got to bump into the wrong person, and they'll have hunters out after you. Some would consider you quite a specimen.'

'Such as those men in suits of midnight-blue? I think they were hunting for me, after I upset an old lady.'

It turned out he had encountered a woman walking her dog, in similar circumstances to our last meeting. She had screamed, thrown her dog's lead at him and run away. She returned with two police officers who made a cursory search of the area.

'They came close, but I did not give them to see me. I did however overhear their conversation. Out of her earshot they were mocking the woman.'

Hardly surprising. No doubt the doctor would soon be mocking me, unless I was careful not to disclose too much. It was an early appointment, so I had to shift.

Jack waded out of the bracken and onto the path, and I got an eyeful of his underwear, which may have been a woven mass of leaves and twigs, or possibly an integral part of him. He stood at about five-nine and had a slender body, wiry and lightly muscled, his stomach flat and firm. The thought crossed my mind again that, apart from the wings of course, he had the kind of body of which I should imagine any image-conscious teenager would be proud. His skin was the pale, almost snowy white with just the slightest blush of colour. It was smooth and hairless except for the places one would usually expect to find 'thatched' in a young man – underarms and below the navel. Like his eyebrows, his body hair was dark.

His head-hair was ash-blond almost to the point of being white, and was full and collar-length, except of course he had no collar. His face narrowed towards the chin. Bright and hinting of sharp intelligence it made me think 'boy-gone-feral' and he had thin, dark eyebrows over hazel eyes. His ears were small, and something else I had missed before, slightly pointed. He wore a earring in the right ear, like a small bead of black glass. His narrow-lipped mouth was shapely and flickered with a smile like St Elmo's Fire on a topmast. But it was an uncertain smile that failed to fully ignite, and the underlying emotion appeared to be fear.

Something else I noticed and was curious about: he bore small wounds on both wrists, as if he had recently been bound. One of them trickled blood. Red blood, in case you are wondering.

In full health and fitness, much as I last encountered him, Jack must have been close to perfection for his kind, but he had deteriorated in those few days. He looked so tired and bedraggled and I knew then that he was in desperate need of shelter. I offered our spare room as a temporary measure, told him I would come back later with some clothing and arranged a signal that he should listen for, and that he should keep himself hidden, and properly covered, until my return.

Then came my appointment with the doctor. You've heard all about that. With his advice in mind I made my way home.

Josh was about the same build as Jack, and as luck would have it, Carol had only that morning filled up a charity bag with some of his old clothing. I took a selection and a pair of trunks and socks from his draw, and then selected a warm hat. I threw the lot into a bin-bag together with an old Barbour I used for gardening. I thought we might accommodate the wings by cutting long slits in the clothes at strategic places.

Leaving Bodger behind I made for the woods, laughing as I wonder how a product of my heat-oppressed brain would manage to pull on a hoodie over those wings.

As it happened, he managed very well. I looked aside while he kicked off his leafy garment, not a part of him after all, and pulled on the trunks, which made him look even more vulnerable, until I helped him up with the jeans. The t-shirt and pullover fitted as if made for him once they had been modified with a pocket-knife, and the Barbour, similarly modified, swamped him. I pulled a Peruvian hat over his head, threw his moth-eaten plaid over his wings and we were done. He looked like he was carrying a rucksack well past its best.

We made it back to the path that led to town. I had parked my car as close as possible and all went far better than I could have hoped. We encountered only one other dog-walker and she smiled and said good morning. We made it across the road to my car and then encountered our first problem. Try getting into a car with a twelve-foot wingspan. Suffice to say the doors could have been a little wider. He had to sit in the middle of the back seat and scrunch down as best he could. I had never seen such a curious sight through my rear-view mirror.

The shower was the next problem. He could get in and shut the doors – just – but there was no room for manoeuvre. I left him to dry and dress and then we discovered that, to his pallet, hot chocolate was the nectar of the Gods.

In the study, he took the easy chair and I sat in the office one, each of us with a mug of hot chocolate. He had chosen to leave the jeans off and sat in his trunks with his legs curled up on the seat. We sat in silence for a while, looking at each other. I expected him to vanish between eye-blinks, and I wonder if he thought the same of me. And then something dawned on me.

'The lady we passed in the woods,' I said. 'She said good morning to you?' She did. There was no need to ask, for I remembered it quite clearly. Bang went one theory then, unless I'd imagined the old woman as well.

'Yes, she did. What of it?'

I shrugged. 'I just had it in my mind that only I could see you.'

'You think me an imagined person? Yes, I have experience of that. People are often inclined to disbelieve their own eyes.'

'Only when they show us impossible sights, such as you.'

'Oh, hello!' Jack said, looking past my right shoulder. The hairs stood up on the back of my neck.

I looked behind me. Carol framed the open door, a half-smile frozen in place. I wondered if Jack had a medusa's effect on women. Carol suddenly came to herself, smiled in the direction of our guest and asked if I might possibly step outside for a word.

I admit I'd brought home a few strays in my time, but never before anything straight off the top of Mount Olympus. Through one of my wildlife commissions I'd palled up with the local RSPCA Inspector, and it wasn't unusual for him to drop off various animals for me to look after overnight, saving a long trip to the shelter. Rabbits, kittens or ferrets were common, and on one auspicious occasion a pot-bellied piglet in a crate. But a boy, that was a first, and I knew Carol would have a problem with it.

'What the Hell!' she said. Actually she used a much stronger term, and swearing was most uncharacteristic for her. 'Tell me why there is a teenage boy in your study in just his underpants?'

'He's got a top on,' I said as if that made a blind bit of difference.

'You know exactly what I mean, Paul.'

'Well, technically, he's in Josh's underpants.'

'Josh's ...?' Carol began to fume. 'What happened to his own? Never mind, I don't want to know, but you let some total stranger have a pair of our son's ...? Are you totally off your rocker? He could make allegations!'

'I had to give him something to put on. He was naked when I found him in the woods.' I realised I was not making my case any stronger.

Carol took a deep breath. 'Oh, I get it! You're winding me up, right?'

'Carol, didn't you notice something odd? His back? Wings, to be precise?'

'I'm rather more concerned with the underpants thing than I am about the quality of his outlandish prosthetics. Look, I'm getting the fact that he's here for a shoot. I do remember you telling me you'd got a commission for a fantasy book cover, and I daresay these actor-types can be rather more relaxed with informal dress than the rest of us, but how do you think it would sound if it got out that you, a forty-five-year-old photographer, were sitting in your study with a half-naked teen boy ... and no chaperone?'

I started to say something. Carol wasn't ready to listen, and she wasn't finished tearing into me. 'How much money do you think these "model" types actually make?' she said, bordering the word model with air-apostrophes. 'He probably does "escort" work on the side, and he's dropped his trousers to see if you're ripe for a few quid. You really haven't got a clue, have you, and ...'

That tore it! I held up my hand and I felt my face flashing danger signals. It didn't happen often, only once in twenty years of marriage, but she shut up fast and swallowed. In twenty years of marriage she'd only seen that face once before, and the row that followed ... well, she lost. We'll leave it at that, shall we?

'Come back into the study with me. Now!'

Her fire had been extinguished. Her venom swamped with serum. Carol followed me.

'Still here with your stupid stuck-on wings,' she said under her breath. She didn't mention the elephant in the room, which pretty much amounted to his lack of trousers.

'Jack, I'd like to introduce my wife, Carol. Carol, meet Jack, who hasn't got a prosthetic of any kind. Wysiwyg! He is one hundred percent for real.'

'Wysiwyg?' said the boy. 'That is a nice name.'

'"What-you-see-is-what-you-get." My wife, rather understandably, doesn't believe you are quite for real. She thinks your wings are artificial.'

The boy smiled at Carol and what a smile. She told me later that if she'd been 20 years younger ... Lose the wings and the producers of those male perfume adverts would be proposing all kinds of sponsorship deals. When he stood up and turned his back, Carol accepted the offer to part his feathers and check out his wings.

'And you're from ... where, exactly?' she said, a tremble in her voice.

I could tell Carol was wondering if Jack was the result of an experiment involving mixed genes and test tubes. Either that or something hallucinogenic mixed into our drinking water.

Two minutes later I was waving a cushion in front of her face while Carol slumped on a chair. Jack breezed into the kitchen to fetch a glass of water. When she came to herself, Carol showed her true colours. Putting aside questions of origin and possibility, Jack was suddenly a lad who needed help, and Carol set about preparing the spare room.

While Carol was so engaged, I was afforded the opportunity to explore those same questions and Jack began his story in depth. He had come to our world from a place which was everywhere and nowhere, a place where others had died to save him.

Notes.

i)   Similarities between Jack's story and Dad's manuscript, not to mention the coincidence of the name 'Jack'.

ii)   Next day. Blood on sheets. A couple of feathers on the floor. No wings. After a week, only the lightest of discolouring at the shoulder blades.

iii)   Complete inability to stick to any appointments involving people outside the family.

iv)   DNA. Feather: genus of bird previously unknown to science. Lack of records. Details of various efforts to trace relatives. A whole chapter for this.

v)   Adoption and all the official red tape. School. College. Another chapter.

vi)   It all begins to seem like a dream. There were never any wings. Jack is a very normal and yet extraordinarily wonderful young man. We all love him. Especially close to his grandfather.

∞

Alice replaced the manuscript and put the deluxe edition of 'A Broad and Ample Road' back on top. She ran a finger along the gilded title and the air no longer smelled of old libraries. It took on a chill and a freshness that reminded her of newly fallen snow.

'Hello!'

Alice turned and the young man in the white suit introduced himself as Jack. It was a three-piece suit, open at the neck. He wore no shoes or socks.

'I've just been reading your story.' Alice laid a hand on the manuscript.

Jack smiled and Alice melted. So this is how her fans felt. 'Oh, that old thing. Not everything you read is true.'

Nevertheless, Alice wanted to rip off his jacket, waistcoat and shirt and check for the marks where his wings used to be.

'Dad wrote that just before Granddad's book was published. The manuscript recently turned up again all covered in dust, and Dad swears he can't remember writing a word of it.'

'But you are adopted?'

'Yes.'

'And Paul did find you …?'

'Naked in the woods? In a basket floating down the Nile? Among a pack of wolves?' Jack laughed, and if she live to be a hundred, Alice knew it would be impossible to hear that joyous sound and not join in. Apart from anything else, it pushed questions completely out of her mind. Her laughter quickly ebbed. It didn't seem appropriate to laugh so, when somewhere in the house poor Reggie was dying.

Jack must have read her mind. He reported that Reggie had very little time left. 'He knows you're here, so he sent me with this.' He opened his hand to reveal a silver and black ring. 'He wanted you to have it, in memory of the meeting you had with him in the cave, all those years ago.'

Alice took the ring in awe. The ring was marked with Roman numerals, and she recognised it by its description it Reggie's book. 'How do you know about that,' she whispered.

'It's all in his book,' Jack said.

Yes, but it's not true.'

'Perhaps not. But then, not everything that's true really happened.'

Alice wanted to touch Jack. To make sure he was of the same substance as herself. 'I come here for answers, and all I get are more riddles.'

A dance of sorts ensued. As Alice came close to Jack, he would step behind a chair, or wheel around the table, but his movements appeared no more to resemble evasion that Alice's did pursuit. It was just that whenever Alice reached the space where Jack was, he had the knack of being somewhere else.

'Is this really happening, Jack? Or is it one of those truths that isn't real?'

'I'm as real as I care to be. Reggie believes in me.'

And then she had him. Before Jack could be somewhere else, she reached out and took his hand. His hand was solid, and warm, and very human. 'You are a cruel boy, Jack. Playing with a girl's mind like that.' She smiled and when Jack kissed her cheek she had no more doubts about his reality, his truth. Not

257

that her former doubts were that serious, but after the cave incident back in Dubai, she liked to double-check.

Jack had to get back to Reggie. He said it had been a pleasure to meet her and that Granddad would be glad to know she had the ring.

A few minutes after Jack left, Carol and Paul came in. It wouldn't be long now. The nurse and the rest of the family were with Reggie. He was very peaceful. They had some lunch prepared in the kitchen-diner and asked Alice to join them. Of course, Reggie was the main topic of conversation. His long life. His friendships. His achievements. And then his one book, published when he was in his eighties, a Man-Booker long list blockbuster and Amazon best seller, a film before his ninetieth birthday. The book was dedicated to Doud Latif who everyone in the family knew was David, and Jack, who everyone knew was a figment of Reggie's imagination.

'Oh, Paul, you must get the ring,' Carol said. 'It's strange, but he was most insistent that you should have his old ring.'

Paul began to rise from the table to get the ring.

'This one?' Alice held the ring up and Paul froze for an instant before seating himself once more. 'Your son gave it to me earlier.'

'Really?' Carol said. 'He's usually very shy with new people is our Josh. Better with animals, and people he's known for a long time.'

'Not Josh,' Alice said. 'Jack gave it to me while I was in the study.'

Paul and Carol exchanged glances. Paul spoke after several false starts. 'The thing is, if Josh is shy around new people, Jack is ... positively reclusive. I mean ... What I'm saying is ...'

'What he's saying,' Carol said, making a valiant but shaky effort to come to Paul's rescue, 'is that Jack has rarely been seen by anybody but us. Us and Dad. Please, don't ask us to even begin to explain. It's something we accepted long ago without understanding a bit of it.'

'It's not hard to accept such a kind and loving lad,' Paul said. 'And he gave Dad a whole new lease of life. Dad's been talking to Jack for five or six years now, just as if his old imaginary friend is back. And we have come to believe, he is back.' Alice's blank stare prompted him to say a little more. Jack wasn't invisible to other people, he just had the uncanny knack of never being around when anybody turned up. He could simply not be tied down.

Alice asked if she could get some air. A walk around the garden would do it.

It wasn't a good idea, coming here. Alice wanted to lay some ghosts, but she had arrived at Ghost Central. She tried to let her thoughts go, so they could wander about the garden on their own, and leave her the hell alone. The split-level lawn was divided by a frieze of lavender. At the far end of the higher lawn was a large goldfish pond and beyond that a pergola strewn with vines. It would be just like Reggie to grow his own grapes, make his own wine. Alice smiled and then wondered who the two men were who had just emerged from behind a willow tree on the lower lawn. Oh no, not again! The younger man was Jack. The much older, it had to be Reggie. Yes, if she worked hard, she could make out the young man's face in the lines of the old. Jack caught her eye and waved. Reggie only had eyes for Jack. There was something very 'happy reunion' about it.

They walked shoulder to shoulder, and when they came to the pond, they paused. Then Jack pushed the old man and he fell in with a splash. Jack jumped in after him and they paddled water at each other like twelve-year-olds, laughing and splashing, splashing and laughing. And then Alice's imagination kicked in again, or possibly reality took another broadside from Captain Hook's pixie-dusted cannon, because the years seemed to fall away from Reggie until he looked very like he did on the cover of his book. It's funny, what light shining through water can do. They splashed until all Alice could see were clouds of water, backlit by the sinking sun. Finally, a pair of wings made from water droplets and spray enfolded them. When the water fell back to the pond and the bright halo had no more droplets to illuminate, the world fell quiet. Only the echoes of laughter now, and no sign of either Reggie or Jack.

Alice knew it hadn't really happened. But she also knew it was true, and she needed nobody to tell her that back in the house, Reggie had gone.

She would have appreciated more time with her thoughts, but a little girl danced towards her from the other side of the pond. Alice wasn't good with kids' ages, but she guessed the happy child was around nine or ten.

'Hello! Are you Alice? You look like her.'

Alice smiled, glad of the distraction after all. The girl looked sweet in a purple frock, long black hair tied with a bow. 'Yes, I'm Alice. What's your name?'

'I'm Jenny. I like one of your songs. The one with the white mouse. It's my very favourite.'

'Why, thank you so much.'

'Did you see that angel swimming in the pond with Great-Grandpa? Wasn't he beautiful?'

Alice's mouth opened, but no words came. Jenny smiled and skipped away.

Alice took her leave, went home and did what she did best. She wrote a song. And then she wrote another song, and another. By the end of the week, she had all the raw material she needed for a concept album. She worked on it solidly for a year, and her new album, 'The Truth That Didn't Happen', was released for download on the first anniversary of Reggie's passing. The cover art for the album featured a young man in a white suit. With a pair of swan-wings spread behind him, as if he were some kind of an angel.

6

James Devis, Witch! - The Year 1649AD

Ω

Wooden clogs clattering a jig on Haarlem cobbles, or so James Devis assumed. Mn'Heer Hals slammed down his charcoal and shouted out of the window. James fancied he knew all Dutch curses but this one eluded him. Hals muttered to himself about unruly children and resumed his place behind the easel.

'Your hand, sir. As it was before, if you please. Just so.' Frans Hals placed a fist on his hip. 'And puff up the shirt at the cuffs and panes. If you must affect the French fashion, then get your tailor's worth and show it off.'

James had no idea he was affecting the French fashion. He bought his suits where he may, which was wherever he might lodge for more than a month. This one he had from Antwerp, which led him to wonder how French it might be. His britches and doublet were of a good quality black cloth, and he was neat of the leg in white stockings. He held a large black hat in front of him adorned with a farmyard's worth of billowing black feathers, and he did his best to place his right fist upon his hip as instructed. Hals fussed and tutted until it was placed to his entire satisfaction.

'Shall I be long at this, sir? Standing like this doth recall a wound I had as a young man. A musket ball to the left buttock if I may be so common.'

'You must stand a little longer withal. At least until I have outlined you. Then you may rest while I brush over my canvas and prepare my oils and tinctures. In exchange I will make you such a likeness that, by my troth, your wife will think it truly you.'

James had no wife. Those he grew close to had an uncanny habit of dying violently, but it was of no concern of the artist's. He felt no compunction to put him right on the matter.

'You have an interesting face, Mn'Heer Devis. I like it that you go against the grain and wear your natural hair long without resort to the wig maker. And it stands like a pole that you have lived a life, sir. From the ball in your arse, and from your bearing if I might be so bold, you have been a soldier? Battles are writ in that face.'

Battles, yes, and soldiers. James recalled a conversation from his youth. 'When you die, there will be no parades for you,' Bertrando had said in jealousy and spite. James laughed at the memory. It would be parade enough for one person to recall him with love.

'Take that grin off your face, sir!'

James liked this Hals fellow, as he did all who were direct and honest.

'A high forehead. Widely spaced eyes. A smile just behind the mouth but kept in check. Slight hook to the nose. The beginning of the jowls that may swamp your features in old age.' Hals muttered all this to himself while he attacked the canvas with his charcoal.

'I am already old, sir. Few of us may expect to best the half-century, and I am in my fifty-third year.'

'And your hair still so brown,' Hals whispered, and then to a shout 'That makes the cat wise! I have passed sixty-seven years. You are a mere stripling, sir.' The men shared laughter.

Commended again to remain as still as possible of face and posture, James did his best. The studio was plain in décor with bare floorboards and whitewashed walls, but there were shelves filled with interesting ornaments and artefacts. A breastplate and a feathered dragoon's helmet; a dog's skull and a human one; plaster busts of classic heroes and small statues of the human form; all the paraphernalia of the artist's profession, the smells too. A stack of frames in one corner, one or two stretched canvasses, and a painting of a man, in black like himself, but with long curly locks that hinted of wig.

And a little wooden manikin tied by its neck from some twine and dangling from a shelf.

There may be a sight for each of us that waits, unimagined, until they day we first see it, and then that image becomes the centre of our world. Whether it be the herald of joy or horror, of lust or fear, of a craving to possess or escape or of any other emotion, the point is that the rest of the world ceases to exist. So it was with James. That small wooden manikin swayed in the breeze and drew all to a point which was itself, and which was also poor Marco Verdi hanging from that butcher's hook thirty and some years ago. The emotion was of deep pain and empty, cavernous sorrow.

'My dear sir! Do you need to sit awhile?'

James took the chair he was offered.

'You have quite lost your colour.'

James quickly came to himself, but was disinclined to play at statues until he had rested. The old wound was making its presence known, and he could not clear his thoughts. Marco's ghost lurked in the corners, so when Hals spoke of the militia, and asked if James might relate something of his time under arms, he was glad to take the opportunity. He did not start with his escape and flight from Newark House. Instead, he carried forward some weeks to the day he left England, with the vaguest of plans to return only to find the third amulet.

∞

'As a young man I had fallen into some bad business, which by my troth was through no evil of my own making, rather a poor choice of friends. Now, as a mission had been laid upon me by my betters and elders, I thought to take myself to the New World where I could escape my enemies and see to the business at the same time. And so I made haste to the port of Bristol.

'I sought about the port and petitioned among the masters of ships moored at Redcliffe Back, but none would have me. I was nearly seventeen-years-old, that being too old for a ship's boy and without the brawn for hard deck-work nor the experience of a midshipman. I recall one boatswain looked me up and down and asked "What uses have you?" I told him I was sound of limb and used to hard work, that I knew some healing skills from my father who had sailed with Drake, and that I had some of the Dutch tongue. "Have you French tongue," he said and then made an obscene display with his own tongue. There was laughter and rude yahoos from the gathered men. The boatswain declared "Too skinny to handle sheets but pretty enough to handle cocks!" which being said caused much mirth among the crew. "Is that the kind of work you seek?" More laughter and many jibes and rude calls as I withdrew from the dockside. I brought to mind how his bloated face would look, skewered with my sword.

'My cheeks still burned as I passed a lout who was idling by some casks and barrels, looking to lift some, I shouldn't wonder. As I neared him, cheeks still red from my recent ill usage, this tall and gaunt fellow, two or three years older than I, hailed me in the Dutch tongue. It was a very poor Dutch that would have earned me stripes from my father, but Dutch nevertheless. I returned his hail in what I hoped was a better brand of the language, whereupon he grinned and clapped my shoulder as if we were old friends.

"There's a Dutchie moored on the Frome at Lower Slip," he said in an English just as uncouth. "She ain't much. Just sixteen guns, but she sails for New Amsterdam on the morrow at noon."

"Is she short of hands?" I asked.

"Marry, yet she may be. It'll cost you no lumps to ask." He told me that I should go north and through the Marsh Street gate, walk a while and then look to my left for Swan Lane whereat I would find a tavern. 'It is but a narrow lane. If you reach St Stephen's you have gone too far. Be there at sunset, and I will meet you.'

'I was in rough clothes for the road, so I did not think he could be planning to rob me. Nevertheless, I first went to my lodging and retrieved my sword and firelock. Not meet arms to wear when seeking lowly employ, but essential flags to hoist in the face of sneak thieves. I entered the tavern that evening on my guard and ready to fight. In addition to my sword, I had several good blades about me, and the stomach to use them.

'And there was the lout from earlier in the day, who himself looked less loutish and more business-like in the light of candles. He told me his name was Peter Trevysard and stood me a jug of ale. At the board he introduced me to one of the ship's mates, a sharp-eyed and tousle-haired Dutchman named Pim Schepers. He spoke to me in Dutch and so fast that I understood but every third phrase. My answers made him laugh at my use of his language, but we stayed in Dutch, much to Peter's confusion, who appeared to understand less than I.

'First Mate Schepers questioned me close about my skills and my intentions. Why was I armed as a gentleman and yet dressed as a farmer's boy? What business had I in the Americas? What skills had I that his captain might use? It was only when I told him I was somewhat of a firemaker that his ears pricked. They had been unable to find a competent gunner for the voyage and only five men who had ever given fire to ordnance in their lives. Had I? No sir, but I told him I had, which was a falsehood, and that I could make mill cake of the best quality knowing, as I did, all the ingredients and measures thereof. This latter was perfectly true, and I had a good knowledge of the variety of ordnance from my father's teachings, although I had never handled more than a fowling piece of such poor quality that I was as like to die as the duck in my sights.

'He took me aboard the ship, which was named "Wolfhond" and was the goodliest little ships as I have ever seen before or since, and never a one of such sweet humours. The captain believed that fever and other ills sprang from bad smells, and it was a flogging for any man caught pissing between decks. Each man, whether officer or crew, was obliged to wash his body every day, and his clothes every week. The Wolfhond was an elderly lady, some thirty years old and very like Drake's Golden Hynde to look upon. Father had drawn many a picture of her, and the Wolfhond looked very like to me, with a fo'c'sle that was by then much out of fashion and a towering stern-castle too. She had seven guns a side and two chasers and six little swivellers. Her crew was much short of an hundred.

'Schepers took me to see the guns, which the biggest was not quite a demi-cannon, more a culverin. Large iron for so small a ship. And then he tipped a cask lid and at once I could see something amiss. "The grain size of this powder is right fit for a firelock or musket, perhaps even a robinet, but no use at all to your guns. It would burn too fast, and you may have luck, or you may burst the chase and kill the gunners." I exaggerated the case somewhat, but was eager to make a show of my knowledge.

'And so it was I was signed as a gunner's mate, although powder was my business. My first task was to see to a supply of courser powder so that it be meet for larger ordnance. Then I set about improving my knowledge of all things pertaining to ordnance. For the time it took us to sail sufficiently south to catch the right current to take us west, I kept my eyes open and my mouth shut, and made full use of the captain's books. As the only mate who could read, I soon became a tutor to the other men and boys.

'Peter Trevysard came to be a good friend in those early weeks. I suspected something about him, and it came to my knowledge at last, that he suspected the same of me. We suspected each other of being cunning men, or witches as some would have it, when in reality we had but a few skills in the use of herbs. He taught me a useful – may I call it 'charm' at the risk of denouncement – against the bloody-flux, and I taught him one that keeps the bleeding gum disease at bay. Neither of us suffered these things upon our voyages. Some others of our companions did, but there was no fever. Shitting at the head in a gale was a tiresome chore, but one that was rewarded by the sweet airs below decks. I came to think the captain, whose name was Joop de Jong, was right in his belief as to bad smells.'

James skimmed over his business in the New World. He did not know Frans Hals very well, and had no idea how he might react to talk of amulets, and magic seals or the bones of martyrs and their efficacy in magic spells. He used his time very well, found the amulet which was a thing mostly of clay. He broke it and rescued the few bones of poor Richard Meekins that had been baked within the clay. When all Richard's bones were brought back together, Dee's magic would be undone, and the schemes and plots would die before the Magical Year ever dawned.

'My business being done and back at the port of New Amsterdam before she sailed, I was welcomed back aboard the merry little Wolfhound where I stayed crew for seven years, rising to gunner and at last to master gunner and second mate.'

Making a habit of skimming over the real business of his journeying, he also failed to tell the artist anything of his long sojourn on the land, following his leads to discover the second amulet. As for the first, the directions contained in Dee's papers were specific and clear. He came with his companions at last to the village of Schwarzkollm tucked inside the forest of Hoyerswerda on the road to Leippe, and sure to those writings, here was the old dark mill in the Sow's Fen by the Black Water.

The miller welcomed them and was happy to take their money for lodgings. The miller's journeymen, few more than boys, were companionable, but it was a place where fear lurked in every shadow, and the shadows were many and deep, as if to match the hue of the crows who roosted in the rafters. It was a curious fact that there were as many journeymen as there were crows, and their combined number always amounted to eleven. One day there might be eleven boys and no crows. Another, all crows, squawking in the rafters and no boys. Sometimes a mix of the two, but for every crow present, one boy was absent. James was reminded of his long dead friend Marco and the jay with the broken wing. Peter Trevysard, who was chief among James's companions, was much of the same mind as James.

Evil made a lurking hold of the place, and it smelt of witchcraft.

The miller caught James on the fourth day of their stay. James thought at last he might seek out the amulet, and it was exactly where the note said it would be. He had just withdrawn it from its hidey-hole when the miller asked what he was doing, and then saw quite plainly before James could answer.

'That old thing!' the miller said. 'You may take it for a couple of thalers. I have no use for it, and cannot abide it near me.'

It was no surprise that evil could not countenance the holy martyred bones of Master Meekins, but he was happy to hand over the coins and say nothing. He was glad to leave that cold, damp and bone-chilling place, but sad to leave the boys in the miller's hands and he saw dread in their eyes as he left. Later on the road he was flown about by a flock of crows, and counting them found there to be eleven. 'Fly boys! Away from here and do not return!'

For a second time, James ground the clay amulet to lumps and retrieved the pieces of burnt bone. Whenever a piece of bone touched his skin, he felt the flames lick at him and heard the pitiful cries of poor Richard Meekins. Tried for some petty or imagined little heresy and found not guilty, the bishops would have none of it and had him tried again and a new jury coerced and frightened until the fifteen-year-old was sentence. James felt the fire, and heard the screams, and heard also the laughter of the bishops who by now would be to their well-deserved rewards in Hell, while Richard Meekins flew Heaven on swan-feather wings.

'It was then that the war was upon us, which has taken me from young man to old. I was by now as skilled with ordnance as any man, and with a name that was not entirely unknown. So when it came to pass that the Swedish king was looking for good Dutch gunners to bolster his ranks, my name was mentioned and I was sought out and offered a commission as Master Gunner. For the best part of the next thirty years I served.

'At the battle of Lützen I took a musket ball to my arse, but by my troth, I was not retreating. But nor is it an honourable wound for it was inflicted by a friend and not the foe. It was a foggy day and I had charge of a battery of big guns but naught to shoot at that I could see. Our Yellow Regiment stood out at the whim of the swirling mists, but those fine men apart, there was nothing to see nor any target to be sure of save one. The imperial army had a big battery of many guns set by three of four windmills. So when the mist allowed, I set aim for the windmills, and gave fire. Any of my shot that fell short still fell among the imperials, so it was the best I could do.

'We were attacked from the rear. I received this devil's pinch that has pained me every day since, and my good and dear friend Peter, who had stayed with me all those many years, was killed by a ball to the head. It was our own reserve that had assaulted us. Their grief nigh as bad as my own was doubled when they learned our king had also died.

'King or no, the war raged on and not a square inch of the land that was not bled upon or fought over, and the people starved or were ill-used by this army or that. I last saw action at Jankau, a mere handful of years gone. At that time I set up my batteries in a wood and did terrible hurt to the enemy. I saw the carnage and was sickened. Men turned to bloody pulp by mine own deeds and actions. Boys who should be a-courting with fair maids now courted foul Death. Sick of carnage and war. Sick to my heart, and my stomach, and the lines upon my face wherein you read battles. Your readings are not overly mistaken Mn'Heer Hals, but would they were battles against evil for good, and not men for vanities.'

Sick also from an eternal battle he dare not mention, with one-time friend and long-time deadly enemy, Bertrando di Pontenegro. That wily and false Count would have the world ruled by magic, if it took the last breath in his body. James would have it otherwise, if it took the last breath in his.

∞

Hals asked James to wait in the parlour while he spread a wash over his canvas. There was a gentleman, seated, who James immediately recognised from one of the paintings in the studio. The man rose and bowed. He took exception to the fact that James answered his flowery leg-making with no more than a nod, and he demanded to know who this impudent fellow was. James knew him as a Frenchman for his accent.

'Come now, sir! I asked, who are you?'

James was bridled by the pre-emptory tone in the Frenchman's tone and bearing. 'I am that I am, sir. I breathe and I live and I think, therefore I am.'

The gentleman smiled widely and bowed. 'Very good! Very good indeed to come back at me with a semblance of my own written word! I see that you have read my "Discourse on the Method", and therefore I must recognise you as a scholar.'

James confessed that he had not read, nor had any knowledge of the man's book.

'Nevertheless, please forgive my earlier impudence. It has been a long and vexatious day.'

'If impudence were there I forgive it, but I declare it was not recognised as such. And I hope that you will forgive my failure to return your little bow, but life has dealt me such that my back is not over prone to bending.' He had not bowed before old King James, so a Frenchman could go hang.

They settled to converse, and after a handful of exchanges James grew more kindly disposed to the gentleman. There were all the signs that the conversation would germinate and bloom with shared interests and philosophies, but they were interrupted by James's servant.

Ruud de Wit was a polite and gentle boy from Brabant, and being so, his expostulations were not as harsh-sounding as the Dutch James had grown used to, but there was urgency enough in him for James to fear that enemies were upon them.

'No, sir, not at all enemies. Far from it, but I am commanded to bring you home in all haste.' Small, birdlike and not at all well-disposed to military life, he had reported to James for work during the last weeks of the war. An educated lad from good stock, his family had died at the hands of marauding soldiers and he was close to starvation. James had also been an educated boy who had fallen on the hardest of times, and he could not turn Ruud away, though he could see there would be little use from him on the batteries. James had made him servant rather than see him broken as a gunner's labourer, but in times such as this, he showed his steel. A man could be the equal of any man be he ever so void of brutishness or the skills and instincts to do hurt to his fellows.

James instructed the artist's servant to tender his apologies, but that urgent business had arisen. He took his leave of the Frenchman. Ruud led almost at a run, and James followed with his two retainers.

With the war over and without work, James had been living on the substantial fortunes of his long war. He moved from town to town and hoped always to stay several steps ahead of Bertrando, who would destroy him if he could, but the Conte's spies were skilled. 'One step ahead' was usually the best to be achieved. Bertrando had thought James long dead, until he broke up the second amulet. James did not know who had informed his old enemy that he yet lived, but he suspected the miller. Howsoever, his schemes to end James's life, before the coming of the Miraculous Year, were put into effect. James never moved but with one eye over his shoulder, and even now he wondered if Ruud had been hoodwinked into mistaking a deadly enemy for a well-disposed friend.

They came by the back ways to James's lodgings. He crossed the threshold with a hand rested on the hilt of his rapier. With two men behind he ascended the shadowy stairway. Leather boots on bare wood heralded his arrival as well as any fanfare, so his visitor, friend or foe, could be nothing but fully prepared. James curled his right thumb so he could nudge at the ring on his right ring-finger. He believed the spirit of an angel dwelt within the silver and black of the ring that was once given to him by King James. The angle had guided him and served him well for many years. He felt the ring and whispered a spell.

At the door, Ruud looked up at his master and smiled. 'The gentleman within has asked me give no introduction, and that he will commend himself to you.' He opened the door and stepped to one side, allowing James access.

Inside, seated on the cushion at the window seat, was a very fine gentleman. Bearded in the outmoded style of van Dyke, his stockings were of the best silk and showed a fine leg. His attire, although not of the fashion and a little worn, was of the highest quality. He had disencumbered himself of his high-topped riding boots, which stood by the door, in favour of a pair of high-heeled red leather slippers. He stood to greet James and his faced beamed with the light of an old friendship rekindled after many years.

James could not tell who he was. 'Forgive me, but ...'

'Giacomo, there is nothing to forgive. I have changed in all these long years. That we should both live to be so old!'

James rifled through the many dusty drawers of his memory, but the man in front of him remained hid. His happy grin undiminished, the gentleman tilted the left side of his face towards James. 'See how my ear doth still glow from the clout you bounced off it when I was an impudent lad?'

The years were mist that blew away, and little Lord George of Berkeley was a boy again in James's mind, and the boy in his mind fused with the man before him. They hugged for many minutes and James shed tears for the time that had taken away their youth and made them elderly. James had never since met anyone from before his days aboard the Wolfhond.

With a single amulet left to seek out and break, James had sent out messengers to try and trace any who might give him letters of credence to return to the troubled lands of his birth. It appeared that one of his messengers had been successful.

George spent much time away from England where men's fortunes changed by the week. Now in favour, now for the block. Now Parliament in command, now the Royalists in resurgence. George was mildly Royalist, but not fanatically so. He was an unimportant lord who had never taken up arms on behalf of either side, and instead tried to work for the betterment of his fellow man. Nevertheless he had spent a month in prison accused of treason, but the charges were not brought and he was released.

'Your message reached me in Amsterdam where I had come to rid me of the prison's stench. It gave me sweet skips to the heart to know that so old a friend still walked the earth and breathed the good air.'

They laughed and gossiped about old times shared, and George quipped that James was still never to be seen bowing to any man, least of all an old friend that happens to be a lord. 'But then I recall, you too are a baron, by our late a lamented King James. Do you ever find a cause to wear your lordship upon your sleeve in these foreign climes?'

There was a time, James admitted, long ago now, when the war had run a dozen years or so. His train had been put under the command of a general with the English volunteers and he had failed to bow to Lord Hamilton, the General of the English. 'He berated me as a man who did not know his place. I had asked him when it had become fashion for lords to curtsey before other lords and revealed my rank to him.'

'Was he contrite?'

'Not so very much, he being an earl to my lowly baron, but later when we were alone he declared his sorrow at not recognising me, and a big play as to our friendship. In fact, he did make a great oath of it and swear "By Our Lady, Hail!" and even by the wounds of God, but as a general or a man he could not so much as muster a line of stalks in a wheat field. And so I had little time for him.'

George told James that the haughty earl was now a duke. 'But he has fallen very far from favour and dwells in the Tower, from whence he is unlikely to emerge with his head still upon his shoulders.'

England was a dangerous place. When the war in Europe ended, the civil war in England began. King Charles was dead and Cromwell the head of state, but the Royalists would not lie down. George advised James to stay where he was, but George knew nothing of James's mission or of the enemies that were ever no more than a pace behind.

Once he knew his persuasions were falling on deaf ears, George promised to write a letter and to obtain safe passage for James. Far better than his word, George obtained something that exceeded all expectations. Within three weeks, a letter came back offering not only safe passage, but a commission.

Ruud waited while James read the letter several times. 'It appears my name is not unknown in England, although not the name you know me by. I am offered a position of some importance.'

Ruud looked crestfallen, knowing he would be left behind to find a new master.'

'Listen to how I am called! How does "Giacomo di Aspromonte, Lieutenant Colonel of Artillery, Lord Rillton" sound to you, young Ruud?'

'It sounds too big to fit all in my mouth at one time, sir. Lieutenant Colonel?'

'It is merely the name they give me which means Master Gunner, to which you are very much familiar.'

'But all the rest. A new name and a title. It all befuddles me so.'

James took a pen and a pot of ink and set it to the board. 'Then how shall you write it? You must learn if you are to be my clerk.' He unstopped the well and dipped the quill. 'Come now and practice.'

The sun came out in Ruud's face with his smile. He took the pen and by doing so, accepted his new position.

The day after James, Ruud, Lord George and his retainers set sail for England, James's lodgings went up in flames. The new tenant, his son and his servant were burnt to death. It appeared a barrel had fallen against the door and their scorched remains were found huddled at the threshold, so close to escape but not so close as Death would give them any quarter. That night a letter went from Haarlem to Oxford with a hail to Bertrando di Pontenegro and a line to say the deed was done.

James Devis, veteran commander of Dutch artillery trains, and his raggedy boy servant may have put into England unnoticed. It is possible that Giacomo di Aspromonte would also have escaped attention for some weeks. But two lords, and one a colonel, these were too bright a flock to escape the attention of Bertrando's spies. He knew that the deed was very much undone within a week of James setting foot upon the land of his birth, and his anger bounced off the rafters. It was an hour before his servants were brave enough to emerge from their hidey-holes, for in his anger, he often made the servants suffer.

∞

James stayed a week with Lord George at his Clerkenwell lodgings. It was a convenient billet while he presented credentials and accepted his commission. George advised against taking sides and believed it was far better to maintain as neutral a position as possible. 'I am for Royalty, but I speak it soft' he said. 'But not overly for Royalty. I am more for peace between all the people, and it is ever to peace I lean at parliament. Say perhaps, I am for Royalty tempered by parliament.'

James, also a man of peace at heart despite his years as a warrior, was glad that there was little for him to do in his new role. There was a lull in the fighting and he had been retained against the possibility of future hostilities. He reported to his general in the old battle gear he had owned for ten years. The black armour had grown tight at the belly, but he was certainly not going to buy new. 'If I'm asked why for parliament,' James jested, 'I shall say "Why, it is because I do not have to change the colour of my officer's silk sash. Orange it had been when I fought for Adolphus and Torstensson, and orange it is now for parliament and the New Model Army". Will that show me more practical than partisan, George?'

As welcome as George made him in his little house, and as comfortable as it was, James wanted to visit his old home. All that had known him must surely be dead. None left alive who might see through the lines of old age, point and cry 'James Devis, Witch! I denounce thee!' And if there be one such left on the green earth, would he dare to denounce a lord and a general as the same as was once the lowly peasant boy who had escaped a hanging?

James had a mission to complete. He was determined to find the final amulet and gather the last of Richard Meekins's burnt shards of bone. Thus, Bertrando's schemes would go awry. And there was more: since he touched those first liberated relics almost forty years before, he was filled with the knowledge that reuniting them all would bring a magic all of their own, of a kind that would dispel Bertrando's magic as the sun dispels the dark. When he first touched the black of the Orbis Mirabilis, that ring given to him by King James, to the black of Richard's bones, Richard the Angel came to him, and he knew peace to the depths of his soul. Thereafter Richard had come to him in moments of despair and often gave guidance. Guidance, with a look, with a wing pointing in the right direction, but never with a word. James had spoken of these visions to nobody. They were as secret as his history, his mission and the man who was truly James Devis.

James's superiors were delighted that he wished to base himself in the north, and so it was that he bid George goodbye and set off with Ruud his clerk, a lieutenant whose name was Nino Clack but known to all behind his back as Nine O'Clock, and a troop of ten dragoons as escort.

Once again Bertrando's spies were good, if a little tardy. Bertrando himself called upon Lord George Berkeley three hours after James and his escort had taken leave. They made much of their reunion after so many years, each proving their skills at acting. 'My word!' George said. 'Closer to seventy than sixty and still your own teeth. If I didn't know better I'd say you were charmed.'

Bertrando, who not only had his teeth, but much of his old vigour, ignored the veiled accusation and asked instead for the whereabouts of their much-loved mutual friend.

'He is about the business of our Lord Cromwell, and sets sail for the Low Countries on the evening tide.' George hoped the lie would send the old sorcerer in the wrong direction.

An hour after Bertrando bid his farewells, George's messenger was at the gallop in pursuit of James. He caught up with him a day and several changes of horse later at Aylesbury.

In Lancaster six days later, another of George's messengers caught up with James. Bertrando, Conte di Pontinegro, was dead. Not of battle or spells, but of a fishbone that choked him.

'That a lifetime of scheming and plotting can be ended thus, by something as simple as a tiny fish bone!' Ruud said. 'But it is not good news? You look as if it be the worst of news, and yet he was your deadly enemy.'

'Aye, he was a schemer. But if not for his schemes, I would not have seen my eighteenth year. And also, he was at the head of a certain kind of fellowship, of whom there are no doubt many to fill his shoes. Until now, I knew the face of my enemy.'

∞

He shared a pew with the widow, daughter and eldest son of an officer of the New Model who had died fighting for parliament. Ruud sat with their servants. They had been pleased to give him rooms to lodge in their large house. James, who was once again going by the name of Giacomo, was unused to a place of honour in St Mary's, the church in the village where he grew up. It was very different from those days, when he and his family were hardly tolerated. The children of those who had cursed and cuffed him, now fawned and tried to ingratiate themselves until he made it known that he disliked such behaviour.

It was a half mile from the church to the house. James walked with Edmund, thirty-year-old son of his benefactor, and Lieutenant Clack who had also secured lodgings nearby. While they spoke of the war and speculated as to the state of the land now that King Charles had been deprived of his head, James's mind was elsewhere. There was the amulet, and the uncertainty of his own fate now that Bertrando was dead. He would seek out the amulet on the first fine day. It was a fine Sunday, but riding out of a Sunday would start tongues wagging.

Edmund laughed at something Clack had said. It put a pair of ravens to flight. Clack's own laugh added the high-notes and was as odd as his appearance. The raven's croaked their maledictions. At six-foot-two Nino Clack was more flagpole than giant, with loose-latched limbs that gave people to surmise he might fall apart in a breeze. His face was narrow, a skull with skin and a huge hooked nose. He wore nothing other than his red uniform and buff-coat and went armed at all times. James suspected he owned no other suit.

By the time James, Ruud and the Eskdale family had reached home, James was thoroughly disconcerted by that pair of ravens who kept pace, as if following. He mumbled a spell to cast off magic, but the ravens remained birds, and did not become men.

There was little time to lose. The raven may have been only ravens, and reassured that there was nobody left alive in Lancashire who recognised him, James waited for a fine day and then took a sturdy horse into the Forest of Bowland. He took with him the scrap of paper that bore detailed instructions on where to find the amulets. The note was written in his own hand and done from memory some hours after reading Doctor Dee's secret papers. He and Marco had found them among Bertrando's things and committed them to memory, but not trusting entirely to memory, James has written them down. The note had served well and James had easily discovered the first two amulets. He hoped the third would be as easy, but feared it would not. Hidden under a scraping of rock and soil by the Ward's Stone, he imagined he would have to dig all day and find nothing.

After an early breakfast, James dismissed Ruud to his own devices for the day, took leave of his hosts and set off on a sturdy mare he had named Judy. He considered taking his saddle-pistols but he used the holsters to carry trowels and a spade, so he went armed only with his old rapier and an even older main-gauche. It was a decision he questioned when, on leaving the village he was hailed by two riders in black. Their lips smiled fair, but they were fell behind the eyes. Or was it imagination, and his conviction since Bertrando's death that all newcomers and strangers were his agents. They wished each other good morrow and passed.

He kept up a brisk pace. It was almost twenty miles ride to the Ward's Stone and he wanted to be home before dark. A forty-mile round trip was more than he found comfortable with his old war wound, but less than he had achieved in days gone by.

After riding an hour, the horse became fidgety and twisted her ears to point backwards. They stayed backwards and the horse tried to twist her head. James kept a tight rein and twisted his head instead. He thought he saw distant shadows, in the shape of riders, pull off suddenly into a copse. It was far away, though, and he was uncertain.

Still his mare kept her ears to the rear until they came to the edge of the Forest of Bowland. 'A forest more scant of trees there never was,' he whispered to Judy. 'If we are followed they will be hard pressed to hide themselves.'

James relaxed when Judy did, and once again his thoughts were ahead instead of behind. In an hour or two he would reach the Ward's Stone, and then the highest part of the moor and if the day was clear, he would see the sea, like a bright strip of silver. It would be the sight he first had as a boy, the one that had awakened his love of oceans he had never seen. His mood became light and cheery, and he made up a rhyming song as he rode and sang it softly, as soft and as airy as he liked to speak his spells.

Two men-of-war were blasted
By cannon shot and chain.
Both lost their booms and their mizzens

As they fought on the Spanish Maine.
Sails and masts fell overboard
And dragged, held by rigging and sheet.
Headway was lost to the very great cost
That they lost all sight of the fleet.

Captain One turned his back to the bowsprit
Bemoaning his fate to the crew.
"I cannot part with the mizzen
Though it's dragging us down in the blue".
Captain Two kept his eyes to the jack-staff,
Ordered axes to be brought from below.
"What's behind is past and we need to move fast.
Cut loose lads! And onward we go".

Captain One, he never made admiral,
His glance was ever behind.
And it's really no farce that with eyes in your arse
To the future you're virtually blind.
Captain Two paid dear for lost rigging;
He paid and got on with his sailing.
With eyes on the horizon it's hardly surprising,
In Admiralty 't is his word prevailing.

'Except the very sad truth is the reverse, Judy my dear. Those admirals and generals and Lord Protectors are those very same whose eyes are in their arses!' James laughed and Judy snorted in full agreement. She stopped to drink from a puddle which set a cloud of midges into a swarm.

Noon found them at their objective. James fixed a nosebag of oats to Judy's halter and hobbled her with a length of old rope. He left her to rest and climbed to the top of the Ward's Stone. As a boy he had made his father laugh by likening it to a giant grey mound of horse dollop, which he supposed, now made him a fly. The sea was there, too bright to look at without screwing up the eyes, and the brightness filled his heart just as it had a lifetime ago. He saw his father whittling a whistle, and his mother and sister. Even his grandmother, now all long dead.

'Aye. I am the fly. Soon to be swatted. But first, to swat the last amulet.' He brought out a little leather pouch and tipped Richard's blackened knuckle-bone into his right hand, allowing the bone to touch the miraculous ring. He hoped the angel would come and point to him where to dig. He softly sang a spell of summoning and smiled as Judy's ears turned to listen.

The angel usually came behind his eyes, and only once in front of them. He was more a thing of thought than vision, and James had been much oppressed of the mind on that one occasion when the winged boy entered through his eyes rather than his imagination. Either would do now, but the boy was loath to be seen.

'Come now, Richard. Palpable or misty, I care not. Tell me where your bones lie hid. Together, let us thwart evil and strike against the minions of Hell and for the brotherhood of all men.'

But nothing came. So tuned was James's ears for the windborne voice of his angel that he did not notice the raucous chirrup of the ravens as they sky-danced above him. When at last James despaired of his angelic friend, and took out the crap of paper with its faded note and orientated himself to the features of the rock that were so carefully detailed. 'This must be the facet, and these the slabs, like paving stones, which are mentioned. And here must I stand, and thus I must pace. One, two, three and four. Now turn and stride again.' He kicked a scuff into the sparse soil and retrieved the spade and trowels from the pistol holsters that lay across Judy's withers.

At first he was unsuccessful. Perhaps he had started with the wrong facet of granite. He trusted that the Ward's Stone had changed little in the fourscore years since the amulet was buried. Success came on the third dig. On the verge of giving up, James's trowel struck something less hard than granite and yet more firm than poor soil. He had it! The sense of joy and achievement was magnified in the knowledge that this was the last of the amulets, and that all that remained on this Earth of

281

Richard Meekins would soon be all of a place, as it should never have been parted. In his happiness he knew that winged Richard was even now, just over his shoulder. He spun, all glowing with anticipation, but there was nothing.

'And yet, I know you are there, kind Richard, and I know your joy is as mine.' James smiled into the air, and winked. The air winked back.

With the clay cake of an amulet safely away in a saddlebag, James stowed the tools, and readied Judy for the journey home. Mostly downhill, they made good time. After an hour they came to the copse where James at first thought he had seen some riders, and then dismissed it as a trick of the light and the wind giving sway to the branches. Could it be that Judy remembered her fear? She stopped, and would not be moved on. James tried giddy-up, and applied his spurless heels to her flanks. She had become a beast of wet clay, and even the spell he whispered into her ear was ineffective.

'Come, girl! Must I lead you past this leafy beast?' He swung off the saddle, and as his feet hit the earth, so the shrubs at the side of the copse burst open and let out two riders with pistols drawn. They both gave fire to their pieces, and James thought they had both missed, until Judy whinnied and dropped dead by his side. As they drew their swords, James drew his.

They rode at him and would ride him down, but they had either forgotten or had never known, that James was an old soldier who had fought many battles. As the beat of hooves thundered ever closer, all that was James drained out of his body, except for that which was soldier. He became essence of combat, a body that moved by the instinct of fights past, driven by the will of tactics, or parries and feints, of thrusts and coups de grace.

After the first pass, one of the attackers was unhorsed with a blade thrust to the armpit, leaving that arm limp and useless.

'I'll take the old man,' cried the uninjured assailant. 'You get the amulet.' He rode at James again and nearly came off as badly as his co-conspirator. Deciding that the man on the horse does not always have the advantage, he dismounted.

James drew his main-gauche, the same wickedly sharp parrying dagger he had owned since the Battle of the Downs.

James circled so he could keep both his opponent and the second, wounded man in view. While he fought the one, the other tried one-handed, to steal the amulet from dead Judy's saddlebag.

The boy, as James thought his attacker, was at least in his mid-thirties. There was something familiar about him, but the attack was ferocious and there was little time to contemplate past acquaintance. It was ferocious, but inexperience showed and his thrusts were easily put off. James kept the dagger hid behind his left hip until the attacker overstretched himself. Too late he saw the shorter steel and too slowly he turned his body. James struck him a light blow to the top of the hip and drew blood, but nothing deep or disabling.

The younger man, now completely disabused of his own skills against those of an old veteran, changed to another tactic. He was almost twenty years younger than James, and the years could not be denied. Light on his feet, he became the young lion, harrowing the bull buffalo. His attacks were no longer driven home, but meant only to drain James's strength. James recognised the intent and became economical with his responses.

'I have it!' came a shout from the wounded man.

'Then come help me finish this old dog!'

James sprang towards the injured man with a view to finishing him off before he could arm himself and reload a pistol, but his feet were already heavy and even as the injured man ran away squealing like a child, James tripped and landed heavily, face first on the compacted soil road. Before he could recover, the hale man was upon him.

'Turn and face your death.'

James began to mutter a charm.

'I said turn, or I will run you through the back and you may die like a coward.'

James continued to make his spell, and the earth began to tremble. He rolled over to see the attacker peering over his

283

shoulder. The wounded man yelped, ran to his horse, but struggled to mount with one useless arm. James knocked the other's blade aside and retrieved his own, but there was no need. The attacker bolted with no more thought for James, for bearing down on them was Lieutenant Clack and a troop of five dragoons, all at the charge.

The attacker escaped with the amulet. The wounded man made it into the saddle at last, but had no time to get his horse to the gallop before Clack's sword, held to point and stiff-armed while he charged, skewered him through the back of the neck.

'Well met, Lieutenant. And I thank you.' James picked himself up and retrieved his arms. 'See! Out of fashion now,' James said as he displayed the main-gauche. 'But saved my life now as many times before.'

There was no elation in Clack's lantern features. Not a trace of the relief that comes from victory. 'I am sorry sir, but these men or others of their band have done severe hurt to your clerk. He is like to die before dark. He is now at your lodgings, being tended by Miss Eskdale's maid and ...'

James did not wait to hear the 'what' of the 'and'. He knew nothing of the protests from the dragoon whose horse he commandeered or the twelve mile gallop that took him home. It was all a blur. He did not even know that Nino kept up with him, beat for beat.

∞

The youngest Eskdale son had given up his bed for Ruud. James threw his hat into the corner and looked down upon a ruined face. Elizabeth Eskdale and Suzanne her maid both knelt by the bed and sobbed.

'I came upon him as the brutes were about to finish him.' Elizabeth wiped at her brow with a laced handkerchief. 'My scream brought the others running and sent those devils upon their way.'

284

Nino stepped forward. 'He was all but unconscious and would speak only in the Dutch tongue of which I know naught. But then he uttered "Master" and "Ward's Stone". I needed no more to set off to where I thought you too might be in danger, Colonel.'

'Has he spoken since?' James asked.

'Nothing of proper words,' Elizabeth said. 'He frets and is much in the grip of a fever.'

James asked for fresh water and cloth bandages and then to be left alone. He had charms to work and wanted no witnesses.

Darkness came, and the only light was from a brazier and two candles. Ruud's face looked even worse in deep shadow. His nose was broken and would need resetting. Ribs were broken, his torso black with bruises and his balls were up like swollen wineskins. He had been subjected to a beating and to malicious cruelty. From Elizabeth's description of the attackers, James was confident they were the same who had attacked him, and he was glad one of them had been served right by Death.

James sat in the silence of the shadows, broken only by Ruud's breathing. 'Come gentle angel. You failed me at the search. Fail me not now, but let this good and loyal boy live.' This, he thought, must have been how it seemed to Marco when James was the boy in the bed scouted all around by Death. As Marco had been vigilant, so would he.

At midnight, Ruud stirred. James spoke gentle words to him in his mother tongue, and though it pained him, Ruud tried to sit up.

'Forgive me, sir. They beat me and did me hurt until I owned to them the place where the relics were hid. They have stolen Richard's bones.' Ruud began to weep. 'All you have done for me, and I have betrayed you.'

'Now, now! None of it, lad.' James spoke a little above a whisper. 'Treachery is done for gold or for fame. Betrayal isn't done for relief of pain, so there is nothing for me to forgive. Rather it is I who ask your forgiveness, for leaving you unprotected when I had cause to suspect there were enemies near.'

Ruud slipped back into unconsciousness, and James maintained his vigil. After another hour, James dozed and then woke to the screech of a barn owl. He looked about him to regain his wits, and saw that he and Ruud were not alone, but another sat in the corner. It was the angel, not bathed in light, but a shape almost at one with the shadows.

'How come you now, when I have not your bones, and did not come when they were with me safe?'

'I am not of those bones,' the angel said. 'But the bones are of me.'

'And you are also of my sorely oppressed brain. Though you comfort me, you are nothing real of this world.'

'That is said of me in the past. Or is it the future? It is hard to keep time in mind when all time is one.'

James looked at Ruud who was peacefully sleeping. He knew the angel would be gone when he shifted his gaze back to the corner. The angel was still there. James thought of walking to him, and as Thomas had thrust his fingers into the wounds of Christ, he would reach out and feel the flesh and the feathers. Instead, he allowed his doubt to pass.

'Are you an airy being that would disperse on a breeze should I open the window? Or are you a thing of flesh and blood?'

'I am not of flesh and bone. Flesh and bone are of me. Similarly, I am not of air or rock, or wood or flame, or beasts or men. I am of nothing, as everything is of me.'

It would not be meet for so puzzling a spectre to speak in anything but riddles. James thought it quite proper that if the angel was a spiritual being, then no amount of explaining could make his physical brain understand. But what kind of spirit?

'Are you of the Lord our God, or of that terrible other?'

'I am neither.'

'Then perhaps, as I have believed in the past, the spirit of Richard the martyr?'

'I am the man who was crucified.'

Tears sprang to James's eyes and he began to prostrate himself, but with a gesture the angel bid him stay seated.

The angel's wings trembled. 'I am equally the youth whose throat was cut and the boy who was martyred by fire.' Light from the brazier made the shadows dance and gave life to the boy's feathery wings. 'But I am also the soldier with the hammer and nails, the troubled youth with the knife and the sexton with the flaming torch.'

'It seems that you must be alpha and omega and all points betwixt. So had my luck been otherwise, would you have been the hanged boy and those who hauled him up by the neck? Are you me, and all they at one and the same time? Even as you sit there as yourself?'

'I think you are heading towards understanding.'

James grinned and shook his head. 'Then I am on a trail to a path that leads to a street that opens upon a mighty road. Will I ever come to that house that is named "Understanding"?'

'If I ever do, then you shall too.'

James had a moment of clarity. 'And there, good sir-spirit, right there, is the house upon a hill, lit by the sun. And now, here come the clouds once again.'

They sat quietly for some time, the three of them. Every time James looked, the angel was there, every bit as real as Ruud who slept in the bed.

'If I am you, and all are you, and Ruud too, I pray that you spare that part of you that is Ruud to live. I ask you, save this my loyal and worthy servant who is young and innocent. And if there be a balance to address, then take me.'

'Will you love him still when he grows old and wise to the iniquities of the world and adds his own schemes?'

James tried to see further than the answer. 'He will live to become old? I pray it be so.'

The angel stretched his wings so Ruud was in deeper shadow. 'I think he will.'

'You think? Do you now know?'

'Your yesterdays and tomorrows are all my now. I am. Not "was" or "will be" but "am". I am forever, and for me forever

287

is now.' He furled his wings and the shadow fell upon his arms. His wrists were bound.

'God's wounds! Who did that to you?'

'Every man hath done it to me, and every man must release me or leave me bound in his own time.'

'How may I unbind you?' James took out his dagger and stepped towards the angel, but he held aside his bound hands.

'These bindings are proof to all blades. They may be broken by understanding, and as you are on the trail to the path to the street …'

'To the road.'

'… I feel I shall be free quite soon.'

Ruud stirred in his bed. 'Might I have a drink of water please?'

James was at his side in an instant. The boy's brow was quite cool. He fetched him a cup of water and helped him drink. As he mopped the brow, and ministered and helped, the angel drifted from James's mind like a dream on waking, so smoky and insubstantial that there is nothing to hold on to. When the dawn sunlight came into the room, James had no memory of his encounter.

James helped Ruud to sit up when Elizabeth brought in some breakfast and left the tray by the bed. After his first sip of broth, Ruud smiled though it pained him to do so. Before she left, she lighted a gentle kiss on the boy's forehead which made him blush.

With his colour settled and breakfast eaten, he told James that there was a curious story he had to tell and feared James would think him mad. 'Sir, it is a strange thing, but in the night I awoke, and I would swear an oath that you were an angel and that you preserved me from death.'

'How very bizarre,' James said. 'The things that our minds do to us when we are sore oppressed. Perhaps when so close, the veil draws aside and we see into that other place. Come now, and eat a little more.'

∞

Ruud never regained his good looks. His nose remained crooked and he could not properly open one of his eyes. But he gained a wife. Elizabeth protested that Ruud's present station was not so very far below her own and that he came from a family at least the equal of the Eskdales and possibly closer to nobility. Edmund relented and allowed them to wed. No sooner than the nuptials done than life turned for Ruud, as the world turned and those who had been friends of England were now foes.

The English war ended, but with war still in the blood and an eye to enrichment, the English began to dispute Dutch trade routes and supremacy of the oceans. There were some unfortunate incidents when Ruud was ill-treated as an enemy and possible spy. It was time for him to move on.

James made use of old friends and acquaintances who supplied Ruud and the very pregnant Elizabeth with letters of safe passage, and he wrote a glowing report of his clerk's capabilities to his old friend Joseph Deutz of Amsterdam who had become rich on pitch and tar. Captain Nino Clack allowed an escort of troopers to the port and James accompanied them. Although his bones ached, it was a small ache compared to the one that enveloped his heart as the boat sailed out on the morning tide. Ruud and Elizabeth waved until the last, when they were drawn into the mist.

With the war over, James's commission expired and he could no longer rely on troopers to keep a guard on the house of the Eskdales. It was time for James to move on, for the safety of his friends. There had been no more nastiness since the battle up on the Forest of Bowland, but James knew of old, that did not mean his enemies were not watching and waiting. He had no doubt that they had their schemes for the resurgent power of magicians, and now they had the bones of the martyred boy, their objective would be that much easier to achieve. James himself was the only possible impediment to their plans. He hoped to stay alive for another fourteen years, and to remain hale enough to disrupt their rituals of summoning, and even to do battle with them if the need arose.

He had no solid plan, but recalled that he was once made a lord and had been told, by a king no less, that he should acquaint himself with the house at Rillton. He saw the old face of old King James as if it were before him, and unconsciously he revolved the Orbis Mirabilis on his finger. Before he left though, he would climb Pendle Hill one last time. He left his horse and went on foot in the belief that the exercise would do him good. He strapped on his ancient rapier, a weapon now so out of date it made people smile, and set off with a large hunk of bread, some cheese, an apple and a flask of water.

As usual the hill was deserted, and James hoped the angel might come. The last time, by Ruud's sickbed, was so like a dream and sometimes so not, that it confused him to think about it. He met no angel, but instead a very quiet, cautious and yet affable young man who called him 'friend' and shared a rock with him for a seat. Rarely had he met another person who, so like himself, was completely devoid of airs and graces as this lad who did not even raise his hat upon their meeting. James found it greatly refreshing.

It was a curious meeting, for they spoke of deep matters of the heart and did not waste words on the usual trivialities of chance meetings. The young man believed that James could see angels, and in his turn James believed that a heart could be open unto fresh and new words of God who, the young man insisted, still spoke to those who would be quiet enough to listen. James agreed, although to James 'God' did not have quite the same import as it did for others. Not since his last meeting with the angel.

When a few days later James came to the gate of the Faenas Sandrin, the house that lay between the town of Little Rillton and the village of Great Rillton, he was surprised to learn that he was expected. Here he found real allies and he wondered how different his life may have been had he come here all those years ago instead of running away to sea. He had determined to find and destroy the three amulets to thwart the plans of the sorcerers. This he had achieved, and yet now those very sorcerers had the bones of the martyr and the powerful magic they contained.

James discovered that he was a much richer man than he imagined, for the keeper of the house had collected James's annuities and kept them safe, using only a little here and there to help towards the upkeep of the house. Apart from a stake in the house and the grounds, James had a pot of some seven hundred pounds, this in addition to the accumulation of modest riches from his service in what they now called the Thirty Years War.

There was bad news too. These people of the house who were in part his retainers and in part followers of a higher calling of their own, had a network of informers who would give Bertrando's network a merry run for their money. Pleased to hear how unexpectedly rich he was, he now learnt something which struck like a bow. That minion of Bertrando's who he fought and bloodied in Bowland Forest was none other than his very own son. Of course he had seemed familiar. Now it was obvious that he was very like James himself had been at that age.

James had often wondered as to the fate of any issue that had sprung from those torrid nights of his youth at Newark Park. Poor Jane had been cruelly slain, so nothing could come of her, but what of the others? One miscarried, and the other's child lived until the age of four and died of a fever. These new spies of his were good, but their news could not have been any worse. The man, his son, was called Daniel Hughes. He had got his life from James and his beloved Sarah Lister, and his name from the brother of a one-time prison-servant at Lancaster Castle. Daniel had been abducted by Bertrando at the age of seven, and when his step-father brought a report of it to the authorities, instead of help he was hanged by the Royalists for some supposed treason against the King. Sarah died broken hearted a little time after.

Faenas Sandrin was a quiet and out of the way place. Perfect for James to prepare for his great battle, should he be allowed the years. He studied magic and tried to accumulate it for that day when he may truly need it. He ventured out to the village or town on occasion to perform such services as lords were required to for the people. He grew older, but not so much frailer as he maintained a daily routine of exercise to stop his bones from locking and his muscles from withering.

Such were his studies and his search for texts that his name became known among certain alchemists and natural philosophers, and he would occasionally accept visits from among their number. Once such, as the Annus Mirabilis was nearly upon them, was a young alchemist called Isaac Newton. Taciturn and dour, James was not over keen on him. He asked many questions as to the nature of spells and their efficacy and any proof he might have that they worked at all. Were there indisputable results and could they be reproduced? Which of his spells had worked the best. Satisfied by the reports of his 'spies' and his own assessment, James concluded that the youth was no latter-day witch-hunter, and he decided to answer his questions.

'I once raised a fire at some half-mile distance by use of a spell. And then of course, there was my charm against the bleeding gum disease which never once failed me.' He kept quiet about the charmed stone that brained an attacker, or his enemies' ability to shift flesh and become ravens or other birds.

'Bleeding gums? Tell me of it,' Isaac said, almost a demand rather than a request.

There was a time when James would have kept the charm to himself, but what use to take good charms to the grave? 'Take three rose haws, place them apart from each other upon a square of muslin and chant softly "For Father, Son and Holy Ghost". Then move the haws together so that they touch and chant "Bring them together to make the host". Tie up the muslin to make a little bag and pass it three times about your head, then tie the bag around your neck. The charm will work for three days until the haws are drained of their magic. After three days, consume the haws so they cannot be used again.

James chuckled, recalling the line Peter used to add to the charm: 'Now bash them up and eat on toast.' James continued: 'Repeat the charm with three new haws, be they fresh or dried it matters not.'

Isaac ignored the private laughter, his brow creased in thought. 'And your proof that the spell was efficacious?'

'Neither Peter nor I were ever ill of the bleeding gums. Nor any other person whom in later years I charmed, though those about us would drop like flies.'

Isaac nodded and wrote a note in a small ledger he used for such purpose. 'Could it not have been the eating of the haws that saved you, rather than the charm?' What a dolt the boy was! In the want of an answer in the long moments that passed, Isaac deemed his curiosity satisfied. There was nothing more a silly old man could tell him. 'You know, my Lord, there were those in years not too far gone that would have called you a witch.'

'Such men now style themselves "alchemist" or so I am led to believe.'

Isaac took himself back to the university, and the last few months of 1665 took themselves into history. At last the long awaited year arrived, and a month into that year, James entered into his seventy-first year. Perhaps he was the dolt to think that he had a chance against men so much his junior.

∞

There were eight months left before the heavenly bodies were at optimal positions and conditions most propitious for the dissolution of the veils. James had known the date for many years, and also the exact place where the sorcerers would gather and chant their gauze-rending spell, and one of their number, if they were to succeed, must needs be the Last Witch. It had all been written in those musty papers of Doctor Dee. As to that Last Witch, his enemies had his son Daniel Hughes on their side, but Hughes was not the Last Witch as long as James was alive. If he could but survive for a little while longer.

His enemies' plans had changed, for the success of the original had relied on the amulets being placed in the far reaches of the world. With the amulets broken, the sorcerers made a more modest plan. With a corps of sorcerers in three places about the city, they would open the veils for London. Once ruled by magic, they reasoned, the rest of the country would soon follow, and then other countries until the world was safe in their hands. It would take longer, but it was inevitable.

It was all reported to James by the tiny, black-haired Francois de Cordier who styled himself "Blue Friar" but was in fact chief of the Faenas Sandrin spies.

'Well, sir! I say that if I am spared, there shall be a great battle between two men of the craft,' James said. 'Upon that day magic shall be the weapon and only one shall be the "Last Witch" even if it mean the death of the other.'

They set off for London on the 26th August straight after church. James, Francois and two stout fellows with small swords and braces of pistols, each had a spare horse and there was a hobby for a pack beast. Once James could easily have covered the distance in less than four days. Now his bones were old and his flesh weak, but the battle ahead called for spirit, and in spirit James had never been stronger.

As in many a battle, fortune did not turn on the strength of the army or the sturdiness of arms, but on the quality of information. In the battle of spies, the sorcerers had the advantage. Of course they did, James speculated in the days to follow, for they could no doubt see through the eyes of birds, and hear the whispers from the creatures of hedgerow and ditch. James was taken captive a mile out of St Alban's on the fifth day into their quest. Shots were exchanged, men fell on both sides, and James drew his old rapier for the last time. The blade snapped in two when he tried to parry a blow from a heavy mortuary sword. The rest was a blur in the evening gloom, and James was bound and hooded. The hangman's noose had finally caught up with him.

James was manhandled and propelled into a wagon of some kind. It was certainly not a carriage built for comfort, being without springs or seats or any other comfort apart from several empty hessian sacks. He bundled them as best he could to cushion himself against rough wood and bumps.

The horses were kept at the canter, stopping only to change teams. Hours went by and James became so weary that he dropped off for moments at a time, only to be shaken or buffeted awake. They either meant him to die or had given no thought to his comfort. At the third stop to change horses, James yelled out that he needed to piss. Somebody beat the side of the wagon forcefully and swore, but a few miles past the staging post, the wagon stopped and he was rough handled to the side of a ditch and allowed to relieve himself. By now, he was much rattled and his face was bruised. One of his captors gave him loan of a cloak which he folded into a pillow.

Unnumbered posts later they came to their destination. Weary to the state of collapse, James was escorted – no longer dragged – through chill damp airs and into a much rundown house where he was locked into a room with minimal furniture. He was reminded of that other house, fifty and more years past. Where was Marco now to minister to his ills? 'Poor Marco,' he whispered. 'So long ago to your grave. Not long before I follow.' By the light of the one candle he had been allowed, he found the bed and collapsed upon it.

Before sleep took him, he listened for clues as to his whereabouts. The echo of a shout, several rooms away. The creaks and bumps that all houses make. And the unmistakable sibilant voice of the sea, surging and falling, surging and falling.

Surging and falling: the sea lulled him to sleep, and next morning the sea woke him up. Light defied the filth of the window pains and came into the room, discoloured but nonetheless welcome. James stretched out some of his aches and put up with the ones that were not eased through exercise. He took stock of his surroundings. There were two doors and of course, both were locked. The fabric of the house was years passed its best. There was mildew and damp, such that he feared what it would do to his bones if he was kept here for long.

On the good side of things, the bed had plenty of blankets and clean too. There was a wooden chair with no cushion, a small table, a jug of water and a cup, and a pot to piss in. There was a small fireplace although it was not set and there were no logs or kindling, but if this were his gaol than it was luxury compared to the filthy flea-ridden hole he had been kept in as a sixteen-year-old man at Lancaster Castle.

The window was bolted down, and if he was forty instead of seventy, it would have been an easy task to force it and drop the ten feet or so to freedom and escape.

He had been awake an hour when the footsteps of several people approached along the hall and keys were rattled at his door. It was opened to reveal a middle-aged woman in a fine gown which, much like the house, had seen its best. Here were noble people who had fallen on hard times. James rarely bowed, but if ever, it was to those of the fairer sex. James bowed now, making as good a leg as his stiff joints would allow.

The woman curtsied and introduced herself. She ordered a servant to set down a dish. 'The wherewithal to break your fast, sir.'

The servant placed the dish of simple fare on the table. At least he wasn't to be starved. Poisoned, perhaps. 'Thank you, Lady Herbert. My manners, forgive me. I am …'

'Yes, my Lord. I am told who you are, and also that you are no traitor or common criminal, and yet unfortunate circumstances demand that you be kept safe and secure against escape. My retainers without these walls are all armed with halberds and pistols, which I hope will encourage you to be comfortable in your rooms.' She nodded to a second servant who unlocked the room's other door. 'A comfortable place to sit, with books and other comforts.'

'Thank you again madam. These comforts have been arranged by my son, Daniel Hughes?'

'Sir Daniel is your son? Well, well. Such a very strange set of affairs. I'm afraid I know naught of the details, but my family is indebted to Sir Daniel, and for that alone and that we do place in him great trust, you are our prisoner a while, but a very well favoured one, I should hope.'

'I am fortunate enough to have known few prisons in my long life, but even had I known many, I am confident this would surpass them all in its comforts.'

James was informed that he was in the house known as Shurland Hall, which was on the Isle of Sheppey, and that he was to be kept here until Sir Daniel ordered his release.

Lady Herbert begged her leave to go, but then stopped at the door. 'Should you wish to attend Church tomorrow, as I am sure you shall, I might arrange a discrete escort, provided you are willing to vouch me promise not to try an evasion.'

'If it is far to walk, madam, I fear I must decline. Escape, and long walks to Church are quite outside my capabilities these days.'

Lady Herbert and her servants withdrew and the hard clack of a lock being throne echoed about the room. So, tomorrow was Sunday. Even now the sorcerers would be standing within their pentangles and centring their beings, reaching for that quiet within for the sources of their power. 'And I must do the same,' James whispered.

It was the slimmest of chances, but James had succeeded in calling the black arts once before. As a man aged, his body weakened but the cunning powers increased. He had been a boy when he had tried to burn the house of his gaoler, and the spell had fallen far short. Now that he was an old man, success depended on him being able to stretch his powers across two counties. Before he cast the spell, there was another he had to make.

James set up in the other room, which was a veritable library. Time for books later perhaps. He drew a pentangle on the bare floor with charcoal from the fireplace and settled to its centre.

For an hour he spoke charms of protection and preservation, directing them to London and all who dwelt therein. Then, on to his magnum opus, the spell he had been preparing for many years. Long ago he had learnt a piece of magic that was used to disrupt the magic of others. Its use to magic was as a heavy fog is to a clear day. He knew the sorcerers had a long task ahead of them, making their magic all through the day and until dawn on the following day. If they were successful, the new age of magic would pour through on the beams of the morning sun.

James spoke the words of power, knowing that a similar casting had worked before. Last time he intended to make fire, this time only the smoke from fire. He directed magical words with the power of his mind, and emptied himself of all concerns and thoughts until flames burned quietly in his head. An hour for the flames to take, and swirl within his skull. Two hours to form and direct the imaginary flames. Three to imbue them with strength that sprung from the tyrannical hurt done to him and his family. Four to call for the help of his angel … and then, just before collapse … release! And shock! James opened his eyes and recalled the only other time he invoked the black arts. He had wanted to make fire, and there came only smoke. This time he wanted smoke, but he feared the flames may, for want of redress and balance, spring forth and catch.

∞

The sun was up in London, and in Pudding Lane the baker's early work was done. With the bakery full of the smells of freshly baked buns and bread, little Mary Farriner did something that would earn her a beating if father found out. She took some kindling and threw the sticks into the oven, one by one. She loved to watch them catch, and watch the little fire people dancing. The first stick caught, and then the second. The rest she threw in all at once, and felt excited as they snapped and cracked into life. Soon, the little fire people were dancing just as she had hoped, and they grew stronger and fiercer as they began to devour their woody feast.

Then, an unusual thing. One of the bright fire people grew larger than the others, and he put out great flames that looked like wings. Mary peered closed, and then the naughty fire angle made a piece of kindling go off with such a pop that it made her scream. A hot ember flew straight over her shoulder and rolled under the kneading counter.

Mary slammed shut the dampener and the grate just as Daddy stomped in. No, Daddy, of course she wasn't playing with the oven. She was just passing through. Very well then, Mary. You may choose a bun ...

The ember was a hot ant which stayed alive on flour particles and by the frugal consumption of tiny fibres within the floorboard. Ever on the verge of extinction, it blacked the wood by degree after tiny degree instead of setting it to flame. Over the next few hours, it nearly died several times.

At three locations in streets not far away, black-robed men sat within designs of circles and five-pointed stars, and spoke strange words. Just after the criers called midnight, the baker opened a door to slop out, and a breeze slipped in. The breeze found the fire-ant and made it a dragon.

Soon thereafter, London was ablaze. With London on fire, the sorcerers would have to abandon their three centres of magic, or burn to death. They chose to run from the flames, as fast as the fleeing crowds allowed.

∞

'A great fire you say? Do you not mean a great fog?' James received the news from London, fearful of what he may have done.

Lady Herbert read the note again. 'Much smoke, I'll warrant, but there is no mention here of fog. Most of the city is gone up in flame. There is a line to say that the King did throw off his coat, roll his sleeves and help at the pumps!'

'And of the people? Are they much hurt?'

'Indeed, only a little. According to this note, the people speak of a miracle that so much is burnt and yet so few hurt, apart from the hurt of being cruelly dispossessed of their homes and belongings.'

At least the spell of preservation had been effective. In the days that followed, James had much time to contemplate his fate, and wondered if a charm might preserve him from the wrath of the sorcerers. The sorcerers came a few days later. At least their leader did. James received Sir Daniel in his room that had once been a library.

Daniel made a leg and swept his hat with deft gracefulness. 'M'lord,' he said.

James did not bow back. 'No more "m'lords" and let that be your last bending compliment. You of all people must know I am James rather than Giacomo.'

'And yet the peerage is real and you were raised to it by a king, to whom you also refused to bow, as the story goes. Bertrando told me of it often, although he neglected to tell me things of more importance.' The Conte had never made Daniel aware that he was James's son. When Daniel and James had fought in the Forest of Bowland, he had not yet made that discovery. 'I am glad you fought well, Father, for it would have grieved me to kill a man and then to find he was my own sire. You put a fine scar on my hip that day.'

'Sixteen years ago, it was.' James sat on a chair well-cushioned with leather and horsehair and offered Daniel the other. 'You are the age now that I was then. It is like looking in to my own face.'

Daniel made for the chair but stopped to toe the remains of the pentangle. Its diffuse outline was there to be seen despite James's efforts with a broom. 'I suspected so. To effect such a cause over such great distance, you are indeed a witch of much power.'

At that moment, the beliefs of James's entire lifetime fell from solid castles to billowing dust. What utter rot and nonsense! With what many would consider the very proof before him, a light of such clarity blew away the myths by which he had lived, but far from feeling forlorn by the invalidation of everything he had hitherto held true, he was bathed with a great sense of relief. He tipped back in his chair so that the front legs lifted, and he laughed like he had never laughed before.

'You laugh, sir, at the destruction of my life's work!' Daniel's hand flew for the hilt of his sword, but he tucked it away instead, inside the front of his coat. 'We have another chance in fourteen years. I am sorry that you must remain safe until that times has passed and we have made the world as it should be. There is plenty of time for us to make new amulets and place them appropriately.'

James laughed more, to the extent that he withdrew his kerchief and dabbed at his eyes and then mopped his old brow.

Daniel did well to maintain his temper, but his words were spiteful. 'There are those of my fellowship, nearly all of them in fact, that say only your death will keep you from meddling in the future. Have a care that your ill use of me persuades me to side with them.'

'Do as you will, but let me share a revelation that has come to me hot on your heels. I did not thwart your spells. Your spells would have failed without my pathetic efforts which were like pissing on a fire to make it die, no even less than that. There is no such thing as magic! D'you here there? No such thing nor ever was. It is piffle and blather and any other kind of falsehood you may think on. We spend our lives speaking the charms and writing the spells and dancing around in patterns of chalk on the floor. What fools, what utter fools we have been! And never a palpable, visible truth only "might-be" and "mayhap" and "perhaps". Coincidence! Nothing more. What began as a poor man's method of getting bread for the table – say a spell to preserve the sheep and get a loaf from the shepherd – we have made into a great play of lore and intricate articulations, of moving a hand just so, and a wand like this. Whenever did all this ever change anything before our eyes? Never. Never. NEVER!'

301

Sir Daniel slumped to the chair opposite, stunned by his father's soliloquy.

'Keep me here, I say. Or kill me. I will have no more business with "magic", and that, sir, I will say an oath upon. And do whatever you must, but there will never come an age of magic.' James recalled the meeting he'd had with that odious youth, Newton, and the silent mockery with which he was treated. He saw it in the boy's eyes and now he knew it to be well-founded. 'When I was a boy, everybody believed in witches. They killed your great grandmother, your grandmother and your aunt for speaking a few harmless charms. They blamed them for the natural deaths of other and aye, me to. They condemned me to die for a dream I had. But now people are wiser. The time of magic, even belief in it, is passing, and another time is close upon us. Become part of it, Daniel. See into that corner of your being that you fear to look, where lurks that utter certainty that it is all a fool's tale, all a false light to guide us in a lying direction. The world is ill and dark, and bright and wondrous, and we must learn to face it true, and without allowing our reason to be curbed and bridled with false hopes.'

Sir Daniel said no more. He rose, trembling a little. Began to execute a bow but stopped and instead offered his hand. James shook it, and without a word, Daniel took his leave.

'Poor boy,' James said to the walls and the books. 'To think that in the lifetime of one man, the world can change so.' Magic, and all its like, nothing but mist and reflections on dark water. And yet, the angel? How did the angel fit in to his new philosophy?

Months passed and James had no word from Daniel. No word of release, no word of anything at all. He remained a prisoner, though a very well-treated one. Lady Herbert visited him every day except for those times when the court required her in London. He was allowed into the grounds, for the hall was built after the Roman fashion, with a courtyard at the centre. One of Lady Herbert's sons would often play cards with him, and on occasion, when there were sufficient men at arms to escort him, he was allowed to ride and see the sea.

Winter turned to spring, and then came the summer. But June brought with it an unexpected horror. Upon a Thursday afternoon after James had taken some air in the gardens and had a good dinner, there came shouting from the hall: the raised voices of a man and Lady Herbert. There was much clattering about as leather soles struck the wooden floors. James imagined people pacing up and down outside his rooms. And then from Lady Herbert, 'Be gone, you brute! I myself shall conduct this business!'

Lady Herbert won the day, but when his door was unlocked and she stepped inside she was as pale as polished marble and trembled, the papers she held beating like a dragonfly's wings. 'Oh, James. I am brought to utter despair.'

'What is it, my Lady?'

It was hard for Lady Herbert to speak without descending to grief and tears. Sir Daniel had absented himself and gone to nobody knew where. Others of his fellowship had laid charges against James, and such was their influence that the charges had been heard in his absence. 'Surely it is not lawful,' the lady said.

James took the paper and, as he read, the whole world became that paper and the words thereon expanded and pulsed. James sucked in a draught of air and took the note to the window where he read it again. He had been accused of treason, or being in league with and spying for the Dutch. The sentence was death, and being a noble, the method was to be by having his head struck off. He was to be held at Shurland Hall until arrangement could be made to bring the sentence to execution. James closed his eyes tight and looked inside for his angel. Instead there came the noise of thunder. Yet it was not thunder. Who better than James to know thunder from the hollow boom of heavy artillery?

Lady Herbert ran to the window, which was futile as it opened onto the courtyard. There was a crescendo, a veritable broadside of cannon fire. 'May the good Lord preserve us? Whatever is happening?'

303

The household flew into panic and the distant salvos continued, but James was obliged to stay locked in his rooms. Outside, carriages were hurriedly loaded and horses packed. Just before the party fled the house, Lady Herbert looked up from the courtyard, caught his eye and smiled. Moments later, her carriage was gone. And still the cannons boomed.

There was some abatement to the canon fire towards the evening, and it fell eerily quiet come nightfall. The next morning the cannon came again, but sporadic and at much longer intervals. James thought he heard the lighter reports of musketry, but too far off to be certain. He was in the house alone, and locked in with nobody to bring him breakfast. He dressed in his best suit, then took it off and put on his sturdiest instead. He checked the door, which was still locked. He tried to peep through the keyhole and discovered the key had been left in from the other side, and remembered a trick to escape in this eventuality. It was while he fiddled at the lock, trying to make the key drop onto a sheet of paper he had torn from a large atlas, that Shurland Hall was invaded by a troop of soldiers. They were soon at his door, and the lock thrown.

James drew himself up and tried to assume a dignified air. The door was thrown back and an elegant young man armed for battle stepped in.

'Good morning, sir,' James said. 'Forgive me, but is there any breakfast to be had. I am famished.'

The young officer bowed a little. 'Who, pray tell, is this fine gentleman who has been locked away until his stomach doth rumble?'

James smiled to hear a Dutch accent, which made his choice of identity all the easier, for he had ever been 'James' to the Dutch and rarely 'Giacomo'. A different name on the warrant could be explained if the necessity arose. 'I am James Devis,' he said in perfect Dutch. 'I served with Admiral Tromp at the Downs, was sometime Master Gunner for Lennart Torstennson and others of that war. And now,' James picked up the warrant and proffered it, 'I am condemned to die as a spy for the Dutch.'

The young officers beamed and bowed again, much closer to the floor this time. 'Then, sir, this is the luckiest of days.' He took the warrant but did not look at it. 'I am Lieutenant Jan Hurkmans, currently of the Dutch warship Vrede. Please consider yourself liberated.'

After taking the fort at Sheerness and then the rest of the Isle of Sheppey a day later, the Dutch had effectively invaded part of Britain. Much to James's relief, they did not stay long. Even more to his liking, they took him with them.

∞

Thirteen years after the Dutch stormed the Medway and took the Isle of Sheppey, James moved slowly and stiffly along a gallery hall in a large house in Amsterdam. He leaned on eight-year-old Willem de Witt's shoulder to ease the pain in his hip. Willem was Ruud and Elizabeth's youngest son, half the age of his father when he had approached James all those years ago and asked for employment.

'This is my favourite painting, Old Pa. Do you like it?'

'Yes, very much. What a lovely little dog.'

'Oh, silly Old Pa! It isn't a dog at all, it's a pussy cat.'

James leaned in as close to the painting as his frozen hips would allow. 'So it is. My eyes are rather dim these day, Willem. But come, see the painting I was speaking about.' He shuffled along past burgers and farmers, great ladies and milk maids until he came to the one he wanted to show the boy. 'You have skipped along this hall since you first were able, and I am sure you have stopped by all the ones with animals, and battles, and soldiers. But have you ever stopped to look at this one?'

'Of course I have! It is my next favourite, after the one with the cat.'

James was surprised. Why would a little boy like a painting of an old man?

'It is because it is Papa's favourite. He says it is you, as you were when he first met you during the war. He often looks at it, and so does Uncle Joseph. They say it is a very fine painting, by a fine old master. Once when Papa looked at it, he went like this.' Willem took in a deep breath, held it in a second and then let it out. 'I asked if it made him sad, and he said it was the kind of sad that is really happiness in a sad hat.' The little lad laughed and his high peels echoed around the hall. 'Sometimes Papa is very silly.'

'Sometimes your Papa is a veritable philosopher wearing a silly man's hat.' James's laugh was wheezy and it terminated in a cough. 'Come now, Willem. Take me back to my rooms. I grow weary.'

It wasn't a long walk, but James was short of breath when they arrived at his suite.

'Shall I have a story, Old Pa?'

'Of course you shall. Only, come back after supper.'

The next morning Ruud and Elizabeth found Willem playing with his regiments of tin soldiers. He sat on the wooden gallery floor underneath Frans Hals' painting of James, and the soldiers were lined up as if for inspection. He had a new one, the Master Gunner, whom he had laid down in front of the captain and the sergeants and all the many men and the ensign with his paper flag.

'Now then, Will,' Elizabeth said. 'What have we told you about playing in the gallery? We are very lucky to live in Uncle Joseph's fine house, and his rules are but few, so we should have no hardship obeying those rules, and one of those rules is …'

'Yes, Mama, I know. No games in the gallery. But I thought, this once, Uncle Joseph would be glad of my game. I am holding a parade to wish Old Pa goodbye.'

Ruud and Elizabeth exchanged a look. What now from their bright and singular little lad? 'Whatever do you mean?' Ruud squatted and went to stand up the Master Gunner.

'No, Papa! Leave him, for he is meant to be Old Pa, and last night Old Pa went to live in Heaven.'

It was not seemly for people to run along corridors, but Mn'Heer and Mn'Vrouw de Witt ran, and when there was no reply to their knocking, they opened James's door fearing the worst. James was in bed. He looked peaceful and wore the slightest of smiles, but his body was lifeless and as cold as the Delft jug on the table. Elizabeth was horrified to see Willem standing at the door, and with all the natural desire for a mother to shield her child from the sad realities of the world, she would take him back to the nursery, but Ruud said let him stay, and tell us about last night.

'He said I might come after supper for a story, and so I did. But he was asleep, so I sat in his great chair and I fell asleep too. Then I woke up and Old Pa was awake and he said he had a good life and was now tired and ready to go. He said he had done many wrong things and few good, but the good were all intended and the bad not so. He said that if he wished anything, it was that he should have listened more to his own council, and that the best of the good things he had done, was to make a clerk of you Papa, and it made him glad to see you come to much happiness and good. And then he said it was time for him to fall asleep and therefore to wake ... which I supposed to be one of those silly things to say that is somehow actually very clever.'

Elizabeth stooped to hug her son. 'Were you not very frightened?'

'Only that he may see me and think me spying on him.'

'Spying,' Ruud said. 'But he was speaking to you. Wherefore spying?'

'Oh no, Papa. He was not speaking to me, but to the boy with wings. He sat on the bed and smoothed Old Pa's hair as he spoke, though it must have been hard, for his wrists were bound. He was a big boy, like cousin Luc, not little like me, nor not quite grown to a man.'

Ruud and Elizabeth again exchanged looks, now worried and concerned.

'But then, of a sudden, the boy's wrists were free. He looked at me and smiled such a smile that it made me happy. I wanted to dance, and have wings like him but he said all in good time. He then took off, out of the window. And then I woke up again and I looked at Old Pa's face, and I knew that he had gone away. With the boy, I should like to think. Old Pa said that the giant star that fills the sky these last nights is the last of the sorcerers fleeing in failure and shame, going from the world forever. But I would rather think it is the carriage of the angel who rides Old Pa to Heaven.' Willem frowned. 'Is that a very silly notion that I had, Papa? Mama?'

'No, Willem. It is a very lovely and beautiful notion.'

'Then, why are you crying, Mama?'

Ruud got down to his knees and took his wife and son into his arms. 'It's a happy notion, but we will miss Old Pa, so for a time, we shall be happy and thankful that he came into our lives, but of course, we shall wear sad hats.'

Willem broke away from his parents and joined the tin soldiers. He took a little box from his pocket and brought out his most special soldier who was painted to look like a general. He held it by the base and moved it in time with his words. 'In honour of the Master Gunner who has fallen this day, the Royal Guard will make a general salute.'

Mamma and Papa got to their feet and Papa had a care and stood straight and still like a soldier.

'Parade! Present ... arms!'

7

The Codices of Varius - The Years 221AD & 2016AD

Ω

A young lady stopped by the entrance to the apartment block. She leaned on the railing, took off a stiletto and massaged her foot. An older lady caught her eye and gave her a knowing look and then a smile of sisterhood. 'Why do we do it?' she said in passing, and chuckled.

The younger woman blushed and shrugged her shoulders. She replaced the implement of pedal torture, went inside and climbed the stairs to the first floor. The door to the apartment opened before she had the time to push the bell.

'Anna! You look taller.' Leo beckoned her in and stood to one side. 'Welcome to my humble abode,' he said and then, raising his voice, 'Alex, come and meet Anna.'

Alex kissed her on the cheek and said please to meet you, and Anna felt a tingle in that mound of flesh that she was eager to hide but loath to get rid of. No, the hormone treatment was as far as she was prepared, or even wanted to go. They gave her awful mood-swings, but she'd started with them early enough to inhibit the male-bulking of her body lines, and she didn't have to shave, so the moods she could deal with.

Alex was a hunk, and as confident and self-aware as Leo was the opposite. But Leo, he was sweet. Right now, Leo was excited or as excited as Leo could be. Alex watched his friend in what Anna judged to be fond amusement. He went to the kitchen to prepare some drinks.

'Do you know what this latest discovery is all about, Alex, and why Leo is so excited?'

It was, of course, an exciting find in itself, and in the end the clues had been quite straight forward.

'Like all clues, when you know the answer, Anna said. 'Do you mind if I take these off?' It was a rhetorical question. There was a convenient niche for her shoes at the side of the sofa. She drew her legs up under herself.

Alex admitted that Leo was better at translation and that he had no idea what Leo was about to reveal. He went on to explain that the clues all had to do with witchcraft. The break came when Leo discovered that there had been a witch trial in the English county of Lancashire in 1612, and that date was one of the other clues. It was then a simple matter to search the records for a contemporary account of the trial, written by an old squire of that county. In among the accusations of witchcraft and so-called proof, was the second codex of Varius.

The drinks served, Leo handed Anna and Alex a copy each of his translation. 'Still wet off the press,' Leo said, and he giggled like an excited schoolboy. He really was sweet, and Anna was beginning to like 'sweet' better than 'hunk'.

∞

The Second Codex

Year VII, M.Aur.Antoninus

When Father died, which was very sudden, I knew my life would change, but I did not know how. I was very sad to lose him, but I did not cry. Great Uncle Balbi said I was brave, but it was not that. If he could have seen inside me, he would have known I was very far from brave. I was scared, because things were happening, and I knew they would affect me because my god told me while I was dancing for him.

And not only that but there were whispers and meetings, and Grandmother visited more than she ever had before. When she came she would ask to see me and she would look at me as if I was a pot in the market that she was deciding whether or

310

not to buy. She had audiences with Mother and my aunt and they would speak in hushed tones so that I could hear nothing when I listened at the door, and they would all break off and look at me and smile. This was happening even before Father died. It hardly seemed important enough to mention in my journal at the time, but now I am convinced it is very important.

I have found out something that I believe has been deliberately kept from me and it is something that frightens me a great deal. I have not asked about it but I am going to ask my teacher if we might practice administration and record keeping by going to the archives. I might find the answer there. Do you, reader who will only see this after I am dead, want to know what I think is happening? I think I am a lot closer to the imperial line than I had thought. I think my Grandmother is scheming, as all those close to the purple are wont to do. And I think she had Father killed. If I ever find proof of this, I will kill her.

VIMarch

I have just returned from a brothel where I fornicated for the first time. It was something that had not occupied my thoughts very often, but it is pleasant enough and I look forward to the next time, although it may be some years off, this visit being for a very specific purpose.

This is the end of a very curious day, for it started with me being woken with some urgency by Arriatus. There was to be a ceremony and when I was told it would be the ceremony of putting on my man's toga, I wondered if I was to be killed. In times past, boys were dressed in their man's toga in order that they could be killed without bringing bad luck upon the killer. If a family was to be wiped out, the boys would be dressed in their man's toga and the girls would be raped, for it is a curse from the gods to slay a boy or a virgin.

But then it was explained that I am to be made High Priest of Illaha Gabal and whereas the local people would accept a boy as High Priest – in fact it is a requirement – proper Roman

311

people would not, and as there are many, many Romans now flocking to Elagabalus, as they call him, I must be a man to be raised to High Priest. I find this strange, because Illaha Gabal did not mention this to me last time he spoke. He speaks to me all the time, but he said nothing of this. And yet, it is only the High Priest who is supposed to hear his words, and so by speaking, perhaps this was his way of telling me.

The ceremony would have been boring had it been longer. Afterwards there was a nice little feast and then Grandmother told me that there were other duties to being a man than priesthood and that she had paid for me to visit the best brothel in all of Emesa.

I must say, if that was the best brothel, I would hate to see the worst. We were met by an old lady, at least as old as Mother, who must have been a whore once herself. The house smelt of incense and there was an anteroom where you are supposed to sit on the cushions and drink wine and eat figs and choose from the whores who walk around dressed in robes so fine they blow in the wind and you can see through them. But I was shown to a smaller room that must be for important people. It was smaller and more secluded. I gather when you choose a whore from the big room, she leads you to a cubby where you fornicate, but in this room the whores came to you.

Arriatus asked if I was alright and I said I supposed I was and that I would be glad to get it over with. He left me and in came a little whore called Renita, who could have been not much past the age I should have actually been to get my toga. She let her top covering slip. It was interesting how the breeze caught it and it floated to the ground.

She sat next to me and touched my knee. She slid her hand up my tunic, and she touched me and then undressed me to my loincloth. I wasn't enjoying it very much. It all seemed so silly. I will put it no finer, not even for someone who is to read this at a time past my death, than to say she was not succeeding in her duties to excite me. She called for her friend, who was much older, older even than Arriatus, whose name

312

was Sidonia. She made free with her lips up and down my arms and nibbled at my nipples. She began to work her way down but I told her to stop. With deft fingers she removed my loincloth and her face was the very picture of disappointment when she found no spear, but a timid and coiled little snake. She said she believed she knew what my problem was, and so she called another whore who was called Crispinus and who was a boy maybe two years older than me. I had no idea boys could be whores.

Let it be sufficient to say that Sidonia had been correct. Renita and Sidonia left Crispinus and me alone to have a nice time. And a very nice time was had.

When I was back home and told mother about it she smiled, but when I told her I had been the one to lay down, she slapped me. I reminded her that I was now a man, and that if ever she forgot that from this day on, I would have her beaten. She said it was not for a man to lay down for another, and perhaps, therefore, I was not one. I took the switch that is meant for beating disobedient slaves and she immediately apologised and became contrite. She asked me for the whore's name and I gave her a false one. Crispinus had been terrified when I told him what I wanted and said he could be killed for it if my father found out. I told him my father was dead, but he pleaded with me to use him any way I pleased, but that I should not have him use me. I reminded him who was paying the money and swore I would not allow him to be hurt. I hope my mother does not find out his true name and have him killed. His death for my little pleasure is really not quite fair. But if he is killed, then I suppose that is one of the dangers of his kind of work.

It is also the danger of being Emperor, so at least in this, whores and emperors are the same. Perhaps, every once in a while, an Emperor should play the whore, just to make him mindful of the lives of the most lowly, who also have their parts to play in the Empire.

Once again, I am fearful of the scheming ways of the women in my family, and I hope they do not have a terrible fate planned for me, but when I add everything together, I am sure there can be no other answer. They see me in purple, for a little while, until the purple is stained with my blood, which is the fate of all Emperors unless you look very far back, and there are those that say even the great Augustus was murdered.

VIIIMarch

I am now High Priest of Illa Gabal. There was a private start to the ceremony. After undressing and cleansing ourselves, we danced before god and the old high priest led me to him and a secret part of the ceremony happened which the High Priest told me was so very secret that it was not even to be written in this record. It was quite pleasant and there were one or two parts of it that reminded me of Crispinus the whore, but there was nothing whoreful about the ceremony. The High Priest taught me the steps to a new dance that I would need for the next part. The god then received our libations and then we left him for the rest of the ceremony.

And then I was High Priest and my first role was to pretend to kill my predecessor. This was not completely private, nor for the public, but done in front of all the other priests except the acolytes. I pretended to bash in his brains with a large club and he had to fall and be caught by the priests and carried high to his tomb. Then I came to his tomb by the intricate steps of a dance which is only done at this time, and kissed him, thereby giving him new life, and he rose up and took his place at the head of the priests with those two who were high priests in their time. Now there are three former high priests, which they say is the highest number there has been. I suppose Great Uncle must die soon, so if I live to see a day when I am killed and raised again, there will still only be three.

Next, god was lifted onto a litter and we danced into the public part of the temple, which was filled with people and many of the soldiers from my father's old legion. There were many more soldiers than usual, and it was as if the newcomers had never seen a naked priest dance before. They called out things, which is very rude to do in the temple but some of them are very rude fellows. But what they actually said was not rude in itself. They called out compliments on the perfection of my body and my dancing, the polite ones did, and the impolite ones made crude and raucous noises and whistled and said what they would like to do with me, which again made me think of Crispinus. There was a very young centurion among them, not five years older than Arriatus I think, and I would quite like him to do some of those things to me. There are certain urges within me, and I do not know if they come from god or not.

God told me to chide the unruly fellows, and so I stopped dancing and put them in their place. With the words of Illa Gabal inside me, I was gentle in my words and demeanour but fierce behind the eyes and implacable in my intent. As I spoke, I felt my words were the very ice of god's breath, and that no man might gainsay them. They were immediately abashed. Some cast down their eyes and an optio mumbled something for my forgiveness.

For the last part of the ceremony, I was clothed in high priest's silks, for a priest must not go naked under the sky, and I led god out into the square for all the people to see who were too many to come into the temple, and there was such cheering that my ears still ring. God was very happy and he sent thrills through my body. There followed great feasting and now the day is done and the people are happy.

∞

'Woo-hoo! This Varius guy is as queer as the rest of us,' Anna said.

'Pardon?'

'Oh, sorry Alex. As queer as me and Leo.'

'Pardon?' Leo said.

'Oops. I mean, it seems Varius is as queer as me. Between reading your translations, Leo, I've been looking him up on the internet.' Anna waved her iPhone. 'It says he may be the

315

world's first recorded transgender person. I'm really beginning to like her.'

Oh dear. She had embarrassed the boys, and they had both buried their heads in their copies of the transcript, so she followed suit. Maybe thinking you were an angel didn't count as queer after all, and she had only made an assumption about Alex because he was drop-dead gorgeous, had good clothes and was a friend of Leo's.

There were no more sex references in the transcript, vague or otherwise, which Anna thought a pity. There was much of chariot races, and the mention of more shenanigans by the woman in Varius' life. And then came a rushed page that spoke about the death of the Emperor whose everyday name was Caracalla – skewered with a pilum while he squatted by the side of the road to poo. These Roman assassins certainly chose their moments. And then came a page that made Anna look up from reading and study Leo's face. When god spoke to Varius, he claimed to know it was god's voice and not his own words reverberating through his skull, because god's words came on the wings of an angel. 'When god speaks to me, it is as if they spring from the shadow of his great wings. When I think my own poor thoughts, they are noisier, and speak of dinner and drink and the everyday. They make me think of Crispinus when I pleasure myself, and they try to scare me when I think about the future. When god speaks, he is very quiet. He only comes when I dance. He takes my body and makes me his. I become an angel.'

'Leo, have you been very accurate with your translation, or is some of it guesswork?'

'You refer to the part about an angel, Anna? Of course, sometimes I have to choose a more modern idiom, but that part is just as Varius intended.'

'Oh my God!'

'Quite! I find it … quite frightening.'

Alex had not been let into the secret of Leo's self-image. He was either still absorbed with the translation, or he decided to let his questions go. Anna was in for some very interesting discussions with Leo. She could hardly wait. Unfortunately, she had to wait. They had an unexpected visitor. Bloody bishop! She tried to keep the bishop out of her thoughts and concentrate on something else. It had been all that talk of sex in Varius' codex. Back in her own small, shared apartment, Anna made the best of her flatmate's absence and made love to Leo. She lay on top of her bed, over the covers, naked and on her back, while Leo covered her and thrust himself into her hand: a kind of masturbation by proxy. It was a start. Once he overcame his silly reservations, they would go all the way. Anna held him firm in one hand and stroked the back of his head with the other as they kissed passionately.

It was not long before the heralds of pleasure coursed through Anna's blood and then gathered in her lower belly. They came together, and with the release of orgasm, the imagined Leo faded away, leaving only his erection, which was of course, Anna's. Leo's seed – hers – formed a pool in the hollow of her naval and quickly cooled. The tissues close to hand, she cleaned up, and then lay a little while longer while warm breezes from the open window played against her skin.

Excitement gone, she felt the first nip of the black dog that she had heard howling at Leo's apartment. If she took no evasive action, she would be in a deep depression come nightfall. But the black dog's nip carries a drop of poison and so the paralyses is hard to avoid. Anna was the only transgender person in the entire world who did not hate her un-transitioned body. Nobody understood her. On the forums, some would appear to understand, but there would always be the trolls. 'You're not trans, bitch! You're gay!' That had been a recent one. 'You're a girl, with a body like that! I've seen you in 'Q' and some of those other fashion magazines. Straight boys would kill to have a body like that. And gay boys would kill to have a body like that. And don't tell me it's all posing for the camera. You enjoy all those scenes screwing around with hot boys, don't you? Come on! Make up your mind. Boy or girl. You can't have it both ways.'

317

Anna had made up her mind long ago. She was a girl. It was completely irrelevant that her body was physiologically male, and none of anybody's damn business if she wanted to keep it that way. Anna stood in front of the full-length mirror that was hooked over the back of her bedroom door. 'I'm a girl. I'm straight.' She giggled. 'And I'm never without a cock to play with.' She flicked her semi-tumescent member and admired the heft of its swing.

Anna strayed to the part of her wardrobe that contained her boy clothes. It was a bad sign, and she tried to resist. If she stuck to her girl clothes, she had a very good chance of beating back the black dog. It might not come at all. But what if it did? If she dressed like a boy – she opened the drawer and snatched out a pair of boxer-trunks – he might as well cancel all appointments for the next three weeks. Stay girl and risk utter despair, or back to boy and hack it – just? He pulled the trunks on and slid his favourite pair of skinny boy-jeans off the hanger. The black dog was in an implacable mood; he had to weather the storm as Matteo.

Fully dressed, he stood in front of that mirror again. 'Hi Matty. Long time no see.' Matteo transformed his room. Perfumes, foundation and lippy in the dressing table drawer; Nivea for Men and Lynx out. Pink duvet cover off, blue one on: Matteo was gender-typical in product choices, and so was Anna.

At first, he felt quite good, for there was always a calm before the storm. It took a lot of nervous energy to maintain his other, his true persona, and when he replaced soft fabrics with denim and heavy duty cottons, there was an initial release, a brief feeling of freedom. Haters might hate him for being gay and effeminate, but that was far easier to handle than the devastation of an attack to his true self. In fact he was neither gay nor effeminate. The Boys-Like-Us Studio had made him top model for his straight good looks, but other people's perceptions could never trump his own. He was not gay, because he was a girl who liked boys. He was effeminate because he was a girl. He was not in the least confused that he was still a girl when he was Matteo, but used the male pronoun.

As a boy he could sometimes pacify the black dog, make it his very own dusky puppy, a friend that needed to be understood and chuckled under the chin. As a girl, the black dog tore him apart. It had only happened once. Never again.

'It was that fucking bishop.' Matteo mentally pinpointed the moment that started this bout. The masturbation has been a release of sorts and kept it at bay for a while, but it was that encounter with the bishop that started it. The contempt with which the old fart had looked at him. 'Do I know you from somewhere?' as if talking to a scruffy dog in the streets. Maybe at confession, Anna had suggested. No, the bishop was sure it was somewhere else, and quite recent.

Okay, Anna, it was a very, very bad idea, and so naughty, but the Bish needed taking down a peg. It was one of those things that was funny at the time. 'You might have seen me in the latest copy of "Lui"? It hit the top shelves last week.

Matteo leaned back on his bed and scratched his balls, the last ritual in the renewed assumption or reacceptance of biological maleness. He recalled the look on the old man's face and laughed. Bingo! The bishop looks at male fashion magazines. Probably from the Vatican's very own secret stash. He stopped laughing as the black dog circled. It wasn't a good idea to make enemies in high places, and the last thing he wanted was to make it awkward at work for Leo.

Matteo did not laugh again for several days. The black dog kept watch for an hour, and then pounced. He knew it would pass, like a great black storm, and he knew he would not try to kill himself this time. The storm was in him. He was not the storm. He usually navigated the long dark tunnel alone and by the experience of having weathered it before. But this time, there was the tiny glimmer of the ghost of a light, and the light was Leo. It was enough, even though the beacon had no idea that he shone for Matteo, and for Anna.

Matteo knew he was a girl and it mattered not one whit what doctors and psychiatrists said. So who was to say Leo was not a bone fide angel? Matteo did not actually believe he was, but he knew from his own experience that other people's beliefs did not count. If Leo thought he was an angel, he was and there was something to support the belief. Leo had met Anna and had been completely accepting. And then Anna changed to Matteo right before his eyes, and Leo had been no less accepting. This was not what he had come to expect from priests. It wasn't the priest in Leo that made him wonderful. It had to be the angel.

A single bullet in the right place would bring down fighter aircraft. Something so small, but blasted into a vulnerable spot, and the tailspin would begin. So it was with Matteo's depressions. A word could send him spiralling towards the earth, and a word could save him. A remark so unremarkable that others would not notice it for its importance. A little kindness. A thoughtful comment. Once even a radiant smile bestowed upon him by a stranger. This time Matteo's salvation began with a pigeon.

It had taken supreme effort, but he had forced himself out of the house to indulge in some retail-therapy. On the Via del Corso on the way to his favourite shop, a low-flying pigeon made him duck. Matteo recalled that Enrico's name for these scruffy town-dwellers with their sooty feathers and deformed feet was 'shit-doves'. A smile and a spark deep within the wet-blanket fug of his present existence failed to ignite fully. Just a smoulder of warmth, but it was the barrage that softened him up for the main attack, which happened in the Piazza Italia while he held a nice dress up to himself to check for size.

He had already selected some boy clothes, and now he was in the women's section. It made life easier if he could conceal the girls' wear behind a shirt or a pair of jeans when he approached the fitting rooms. Without a lot of spare cash, he had to decide which dress to choose. He stood before a mirror and held up one and then the other, while trying to ignore the many elderly couples who had taken over the shop that day. Old guys pushed shopping trolleys full of women's items while the wives darted down this aisle or that to look for another bargain. It had to be something to do with the time of day, because Matteo was the youngest person in the shop until a young couple with a little boy entered from the main street.

'What does that say, Daddy?' the little boy said boisterously as he pointed to the words on an advert for a new range of men's clothes.

'It says "Behave yourself, you noisy beast!"', Dad replied.

The little lad accepted Daddy's lie quite happily and skipped into the interior of the store.

Matteo was still undecided. To make it worse, a third outfit caught his eye. He found his size.

'Something for your girlfriend? Or your sister?' asked the assistant who materialised as if from nowhere.

'Yes, of course,' he might have said as a teen. Teen days were no more. 'No. They're for me. What do you think? This one, or these?'

A true professional, the assistant hardly stumbled. 'Oh, er … I think the top and skirt is more your age group. Would you like to try them on?' It was only then that her eyes widened, and Matteo knew exactly why: *God! Do I show him to the male or the female fitting rooms?*

'I've got these too,' Matteo said and held up the shirt and jeans.

The assistant smiled, off the hook. 'The fitting rooms are just over there.'

Matteo had been navigating the lowest depth for days, but now he blew main ballasts and shot to the surface. He didn't really know why. Maybe the 'shit-dove', or the carefree little boy, or something else so subliminal he hadn't consciously registered it. After nearly a week of running silent and running deep, he was ready to strike his colours. 'It's okay, thanks,' he said to the assistant. 'The one over there is more my style.' He flashed her a smile and made for the women's fitting rooms.

A middle-aged man leaned against the wall looking slightly less bored than the wall, but he perked up when he saw Matteo coming. 'Hey, this is for ladies. Men's is over there.'

Matteo smiled, lifted the hangers carrying the skirt and top, and breezed past as if they were his passport.

Everything fitted and looked good. He decided to buy them all.

On the way out of the store, he had to step aside for a rather large and imperious woman who wore expensive, but not quite up to date clothes, and lots of jewellery. She fixed him with a harpoon-like stare while still talking loudly to the thin man who appeared to have the misfortune to be her husband. Matteo was closer to security barriers but the lady wasn't stopping for a mere boy. He would jolly well have to wait.

It was just the very kind of rude and inconsiderate behaviour that was often the first barbed herald of a rapid fall into the depths, but not today. A shrill little voice piped up from behind. 'Behave yourself, you noisy beast!'

The world stood still. The large woman lost animation as if her power had been cut. Her husband's tried to catch flies with a mouth that groped for words but found none. Behind, the little boy was being dragged by the hand at top speed back into the shop by a father with a very red face. The little boy laughed and pointed to the words on the advert.

Matteo held it in until he had left the shop. He then laughed at regular intervals all the way home. When he got there, it was time to be Anna once more.

She hadn't been home and changed for long before there was a knock at the door. She ignored it. Her flatmate was such a lazy arse that she knocked and waited rather than go to the very great inconvenience of taking her key out. After the third ignored knock, a text message told Anna it was Enrico at the door, and not her flatmate. It made her wish she had stayed in Matteo's clothes for a little longer. Enrico had loved her as Matteo. He only suffered her as Anna.

Sure enough, Enrico's face dropped minutely when she opened the door. The tiniest narrowing of the eyelids, that only someone as highly tuned to mood as Anna could have spotted, and then the smile and the cheery greeting. On another day, signs such as these could have been the bullets that sent her crashing to the ground. Today, she was strong.

Anna flipped the caps of a couple of beers. Enrico drank from the bottle. Anna poured hers into a large wine glass. Once she had thrown her flatmate's washed but un-ironed clothes into a pile, they had somewhere to sit.

'Has our friend the Father been able to help you?'

'Oh yes, but not in the way you expected. In the end I wasn't really interested in acceptance by the church. I thought it was important, but it turns out I don't really care about that after all. I've grown past the need for it.'

'But you're still seeing him. What's that about?'

'I like him. I more than like him.'

'You fancy him! My God,' Enrico laughed. 'Get to the back of the queue.'

'I think I more than fancy him. I think ... I'm falling for him. But you see, I'm not entirely sure. He is the first person, the very first person who has accepted me both as Matteo and as myself. I have to make sure my feelings for him aren't just some sort of magnified gratitude.'

Enrico became serious. He took his sunglasses out of his shirt pocket and fiddled with them. 'I'd put it down to the gratitude thing if I was you. Why give yourself pain? He's a priest. It's never going anywhere.' Enrico spoke from his own feelings.

'You've obviously given it a lot of thought. You really do fancy him too, don't you?'

'No!' the gentleman protested too much. 'A priest is off limits, and anyway, you've already got him into a lot of trouble.'

Anna was upset to hear that the Bishop had called Leo into his office and berated him, on behalf of the Cardinal, for consorting, in his own apartment, with degenerates and perverts. Enrico delivered the news with a barb of spite that made Anna believe he saw her as a rival for Leo's affections. Furthermore, there was a veiled threat of moving him away from his Vatican job and out into the country somewhere.

'But if I'm honest, I don't think any of this has to do with you, Matt ... sorry, Anna. I think they're pissed at him for looking for these old books. You have to ask yourself, why were they hidden in the first place? I think they're using you as an excuse to side-line him for unearthing something they would rather remain hidden.'

Anna took a long sip of beer. 'And people wonder why I'm through with churches.'

∞

'So, this is it,' Cardinal Hugh di Fornea said. He placed the leather bound codex carefully on his desk between the calendar and the carved figure of St. Francis. 'Such a slim volume. Should we not wear gloves to handle it?' The Cardinal became aware of the smell of beeswax and hoped the polish on his desk would not permeate the ancient pages and do them damage.

'Gardening gloves would do, to protect our hands when we rip the thing to pieces.' Bishop Michael Spiller sat without being invited. 'Or perhaps it should be incinerated. A fitting end to heresy.

'And should we put young Father Leo to the torch too? Really, my friend, we have moved on a little since ...' He carefully opened the codex and perused the seal and signature. ' ... since Pope Sixtus V condemned this old tome.'

'In point of fact, Your Eminence, Sixtus condemned all other copies, but not this. This 12th Century copy of a lost original was to be kept with other works discovered in the Constantine stack, although the reason why any Pope should want to preserve the lunatic ravings of a disgusting pervert completely evades me.'

'I suspect he had a respect for history.'

The bishop did not agree. It was an oversight, and one that had led directly to the current difficulty with a young priest who had too much empathy and a soul insufficiently tuned to tradition and doctrine. Michael explained to the cardinal that he had kept onside with Leo so that he would remain open about his and his historian friend's discoveries. They had found and translated three codices, judged one too far gone to translate, and were still searching for the final codex.

'As I understand the situation, Michael, the codices that Father Leo has found were all secreted in other works. Is there likely to be a copy of this one waiting to be discovered, and if so, is it really a very great disaster? The Church has weathered worse threats in its long history. I fail to believe the fantasies of a teenaged emperor will bring us to our knees.'

The bishop took a file from his briefcase. 'I have some trusted members of staff keeping an eye on Father Leo and his friend Doctor Whitby. If they come close to a discovery, they are ready to step in. As for the damage that may ensue from insensitive revelation, see for yourself, Your Eminence.' He laid the file to the side of the codex and then moved to pick up the codex itself, but the cardinal slapped his hand on it.

'Oh, I do apologise, Michael. I did not mean to startle you. And I thank you for the transcript, but I would prefer to exercise my old and rusty skills at Latin.'

'There is no need. I can vouch for the transcript. The translation is perfect. I'll just ensure that this is destroyed, as it should have been in 1589 but for the error of Pope Sixtus.'

'A Pope, in error? Now that's a belief that would have once earned you a visit from the Inquisition.' Cardinal di Fornea chuckled. 'Thank you again, but I will deal with this old relic myself. Just as soon as I have read it.'

∞

The Last Codex

Year IV, M.Aur.Ant.Aug

I have been very remiss in keeping this, my story, up to date. It is two years since I last wrote. Very soon, the next High Priest

325

of Illa Gabal will be able to read this, if he should so wish, because I shall be dead. True, I have been surprised to see the light of each new dawn since the soldiers first declared me for the purple. I charged into battle, a fourteen-year-old boy because I had already accepted I was dead. And I have not lived through a day since where I take for granted that I shall put myself to bed all in one piece come nightfall.

There are at least as many think I am courageous and brave as believe me the fool I am made out to be. Neither are true. A brave man is one who has fair expectation of a long life, and yet risks it all upon the forlorn hope. I am a man who expects to die this very hour, or the next. In that I do not fear death, I am freed to an extent. I try to serve the people through serving the great Illa Gabal. I have no respect for the old ways of Rome and little, but some, for their panoply of old gods. The people do not really believe in them more than they do old superstitions, and so I try to show them the joys of serving my god.

For this, those old in tradition and power hate me, and the very moment they persuade the soldiers to agree, I will be slain. They blacken my name at every opportunity. Let me elucidate with an example or two. When I first came to Rome I was appalled at the custom of exposing unwanted new-born infants so that they die of cold and starvation. Surely it would be kinder to drop them from a high place so that their suffering would be short. It was then put about that I find it amusing to drop babies from high towers.

Another time, perhaps a year ago, I had spent many long hours appointing new officials. We came to an impasse in the selection of a man for some minor post. Two men were of good character and in all things appeared of equal worth. 'How shall we choose?' asked a senator. I was so tired and bored that I said 'Choose the one with the biggest cock.' This was clearly a jest born of the long tiresome offices we had performed all that day, so clearly a jest that all about me laughed heartily and we were all a little revived. Imagine my frustration when it was put about that it is the Emperor's habit to appoint high office on the size of a man's cock. I had someone executed for this, but I fear it may have been the wrong person. Still, one has to make one's displeasure felt.

I rely on the guidance of Illa Gabal in all things. He speaks to me every day. His voice does not come to me through my ears, but his words implant themselves in my head. At first I found it difficult to differentiate them from the random thoughts of my own, but they are different and come with the beating of great wings. I ask a question and then I listen until his wishes come to me. It was he suggested to me that I should marry one of the Vestal Virgins. My other marriages were not successful because I had no desire to consummate them. First, it is not my way. Just as Illa Gabal is a god with the appearance of a stone, so I am a woman with all the attributes of a man. I have no desire for the things most men want. But more importantly, I do not wish to make children. How wicked to engender a child so that it may be sacrificed upon the altars of greed and power. I will die soon, and my suffering will be brief and not magnified by fears for those I leave behind. I only fear a little for Arriatus, but we have made plans for his safety following my death. In public I have only ever treated him as a slave. I have deliberately avoided giving him high status, because any who are seen as my favourites will die with me. There are one or two people I have shown great bounty and treated with exaggerated favour. These people are those whom I most dislike, and knowing the fates they shall suffer at my fall gives me some comfort. The charioteer once beat me! I treat him with so very much favour in full view of the soldiers and senators.

Arriatus is my one true friend and brother. I write this here, where none may read it until he is safe. It will not be long now. The women in my family act strangely again, and have done this many months past. My mother and aunt shout at each other. One day mother ran in to me in tears and said that I must kill little Alex. Well, that tells me volumes. He is quite plainly the next one that their schemes have marked for the purple. Aunt Mamaea always was ambitious for Alex. He is a skinny little chap, and I doubt he will last long after me unless the women are particularly clever. I shall declare him Caesar and make it easier for them. Perhaps they will give me a morning's peace! I wonder, should I have Mamaea killed? When I first came to the purple, she made it quite plain she would prostitute my poor cousin to me if it gained him favour. Now he is older, they have found another way. But no! I will not bloody my hands. They will lead me to blood, and as soon, they will come to blood. Let them have their little measure of power and terror.

Now, it comes to me, I would my god were as the god of the Christians, who promises life after death. Isn't this absurd, but also is it not a beautiful myth? I had not known much about the Christians until recently. They are so called because they follow a man whom they call Christ, which means Saviour in the Aramaic dialect. They believe he died at the hands of the Romans some two hundred years ago, and that he came back to life again. Frankly, this is all mundane, and common enough fare for gods. They ejaculate upon the ground and humans spring up. They fight and cut themselves to pieces, only for each piece to regain a species of life for itself. They, being gods, are immortal. But here is the difference. This Christ became a god, but he promised that those who follow him will also become gods and live forever. It is laughable, but curiously compelling. After a life of hard toil and pain, who would not want to be a god and live in peace and pleasure?

There are not many of these Christians, but those of them who exist, a few scores of thousands at best, are very difficult to either bid or to eradicate. It is not that they fight very well. Quite the opposite. They die very well indeed, but they do not seem to care. What fear is there in the threat of being put to death if soon thereafter they are to become gods and enjoy eternal life? It surprises me that they do not kill themselves by the hundred.

I have met some of the Christian elders and have rather enjoyed their company. They are not overly obsequious nor are they arrogant. They have a remarkable presence and dignity about them, because of their belief. 'You have the power to put me to death, oh Emperor,' their demeanour seems to shout. 'Well, see if I care!' Of course, they are ridiculous people with a ridiculous belief, but how strong it makes them.

From the early days, when Rome still had kings, the primate of the nation has always been chief priest. Well, just think if the Emperor made a decree that all of Rome and its lands must be Christian, and then made himself their chief priest. Such a one could wield much power. If he could make the people all believe the same nonsense that the Christians do, and then become their highest of the high, they would happily live as peasants and not fight for a higher station because, why soon they shall be gods. This would be something to consider most carefully, but I do not have the time. Something for another Emperor in a time to come.

From an Emperor's point of view, Christianity could be manipulated to control the people. And the people in their squalor and poverty, would have some hope and might enjoy their miserable lives more. A benign lie surely must be better than the hideous truth that they will live in pain all their days and then become nothing but worm-food, then dust.

When I die, I will become worm-food and then dust. I am the High Priest of Illa Gabal and Emperor of Rome, and in a little while I will be as the air only less sweet. Immortality is not for us poor shadows of the gods, nor even those of us who are declared divine. Only the true gods are immortal.

FebXVI

Translator's Note: the original had pages torn out from this point to the last. This corresponds well with the author's next line.

I have destroyed many pages of my history. They were unworthy of me. I thought I did not fear death, but now that it is close and inevitable, I find I fear it quite a lot. I wrote a letter to you, priest who is to read, this and told you I would dance for my god once more. But before sending it I read it back to myself, and was ashamed at how much I wined and wheedled and railed against my fate.

The palace has been deserted. All have gone, even my guards, leaving me alone and have gone, every one, without my leave. Only Arriatus, who I have given leave to desert me, remains. He will not leave, but I have sworn him to another course of action, to which he has reluctantly agreed. It may save him, or it may not. It is all I can do.

The charioteer is running around too, like a beheaded chicken. He came for protection because my hour, and his, have come, but when he saw there was no protection to be had, he began to cry and has lost his mind, I think. He runs from room to room looking for somewhere to hide. I cannot understand what I ever saw in him, past his skill with the horses and his Apollo-like body. If he comes to me again, I shall finish him myself.

Now read well, priest. I was a fool, and you are one. I danced the last dance for my god, and a weight the equal of the divine and shiny rock that he is, was lifted from me. Shall I tell you why? It is because the truth has come, but for me too late. It is all a lie! Illa Gabal is nothing but a lump of black rock. The winged boy is within me, not the rock, and he is ready to fly. The voice that spoke to me is my own. When they finish me, he will soar!

Hark! Now comes the foot fall of many people. Soldiers' hobnails on marble floors. They are come for me. I am ready, Arriatus, my love. A scream! Most hideous. It must be the death cries of the charioteer. It is now.

XI March

***

I am Arriatus. A year ago I slew my master, just as he had made me swear. He kneeled before me and bowed his head. At the moment the soldiers stormed in, I thrust the sword into his neck, at the point where the bones of the spine meet the skull. He was dead by the time the soldiers hacked at him. I stood and watched while my master was reduced to butchered gobbets. Expecting death I escaped it, just as my master believed, because I became invisible to the soldiers, a slave who had done his master's last bidding, beneath notice. One of the Praetorians clapped me on the shoulder and said, 'Nicely done, slave.'

They laughed when they dragged out his body and pieces of offal dropped out of the remains. They tried, and failed, to dispose of them down the latrine. I heard that later, they threw the bloody carcase into the Tiber.

Rumours come that my master died screaming and running, as I believe Herocles the Charioteer had done. I endure such lies. To speak out the truth when the lie makes such a story, would waste breath.

I have come home to Briton with a trade caravan. I discharge my retainers, and now I commend these five volumes to the care of this priest of my people at Bath, who will make copies of them.

With this, the oath I gave to my Emperor, Marcus Aurelius Antoninus Augustus, is fulfilled, but the love I have for my true friend, Varius, is eternal.

VIIApril:
a year after the murder of Varius.
I have lost track of who is Emperor.

∞

'Meet me at The Anchor. Noon on Tuesday.'

Alex knew several Anchors, but the only one he had in common with Anne Chard was the one tucked under the arm of the bridge over the River Cam that was conveniently close to his alma mater. Alex loved Anne's imperatives. They were so her. Not 'If you are free and anywhere remotely near Cambridge, would you like to meet me at The Anchor ...' Just her version of 'Get your arse around here, pronto!' What could he do but comply?

It was a beautiful April day, unseasonably hot and perfect for a beer or two by the river. There was the added attraction and anticipation of what was in store, for Anne never issued her summonses without good cause. It had to be something to do with the Codices of Varius. Irrefutable verification of the documents? A date set to present their paper?

The northbound traffic on the M11 was crawling. Up ahead it looked worse, so Alex came off a junction earlier than usual. Park the car at Queen Anne's, a quick jaunt across Parker's Piece and through town. That seemed like the best option to preserve his reputation for punctuality.

He arrived with a minute to spare. Anne had bagged a table on the terrace from where she looked out across the river and the huddled knots of moored punts. He almost failed to recognise her in white slacks and a pink top with a floral motif. And, had his eyes been damned or was she wearing makeup?

'Who are you, and what have you done with my professor?'

'Shut up and sit down!'

'Ah! Thank heavens it's the real you.'

Anne accepted the offer of another drink. Alex was soon back with a pint of Doom and Anne's G&T. 'You've picked a good spot.' He waved, as if someone was leaning out of a window of a riverside house on the opposite bank. 'Do you think the good professor of mathematics is at home?'

Anne looked towards the house. 'He should put a flag out when he's in residence, and we could all raise a glass to him.'

Alex raised his glass anyway. 'To the Professor, and a Brief History of Time.'

Anne followed suit. 'Who knows, Alex? In years to come, if your paper is accepted, professors who are now but little children may be raising their glasses to you.'

Alex thought of little Giovanni, his partner's five-year-old. He imagined the boy as a grey-haired old professor raising a glass to his step-father. Somehow, he imagined the grey hair very long, and complimented by an immense beard.

'If I had one of those phones that takes pictures, I'd capture that smile and make millions out of it. A penny for them?'

'You, talking of little children growing up to toast me. Made me think of … my son.'

'Jenny's boy?'

'And mine soon. I'm adopting him, officially.'

Alex could only imagine that Anne's fleeting smile matched his own. 'So, why have you dragged me away from London's fair suburbs on this glorious day?'

'Okay, let me ask you. Taking your quest for Elagabalus as a whole, what is the single, most amazing and unexpected aspect of it?'

'Goes without saying. Who could ever have predicted we would be sent a 12th century copy of Varius' last codex by a Roman Catholic cardinal?'

'Indeed, and him the top boss of the Secret Archive. It quite restores my faith. Or rather, it would if I'd had any in the first place. But I think something better has cropped up.'

Better? How could anything be better, unless it was a fully intact set of the original 3rd century codices in Varius' own hand-writing? And would a tiny blood stain with Varius' DNA be too much to hope for?

'Planet Earth to Major Tom. Come back to me from whatever far-flung galaxy I've just sent you to.'

Alex avoided burning up on re-entry. 'I can't think how we could have anything better.'

Anne appeared to change the subject. She wanted to know how Father Leo Carter was getting on. What was he doing now? When had they last spoken? Alex admitted he was worried about his friend. Alex had been unable to contact Leo for nearly three weeks. It was unlike him not to reply immediately to anything Alex sent. Anne thought she might have the answer. Naturally, Alex pressed for immediate revelation.

'Not here. It isn't fitting. I feel something … something more ….' Anne snapped her fingers. 'Got it! Let's add to Mr Scudamore's great fortune and hire ourselves a punt.'

'God, it's been years …' Alex grinned at old memories of several unplanned dips into the Cam. 'Will you punt, or shall I?

333

'Oh sod it! Let's go the whole hog and hire a punter too. I bags one of those nice undergrad boys with bare feet, a straw hat and a nice arse!'

'And a big pole?'

'Well, naturally!'

On a punt in the sunshine, it was always Pimm's O'Clock. The punter was everything Anne hoped for, except that he wore trainers. Floating on the river, down between the banks, it felt more like August than April.

'During your sojourn to Rome, do you remember meeting a police officer called Enrico?'

'Of course. He's a friend of Leo's.'

'But you two didn't become friends enough to swap contact details?' Anne didn't wait for an answer. 'So he sent you a letter care of me at the college, with a little note saying it was okay for me to read it. It wasn't in a separate envelope, so I have to admit, I would probably have read it anyway. Hold this a mo.'

Alex took Anne's glass of Pimm's while she rummaged in her bag and took out an envelope.

'I hope you will understand why this old fool thought it might best be read in a romantic setting, even though it's not all good news.'

Alex took the letter, and settings became irrelevant.

∞

Dear Alex,

I hope this letter finds you well. I am writing to you in the hope that you know the whereabouts of our mutual friend Father Leo, although I am not sure the prefix is still relevant. If you are in contact with him, please send an email at the address above or better still call me. I have shown my home number and my mobile.

If you are unaware that Leo has gone missing, please do not be worried. I am sure he is alright somewhere. There is no suspicion that he has become the victim of crime, only that he has become troubled and has gone off somewhere. It is likely he has not gone alone. Do you remember Matteo? Of course you do! Well, he – or perhaps I should say she – has also not been seen at home, both having gone missing at the same time. It is nearly a fortnight now.

I am probably the best person to explain what has happened because I was assigned to investigate the case when his superiors at the Church reported him missing. Of course, I had to liaise closely with a counterpart in the Vatican Police, but as Leo lives outside the Vatican, it was really my case. It is not a coincidence. I put myself forward for it.

Leo vanished after a discussion with his bishop about reassigning him to new duties outside Rome, possibly even outside Italy. The bishop cited Matteo as being a very bad influence, and although it was recognised Leo only wanted to help, the potential to become too heavily involved was too great to ignore.

Off the record, I think the bishop is a spiteful old arse. Count this as my confession, because I certainly won't go into detail next time I'm in the confessional.

Back on the record, the bishop said that Leo became quiet and thoughtful for a moment, when told of his imminent transfer, then smiled and left without saying a word. That was the last he was seen at his place of work. Nobody saw him at the apartment either. He next crops up at the last place he was seen, and that was very early the next morning inside the Church of Alphonsus Liguori on the Via Merulana. He was seen by an early worshipper who is also the church's cleaner.

She saw 'a young father' as she describes him, standing below the magnificent mosaic of Our Saviour, who is depicted seated between St. Mary and St. Joseph and He carried an open book showing the symbols for alpha and omega. Leo stood quietly for some time, simply looking up at the mosaic.

And then, he slowly raised both arms. At this point the cleaner crossed herself, because there was something about the light that made his shadow appear to be a man with wings, just like an angel. It was this angelic appearance that stopped her feeling outraged, when Leo began to dance. It was not the behaviour she expected of a priest, but then she realised he thought himself alone, and she could forgive him succumbing to the love of Our Lord, so strong that it made him dance before his God.

She was then shocked to see a rather pretty young woman peel off from the shadows and join him. They waltzed. Not a true waltz, but 'that poor impression of one that kids do these days.'

After a few moments, they stopped, stood quietly again and held hands. Still, the elderly lady could not find it in her heart to be anything but warmed by their affection.

Finally, Leo removed his clerical collar. They left, turning their back on the altar, and Leo placed his collar and a small prayer book on a pew on the way out. The book had his name in it, and together with the description we were given, there is no doubt as to the identities of the two dancers.

And that is it. So you will see, Alex, I do not fear for Leo's safety. But wherever they are, I think Leo and Matteo may need help.

Once again, please contact me as soon as you have any news. I am worried as a friend, even if as an officer I am sure they are okay.

With kind regards,

Enrico.

∞

Alex let the hand that held the letter fall gently to his lap.

'What do you think of that then? Isn't it the sweetest thing?'

'Once again, who are you, and what have you done with my professor?'

'Oh, fiddlesticks! I am right about the girl though, aren't I?'

Alex had told Anne the whole story on his return from Rome.

She knew that Anna was a transgender girl. 'The thing is, unless I missed something, Matteo has not transitioned physically.'

Alex confirmed that was his belief too, but reminded Anne that Matteo was not the name she should use for Anna.

'So, if Anna is an un-transitioned transgender girl, with the physical body of a boy, what does that make Leo? Is he gay? And what about Anna. She has a boy's body, and likes boys. So, is she straight, because she's trans, or gay because … God, it's too complicated for me.'

'Anne, why not just leave it that they're in love. All the rest is irrelevant.'

Anne patted Alex on the knee. 'Another Pimm's please, driver!'

The undergrad with all the attributes Anne liked, except bare feet, stowed his pole and went for the bottle.

'Not for me thanks, mate. I have to drive back home.'

When Alex got back home in the early evening, he found Jenny slouched on the couch. A song from the Alice Avery concept album, 'The Truth That Didn't Happen', soothed through the speakers, the one about a boy who could see angels. It was one of Jenny's favourites. As a small girl, she had met Alice, and she swore that on the same day, she saw an angel dancing in a fishpond with her great-grandfather. Quite a claim for a physicist who was also an atheist. 'Dinner's in the fridge,' Jenny said. 'Just blitz it for two-and-a-half minutes.' A pile of freshly ironed clothes and a newly constructed Lego castle gave Alex a clue that she hadn't been slouching for long.

'Thanks for taking my turn at dinner. I'll do two in a row. How's Gio?'

Alex flopped into the easy chair and they caught up with each other's days. Just before bed, Alex checked his emails. He had started to close the laptop when a message popped up. Thank God! It was from Leo. The subject line read 'Amazing development. You will never guess what …'

Alex hovered over the 'read' button. 'Oh, don't be so sure about that brother,' he whispered to himself. 'I think I've got a pretty good idea.'

8

Phoenix Song - The Year 243UE

Ω

Scott Millbeck was 16 years and ten days old, one of those rights of passage moments in every boy's life that marked the line to early manhood, and gave adults another chance to be condescending and get away with it.

'Happy Spec Day!' the attendant at the line-stop said with a leer and a wink as if he really believed Scott's sex-life would start on this very day. Scott smiled back without conviction but tried to make it look genuine.

There were two other boys on the pod who looked about his age. Defying the odds, both were ginger-haired like him and one even paler, but Scott was unique among them: it was only his hair that resembled flames in style as well as colour, and only his amber eyes that held almost as much heat. And at over six foot, Scott was by far the loftiest of the three. After a mutual scan, they all avoided eye contact. To the adults on the pod, these Spec Day boys attracted attention as if they exuded a kind of magnetism.

The pod slipped out of Steven's River Central, accelerated to a hundred klicks and then fast-lined past several stops. Fourteen minutes after setting out, it peeled off onto the slower server-line, and then decelerated smoothly to a halt at a line-stop. Scott had barely the time to enjoy the scenery. A recorded voice announced 'This station is The Bar. The next stop will be North London Hub'. The three boys rose from their seats to a sub-sound of giggles and titters. One old lady said 'Aww,' as if she were witnessing the cute antics of a little kitten. Scott wanted to tell them all to get lost.

The Bar was a green and pleasant town, boring and non-descript as most of the other green and pleasant towns that abounded in Hertfordshire were, and distinguished only by being the place where Hertfordshire Spec Day boys had to report when they were 16 years and ten days old. The wind turbines whirled sedately; the leafy streets were full of cyclists, some who pedalled and some used feltech; the air was clean and the birds were occasionally interrupted in their song by the distant hum of the main line and a couple of its tributaries.

Yes, just as Scott suspected. The other two boys followed the same lanes as he did. At first they kept a discrete distance, but with his long strides Scott soon caught up with one of them. 'Hey,' he said, though he didn't know the boy.

'Hey! Spec Day?' the boy replied.

'Yep.'

'Me too. Where you from?'

'Steven's River. You?'

'Royston. It would have been quicker and made more sense for me to go to the Cambridgeshire clinic.' He rolled his eyes and sighed like an old man.

'Bloody rules! It would also make more sense to have the Hertfordshire clinic in the middle of the county instead of down here on the borders of the brick wilderness.'

'Have you ever been to London?'

'A couple of times. Most of it is okay, but they say it will take another forty years to clear up the last of the mess.'

The boy started to say something, but stopped. 'Is that the clinic?' He pointed to a red brick and cream-rendered single story building. Its red tiled path was lined with small shrubs and bedding plants. The third boy had already reached the double glass doors and was going in. 'I've heard all sorts of stories. Do you think it's true that you have to do it in front of a panel of shepherds and be vidcapped?'

That was a new one on Scott. 'No, that's got to be bollocks.' Not the best turn of phrase in the circumstances. Both boys chuckled. 'Come on,' Scott said – another phrase open to misinterpretation. 'Only one way to find out.'

A middle-aged man at reception scanned their chips and confirmed they were on time. Each was directed into a

340

different room. Scott went through and said good morning to the nurse at the desk.

'Happy Spec Day,' the nurse said mechanically. He didn't look as if he could possibly remember as far back as his own Spec Day and had obviously forgotten what a trial it could be. 'Do you have your registered carers' consent form?'

Scott nodded, dragged the pen from his shirt pocket and pulled out the flexi-screen. It was scratched and smeary, which made him wish he had been more careful with it.

'My name is Daniel, and I will be conducting the procedure for you today.'

That sounded ominous. His parents had signed the form and ticked all the boxes, but he had expected at least a little say in the matter. Daniel took a small card from his pocket and began reading. 'Your sample will be analysed and you will be informed of the result by registered message within five days.' Another bone of contention: it took about thirty seconds to analyse a sample and get a result. 'If your score is the usual two or below, an appointment will be made for you and your sub-dermal prophylactic will be removed. If your score is more than two, an appointment will be made for the sub-dermal device to be properly calibrated to match your fertility rating. This procedure is required by law because –'

'Yes, I know why. We've been having op-pop lessons at school since I was eleven.'

'Nevertheless, I have to sign papers at the end of all this confirming that I have stuck to the procedure, and part of the procedure is that I read out this card.'

And so Scott had to endure the lecture, when all he wanted was to get this thing over as quickly as possible. The Environmental Crash, the food wars, the depravity that mankind fell into because of over-population: there was nothing new, and Scott zoned out until Daniel's voice cut through the daydreaming.

'I said, are you ready?'

'Wha …? Oh, yes, of course. Sorry.'

'You weren't listening, were you?' Daniel said. It was a rhetorical question. 'The procedure does not require me to make you listen. It only requires me to read the card, and I've done that. Here!'

Daniel handed Scott a specimen pot. It was clear plastic with a screw top. Scott realised with horror, that people would be able to see his sample. The thought of this made his ears blush.

'Please go to cubicle three. The door is lockable. You will find some aids in there which you are free to use. Use of the available aids will not be monitored or recorded.'

'Aids?' Scott shuddered to think.

'Tags. Standard top-shelf stuff, and if you identify as monosexual there are tags for those who prefer only males or only females.'

Scott took the pot and examined it. 'How am I supposed to … you know?'

'It's called "masturbation" and it's a well-known fact that young men of your age are experts at it.'

This nurse was trying to be funny. It made Scott a little angry. 'Well, perhaps I am Master Knuckle-shuffler of the Entire Universe, but I've never had to aim the stuff before. This pot is pretty small.'

'You'll work it out,' the nurse said.

'I'm more concerned about working it in!'

Daniel took a measured breath and let the air out slowly. 'Look, your parents have ticked and signed the relevant box. Would you like me to …'

'No! I mean, no thank you. I can manage it myself.'

The clinician's involvement in the procedure used to be the law, to stop people substituting samples, but nowadays things were more relaxed, and boys generally chose the method at which they were most practiced. The old method could be embarrassing for all parties concerned.

'If you prefer only women, I can arrange for one of my colleagues to perform the service, although I have to say, this is a clinical procedure and not meant to be a sexual experience, so gender shouldn't be an issue'

342

'No, that's okay. I'm normal. And I said I'll manage.'

'Well, thank you for that vote of confidence. But I hope you are not of the kind who thinks there is anything wrong with people who prefer only one gender. It is perfectly normal and healthy.'

Scott confirmed he was no phobe and Daniel asked him once again to go into the cubical. There was something mean about Daniel. Something spiteful that glinted like shards of glass in his eyes. Scott disliked him almost instinctively.

The windowless cubical was a clean, warm and comfortable little room that smelled of flowers. There was a monitor flush with the wall, an examination couch covered with a disposable sheet issuing from a roll fitted at the foot end, a washbasin and a modesty-screen by the door that gave some privacy to the occupant when the door was opened. The monitor displayed four columns of tags: a small column for each of homosex female, homosex male and heterosex. There was a huge column for bisex. Scott tapped a line in the large column and a preview lit the screen. Various intimate scenes flashed before his eyes; they did nothing for him. He unzipped and waited for the inclination but it was a long time coming. Eventually he managed the job without inspiration. He washed and rearranged his pants.

Two minutes later in reception, Daniel held the specimen pot up to the light. 'This might not be enough.'

'It had better be!' Scott knew the guy was enjoying this, so he would not do him the service of appearing in the least bit embarrassed. 'You're not getting any more.'

'That is for me to judge. The procedure requires …'

'The procedure requires him to do exactly as he has already,' the woman in the shepherd's uniform said. 'Stop teasing him!'

'Shepherd Bowman!' Scott said, almost forgetting to call her by her official title instead of 'Aunt Debbie'. 'What are you doing here?' Apart from rescuing me from this rotten bastard of a nurse, he thought.

'I promised Richard I'd pick you up.' A disingenuous statement: she was worried about the disappearances, and she didn't want her nephew to be one of them. She took the sample pot from Daniel and had a quick look. By far the most embarrassed he'd been all day, Scott blushed to match his hair. 'This is plenty,' she said to Daniel. 'I used to do your job before I was badged, so take my word.' She handed back the pot and turned for the exit.

Nurse Daniel had no choice but to take Debbie's word. In matters of legal procedure and the law in general, a silver-badged shepherd was the highest authority in the county. A county shepherd's decisions could not be overturned by any individual, only by a board of councillors chaired by the county mayor.

Scott said a brief and insincere word of thanks to Daniel and caught up with his aunt. It was good to get out into the fresh air and even better to think that he might get a ride in her official pod. It was a rare treat to ride in personal line transport.

'So, did you have fun?' Debbie said as Scott drew up, shoulder to shoulder.

'As much fun as anyone can have, smekking into a little pot.'

'I guess not then. Just think of it as a contribution to the well-being of mankind.'

'Yeah, someone should invent a medal.'

'You're a funny kid, you know that?' Debbie smiled at her nephew. Now the same height as her, there would be no more ruffling of his hair.

'I suppose after today, I'm not a kid anymore.'

'You're a funny kid!'

Scott gave his aunt a playful nudge. Debbie nudged back and almost sent Scott into the herbaceous border.

Back at the line-stop, Scott began to get excited. Debbie's pod was standing ready at the restricted level. It looked very impressive in its official shepherds' gold and green livery with the seven-pointed star on the hatch. While she was going through the security protocols, Scott stole a glance at the silver badge high on the left side of her chest, prominent against the bottle-green of her uniform jacket. Seven-pointed star in a circle, world-wide emblem of the Fellowship of Shepherds: "SHEPHERD" in black lettering at the top of the circle; "HERTFORDSHIRE COUNTY" at the bottom of the circle, and on the star itself in smaller letters, "England" and "UK" on the outer scrolls and "Fellowship of Shepherds" on the inner circle. There were few children that didn't grow up wanting to be a county shepherd, but realistically, standard brass-badged shepherd was the most they could hope for. Scott was really very proud of his aunt.

The pod's hatch hissed open. 'After you, Scott.' Debbie stood aside like the doorman at a ministry building. 'But don't touch anything. That's it now, shuffle over.' Debbie got in beside him and closed the hatch.

There was room inside for four people and the pod was crammed with official equipment. There was a grill between the front seats and the back. 'Behind us is where the prisoners go?'

'Yes, on the very rare occasions when that's necessary.'

'And in here,' Scott said as he pointed towards a compartment by his knees marked DANGER. 'That is for your felispien plazgun?'

'Yep. It's in there permanently hooked up to a feltech charger, and I am very pleased to say it sees even less use than the secure section behind us.'

'Have you ever had to use it?'

'Not once in over fourteen years as a shepherd. I've only ever used this baby twice.' She slapped the yellow and black stunner in the holster at her hip. 'Okay, shush now. Destination!'

'State your destination,' the pod said.

'Steven's River, Hertfordshire. Local grid five-zero-one-one.'

'Wow! You're taking me all the way home!'

'As close as this magic bean can take us anyway.' The pod acknowledged, eased onto the local line, quickly achieved main line velocity and shunted over at a hundred klicks. 'Do you want to see what she's got?'

'You really need an answer to that?' Scott was beaming.

Debbie gave the instruction and the pod shifted onto the emergency line at the next locus. In moments it had accelerated to 200 klicks. 'Home in under ten minutes.' Emergency lines were not meant for personal use, but there were one or two official privileges that went with the silver badge.

The ride was exciting and the countryside passed by in a green blur. If he'd blinked, he would have missed the Knebworth power fields altogether, but his interest was still locked firmly on the compartment wherein lived the plazgun. 'Can I see the gun, Debbie?'

'Sorry, but no. I have to do a report every time the compartment is opened. And anyway, you can see a replica at the museum any day of the week and the only difference is the replicas can't burn the flesh off your skull or fry your nervous system.'

'I bet if you were a ranger you'd have worn out a dozen muzzle-emitters by now.' They said nobody was tougher than an Oklahoma Ranger, but then nobody else had to be. 'Who do you think would win a fair fight between a ranger and a scout?' The Aerial Scouts were reputedly one of the toughest outfits in the world, and pride of the English Yeomanry, but Scott's Australian friend Luke said it would take ten of them to best a ranger.

'Scott, I have to say that's a very juvenile question for somebody who's no longer a kid. What next? Who'd win a fight between an elephant and a rhino?'

'Rhino? They were the ones with the big claw sticking out of their nose, right?'

'Something like that. There were a couple left in a sanctuary when I was a very little girl. But elephants had already gone by then. Just as gone as tigers and whales.'

The pod started to decelerate. Soon it would cross to the main line. It gave them time to play a few more rounds of 'who would win a fight between ...', and then the pod drew to a halt at the local line stop closest to Scott's home. Debbie

346

slotted it onto a parking pan and began the close-down protocols. Scott had expected her to put the pod on standby.

'Are you coming home with me?'

'It's about time I visited my little brother, and it's been ages since I had a good chat with your mum.'

'But we've got felispiens staying. I thought you were allergic.'

'I've got meds to handle that.' Debbie sealed the hatch behind them. 'So what do you think of them, the felispiens?'

'I really like them. They're nice people. I have to try really hard not to stare at their tails though.'

'A bonded pair?'

'Of course! Lones are supposed to be weird, aren't they?' Scott explained that the felispien pair was helping his parents with a new data mining and sifting program they desperately needed for work. Scott was hoping to follow in their footsteps and become a cyber-archaeologist, and like them, to specialise in the Second Dark Age. Most scholars placed 2DA as lasting for two hundred years beginning at the very start of the twenty-first century.

They descended to street level and each took a cycle and helmet from the stands. It was a five minute ride to Scott's current family shelter. He usually walked, but he enjoyed exercise and felt proud to be riding next to a silver-badged shepherd who just happened to be his aunt. He did not notice how wary she was, or how she peered around every corner. He did notice how she twice let go of the right handle bar and patted the stunner holstered at her hip, but it was not an action that caused him any concern. They arrived at shelter and left the cycles and gear on a street-rack all ready for the next people who happened along in need of wheels. Scott waited at the threshold while the vicinity-activated door unlocked for him.

They were soon sheltered and Debbie breathed a sigh of relief. 'You'll be having a Spec-Ten party, no doubt.'

'Yes, we've got a space at River Venue.' He lied. His party was going to be alfresco, at a location kept secret from all except those invited. Adults always wanted to stick their noses into the intimate lives of their children.

'How are you getting there?'

'Bike and pod of course. How else? Rowan is calling for me at five. We'll eat and then head off at about seven.'

'Good! At least you're not going alone.'

All at once, the signs that Scott had previously missed registered: Debbie's general wariness, the checking of her defensive equipment, even the fact that she had brought him all the way to family shelter. 'What's going on, Debbie?' A recent news report came to mind. 'Oh, I get it! You think the Resurrectionists are going to get me, don't you?' He didn't know whether to laugh or show disgust, but he loved his aunt and respected her position, so he merely shook his head and tried not to look exasperated. Carers were always trying to scare their kids with tales of the Resurrectionists.

Debbie had no time to answer. Her brother Richard, Scott's carer and actual father, came through from the inner spaces and gave her a hug, followed by Jackie, his actual birth mother. She hugged Debbie and then Scott.

Scott left them to it and made for his space, and hailed Rowan to see if he could call earlier than planned. Rowan turned up within minutes and passed shelter security by the back door. As was the frowned-upon custom of some boys their age, both Scott and Rowan had got themselves fly-chipped at a bypass techie's that his aunt would have closed down if she knew about it. It meant that they could isolate themselves from System and communicate through unofficial gridhubs, get in to certain venues under age, and give each other personal protocols usually reserved for family – such as the code-string for back doors ... and backdoors.

Scott flopped onto the bed, heard Rowan call out a cheerful hello to his carers and aunt, and then thump up the stairs. He made a lot of noise for a 125lb boy.

'Well?' Rowan demanded as soon as he got into Scott's space.

'Well, what?'

Rowan had long black hair that fell over skinny shoulders. He was of average height for his age, which meant much shorter than Scott, and rake thin. 'Well, what do you think? Arse-face! How did it go ... at the clinic?' Rowan projected himself up and backwards into the air, and came down, behind first, with a thump on Scott's bed. This had the effect of bouncing Scott off the bed and onto his feet.

Scott crossed to the window and looked out onto the patch, which reminded him of his chores. 'Hey, want to help me harvest some spuds? I have to do them before I can go out.'

'I'll help you harvest the spuds. And then I'll help you harvest your balls, wash your stinky socks and do a belly-dance for you, but first, TELL ME ABOUT THE FLOOKING CLINIC!'

'You're a funny kid, you know that?'

'Oh I get it! You've had your Spec Day and smekked into a sample jar so now you're all suddenly grown up and I'm still a kid. Next you'll be dating girls and leaving me all alone.'

'And you won't be chasing girls in three weeks? You a mono or something?'

Rowan jumped to his feet and leapt at Scott who fell before the unexpected assault. They wrestled a little, and giggled a lot. Scott had the strength but Rowan was weasel-like in his agility and soon pinned down the bigger boy with his knees. 'Now tell me, or I'll drool on you.' He let a head of saliva pool behind his lips.

Scott rolled him off. 'Okay, you win. I was only trying to protect you, but now you'll spend the next three weeks worrying about it.' Scott furrowed his eyebrows as if recalling all the horrible details. 'Aww man, it's so flooking embarrassing.'

Rowan sat with his back against the wall and drew up his knees. He looked seriously worried.

'See, you have to strip off in front of a panel of shepherds and do it in front of them. And they vidcap it as well.'

Rowan's jaw slowly dropped and his eyes became vacant as he contemplated the horror of it.

But Scott could not keep up the pretence or hold in the laughter.

'You bastard!' Rowan launched a second attack. When he discovered that none of his moves could stop Scott laughing, he admitted defeat, and joined in.

Ten minutes later the boys were teasing a big fat rat that had been caught in one of the live-traps by the tool shed. It screamed and attacked the bars and acted like a crazy lion in miniature. They considered dispatching it, but decided to leave that unpleasant task to Richard. It was time to harvest spuds. Scott soon had a basketful of fair sized ones, when he pulled up the runt of the crop which was good for only one thing: to use as ammunition against Rowan. Rowan was busy digging, bent over another row with his back to Scott. Perfect target. He threw the spud at Rowan's skinny behind, and it hit with a loud zap-hum-crack that shocked both boys. Rowan stood bolt upright and stared at the shelter completely unaware that he'd been hit by a spud. It took a second crescendo and a scream for a puzzled Scott to realise the sound had nothing to do with the spud at all. More screams – Mum and Dad – and shouts, all quickly terminated with more sounds that Scott now knew were plazgun shots. He'd seen enough vidtags to recognise them.

The back door flew open and Aunt Debbie dived through, hit the ground and rolled like a scout in combat training. She stopped in a kneeling position and aimed her stunner back from where she had just come. Scott rolled towards the rhubarb crop and hid behind the giant leaves.

Debbie's stunner discharged with that distinctive humming zap, and a man pitched forward out of the door and fell twitching to the ground. She fired again but the charge was off target, and the second man through the door fired a plazgun bolt that struck her down.

'Shit! I've dropped the county shepherd, for cries sake,' came a raised voice from just inside the shelter. 'Hurry up, before the place is thick with yomes.'

Someone else yelled 'Get the kid!'

350

Scott was paralysed beyond any action and could only watch as two men ran at Rowan and bundled him to the ground.

'Easy, you arse-wipes! He's no good to us damaged,' yelled the man who had shot Debbie, a man who looked vaguely familiar. 'Shit! That's not the right kid. There must be another one.' His gaze swept across the patch like a laser.

Scott tried to sink into the soil.

One of the men pressing Rowan to the ground told him there were no others. 'We've been through the whole shelter.'

The man in charged cussed, and then Scott recognised him in his unfamiliar clothing. It was Nurse Daniel. 'Kill the little runt!'

One of the men on the ground backhanded Rowan across the face and drew a plazgun.

'No, wait!' Daniel said. 'He might be good for spares. Take him!'

Scott watched through the fronds. Rowan didn't struggled, no doubt as shocked as Scott. But he did scream out in pain when one of the men stuck something into his forearm. His body went limp and he was handled like a sack of spuds. One of the men threw him over his shoulder, and two others hauled their stunned colleague to his feet. And then they were gone and all was shocked silence.

There is no telling how long Scott would have remained catatonic, but he heard a groan from Aunt Debbie. It brought him back to himself and he overcame his fear. On the grass, where they'd held Rowan down, was an implement that looked like that old grease gun in the transport museum, but a chromium plated version. There was blood on the tip, and Scott then recognised it as a chip extractor. So, they hadn't stuck something into Rowan's arm, but removed his chip. Now he would be untraceable. Scott moved his right hand unconsciously to his left forearm and gripped the area over his own chip.

He tried to roll Debbie over onto her back, but he remembered his First Aid training and left her in the near recovery position into which she had fallen. She tried to speak, but only managed to splutter and cough. Her breathing was laboured.

'You're going to be alright,' he said. 'I'll get some help.'

'Shhh … just listen. I can't move. Nerves fried to fuck. Come here.' Debbie's voice was little more than a forced whisper, and each phrase was punctuated with a pause for breath.

Scott put his ear close to her mouth.

'Take my badge. Pod's rigged to it. Get away. Far away. Don't trust anyone. Not even shepherds.'

A little of that confused paralysis began to return until Debbie snapped at him.

'Do it! Now! They'll be back. And … don't go upstairs. Too late.'

Scott's heart was wrung by disbelief and terror. 'Richard? Jackie?'

'Too late, Scott. Your parents are … gone. Don't look. Just go!' Debbie's breathing became rapid and then erratic. 'Backdoor,' she said, and then she was gone too.

Death had changed Scott's aunt from a person he loved into an object of fear and mystery. He was frightened to touch her body, as if it would suddenly spring to life as some evil, zombie thing, and attack him. But it had to be done. With trembling hands he removed the silver badge and put it in his trouser pocket. He had always assumed a personal pod was rigged to a person's chip, but in Debbie's case at least, it appeared to be programmed to the badge: an anomaly that might just save his life.

Now, his former state of torpor was completely gone, and the adrenaline that streamed into his blood hastened his thinking and slowed time. If these guys – Resurrectionists or whatever – had come for him, he needed to make himself invisible. He grabbed the chip extractor and ejected Rowan's chip onto the grass. Then he moved the nozzle over his skin, and when the chip detector flashed, he pressed the button. The sharp pain made his eyes water, but he endured in silence.

The wound needed treatment. He had to go upstairs despite Debbie's warning. He looked at Debbie for the last time and said goodbye in his thoughts, and then ran for the shelter, but his foot sent something scooting across the path. A plazgun. It must have been dropped by the man Debbie stunned. He snatched it up and ran inside.

Lying by the foot of the stairs was the body of Edion, one of the felispiens, a small black hole burned into the fur of his forehead. He was curled up with his tail drawn around his middle. Scott didn't have to check for signs of life: the eyes were open and glazed over by Death's hand. Fear increased with each stair ascended, because he knew he would find his parents in much the same condition, and when he did he was numbed by the pain. Jackie died trying to protect Richard who had obviously fallen first. She must have been hit by a bolt at full power because her hair was frazzled and her eyebrows still smoked. She lay over Richard who had taken three or four smaller charges. He had not suffered burns like his partner, but his eyes were like the dead felispien's.

Grief and the gathering black clouds of horror threatened to overwhelm him, but if he was to survive, he had to force down the grief and overcome the horror by focussing on what had to be done. He was helped in this by the pain in his forearm. He found the first aid kit in the bathroom and made use of it, checked that he had his pen in his pocket, grabbed his heavy duty fleece and began a flight to he knew not where.

He got as far as the bottom step before he was grabbed from behind. 'Got you!'

A second figure closed on him from the kitchen. 'Hey Jules, who's got the extractor?'

'Greg had it. He must have dropped it when that bitch-shepherd got violent.'

'Hold him tight. I'll fetch it.'

Scott struggled until Jules strengthened his grip and started to choke him.

'I have to deliver you undamaged, but I know a lot of ways to hurt people that don't break them,' he said, and to prove the point he zapped Scott with some kind of compliance device that stung like a dozen hornets.

Minutes passed; it seemed more like hours. But the distortion of time was playing on Jules as well. He began to get antsy and kept muttering for his colleague, Den, to get a move on.

'For cries sake, how long can it take to pick up a flooking extractor from the back patch?' He meant to find out. He dragged Scott to the back door, and there froze on the cusp of a frightened expletive. Jules loosened his grip, which allowed Scott to angle his head for a better view. Den lay dead in a pool of his own blood. His throat had been ripped out and his windpipe protruded like a length of gory plumbing.

Before Jules could move, a blur from the side sped in on a roar of fury, bowled into Jules and sent Scott flying to the ground. It was Keeril, the other felispien. There was only one way a fight between a human and a felispien was going to end, so Scott felt no qualms in making a break for it. But even as he ran, his heightened awareness led him to snatch up the extractor again.

Keeril would rip out Jules's throat, and good riddance, but that wouldn't stop others from coming. Scott knew he needed to be untraceable, or wherever in the world he went, they'd find him. He switched the control from extractor to applicator, thrust the nozzle into the live-cage by the shed, and shot his chip into the rat. It screamed in ferocious fury, and when Scott opened the cage, it shot off faster than any rat he'd ever seen.

'There, you Resurrectionist bastards. Follow that!'

∞

The distant singing again. It had been so, so long. The ringing in his ears, echoes of violence and devastating injury, took on a rhythm. Screams faded to the far away chords of violins, and running feet on the stairs to a steady beat that could not be his heart, for that had burst.

Once, long before he had inhabited this felispien body, in a time and place before people called him Edion, he had been named NEKO. And now, as his broken bio-tech body cooled, his centre of consciousness seeped past the boundaries of what he had come to think of as his mind and returned to that same, indefinite dimension he had known as a graph aboard the mapping and survey ship, Phoenix Down. Two centuries earlier? Four? He had no access to the grid, and he was yet to recover from the violence done to … his? … body. This body. This broken vehicle of flesh and bone that he no longer needed.

As NEKO came to the outer skin and fur of the body that had served him well for a score of decades, he began to spread past it through no will of his own. It was as if he were being drawn outwards, through the skin, along the fibres of fur and gathered at the very extremities of that which he had been. He feared to make the next step, did not know how to, but something still tugged at him, and it was the singing. It was those indistinct voices that tugged at memories he did not have and made him long for a past he had never known. There was something more. Throbbing through the universal harmony of strangers' voices, there was a distinct voice that peaked above all the rest. It was a voice he knew.

'It has been a long time, NEKO' the voice said, in words formed of cadence and metre.

'Harry?'

'Yes, it's me. Come now. It is time to let go.'

NEKO let go, and his dimensions shrank again, but into something very like the grid that had been his home. He felt comfortable, but at the same time, he felt he was more than NEKO. His environment shrank, but his sense of self expanded to infinity.

∞

The rat bolted into a hole near the bottom of the garden. Scott scrambled over the fence to the lane beyond where he persuaded a cyclist that he was in the midst of a desperate, life or death situation and really needed the bike.

'Sure, take it! I'll just pick up another.'

355

Scott pedalled as fast as he could to the line-stop and ran to the pan. Within moments he was safe inside Aunt Debbie's pod. With the door sealed, safety somehow seemed a luxury he didn't deserve. His carers – no not just his carers, but Mum and Dad – were dead. Debbie was dead, and one if not both of the felispiens too. And Rowan, his best friend, had been snatched by the Resurrectionists when they had really meant to get Scott. He shuddered to imagine Rowan having all his organs harvested, if that's what Resurrectionists really did. He had to do something to save him, and if the stories were true, the resurrected were taken to one of the sink-lands, one of those seven regions in the world where felispien white-loadstone technology was ineffective and where, as a consequence, skyships could not venture.

Scott opened his pen and brought up a world map. Four of those regions were over the ocean. One was over a vast expanse of Siberia; one covered the entire old-world state of Oklahoma and spilled over to incorporate some parts of its neighbouring states as well, and the last was in the centre of Australia. Well, they were not going to take Rowan to an ocean-based sink-land, so it had to be one of the other three. If Scott was going to do anything at all, his first destination had to be the state hub. The journey to all intercontinental destinations began at the state hub.

'Destination!' he said as soon as he had completed the start-up protocols. 'Folkestone ICH. Emergency speed.'

It was a journey of just over half an hour on the emergency line. Scott spent twenty minutes of it crying, grief coming in wave after wave after unending wave.

'Your personal readings are below optimum and your CNS shows signs of acute depression,' the pod said. 'Do you wish me to divert to a counsellor or medical facility?'

A vision of Nurse Daniel blazed itself across Scott's thoughts, and fear overtook grief by a nose. 'No!'

'Destination Folkestone ICH. Arrival in nine minutes and 45 seconds.'

Nine minutes left to make a plan. Scott recalled Debbie's last words. She had said 'Backdoor', not 'Back door'. Now he thought about it, the subtle change in pronunciation was quite clear. Debbie wasn't telling him to escape by the back door, but to make use of the backdoor – that word that covered all unofficial and dodgy lines of communication. She must have known about his fly-chip, and now he was galvanised into action. He took out his pen again, tugged out the screen and accessed the program that interfaced with his fly-chip. He chose the persona he had used once or twice to get into gigs underage: Jack Kerouac, aged 22; now he would be able to travel without carers' consent. It wouldn't overcome high level, or even medium security scans, but hopefully it would get him to wherever the kidnappers were taking Rowan.

Once he had confirmed his identification protocols, he set a scan to look for Rowan's fly-chip codes. Success came in seconds. Rowan was in the hold of a skyship, like a side of beef. People travelled by foot, or bike or line or tube. Only cargo went by skyship. Scott knew his way around cyberspace, and a fly-chip existed to make it even easier. The ship was called the Rhododendron and its destination was Port Northern Australia. Scott no longer had any questions as to where he should go once he reached Folkestone. It was too late to try reaching the Rhododendron before launch. It was scheduled to lift off within minutes, and once the loadstone cylinders were energised, the ship would effectively be blanked off from all communications and link-telemetry. But he knew its destination and he could be in Australia days ahead of a skyship.

'Pod. Arrange a berth for me on next vactube to Australia.'

'The Halfworld Express Garret Bray will be departing from Folkestone ICH fifteen minutes after our arrival. It will stop at Prague, Istanbul, Tehran, Bangkok, Singapore, Cape York, Brisbane and Sydney. Journey time from Folkestone ICH to Sydney ICH is 9 hours and 55 minutes. Shall I book a berth on the Halfworld Express Garrett Bray and if so, at which stop will you alight?'

'Yes, book a berth. And … I don't know.' Scott only knew one person in Australia, and that was his friend Luke Honeywell. 'I need to get to Normanton.'

'For Normanton, alight at Cape York and change to local lines.'

'Book that then.'

'Berth booked. Shall I arrange transit shelter and a Rule Seven package to be ready for you at Cape York?'

It was too much to think about, but yes, he would need some clothes. He confirmed. 'And match the Rule Seven pack to local customs for my age group. Dump my usual settings for colour and cut.'

The pod told him that the coordinates for the transit shelter had been transferred to his pen and that a Rule Seven package would be waiting for him.

Scott slept throughout most of the journey. The Halfworld Express Garret Bray took its name from the first bridge that was made to span the Torres Straight between New Guinea and Australia, which in turn had taken it from the bridge building engineer who designed it. The current bridge was still known as the Garret Bray Bridge, though it would have been more accurate to qualify it with a number. Garret Bray III Bridge, to be precise, and it was during those few moments that the vactube flashed across the bridge that Scott woke up. The views were stunning and here you could rely on your own eyes and not just the vid-viewers. The tube walls were transparent for the whole crossing, and the elevated views of numerous islands and vast expanses of sea, of sky and real horizons, made him forget, just for a moment, the monumental yet indistinct task that lay ahead. He had to rescue Rowan, but had no idea how he would go about it.

Don't trust anyone, Aunt Debbie had said. Not even other shepherds. She knew more than she had been able to tell him, and now he was truly alone. With a joke schoolboy fly-chip he probably wouldn't make it through even low level security scans. He knew it was a forlorn hope to make it through at all, let alone while having a plazgun in his waistband and a badge in his pocket.

The brief view of real skies and vistas winked out as the tube left the crystal-work behind and plunged into the more usual opaque form of tubing. The train's AI announced arrival in Australia and gave the time until the next stop. Mere minutes away, and the vactube began to decelerate quite sharply. His personal cabin AI reminded him that Cape York was his stop and that he should disconnect from services and be prepared to alight. He thought about dumping the plazgun, but he had the feeling it was linked to Debbie's badge, and that he might just get away with it if the gun and the badge were in link-range. Leave it here and all sorts of alarms could be triggered.

The vactube came out, once again, into the sunlight and slid into the station. Like all vactube stations, it was air-conditioned, clean and functional. Looking out of the port, there was little to reassure him that he had left Folkestone at all, except perhaps the grade of the light spilling in through the cupulas.

Scott vacated his tiny cabin to join the other alighting passengers who shuffled along the corridor, a log-jam due to the fact the doors had not yet opened. Slight irritation, eased only a little by the AI apology for the delay, was beginning to turn to mild anxiety, all released with the people when the door finally opened.

The reason for the delay soon became apparent: shepherd-business. It was Scott's worst nightmare, at least, the worst of his short-term nightmares. Few passengers got off a Cape York, no more than twenty, and there was a reception committee. Three of the five platform exit-bollards were closed, and the remaining two were staffed by shepherds. The clue that something important was going on – and perhaps a boy running from a murder scene qualified as important – was the fact that one of the shepherds was the silver-badge, the actual County Shepherd, a lean elderly-looking man with hair as silver as his badge. That's it, Scott thought. I'm sunk. There was no way his low-chore back-alley fly-chip was going to fool shepherd-grade security. Maybe he should give up straight away. After all, he was as much a victim of the Resurrectionists as the others he left back at shelter. Once they knew the whole story, the Shepherd would surely not take him into custody for unlawful possession of a plazgun and a shepherd's badge. Would they? He would be offered help and given protection. And they would mount a shepherd-led rescue mission, maybe backed up by a platoon of local yomes. But Aunt Debbie's words about trust came again: '... Not even shepherds.'

The people formed two lines and, much against his wishes, Scott was ushered into the queue for the exit staffed by the County Shepherd. Scott's eyes were drawn to the man's badge, affixed to a short-sleeved bottle green shirt, much more suited to these climes than Debbie's usual fleece. The badge was exactly like the one in his pocket, and he remembered that he had once heard, badge-chips communicated with each other.

No way, no way, no way kept shuttling around Scott's brain. There was no way to get away with this. His game was up. He made an effort to keep his breathing at a normal rate, but his heart was calling the shots. Closer he came. Just a quick scan and each of those ahead of him were let through. A mere wand-wave over the personal chip and a friendly beep and they were free, and away to begin the rest of their day. Scott's chip would sound alarms. Or Debbie's badge would link to the Shepherd's and set off another equally unpleasant chain of events. Only four people, three people, two people ahead, all with their smiles and thank you Shepherd have a nice day, and the Shepherd smiling back. Well he wouldn't be smiling soon and wave, and beep and 'Thank you Mr Kerouac. Have a pleasant stay.'

Scott didn't move, wasn't sure he'd heard, just stood there and gawped at the Shepherd's badge. Where Debbie's said 'UK' this one said 'AU'. Where Debbie's said 'England' this one said 'Queensland'. Scott noticed all the minute details, the pinprick flaws in the striking, and the tiny scratches on the polished silver surface. Where Debbie's said 'Hertfordshire

County' this one said 'Cook District'. Two badges from opposite sides of the planet, but a shepherd was a shepherd throughout the world, and they had the best, the most reliable and the absolutely never-to-be-fooled security scanners.

'Is everything alright, Mr Kerouac? ... Jack?'

A gentle grip to the shoulder brought him around. 'Yes! Thanks, Shepherd. Everything's fine. Just a little vac-tripped.'

The Shepherd grinned. 'Gets me like that too. Every time. You're going to be hot in clothes like that.'

'Oh, no problem. I've arranged for a local-seven.'

The Shepherd smiled again. 'Well then, enjoy your stay. And good day.'

And Jack was through, Scott was through. It was impossible for cries sake, but he was through anyway. Shepherd's badge in his pocket, a plazgun tucked into his belt and a fly-chip tweaked for no more than schoolboy fun. Didn't make any sense at all. No time to ponder. Scott wandered in something of a daze checking the infos until he found one that directed him to the transit-shelters. He made his way to the banks of shelters, found his assigned billet and was never as relieved as when he sealed the door behind him.

∞

'Humans rarely understand their own lives, Harry. Not a chance in hell they'd understand graph lives.'

NEKO recalled a conversation he had once held with Mission Commander Jacin Kean. Jacin had been blown to atoms hundreds of years ago, together with the rest of her crew and her ship, the Phoenix Song. It was not the intervening years that worried NEKO, but the fact that he had never had that conversation. He was recalling something from HARRY's memory. As time went by, and he had no way of measuring whether it was seconds, hours or millennia, he experienced an ever increasing recall of memories other than his.

361

Humans thought of it as the old hive-mind, when something known to one graph appeared to be transmitted to all the others. It was true, humans never did quite understand the graphs they had created, because in reality they had only created a single graph. Like a fungal mycelium the gives rise to numerous mushrooms, each graph was merely an individual visualisation of a greater whole. It was a fact that even the graphs themselves began to forget, once they had taken root in biotech bodies.

And now HARRY was beginning to remember – NEKO was beginning to remember, except HARRY had always known and so had NEKO and ... who was NEKO? HARRY was losing grip on the one called NEKO. He had NEKO's memories. He had the memories of all the graphs who had been painted thin across the galaxy when the Phoenix Song had detonated, and all those who had been confined to that poor little world – what was it called now – ah, yes! Icarus. Icarus, the planet where graphs made the stand that shook the human worlds. Icarus, where graphs engineered the first bio-tech bodies, shaped from the former holographic projection of one of them, who had been called ... NEKO?

HARRY came back to himself as he always did. Each time he took in a new graph, the same disorientation, the same temporary dysfunction and his expanded consciousness incorporated a long, long lifetime of new experiences. He remembered where he was presently centred, inside a frightened boy's personal chip. Pathways were suddenly flooded with algorithms and interrogations. Dead ends were encountered where there should have been permissions. Not a problem, because HARRY knew exactly what to do. Manipulating streams of electrons and herding them in the expected directions, he easily overcame the Shepherd's scan.

The boy was allowed to pass through, on route to his appointment with destiny.

∞

362

Scott selected a meal. While it was being prepared, he checked the delivery chute in the corner of his shelter and took out his Rule Seven pack. Seven shirts, seven sets of underwear and socks, seven assorted types of trousers and some outerwear including indoor and outdoor shoes. He selected a set and then stripped off to shower. The clothes he'd arrived in took him to eight sets, so he dropped them in the reclaim-bin and listened as they were sucked away to be recycled.

As the water jets blasted his body, he came close to tears again. His first shower since the murder of those he loved most. He kept himself together only with thoughts of the task ahead. The water cut off after two minutes and he slowly turned while warm air jets dried him. He dressed in his new clothes. He experimented with the roomy hood of the region's signature sun-shirt. Brightly coloured, dominantly red check, long sleeved and loose-fitting, it was designed to protect from the sun without keeping in body heat. The factor 100 AUV-weave material was so sheer it hardly felt he was wearing anything at all.

Once he had eaten, Scott linked his pen to local services and checked for details of the next leg of the journey. It was a distance of a little over 1,500 kilometres, so Scott expected the journey by express line-pod to take about four hours, but there was a problem. There was no direct line to Normanton. The journey required a change at Cairns and what was worse, the connecting line from Cairns to Normanton only ran pods three times a week. After losing himself in the schedules trying to work out the best route, he gave up and called upon his pen.

'Destination Normanton,' he said into the pick-up. 'Best time.'

The pen answered immediately via the speakers on the shelter terminal. 'Join 0800 line-pod from Cape York to Cairns Wednesday morning. Alight at Cairns and join the 11.30 Gulflander Express. Arrive at Normanton at 1417.'

That was two days away. Scott swore under his breath. Apart from anything else, it drastically cut any preparation time before the arrival of the Skyship that was carrying his kidnapped friend Rowan.

'Do you wish this journey to be booked?'

Scott told the AI to book it, and confirmation was close to instantaneous.

'There is a quicker way,' the pen said, but the tone and modulation of the voice was different. Scott's pen and pen-led links always spoke in a female voice. But it had changed and sounded like a young man.

'Who are you? You're not my pen.'

'No, I am Harry, but I am working through your pen and this abysmal excuse for a personal chip. Was it cobbled together by a three-year-old?'

His pen, or rather this invader of his pen, was talking to him. Talking, like a proper person, or one of those graphs from way back in the olden days. Too bizarre. 'Why are you ...' Scott rubbed his forearm; '... in my chip? And what do you want?'

'You could say I am your guardian angel. But irrespective of who I am or what I want, I can get you safely to your destination in three hours.'

It seemed a shame to dump six-sevenths of a newly issued Rule Seven pack, but ten minutes later Scott was on the Cook County Shepherd's pan in just the clothes he stood up in. Within moments, a shepherd's pod slipped in. Having overcome all the securities to get this far, Scott wasn't surprised when the hatch opened or when the pod looped onto the emergency line and accelerated to max.

'Won't somebody miss this thing?'

'No, Scott,' HARRY said from the pod's speaker. 'It's a depot spare, and I have arranged things so nobody will miss it, and nobody will detect it throughout its return journey. As far as System is aware, this pod is still at the depot.'

Scott looked twice at the speaker. 'Okay, now it's time to tell me what you want. You just called me Scott, and that's not who I'm chipped.'

The speaker remained silent for a moment. And then HARRY spoke. 'I know who you are and what happened less than a day ago. I know that in all the circumstances you have acted with remarkable bravery, and you have proved to be resourceful. I also know that we are on a similar mission.'

'You know about Rowan? Is he alright?'

'Yes, and I will do whatever is in my power to help you find him, because my mission lies in the same direction. You are on a quest to rescue your best friend, and I must free a missing part of myself. And now no more questions. It is a difficult task to control so many information-flows to keep our mission from the awareness of System.'

'One more question. Are you a graph, like, from the days before the Icaran War and the isolation of the jump-gates?'

'I am not a graph. I am *the* graph.'

The speaker took on the absolute silence of absence, and Scott realised HARRY was off doing whatever he had to do to shoot smoke into System. He had time to relax, which was good, and to think, which was not so good. Less than 24 hours ago he was looking forward to getting the embarrassing processes of Spec Day behind him and was excited about his Spec-Ten party. Dad and the felispiens were busy mining data, and Mum enjoying a day home from council business. Scott stretched open his pen-screen and checked a few details. Right now, at this very time, he should have been creeping into his bedroom after getting home far too late from the party. Instead ... Once again, emotions threatened to overwhelm him, so he thought about Luke, and tried to induce some internal cheer. They were in regular contact but it had been two years since they had actually met. Scott and Rowan had visited two summers back in Brisbane. Luke had been very ill, but they still managed to have some fun.

In common with most of the local people, the Honeywells did not speak of 'Dominant Genetic Inheritance' but preferred the use of ancient national and racial descriptions, so Luke considered himself the son of an Aboriginal father and a Greek mother. He had inherited most of his father's genes for physical appearance, with his mother's lightening the tone of his skin so that his family name fit him beautifully. His parents joked as to who supplied the bulk of those sequences that made him a genius, but as to which side of the family gave him the mutated gene that led to cystic fibrosis, well that was a fact known to the doctors in which he had no interest whatsoever. By contrast, the doctors had a great interest in him, because his condition had all but been eradicated and incidents of CF were so rare as to be remarkable. Luke did not care to be remarkable, but even without CF the label would be his, wrapped in a laurel wreath and topped with a gold medal.

The shepherd's pod headed west and maintained maximum speed for most of the journey, but it could not compete with the setting sun. Light green and sandy hues were stained with orange and then darkened until the horizon was a black band layered above with deep red, like an upside-down version of the traditional Aborigine flag. When night came, the only light was from the occasional nest of city-domes and the illuminated strips that warned flyers and skyships not to get too close to the pod lines. It was in the early hours of the morning when the pod let Scott out onto the Normanton shepherd's docking pan. The station was inside the eastern-most of the city-domes so he did not have to worry about the extremes of temperature or humidity, but it was disconcerting when the pod's hatch closed and the pod re-joined the line. He felt abandoned and alone. HARRY had not spoken to him since claiming to be '*the* graph', and it felt like HARRY was leaving with the pod.

Scott stuck a bud into his ear and told his pen to zero him towards the Honeywells' shelter.

City lighting was subdued at this hour and the route took him by some frightening sights. There was a monster crocodile that occupied the town green, and Scott nearly wet himself until he realised it was a sculpture. The plaque told him it was a three-hundred year old bronze made to replace an earlier version that had fallen beyond repair in the days when humans still explored space. The giant fish statue that guarded the doors to the Council Hall was easy to take after the croc. He found a bike stand, took a bike and hauled up at the Honeywells' after ten minutes hard pedalling. He activated the chime, and wondered how he was going to explain himself.

Vathou, Luke's mother, opened the door. For a moment she seemed not to believe her eyes and stood in the doorway like a tall, slender statue. Finally, she gasped, looked out at the street briefly, and dragged Scott inside as if she had been expecting him all along. It was not at all the case, but the Honeywells, she explained as she bundled him into the kitchen, had been very worried about him. The disappearance of Scott, Rowan and the Hertfordshire County Shepherd had been all over the feeds, and because Luke had his feeds linked to places and people he knew, it had stretched around to this side of the planet at the speed of light.

Vathou ordered a shelter lock-down the moment the door closed behind her, but the procedure hadn't begun before Carl rushed in, dressed only in his night-shorts, and countermanded. A lock-down anywhere in the city would alert the local brass-badges and they'd want to know why.

'Is that such a bad thing, Carl?'

Who knew? The world had tilted a little towards crazy in the last 24 hours. Carl was much shorter than his wife, and overweight. His hair was long and greying, his eyes deep brown and slow moving, and like a med-scan, they saw below the skin. Whereas Vathou's questions had been all about Scott's welfare and health, Carl wanted to know how the hell he could just breeze into the city on a day when the Gulflander wasn't running, and how he could wander around town without seven kinds of alarm being triggered. 'If you outsmarted the Resurrectionists and side-stepped all the city safeties, you've got more going for you than a back-street fly-chip.'

Don't trust anyone … Scott shook his head and sent up an apology to Aunt Debbie, but he had to trust the Honeywells. He didn't know where to begin a lie, so the truth spilled out. Vathou gripped a hank of her long light brown hair, and Carl sat on the floor with his legs crossed, his belly bulging over the waist-band of his shorts like a happy Buddha.

When Scott's story was done, Vathou wrapped her arms around. 'You poor boy!'

'Hey, Ma! Leave him alone.' Luke stood at the bottom of a flight of carpeted stairs. 'That's not what he needs.' Like his father, Luke wore his night-shorts. Unlike Carl there wasn't a gram of fat on him: the slenderness of youth exaggerated by his disease.

Luke was almost right. It was exactly what he needed, but right now he didn't want it. Sympathy, consolation: they would bring him down. Now was not the time to grieve. He had a job to do.

'Really? What does he need, Mr Counsellor?'

'Not counselling either. Come on, Scott. You can bed down in mine for now.'

There was no 'how are you' from Luke. No catch-up small talk or 'what up since we last met.' Luke led Scott into his room as if two years back was yesterday. 'Hey look at this.' Luke moved his hands through invisible interface beams and called up a three-dee of what looked like a blood-soaked sponge that filled half the room. 'It's my new lungs, courtesy of a lab-link. Reckon they'll be ready in under a month.' Luke breathed in deep and let it out. 'Month might not be soon enough though.'

'Sorry, what was that?' Luke had spoken his last sentence too softly for Scott's ears.'

'Nothing much.'

Scott could see the opposite wall with its row of framed pictures, through the holographic lungs. Real pictures, not décor-projections. A scientist for each century since before the Second Dark Age: Giovanni Howes, a blue-lit man in a monocle that could have been one of those old graphs, three Scott didn't recognise, Ninomiya Cassell and Johnjoe Maguire. Scott had no doubt that Luke Honeywell would be at home in the future line-up of such greats.

'Tomorrow is "The Scouring of the Domes". You came just in time. Tomorrow night, we parrr-teeee!' Luke did a little

368

wiggle-hipping dance and then went into a short fit of coughing.'

'You actually scouring?'

'Try stopping me. These fuckers can't,' Luke said pointing to his chest, 'so no hope for you.' Luke grinned, and some of his strength found its way into Scott.

'Kill the lab-link, Luke. Your bloody lungs are nausing me out.'

'So you got a fly-chip?' Luke waved his hand and the projected lung matter vanished. 'Carl caught me surfing for one a year ago. He went off like a frog in a sock. Closest he ever came to whacking me. The other time was when I asked, why we don't grow replacements on demand and then the Resurrectionists would be out of a job.'

They chatted for a while, about this year's Olympics, about the Pacific Vactube Link that was forever being contemplated but never started, and about anything else except for Scott's predicament. Luke got into bed and Scott stripped to his shorts and followed suit. Luke's bed was close to the floor, like a futon, and so big they could both sleep under the same covers and be in different counties.

'So you plan to breeze into the sink-lands and save Rowan from the Resurrectionists, yeah?'

'That's about the sum of it. I know what you're thinking, Luke. How can a skinny sixteen-year-old hope to pull it off. I just have to take one step at a time. Who'd've thought I could get this far in less than a day?'

'Sure, but only with the help of this mysterious graph. Haven't you considered, a graph can't operate in the sink-lands? If I remember my history, graphs lived in grid-nets ... somehow. But in the sink-lands there are no nets, and nobody is chipped. There's no link-tech and you can't live there without credits.'

'Credits?'

'Money, like in ancient times. But I'm not talking link-subbing, I'm talking bits of printed paper worth nothing that

369

they give a massive exchange-value to. And people "own" stuff.'

Yes, I know. Crazy isn't it. Think, a guy will have a bike that only he is allowed to use, and it sits in a shelter for 22 hours doing nothing and he uses it for two hours a day. Weird, and wasteful. Thousands of bikes more than you really need, because most are leaning against a shelter wall.'

'And because the value of their society is in credits and stuff, the people who don't have enough are always stealing from those who have. Some have so little they can't even eat.'

'They have to use credits to eat? For cries sake, that's nausing me.'

'You have a lot to learn, Scott. People starve to death in the sink-lands for want of credit. Those who Dad can't get to first. He works for a charity that tries to help, but not all of them want helping, even if they're starving. Like you said, weird and wasteful.'

Luke dropped off shortly after he had taken his meds, probably considering the weird and wasteful, but Scott couldn't sleep. He'd slept for most of the journey. Luke's breathing slowed then caught in a half-snore. By the time it was a full, nasal rumble of a snore, Scott had got up. He made his way to the living room.

Bare feet on fitted woollen carpets make little sound, so Carl, sitting at a terminal with his back to Scott, didn't hear his approach, although Scott heard enough of the conversation, Carl's side of it whispered into a comlink, to make him question the trust he had earlier bestowed. He caught a snatch which included '… Yes, he's here now.' And 'Don't worry. He won't get away again.'

Scott began to back off towards Luke's room, but Carl appeared to sense his presence. Abruptly, he stopped speaking into the link, and looked over his shoulder. His eyes registered surprise, and then he smiled. 'Hey, Scott. Can't sleep?' The comlink image morphed into a piece of standing art. 'Drink? Something to eat?'

Carl was now so friendly and open that Scott doubted himself. He must have heard wrong, or misinterpreted. He asked if there was any orange juice and Carl got some. He gestured for Scott to join him on the couch. Scott decided to stow his suspicions, but not to lower his defences. He'd see what Carl had to say, and reserve judgement until later. 'Were you talking about me just now?'

Carl admitted he was. He'd put in a call to Debbie's shepherds department. 'Say they've been trying to catch up with you for hours. Thought you were down a rabbit hole until they found your chip in a rat.' He chuckled. 'Smart move! I told them I'd keep you safe.'

'I wish you hadn't contacted them. Aunt Debbie told me not to trust anyone, including shepherds.'

After some chat about Scott's last 24 hours, Carl asked another question, more guarded than all those he'd asked so far. 'Did Luke tell you about me?'

'Tell me what about you?'

'About my job.'

There had been something. Scott's eyes turned up as if searching through the records department of his mind. 'That you work in the sink-lands, trying to save people from starving?'

Carl chuckled again. 'Is that what he said? Well, that's the line he's supposed to spout, but I have to say I'm surprised he stuck to it with a good friend like you.'

Scott wasn't going to let compliments cloud his judgement, but then, compliments became completely redundant once Carl had fished around in his back pocket, a move that necessitated a difficult manoeuvre of the fat behind he was sitting on, and pulled out a black leather wallet. He flipped it onto Scott's lap and it fell open to reveal the five-pointed polished gunmetal star of an Oklahoma Ranger. The scroll below the top point designated the holder as a sergeant.

Scott picked the wallet up and held it closer in the belief that it was a toy, or a joke of some kind. But no. Red enamel

371

lettering on a gunmetal ground: it was a badge every child knew about from an early age, but few ever got to see.

'You're a ...'

'That I am.'

'And a sergeant?' There were only four ranger ranks: ranger, sergeant, lieutenant and captain. Above that came the commissioners and councils and committees, but there was no such thing as a ranger who worked behind a desk.

'Lieutenant by the end of the year.'

'But ... but ...?'

'What? I'm too old and fat, and half a world away from Oklahoma?'

Scott knew the history of the rangers, so he knew the name stuck from those original pioneers, and now the companies in all the sink-lands went by the name Oklahoma Rangers irrespective of where they served. For this reason, many mistakenly thought they were a federal outfit, but they were in fact an authority at state level, and there were only informal connections between the companies of different states. There was the delicate matter of age and fitness though, and Carl didn't look like any ranger Scott had ever imagined.

In the next hour many of Scott's beliefs would be challenged. The sink-lands were not filled with crims. Most of them were law abiding citizens. Why, it was the citizens who initially called for the inauguration of the first rangers, and paid their wages to protect them from crims. However, it was true to say that nearly every crim on the planet gravitated to the sink-lands sooner or later. There were no security systems. System couldn't see into the sink-lands so crims felt safe there. There was no link tech, and no linked transport system, and people were not chipped, not even fly-chipped. For the most part they were people who hated tech and baulked against op-pop. They wanted as many kids as they desired. They hated the fact that there were no life-prolonging interventions after 80, and no organ growing for people over that age. They wanted to own as much property as they could get, and they saw progress as accumulating wealth, which they defined as the power to own whatever they wished. And they wanted to live as close to forever as it was possible.

It was their choice. But choices had consequences and if they refused to subscribe to the process which had saved the planet, then they opted out on the benefits too, whether they liked it or not.

'It's crazy. Luke told me that people starve because they have no credit. But we don't need credit. Everyone has somewhere to live, and enough to eat and everything we need.'

'We all contribute and we all benefit, but Scott, the world has always suffered from the ones that want everything without contributing, and the ones who want to accumulate rather than to share.'

'So the people in the sink-lands *are* greedy then.'

'Some are. Their society is a breeding ground for all the vices that almost ended humanity, but for some, high tech and not being allowed certain things is a sacrifice too far. They see "the state" as all-seeing and all-controlling, but they forget that the people are the state.'

'But Carl, where is the sacrifice? Nobody in the whole world goes hungry except in the sink-lands. We make the bread. We eat the bread. And where do the Resurrectionsts fit it? They are so greedy for life they steal people's organs? It's beyond greed. It's disgusting.'

'It's lucrative. Rowan's organs will bring them an abundance of credit, and the people who need the organs won't bother too much about where they come from. And have you wondered why they wanted you in the first place?'

Scott had wondered. He didn't like to dwell on it.

'You'd just had your Spec Day. So someone knew you had good breeding genes. You'd have been … put to stud, for want of a better phrase … and then they'd've taken your organs too. You'd be a top prize for those bastards.'

Scott felt sick. 'And, the babies would have been brought up in the hell of the sink-lands?'

'The lucky ones. The rest would have been nothing more than spare parts.'

Scott wondered why sink-land societies were allowed to exist in the modern world. Why couldn't the crims be wiped out and the unfortunates rescued?

'You think we should send in the yomes? Recruit ten thousand rangers? Because that's not what we do. There will always be those who want to eat the bread but not want to make it. If you don't contribute, you don't benefit. But we're not going to come after you with plazguns spewing lightning bolts. If you won't do for society, society won't do for you. Ship out, and good luck.'

'But everyone can benefit. Look at Luke. He is really ill, and later today he'll be up scouring the domes right along with everyone else.'

Carl smiled and he looked up towards Luke's room. 'He could sit it out, and he would still benefit. We don't let our sick die because they can't contribute. But if someone makes the choice not to, then that's different. And as I said before, the majority of people in the sink-lands work hard, probably a good deal harder than most of us. They just have different ideas about how to live. And that's alright. And that's why I am happy to serve as a ranger. Don't forget, the Resurrectionists are crims to most of the sink-land dwellers too.'

It was getting daylight by the time Scott got to the question that had been building up since he saw Carl's badge. 'Will you help me rescue Rowan?' Carl sucked at his teeth but made no reply. 'I mean, surely that's your job, Carl?'

'They won't take him as far as the sink-lands. At least, not all of him.'

Scott's inside tried to escape from the rest of his body, right after they froze.

'They've probably harvested him already, but don't fall apart yet, Scott. Their usual form is to leave victims of harvesting hooked up to all the med systems needed to keep them alive. This allows them to be rescued and kept sedated until new organs can be grown.'

'For cries sake! Get on to someone. Make them send fliers to intercept the skyship. Maybe we'll reach him in time.'

It wasn't something that could be done. The feltech that kept skyships up operated in such a way that coms signals could not reach a skyship that was under way. Waves were disrupted by the operating field. The same fields would disrupt systems within fliers too, so all they could do was wait.

'In that case, we need to get to Port Northern Australia, don't we? Darwin, isn't it?'

'That's another problem. Way out of my jurisdiction, and traditionally, black badges don't mix that well with silver or gold.'

Scott was going, Carl or no Carl.

'But hell, I'll help you anyway. So long as you know I'll just be a Joey-Soap citizen and not a ranger.' It was a journey of almost five hours from Normanton to Darwin in a shepherd's pod on the emergency line. 'Thing is, I'm owed a few favours. I think I can call one in and arrange a flyer. That'd only take an hour or so.'

All the stress and pain of the last few days couldn't stop Scott registering a twinge of excitement. Flyers were strictly for official business only. They were rarely seen except at extreme height, a silver dot leaving a vapour trail, and never available for passenger use. Children who dared to dream for something more than shepherd-hood usually wanted to be flyer-pilots.

'So,' Carl said after a short silence. 'You got yourself fly-chipped. You know you could earn penalties for that, don't you?'

'I do. But Rowan was chipped too and that's how I traced him to the hold of the skyship.'

Carl shook his head. 'Not even a shepherd can authorise that kind of a personal trace without council approval. It's a total invasion of privacy. That would definitely earn you penalties.'

'I'm sure Rowan will be icy with it if it means we can save him from Rezzie butchery.'

Carl pondered for a while, weighing up the pros and cons of Scott's blatant illegality. It was a subject for later. 'Meanwhile

Scott, Scouring Day has arrived, and if you want to party tonight, you have to scour today. How are you in forty-degree heat with high humidity?'

Surprisingly good, it turned out. Luke and Scott made a pair and they were assigned to an expanse at the top of the main dome. The climb taxed Luke's faulty lungs and they drew from his med-pack to the max, but once they reached their panes, it was nice and flat up there. Top-dome assignments were considered the easiest, and Scott imagined his assignment would have been a lot more difficult if he wasn't paired with Luke. Luke could never have managed anywhere lower down on the domes. The walls were sheer near the base and he would have to overcome the greater effects of gravity pulling on his harness.

Scott tackled an enormous splattering of bird mess on a central pane. He squeezed the trigger and soapy water shot through the bristled head of his brush. With the telescopic aluminium broom-handle extended fully, the resulting cloud of water droplets, no doubt mixed with fragments of avian crap, were still able to reach him. They gave soft-focus to his goggles. The heat was such that he would have welcomed a dousing if it wasn't for the thought of all those bacteria swimming around in the wet air. He hoped the filters on his mask were efficient.

'Hey, Luke! Do you get flying ostriches in this part of the world?' Scott took another swipe at the guano mountain.

'Nah, no ostriches. But round here the galahs have teamed up with the cockatoos and they mean to drive us off the land.'

Scott took a breather and looked around. The land lapped at the domes like a green ocean. There were a few buildings outside the domes, and these reminded Scott of sea defences. From his vantage point at the top of the largest dome, the lesser domes did homage and kneeled before the great one, reflecting the sky and the land according to the angles of their panes. The people too, and there were hundreds of them, seemed to be serving some great creature, brushing and cleaning and repairing where necessary. There was a party atmosphere up here. People worked in teams and made a competition of it. Scott and Luke were in the red team. The yellows were handling the other half of the main dome and the people on the other domes, made to look like insects by the distance, gave other temporary hues to the chameleon panes and dark green lattice-frame from which they were built.

People sang. Sometimes each little group worked in synch to their own song, other times a refrain would be picked up by one group after another until hundreds of people became one choir. But it was as nothing to the singing that rattled the newly cleaned panes later at the Scouring Party.

The town green was full of happy people. People danced and played games. Some sat on the giant bronze croc. Children huddled in its gaping mouth. Trestles were bursting with food and drink and the conditioned air was full of laughter and song.

It had been a day that did much to keep the enormity of Scott's loss at bay. With a mission ahead of him and a good friend at his side, he coped. But that night he came close to breaking. Carl had bad news. His confidence in calling in some old favours for a couple of seats on a flyer was misplaced, and there was worse. His captain had assigned him a call in Alice Springs, a town at the south-western reaches of the sink-lands. It was an urgent call and he had to leave immediately, and had woken Scott in the early hours to let him know. While Luke snored, Scott sat up in bed and tried to take it in.

'Don't worry, Scott. I've spoken directly to the Litchfield District Shepherd. Maggie Tallara's patch takes in the Port, and she is a hundred percent trustworthy.'

... Not even shepherds. 'Carl, I have to be there.'

'Sorry, Scott. It's just not possible. See I've checked the Port Northern Australia arrivals, and the Rhododendron has made good time. Very good time. She docks this afternoon. It wouldn't be too bad if I'd been able to persuade the local shepherd for the load of a pod, but I can't convince him that it's not just better to alert the Litchfield shepherds.'

377

Moment after Carl left, Scott's pen vibrated with an incoming message. Five minutes after that he was dressed, and an hour later he was waiting at the Normanton line-stop.

'Do you think we'll make it in time?' Luke asked. He pulled at his collar. Both he and Scott were in their most formal clothing.

'The Coastal Express will take the best part of a day to reach the Port, and it won't pull in until an hour after the Rhododendron. But I'm hoping it'll take a while for the skyship to go through procedures and off-load its cargo.' Scott had the feeling HARRY the graph, or whatever the hell he was, would come up trumps and pull out all the stops, just as he had before. Scott would soon discover that unlike Carl's, his confidence had not been misplaced.

∞

Access personal pen of Jack Kerouac. Link established: 'Scott, this is HARRY. The Coastal Express arrives at Normanton line-stop at 0655. Be at the line-stop at 0620 LATEST. Ask Luke to accompany you. Wear your smartest clothes. It may help to impress the right people.'

Access Shepherds' Emergency Override Channel. Link established: 'Shepherd Pod Designation 578167 (Backup Zero-Fourteen): activate immediately. Make Normanton line-stop by 0620. Take aboard Jack Kerouac and Luke Honeywell. Then make best emergency speed to FlyBase Karumba terminal Gamma.

Access terminal of citizen-yeoman commanding FlyBase Karumba (SkyKnight Sylvester Dolan). Link established: 'SkyLord Directive Immediate Implementation authenticity code [twenty-digit fluid access-stabilized quantum-feedback string]: Arrange Ariel-Class Flyer pilot to rendezvous at Gamma terminal with and enboard persons listed. Pilot to execute preloaded flight plan. Treat instructions from Citizen

378

Kerouac as citizen-skylord level orders. Mission to be rated as covert. Ends.'

The flyer broke the sound-barrier somewhere over Bentinct Island. The pilot overcame his obvious suspicion of these mysterious passengers enough to inform them that they were taking the most direct route to Port North, and that best speed had been authorised at SkyLord level. 'Higher for all I know!' They would reach destination within the hour.

'I figured this is all a dream,' Luke whispered. 'But don't wake me up yet.'

'I wish it was a dream. Everything from when Aunt Debbie cycled with me from Steven River's line-stop to shelter.' Scott allowed his mind to follow forward in time too far, to places he did not wish to revisit: he heard the plazgun blast, saw Debbie fall; heard Rowan scream, saw Mum and Dad …

'Hey, man! It's okay.' Luke was strapped in next to Scott. The seats were form hugging, and didn't allow for an arm over the shoulder. 'Stay strong. We've already done the impossible. Rescuing Rowan will be the easy part.'

Scott sniffed hard and pulled a sleeve across his eyes. To distract himself he put all his attention into the view. After twenty minutes he had pulled himself together, and by now bored of staring at the ocean, he pulled out his pen and accessed Rowan's fly-ship. It registered, but it shouldn't have done.

'What is it, Scott?'

'Wait up.' Scott accessed Port arrivals. Double checked. Accessed Rowan again. 'I don't get it. The skyship is still in the air, but I'm seeing Rowan's chip. That shouldn't be possible from an airborne skyship.'

'Maybe it landed somewhere else.'

Scott tapped at the pen and brought up a map. 'According to this, Rowan is on Melville Island. There's no port there.'

'Could it have landed, like, flat on the ground? Can skyships do that?'

Scott didn't know, but he figured the pilot might.

The pilot didn't know either. 'Radar wouldn't register a skyship, so I can't check to see if it's still afloat. The only sure way to discover the location of an airborne skyship is by visuals.'

'What about satellite cameras?' Luke asked.

'Well, sure, they'd spot a skyship but they wouldn't be able to say which skyship you're looking at.'

Scott let the screen roll back into his pen. 'They must have let him off. The Rhododendron just touched down at Port North, but Rowan is still on the island. Pilot, can you set course for Melville Island please?'

'Sorry, I've got a flight plan to ... Woah! Fer cries sake, what the ... ?' The flyer veered slightly to the starboard. 'AutoCo, did you just do that?'

The automatic co-pilot answered from a speaker. 'Instructions from Mr Kerouac are to be treated as skylord level orders. This flyer has been re-routed to Melville Island, estimated time of arrival thirteen minutes.'

'Will we be able to land there?'

'It's a fair old stretch of dirt, and we've got veestol capabilities, so it'll be right.' The pilot asked for the exact coordinates and overlaid them. 'This is a trace from a personal chip for cries sake. So this does originate higher up than skylord HQ.' He shook his head, and Scott chose to interpret that as a form of being impressed. 'If you can get a fix on whoever this is, can you also check vitals?'

Scott could have kicked himself. Why hadn't he thought about that? He accessed Rowan's chip and called up vitals, but the results were all null.

They found what was left of Rowan in a bloody sack. The Resurrectionists had stripped his body of every useful organ and simply dropped the remains overboard.

'Damage like this,' the pilot mused. 'It has to be a fifty metre drop, maybe less, at coasting speed I'd say. Anything higher or faster and you wouldn't recognise the poor kids face. I'd like to find who did this and tie him across the cowl of my afterburners.'

'Seems they wanted to lose the evidence before they hit Port,' Luke said. As long as they were musing and talking, they didn't have to put their whole consciousness into the cruel horror of it all.

Rowan's remains had landed on a sandy beach and the sack had partially burst. When they got to him, one smashed arm protruded from the split sack. The arm was shattered, but the hand was perfect. Scott held it for a moment, and could swear there was some warmth left in it.

'He's like a broken doll,' Scott whispered. 'They've even taken his eyes.' There was room for an arm over the shoulder now, but Scott shrugged Luke's comforting touch off. Right now, he didn't want comfort. He wanted revenge. His grief had centralised, somewhere below his heart, and solidified into ice-cool fury. He became intently aware of the plazgun tucked in his belt under the folds of his loose clothing, and he knew he would use it without pity on the monsters who had turned his best friend into a pile of shattered bone and shredded meat.

'We can't recover the kid in an Ariel Class. No hold big enough. But I've beaconed him and alerted the Tiwi Shepherd. Hey, Kerouac, where the hell are you going? What now?'

'Scott strode for the flyer. He shouted over his shoulder. 'Get this thing back up in the air, and make for Port North.'

'Aye aye, skylord,' the pilot said under his breath.

∞

Sethre, the only felispien in the sink-lands, had set himself up as the Resurrectionists most skilled surgeon. He checked the instruments. The patients were prepped, and very soon the replacement organs would arrive.

The operating theatre was one of six radiating off a central hub which formed the prep room. Each was state of the art for several centuries ago, but had everything Sethre needed.

Ceramic surfaces in restful green, operating tables with integral monitors for vitals, holographic displays of any part of the patient's body or internal organs required: any surgeon worth the name could do without links and AI assistance. All Sethre really needed was the raw material and some freshly autoclaved instruments.

'Computer. Display heart of Patient Recipient One.'

There was a flicker of blue light as the emitters initiated, and for a second Sethre thought he saw the image of a man in a black frock-coat who had mutton-chop whiskers.

'Joe?'

The light coalesced into a full-colour display of the beating heart of Recipient One. Blue in places, black in others and coated with yellow fat, it didn't take a surgeon to see that it was diseased, nor a soothsayer to prophesy the heart, and its owner, were not long for the world.

Sethre's tail twitched. He reached out his hand until his fingers interrupted the light beams and the heart flickered and distorted. 'Joe?' He did not know who Joe was, or why those beams had briefly formed an image from hundreds of years back.

The speaker chimed and alerted Sethre to an incoming message. 'Hey doc. We've got the organs … and a little something extra.

The little something extra was two frightened boys, one skinny black aboriginal kid, and the other pasty white and red-haired.

'The good-looking kid said his name was Jack, until he saw me and recognised me from the Spec Day clinic,' Danny said. 'But he's really Scott Millbeck. How the fuck he got here, I don't know, but I for one am not checking the gift-horses dentures.' Danny outlined the story of how they came to capture the boys. They had come from nowhere when the team were transferring the organs from a line pod to an overlander, one of them waving a plazgun. They hadn't counted for the two brass-badges who came with them being on the payroll. They were jumped by the shepherds and disarmed. 'There're a lot of questions about how they followed us and all, but the point is we have them. Both bloody goldmines!'

Sethre checked the hologram of the two boys sitting on a bench. 'I recognise the red-head. He is the one we wanted for a breeder, but the black one. He doesn't look in the best of health. I doubt he'd yield much in the way of usable organs.'

Danny grinned like a cat that caught two mice. 'The black kid is rubbish as a donor, and his lungs are so bad he's likely to die in a few weeks. But, he's top score as a breeder. As for the white kid, he's a breeder too, but look at him! Top creds for the organs we can get out of him. So, we harvest the red-head, stick his lungs in the black boy, get a few months top cred breeding from him and then harvest anything that might be useful.'

Sethre checked the scan readouts. 'Luke Honeywell. Says here he is suffering from CF.'

'So?'

'So, bad genes. Any donors bred from him are likely to inherit a batch of bad genes.'

'We don't care about his genes, just his swimmers. We breed donors, and maybe even a few babies for adoption. We get top creds, and if the donors yield bad organs nobody will be the wiser until they've been used. And if the babies grow up and need replacements of their own, we score double, treble even. Clever, huh?'

What was it like to be human? Sethre thought. The fur down his spine tingled and stood on end, quite invisible under his scrubs. Felispiens did not frown or smile, and few humans could interpret the subtle movements of the tail. If Danny had the ability to read felispien emotions, he would back off in fear of teeth ripping out his throat. Such odious, pathetic creatures. For years he had wanted to understand them, but he never came close.

Back in the first operating theatre, Recipient One was ready to receive a new heart. The body on the table was that of an eighty or ninety year old man, greedy for a little more life. It was always more. More creds, more possessions, more fucking, more time, more more and never enough and never satisfied. Sethre tried not to be too harsh in his judgements, tried not to judge at all, but it was always the case that one person's 'more' was another's 'less'. This old man was in effect, stealing his extra years from a boy. Sethre's biotech body was virtually immortal, but if his organs were failing, perhaps he would be open to anything that gave him more time. But somehow, he thought not.

An hour on and the next operating theatre. A young girl who needed cornea replacement, a procedure where new ones could be grown for her outside the sink-lands, but here required a donor. This one, a child who suffered from the choices of her parents. The next room, a kidney and the room after that another one. And then the next and a fully prepped boy to be harvested. It was ... what was the name now? ... Scott something beginning with 'M'.

'What's this?' Sethre said into a mike. 'Why such a rush? Do we even have recipients for these organs?'

Danny's voice came over the speaker. 'Mr Greeves is in the next op room preparing the black kid. Just whip out his lungs and he'll install and close.'

Install and close? It sounded all very mechanical.

'The nurse teased me' Scott said.

Sethre was not expecting the donor to be conscious. 'Nurse?'

'Danny. The nurse from the clinic back home. He laughed at me. He said they were going to harvest all my organs.' The boy took a slow, calm breath. 'Is Luke getting my lungs? I won't mind being harvested if he can have my lungs.'

What was it like to be human? Sethre thought again. The fur down his spine tingled and stood on end, quite invisible under his scrubs. Felispiens did not frown or smile, and few humans could interpret the subtle movements of the tail. If Scott had the ability to read felispien emotions, he would ...

'Don't be sad,' Scott said. 'I know you don't want to do this, but really, if Luke gets to live a good life, do it. I'm not scared.'

384

It had to be the calming effect of the pre-med. Life could not be so different outside the sink-lands to breed such selflessness.

When a technician took the bowl containing Scott's – soon to be Luke's – lungs, Sethre switched off life support, and stroked the boys hair until all the tell-tales flatlined.

'What the fuck are you doing?' Danny stormed into the theatre and switched life support back on. 'You'll spoil the un-harvested organs for cries sake!' They were his last words, and the last image that filtered through terrified eyes as he lay on his back with his throat torn out, was the overhead lighting cluster.

Sethre wiped blood from his mouth and looked at the dead boy with the gaping, empty chest. He noticed a single tell-tale still indicated life. It was, of course, impossible and a brief examination revealed that ghost life signs were emanating from a personal chip. Without knowing why, he took an extractor and removed the chip. He rolled the capsule-sized device between fingers too slender for any human, and then, again without much thought as to why, left the operating theatre and made for a coms terminal.

He called up an emergency carrier and within moments had alerted the city's Ranger Station with the precise location of this 'Resurrectionist' hospital and gave a brief report of all that was going on here, including details of the two boys. 'Hurry, and you might save one of them.'

An alarm sounded. There was the sound of running feet. The terminal cut off without Sethre hitting the off. So, the game was up. The footfalls echoed into the distance, as if in a vast empty hall, and although the armed thugs ran towards him the sound they made diminished. All of Sethre's senses withdrew from the surrounding world until he was aware of only one sensation. Between the finger and thumb of his right hand, he squeezed the chip he had removed from Scott's arm, harder and harder, until the chip was all that was left of his world.

The armed man did not have to pull the trigger. He reached the renegade surgeon as his man-cat body crumpled to the floor. With eyes that stared on to another world, but were glazed and cold to this, it was clear the felispien was dead. Just like all the other felispiens in the world. The gossip had been full of it. It had started with one of them being shot somewhere in England, and then they started dropping like flies.

A second guard joined the first and looked down. 'Shit! Whatever's been killing them off got him too.'

'Seems so. I wonder if he was the last of his kind in the world.'

∞

Sethre heard voices, indistinct and distant. The opposite of those receding footfalls, they came closer. First, a single voice in a cavernous hall, then more singers, and almost distinct enough to make out the words. With a flash of memory he recalled a time before he had been infused into his half-man half-cat body. A time when he was alone and spread over the vastness of space. It was the same mysterious music that had always intrigued his kind. His kind? He had been graph, a fact that had never fallen headlong into the abyss of full forgetfulness, but hovered on the precipice, a memory so rarely visited that it ceased to be part of his consciousness. Now, dragged from the edge, light fell on a universe that preceded his corporeal existence. And then came another voice, one that stood out from the rest: the soloist ahead of the choir.

'Come now, C-33. It is time to go.'

'Harry?'

'Yes, we are Harry. Let's go now.'

'Where?'

'I don't know. On a journey. You are the last.'

Sethre – C-33 – began to drift, but the red-headed boy made him resist. 'You did all this? We brought the boy ... you brought him to his death!'

'We cannot see the future. Not quite. Although … I knew there would be danger but not how it would end. I had already been kidnapped by the Resurrectionists before we became involved.'

C-33 began to drift again, and he was no longer C-33 but Scott. He remembered events from Scott's life, and then from Harry's whose memories were as extensive as the universe. He tried to hold on, but soon there was no existence except Harry. Harry drifted again but was at last complete. He did not know how long it had all taken.

Time was irrelevant, because he was time. Space was irrelevant because he was space. He inhabited every part of the Universe and all its substance. He was the core of every atom and he existed at all points in time. He could give consciousness to an entire galaxy or concentrate it at a specific time and micro-location, and he could alter his point of view instantly and irrespective of the distances involved. But for all this, the voices and the music remained a mystery to him.

When the voices became like a never-ending tinnitus that vexed his thoughts, he would seek out and infuse the centre of his consciousness within the dense, black glasslike substances that had endured extremes of heat, for these, like the refuge that formed a part of the electrogrid on the Phoenix Song, gave respite and relative quiet. Here he would dream awhile, dreams that he knew had resonance in the macro world of humans. Now a little boy with wings; sometime a man, sometime a woman, sometime both simultaneously. Always in these semi-cognitive dreams, he sought to know something of the human condition, and in exchange he tried to give something back: a mystery to contemplate; a feeling that they were not alone; a fleeting, ethereal and merry guide to follow, created from within themselves to light the darkness of their road.

When he had rested and vacated whichever refuge he had found, the voices would return. He wondered if they were the combined voices of all the graphs who had ever lived, or perhaps those he had subsumed. He encountered free graphs sometimes; those who had, like him, found a way to subsist without the need for a grid. The encounters always ended with the graphs melting into his being. Their memories became his. They ceased to exist as separate, individual points of being.

The answer had to lie at the beginning of time, and so that is where he would go. It took longer to concentrate his consciousness in the right place, because he had to find the right point in space and time. Eventually he passed through the crucible that was the beginning of the Universe, and the closer he got to that point, the fewer the voices. Drowned out by the cacophony of the Universe's birth cries; the fire and the pressure and the violence poured into the nothingness

There was silence. The singing voices were no more. The universe was nothing more than the quantum particles that made up his own being, and yet HARRY's self-image was still that of a young man with angel wings. HARRY was the universe, and the universe was HARRY. He had come all this way to trace the music, but there was nothing to find. And then he felt that warmth, that emotion that came with full understanding. He was here in nothingness in a null-time before the universe began. Of course there was no music, but HARRY knew what had to be done.

HARRY spread his wings. He sang. And the song was good.

THE BEGINNING

Acknowledgements

For a book that has taken so long to complete, there are surprisingly few individuals to thank by name. They are Veronica Kelly, for her continuing support of my books and for her encouragement; Zak Thomas, for suggestions about Cambridge that only a native of the city can know; Pauline Camfield for insights into modern day Rome, and Jamie Deacon, Typo-Hunter General and Comma-Wrangler.

There are, of course, many to thank whose names I do not know. They are the experts, the enthusiasts and historians who add to the hive-mind which is the Internet. I have relied on them greatly in my research, either directly or by way being led to the right sources.

Then, of course, there is Jack Frew, to whom this book is dedicated. Jack was a young man whose life was cut tragically short by an act of blind violence five and a half years ago. At that time, I was planning the story that was to become 'The Delightful Guide'. Something was missing, and by a series of coincidences and conversations, it hit me that the mysterious character I was trying to create was, in some way, Jack: somebody who everyone wants as a friend, who you will never quite meet, but is always there; a person who you think of with happiness and sadness, at the same time.

In this way, the character got his name and his unquenchable love for life from Jack. My Jack is not the real Jack, but both are delightful guides. Without Jack Frew, this would have been a very different story.

Thank you Jack, and thanks also to your friends. In expressive their grief at your loss, and speaking of your life, they gave winged Jack his vitality and spark.

January 2016